DATE DUE

DEMCO 38-296

The Labyrinth

Enrique A. Laguerre

The Labyrinth

Translated from the Spanish by
William Rose

Introduction and Bibliography by
Estelle Irizarry

Waterfront Press

INTRODUCTION

Enrique A. Laguerre's novel *The Labyrinth* cannot be read quite in the same way today as it was when first published in Spanish in 1959 amid wide acclaim, chosen book-of-the-month by London's International Book Club, and immediately published in English. It was then, as it still is, unique in several ways. It was one of the first Puerto Rican novels to be made available in English translation.[1] The experience of the Puerto Rican in New York was still a relatively unexplored novelistic theme,[2] as was the regime of the Dominican Republic's dictator Trujillo that had provoked books of a documentary nature rather than fiction. Extremely timely and linked to current events that made its translation into English urgent, *The Labyrinth* was a bold and even dangerous undertaking, given Trujillo's reputation for having his enemies in foreign capitals eliminated. It is not surprising that most critics at that time discreetly refrained from overtly identifying the "Santiagan Republic" of the novel as the Dominican Republic.[3] Now, some twenty-five years after the book appeared, and twenty-three years after Trujillo's assassination, what was previously current events is now history. We can step back and view the novel with the distance and hindsight that only time can provide. The result is even more fascinating; the imaginative and artistic dimensions are clearer and an element of prophecy emerges. In his ability to extract and refine material produced by a concrete historical situation, Laguerre created a novel whose stature has grown and whose relevance has matured from timely to timeless.

The Labyrinth is also unique within Enrique A. Laguerre's fiction, which includes ten novels to date. Laguerre is not just a writer from Puerto Rico; he is a profoundly Puerto Rican writer who has seen many of his works become classics. His first novel, *La llamarada* (The blaze), an instant best seller in Puerto Rico in 1935, has already seen its twenty-fifth commemorative edition. As a prominent member and the most consistent cultivator of the novel of the "Generation of the 1930's," he responded to mentor Antonio S. Pedreira's call for an authentic Puerto Rican literature, dedicating his pen to portraying the history of Puerto Rican life in this century. Among his novels, however, *The Labyrinth* is the only one that takes place wholly outside of Puerto Rico.

Puerto Ricans have been accused—and have accused themselves—of what Pedreira called *"insularismo,"* a tendency toward introversion, isolationism, and preoccupation with their own problems. He advised writers, "we also form part of what we call the 'universe' and it is necessary to cultivate our letters from within to the outside so they will have an open road."[4] Laguerre's protagonist Porfirio Uribe, even living outside the island, seems to be an example of *insularismo*. Like so many of his compatriots of the time, his "Puerto Rican dream" is to find economic security, return to his island, join the majority party, marry, and live happily ever after, but just as he is about to realize his dream, something happens that changes his course drastically. By taking Uribe outside himself and outside Puerto Rico, Laguerre shows us that indeed "no man is an island" and that above all, the Puerto Rican should not be.

History in the Making

Two distinct historical experiences form the substance of the novel, namely that of the Puerto Rican in New York and that of the Trujillo regime in the Dominican Republic. In treating life in the United States, Laguerre paints a varied picture of how a sustained sojourn affects different countrymen. While some immigrants continue to be "uprooted plants," echoing the metaphor of his previous novel *La ceiba en el tiesto* (The ceiba tree in the flower pot), others, like Luis Pororico (whose name is a distortion of "Porto Rico"), feel more at home, in his case with an established territory of organized rackets. In Porfirio Uribe's case individuality disappears before the larger fact of being considered a "Porto Rican," which makes him suspect before the police, and even professors and superiors who had esteemed him have their doubts. Boredom, epithets, prejudice, indifference, poverty, life in boarding houses, and loneliness, alleviated by the spontaneous generosity of a friend, the promise of romance, or a dream of success, are all part of the picture.

The major Hispanic theme of the tyrant that dominates the second part of the novel has been cultivated since José Mármol's Argentine classic *Amalia* in 1851, by Miguel Angel Asturias, Valle-Inclán, Francisco Ayala, Roa Bastos, E. F. Granell, Miguel Delibes, Gabriel García Márquez, and a host of other writers. If the number seems excessive, it may be because the state of affairs which inspires such novels is excessive. Laguerre's novel is bound to be different from others of the genre, reflecting his own perspectives and sensibility. His subject is the military tyrant, and the continued relevance of the novel may be appreciated in light of the fact that "there are forty such self-elected rulers today, running a quarter of the world's governments."[5]

While *The Labyrinth* is not in the strictest sense a historical novel, it was evidently inspired by real events: the hunting down in New York of two Dominican exiled writers who had offended Trujillo. In the first incident the journalist Andrés Requena was "killed shortly before midnight . . . in the ground-floor hallway of a tenement . . . on the lower East Side" on October 3, 1952.[6] The second victim was Jesús de Galíndez, who "disappeared" as he entered a subway station on March 12, 1956, on his way home from Columbia University, where he taught. Galíndez was a Spanish exile who had sought refuge in Santo Domingo in 1939. There he taught in the Diplomatic School and worked in the Department of Labor and National Economy, where his arbitration of strikes in favor of workers displeased Trujillo. Fearing harassment, he left for New York in 1946, where he wrote articles for the press and a doctoral dissertation for Columbia University entitled *The Era of Trujillo*, an exposé of the regime. His kidnapping and presumed murder became an international cause célèbre, exacerbated by the untimely deaths of all witnesses and the mysterious disappearance in the Dominican Republic of a young American aviator, Gerald Lester Murphy, thought to have flown the drugged Galíndez back to Trujillo. This was followed by the "suicide" of Murphy's alleged killer. There was an outcry to re-assess United States policy toward support of such regimes in Latin America.[7]

The description of Adrián Martín's slaying early in the novel closely follows the details of the Andrés Requena assassination (the names Adrián and Andrés are similar), while the public protests reflect the Galíndez affair. In the ensuing years, many books purporting to tell the "true facts" for and against Trujillo were published. It is indeed remarkable that Laguerre was able to distance himself from these complicated events and project them into the realm of fiction. While Robert D. Crassweller, author of a 1966 book on Trujillo, recognized the unreal quality of the terrible events he described,[8] Laguerre on the other hand created a fictitious account which seems all too real, one of the ironies of life and fiction.

Historical accounts of the Trujillo era confirm many details of the novel. In a book written in Puerto Rico the year before publication of *The Labyrinth* in Spanish, Germán E. Ornes cites the tyrant's "special affection" for the University, the ubiquitous portraits of the Leader as a sign of loyalty, the lowering of voices in conversation, and the sinister operatives of the espionage network.[9] Arturo R. Espaillat assures us that "no single ruler of modern times has held the absolute power that Trujillo wielded over his three million people for thirty-one years."[10] Crassweller supplies details about the tyrant which appear in the novel: his love of horses, cattle, and young women; his superstitious beliefs; the tendency of his voice to rise at times to a falsetto (Laguerre speaks of his "voice like a baby's rattle");[11] his uniform bedecked with medals; his desire to humble the mighty; and his resentment of social aristocracy. Don Ursulino in the novel seems to closely resemble Trujillo's father, pleasant and amiable, "not evil in a criminal sense and his ingenuous good will and merry spirits endeared him to many."[12] Other correlations between real life and the novel are the long-standing division of the political scene in rival factions, affirmative achievements with regard to order, fiscality, and public works; adulation to the point of deification, enlistment of active feminists into the ranks of Trujillo's supporters, frequent promotions as an ominous sign, and "suicides" in prison. The fate of Trujillo's personal physician and Secretary of Health, Francisco Benzo, who fell from favor and was jailed in 1940, and the personality of a famous hit-man called "El Cojo" (the lame one) seem combined in the figure of Jaramillo.

One of the most surprising aspects of *The Labyrinth*, however, is that several subsequent events, situations, and characters are foreshadowed in an almost visionary fashion. The reader will note the similarity of events in the novel to the following facts which occurred *after* its publication: When Trujillo was assassinated two years later, in 1961, there was an element of superstition involved, as in Don Joaquín Valverde's manipulation of Leader Augusto in the novel. Olga Brache, daughter of Trujillo's former Minister to the United States, had had a dream foretelling the assassination. The Action Group of conspirators who carried out the act included a member of the Military Corps attached to Trujillo in the National Palace, together with a man whose brother had been killed by the government because of his involvement in the Galíndez case. Another conspirator, Manuel Cáceres Tunti, like Lorenzi in the novel, was in another place and saw none of the action, which had been prematurely and hastily contrived by Antonio de la Maza.[13] The superstition, method of infiltration, revenge motive, and even the initial and surname of the mastermind of the conspiracy: *A. Maza*, so strikingly similar to those of Laguerre's character *A. Laza*, are all foreshadowed in the novel.

Laguerre departs from the traditional procedure in historical novels of mixing fictional characters with real ones. Instead, he fictionalizes all the characters, incorporating names and details which echo prominent figures associated with Trujillo, providing an atmosphere of authenticity without attempting to copy reality. The following are a few of these "real people" with the fictitious counterparts mentioned in parentheses:

> *Joaquín Balaguer*, Trujillo's fawning Secretary of Foreign Relations (*Joaquín Valv*erde, reflected in his name, since the *b* and *v* are pronounced similarly in Spanish)
>
> Rafael *Brache*, Trujillo's Minister to the United States, later turned enemy of the regime (Jacinto *Brache*)
>
> *Jacinto* Reynado, Trujillo's political puppet who had a leg amputated because of diabetes (*Jacinto* Brache, Joaquín Valverde's one leg)
>
> *Jesús Martínez Jara*, nicknamed El Cojo, originally a Spanish refugee, famous in the exile world as a professional Trujillo assassin (*Jacinto Martínez*, Spanish refugee, designer of the Trujillo myth, and Luis *Jara*millo, who limped)

Augusto *Sebastián*, Trujillo's Secret Police Chief (*Sebastián* Brache)

*Porfirio Rubi*rosa, flamboyant playboy diplomat and first husband of Trujillo's eldest daughter Flor, famous for his love of "the good life" (*Porfirio Uribe*, with the surname shortened and transposed, whose comparison to Rubirosa is ironic in view of his low-keyed character but nevertheless evokes the attraction of material things)

Martín de *Moya*, for many years friend of Trujillo, later exiled (Porfirio's Santiagan uncle Florito *Moya*. Mention of his name produces ambiguous reactions, so Porfirio avoids the subject)

Luis de la Fuente Rubirosa, cousin of Porfirio Rubirosa, who escaped to the Dominican Republic after being indicted in New York for the murder in 1935 of Sergio Bencosme, mistaken for former Dominican vice-presidential candidate *A*ngel *M*orales (*Luis* Jaramillo; and the initials of the intended victim are the same as those of *A*drián *M*artín, the victim in the novel).

The number of names and other similarities reflected in *The Labyrinth* would seem more than just coincidence. Other plays on names are ironic, such as the observation about the initial "C" in the tyrant's name: "It won't surprise me if one day he changes that 'C' to Caesar" (139), which in fact became a popular epithet in books about Trujillo. Finally, the play on the name Jaram*illo*, ending like Truj*illo*, suggests that where lust for power is concerned, there is little difference between a Trujillo and a Jaramillo.

As we have seen, Laguerre draws on reality but makes significant changes which make good reading. To use the terminology of Vladimir Nabokov, we might say that Laguerre is more attentive to "the facts of fiction" (the internal demands of a novel) than to "the fiction of facts" (adhering to reality).[14] He disguises the Dominican Republic slightly as the Santiagan Republic, a prudent precaution in the heyday of Trujillo foreign intrigue, and times events imaginatively. While Dominican agents hunted down enemies in New York in 1935 and in the 1950's, the analogous incident in the novel takes place in the 1940's, to coincide with the German submarine blockade in the Caribbean and the intensification of anti-Trujillo conspiracies, so that the end could correspond to the 1947 Cayo Confites invasion or that of Luperón in 1949, both of which failed. The strike mentioned in the novel would be the only successful one of the Trujillo reign, which occurred in 1946.

The reality of Trujillo's Dominican Republic, according to the documentary evidence, was filled with terrifying atrocities, physical violence and torture, an aspect largely absent in *The Labyrinth*, undoubtedly because the author's primary interest lies in the emotional, moral, and spiritual damage inflicted on artists, education, youth, individuals, and families. As Lewis Richardson noted in an early review, Laguerre "is not interested in unearthing the sordid and exploiting it in the name of realism."[15] He does, however, communicate the tragedy and suffering of people under such a regime without resorting to sensationalism or *tremendismo* (an accent on horror and violence)—long a Hispanic literary tradition—which his personal sensitivity obviously rejects.

Greek Mythology in *The Labyrinth*

The novel's title refers explicitly to the labyrinth that King Minos of Crete ordered Daedalus to construct in order to enclose the minotaur, fierce monster with the body of a man and the head of a bull, who exacted human tribute from the Athenians. The brave Theseus risked his life to deliver his countrymen, helped by Ariadne, the king's daughter, who provided him with a sword to kill the Minotaur and a clew of thread to find his way out of the labyrinth. Laguerre extends the myth to multiple labyrinths in which Porfirio Uribe is embroiled: that of New York, with the Ariadne's thread of education promising material security; the unseen labyrinth in the recesses of his own mind with its confused values; and the worst labyrinth of all, the Santiagan Republic where "it was unthinkable that a monster was running loose in this paradise" (119). The tyrant's portrayal as a Minotaur of unbridled instincts is appropriate, recalling Trujillo's well-known fondness for cattle and horses. Allusions to the monster's taurine component appear in the episode in which a heifer escapes from its halter and charges Leader Augusto and in Don Joaquín Valverde's offer to try to "distract the bull with his cape," referring to the tyrant (182).

Since Laguerre's use of Greek mythology is explicit and straightforward, it may appear disarmingly simple. It is, however, more complex than it may seem on the surface because the mythological vision functions on several separate but related levels involving author, narrator, characters, and readers, each perceiving it in a different light. The author orients us with the title of the book and its two parts, "The Maze" and "The Monster." The characters often describe their experiences in terms of Greek myths. The narrator in turn offers comments and finally the reader makes further deductions.

Although characters themselves recognize their symbolic use of Greek myths, their reasons for such expression differ. Jacinto Brache simply says, "I've always liked the stories from Greek mythology," to which Porfirio Uribe adds: "I do too. They have a great deal of wisdom in them" (109). The narrator makes it clear that Porfirio's use of myth is a very personal and private affair. His two new Santiagan friends aboard the San Jacinto call each other names from Greek legends. For Luis Jaramillo, his brother-in-law Jacinto Brache is an Orpheus "counting on his magic music to hypnotize the infernal deities" and marry his Eurydice, Hortensia Valverde (109), while Brache sees Jaramillo as Bellerophon bent on conquering the Amazons and the Chimera and on reaching the very doors of Olympus. The narrator explains that this is "a delightful game" and "merely a way of disguising reality" (109), but the reader discovers that it is instead a necessity imposed by the reign of terror in the Republic, in fact, a sort of cryptographic, evasive language. Such symbol using, according to S. I. Hayakawa, often "exists to fulfill a necessary biological function. . . , that of *helping us to maintain psychological health and equilibrium.*"[16] Consequently, when Jacinto no longer speaks of Orpheus and Eurydice, it marks his mental decline and means "he's accepted a reality which for him is horrible" (162).

The reader can further appreciate other aspects of the myths of which the characters themselves remain unaware. If the wary reader recalls that Bellerophon had killed a countryman (or in some versions, his brother), he will be less surprised to find out what Jaramillo's role was in New York. Bellerophon's fate should also stimulate conjecture about his future.

The informed reader can discern that Porfirio Uribe's understanding of the Greek myth is faulty, and at best partial and egocentric. At first he equates the labyrinth with confusion and the monster as poverty. Both in New York and in the Santiagan Republic he misinterprets the story of Theseus merely as a struggle to get out of the labyrinth rather than as a willingness to sacrifice oneself. Theseus had resolved "to deliver his countrymen from this calamity, or to die in the attempt."[17] The reader can see how far Uribe really is from being the Athenian hero and how others who are caught in the Santiagan labyrinth, like Joaquín Valverde, ironically consider him their Ariadne's thread. Uribe has completely forgotten another of Theseus's adventures which characterizes his own situation in the Republic—Theseus's descent into the underworld, where he was stuck onto the Chair of Forgetfulness by the Lord of Hades until Hercules lifted him from the seat and brought him back.[18] Uribe likewise seems rooted to silence and conformity until, through Laza and Lorenzi, he recalls forgotten values and rises from his "Chair of Forgetfulness." In the course of the novel we see Uribe approach a more complete appreciation of the Theseus myth than he had ever imagined.

The myth of Orpheus, the master musician who tried to rescue his wife from Hades but looked back and lost her, can serve as a clue to Jacinto Brache's fate and can be further extended to view Porfirio Uribe as another musician without an instrument descending into a Hades where the Eurydice of freedom is held prisoner by a monster. Additional Greek legends function simply as metaphors that envision Leader Augusto as the "Greatest of Titans" (183), Jaramillo as sharpening his arrows to seek the Achilles heel of a rival (217), and Rosana as a Cassandra.

The reasons for Laguerre's extensive use of classical allusions in the novel are open to conjecture. Jung would say simply that it is natural for the artist to do so:

> It is . . . to be expected of the poet that he will resort to mythology in order to give his experience its most fitting expression. It would be a serious mistake to suppose that he works with materials received at second hand. The primordial experience is the source of his creativeness; it cannot be fathomed, and therefore requires mythological imagery to give it form.[19]

It may also be considered a conscious literary device to clarify events or provide ironic contrasts. As an expression of collective man and community, mythology is appropriate in a novel not only about an individual but about groups of people and even a whole society caught in the labyrinths of New York and the Santiagan Republic. Laguerre's use of myths represents a tribute to their continued relevance, and finally, their recurrence serves as a thematic pattern which is both intellectually stimulating and aesthetically pleasing.

The author contrasts these solid myths of the past with other self-serving myths invented by individuals and societies, which are false, empty and even dangerous. The Santiagan Republic subscribes to social "myths" of super- stitious family hatred and class differences and falls prey to the self-mythification practiced by Leader Augusto, complete with exaggerated titles and legends of "heroic" feats. Such deleterious myths should be destroyed to re- veal the tyrant for what he is, "a man in a hurry to empty his bowels" or a "digestive tube" covered with medals, and to show "that the fiction created by historians and bi- ographers was actually this man of flesh and blood" (184).

Psychological Depth: Symbols and Jungian Archetypes

One of Laguerre's outstanding achievements in the novel is the creation of solid characters whose dialogue, behavior, and responses to events, even when unexpected, are convincing. What makes them so "real" for us lies be- neath the surface, since there are almost no physical de- scriptions. They have great psychological depth, for as Lewis Richardson noted in his review, the author "shows a deep understanding of hidden motivations but indulges in no psychoanalytical jargon."[20] While I believe this is the result of innate sensitivity and intense observation of real people, as an artist Laguerre conveys psychological depth by means of symbols, among which appear, surprisingly, certain identifiable archetypes.

Laguerre frequently resorts to animal imagery to show the instinctive side of man's nature. In *The Labyrinth* are allusions to spiders, moles, turtles, worms, elephants, dogs, fish, pigeons, mollusks, foxes, bulls, cuckoos, hawks, and horses. Some animals appearing in the first part of the novel reflect Porfirio Uribe's solitary underground "spider's existence" or life as a "Dead Letters Office mole." Sea imagery and aquatic animals abound in the second part with clearly symbolical connotations: Paulina's similarity to fish who have lost their sight from living in dark caverns deep under the sea (173), Valverde's "mollusk-like soul" which has suddenly lost its protective shell (180), a fallen fish tank resulting in suffocation of the fish, and a conspirator's recollection of an African fish that buries itself in the mud to await the return of the rains to swim out of its hole. Some animal allusions underscore man's bestiality to be overcome; as Laza states, "I'm also conscious of my animal nature, but I defy it with an ideal" (83). Laguerre's evident knowledge of animal curiosities in this and other novels is probably as much a reflection of his rural experiences as an intent observer of nature as of his artistic propensity toward imagery to describe human behavior.

A reiterated symbol of a decidedly personal nature similar to a thematic motif in music is the baritone horn or *bombardino* bequeathed to Porfirio by his godfather Estefano. It has, like most symbols, dual possibilities. The broken horn, enmeshed with his "very consciousness" (33) is a sort of talisman and at the same time a weight associated with original sin, guilt, expulsion and abandon, since Estefano had killed his wife Catalina in a jealous rage and with his imprisonment, Porfirio had to leave the security of his godparents' home in Coamo, Puerto Rico. The sounds of the horn, his companion during twelve years in New York, recall Estefano's sobs and his own tragic feelings and mix with the incessant wailing of foghorns in the city's harbor and the sound of his heart throbbing "its two organ notes." The *bombardino* also symbolizes his amputation from Puerto Rico, since it is a solo instrument in the native *danza* music. When it is engulfed by the sea, Porfirio experiences a sort of liberation: "When we are isolated for years on end, we become more conscious of the objects which accompany us. He had let the sorrowful old soul of the poor bombardino influence him!" (122) Having lost the horn—talisman and curse—he becomes more aware of people than objects as he embarks upon a new adventure.

Another major motif is that of the netherworld, which for the ancient Egyptians was depicted as a labyrinth. It is accompanied by a constellation of related images: darkness, abysses, and the sea, which together suggest the unconscious, despair, and death. They are ominously present in the dark staircase of the first chapter, the dense blackness of the nocturnal waters that swallow up the San Jacinto, the "mass of rolling shadows" that is the Santiagan sea, and the sensation of endlessly falling expressed by several characters.

In addition to descriptive symbols (animals), personal symbols (the *bombardino*), and those which reflect state of mind (darkness, abysses, the sea), a number of characters themselves correspond to what the great psychologist Carl Jung called "archetypes of the collective unconscious." These are certain primordial or first images man has inherited from his ancestral past much in the same way that physical characteristics are inherited. In this form of psychic heredity, images retained from earliest times in the reservoir of the collective unconscious may be drawn into conscious reality by identifying them with corresponding objects or people in our experience. Functioning separately or in combinations as predispositions, these inherited models or archetypes shape our personality and behavior.[21]

The fact that a good number of archetypes identified and described by Jung manifest themselves clearly in Laguerrean characters in *The Labyrinth* makes an archetypal reading of the text not only enlightening but, to my mind, essential to fully appreciate the author's instinctive psychological understanding, which makes for credible characterization. Surprisingly, one of these Jungian archetypes is explicitly named in the novel: the *shadow*. Porfirio Uribe asserts that his ambition for personal success "is much a part of me as my shadow, and a person can't jump over his own shadow" (47). References to this shadow are repeated several times in the novel, in consonance with the qualities Jung assigned to the shadow as the source of the best and worst in man, his basic instincts which appeal to survival, in Uribe's case, a call to material security. He is confronted with a dilemma, for as Jung observed: "Divining in advance whether our dark partner symbolizes a shortcoming to be overcome or a meaningful bit of life that we should accept—that is one of the most difficult problems that we encounter on the way to individuation."22

Another archetypal component of Porfirio Uribe's personality that is clearly visible is the "conformity archetype" or *persona,* which enables one to portray a role expected of him in order to achieve material rewards or survive. Thus we see Porfirio, characterized by Laza as an innately generous person, adopt in the Santiagan Republic a facade of silence, acquiescence, conformism, and even collaboration in conflict with his nature, so that he lives in a constant state of psychological tension exacerbated by that of his environment. This brings us to the self archetype that is only fully realized when it organizes the other component archetypes into order and harmony. When Porfirio manages to jump over his shadow and take off his mask, he is on the road to self-realization.

He is helped along the way by another Jungian archetype, found outside himself, the "spirit type" or "wise old man figure," who may not always be old, but has the wisdom of old age and influences the protagonist. A common figure in world literature, he can be found frequently in Laguerre's fiction, from Don Polo in *The Blaze* to Adalberto Ortiz in *El fuego y su aire* (Fire and its air), and "always appears in a situation where insight, understanding, good advice, determination, planning, etc., are needed but cannot be mustered on one's own resources. The archetype compensates this state of spiritual deficiency by contents designed to fill the gap."[23] Porfirio, for example, reflects that "in moments of danger or triumph he had always turned to his friend, Alfredo Laza. Alfredo had warded off trouble in the old days" (15). Laza, who perceives that his role is "to awaken Uribe's conscience" (32), represents, in accordance with the universal archetype, "knowledge, reflection, insight, wisdom, cleverness, and intuition on the one hand, and on the other, moral qualities such as good will and readiness to help."[24] "The tendency of the old man to set one thinking also takes the form of urging people to 'sleep on it'," rather than rushing them into action.[25] In the same fashion, after his conversations with Porfirio in the first part of the novel Laza virtually disappears from view as an active character until the moment is ripe to mobilize the moral and spiritual forces needed to drive the protagonist to action. As Jung observes, "not only in fairy tales but in life generally, the objective intervention of the archetype is needed."[26]

Another Jungian archetype, the *anima* or eternal image of woman carried within every man and projected as unconscious standards by which specific women are measured, seems underdeveloped in Porfirio. Perhaps this is because the first projection of the image is always on the mother, in his case absent, and because of the traumatic memory concerning his godmother. It takes the form of a triad of women in the novel that contains the well-known threefold range of feminine qualities: maiden (Hortensia), mother (Paulina, the tragic mother), and sorceress (the superstitious, "clairvoyant" Rosana).[27] Each is surrounded in turn by a triad of men: Rosana loves Laza but flirts with Porfirio and Lorenzi (as with Adrián Martínez before him). Paulina loves her husband, is victimized by Leader Augusto, and consoled by her brother. Hortensia is involved with Brache, Jaramillo and Porfirio.

The triad is itself an archetypal element. For Jung, fourness is a symbol of wholeness while threeness is not: "If one imagines the quaternity as a square divided into halves by a diagonal, one gets two triangles whose apices point in opposite directions," just as the divine Trinity functions in opposition to the chthonic or infernal triad.[28] Porfirio is always the "third man" in the love triad, marginal and expendable, and forms with Laza and Lorenzi a triad in which each one alone is an incomplete hero. There are also three labyrinths, three major male victims of Leader Augusto (Brache, Valverde, and Jaramillo), three Jacintos (Jacinto Brache, Jacinto Martínez, and the San Jacinto). The group that tries to carry out a mission of justice at the end, however, is the quaternity that restores order: "They were four men hunting the monster" (266). The wholeness of four is achieved by the presence of Purificación López, "son of the Antilles, in whose veins ran the blood of three races" (272). His symbolic name, meaning "purification" and his representation of a fourth "cosmic race" (described by Mexico's José Vasconcelos as the culmination of racial mixture in the Americas) contribute to the quaternary impression of wholeness.

The psychological structure of other characters in the novel can be viewed in terms of traditional Jungian archetypes. Leader Augusto is a combination of the hero and demon archetypes resulting in the ruthless leader. Jaramillo fits the pattern of the "trickster-figure," whose other side is his vulnerability to being outwitted. His cunning manipulation of people in the Santiagan Republic and his subsequent fate conform to the trickster's archetypal combination of wisdom and folly.

Perceiving people as archetypes or symbols in fiction does not weaken the sensation of their "reality" any more than it does in life. In fact, their persistent presence in myths, legends, and tales throughout the world gives further credence to their universality. One prominent symbologist has observed that "other people can play a symbolic role in your life, supporting and confirming your Ego by their similarities; or confronting and opposing you as Shadow figures; or they may appear as the successful fulfilment of your true SELF. Just as people play symbolic roles in dreams, so they do in life. We select friends, and even husbands or wives, for symbolic reasons."[29] The novelist, however, must be careful not to make his characters *merely* symbols that could detract from their human dimensions. Fictional characters can be convincing as people and *also* function as symbols drawn from the archetypes of the collective unconscious, adding another dimension of psychological depth. Porfirio's friendship with Laza may well lie in his need to hear the counsel of the spirit type, but he also admires Lorenzi, the invulnerable hero type. Laza and Lorenzi, whose names containing L and z suggest association, complement Porfirio and lead him to the eventual finding of his real self, combining the ideals of the one and the daring of the other.

Narrative and Irony

Among Laguerre's novels *The Labyrinth* is probably the most narrative and fast-paced, with romantic intrigue, a good deal of action, suspense, and surprising revelations, all enhanced by William Rose's excellent translation. The almost total absence of landscape is very unusual in Laguerre, but understandable, since Leader Augusto "even overshadowed nature itself" (184). The strengths of the novel's prose lie in the lively dialogue and masterfully handled narrative that switches smoothly and even imperceptibly from one point of view to another, from introspection to action and from past to present, and events are easy to follow.

Linguistic and situational irony convey the repressive atmosphere of the Santiagan Republic without having to resort to description of atrocities. The exaggerated laudatory epithets like "glorious statesman" and "Father of Their Country," which were commonplace in the Trujillo era, become ironic in the novel. Ironic intentions are evident in the seemingly rhetorical question, "What other illustrious chief of state, no matter how glorious he might be, could compare his deeds with those of Leader Augusto?" (91). Ironic too is the statement that "the Leader's private secretary and counselor was Jacinto Martínez, a man who had fled from 'the bloody dictatorship' in Spain to enjoy the benefits of the excellent democracy presided over by Leader Augusto" (138), but no more so than the truth that many Spanish Republicans escaping the tyranny of Franco sought refuge in Santo Domingo. The Santiagan Republic is characterized as a "free country" (107) in contrast to Puerto Rico's status under the United States flag and as "a country with many more opportunities than Puerto Rico" (110), but the irony doesn't become evident until later.

Galíndez relates in *The Era of Trujillo* that "sometimes sycophancy becomes bitter irony as the sign at the entrance to the insane asylum at Nigua: Todo se lo debemos a Trujillo (We owe everything to Trujillo)."[30] A similar sign at the insane asylum in the novel announces, "We owe everything to Leader Augusto," which is unfortunately true, while Augusto's assertion that "no one is responsible for another man's madness" (236) is not, as we see more than one of his victims driven to madness. Also ironic is the fact that Porfirio, whose ticket to success is a degree in law, goes to a place where there is no law but the tyrant's will. The final irony of the novel comes in Augusto's enraged order to "Kill those corpses," which is not only impossible in the physical realm but also in that of collective memory, where they will live on. Yet the most tremendous irony of all was provided by history; the assassination of the real-life tyrant was a fitting epilogue to *The Labyrinth*.

The Laguerrean Vision

Porfirio Uribe conforms to a general profile of Laguerrean protagonists who are separated from one or both parents, subjected to a traumatic childhood experience, attracted by material gain resulting in a moral decline, and changed through experience and dialogue. Laguerre's faith in the innate goodness of man makes him loathe to condemn his characters, showing instead both their light and dark sides influenced by circumstance and social interaction. Even Augusto might have been quite a different leader, as Alfredo Laza, ever the idealist, observes:

> Prejudices and the urge to power are not innate, they are not an inherent part of man's incorruptible conscience, but are the result of social competition, the effort to keep up appearances. Even Augusto might have been the leader in a good cause if he hadn't let himself get all balled up in his superstitious hatred of the once powerful Valverde and Jaramillo families. (258)

Like the giant or monster in folk literature he "is not unlike a negative form of the Cosmic MAN or the cosmic man gone wrong."[31] Leader Augusto is as much a creation of the rival families as of his own instincts carried to excess; he could not exist without the forces which created and supported him. The ultimate hope is the possibility of change in man: "We human beings change more than we like to admit" (206), as one character observes. We are witnesses to this change in several people, and in Porfirio it is both convincing and natural.

As a profoundly Puerto Rican writer, Laguerre is con-

cerned with questions of Puerto Rican identity and consciousness. Is identity to be determined by birth,
parentage, residence, or feeling? Porfirio, of Mexican and
Santiagan parents and brought up in Puerto Rico, consid-
ers himself Puerto Rican. On the other hand, Jaramillo is a
Santiagan born of a Puerto Rican mother in Puerto Rico.
Other islanders have made their permanent home in New
York. The author seems to imply that it is a matter of self-
identity and that, in any case, the Puerto Rican should also
identify himself with his Caribbean brethren, in line with
the ideas of Eugenio María de Hostos (1839–1903), the
enlightened Puerto Rican educator and writer who envi-
sioned a Caribbean Confederation. Interestingly, Trujillo
ordered a 1956 symposium on Hostos, who in his last
years had supervised education in the Dominican Republic
and had been revered there for four generations, designed
to downgrade him and destroy his reputation.[32] It is likely
that this event contributed to Laguerre's point of view in
the novel. It is also very significant that the author, who
takes a consistent stand against violence as a way of resolv-
ing Puerto Rico's political status in his novels, seems to
condone it as a means of fighting tyranny. Lorenzi, who in
Laguerre's previous novel *The Ceiba Tree in the Flower Pot*
would not subordinate his fiercely independent nature to
serve the Nationalist cause in Puerto Rico, now lends his
support to the cause of freedom repressed by a tyrant in a
neighboring republic.

Porfirio Uribe's motto of "listen, and don't commit
yourself" (178) and his resolve "not to become involved
in anything" (157) is not only the voice of geographical
"*insularismo*" but of an all too common contemporary attitude. "Why did this have to happen to me? To *me?*" (4) is
not the question of a hero but rather of any man and how
he learns to deal with that question forms the material of
the novel. The process of his individuation is inextricably
linked to the struggle of others, of community and collec-

tive man. Attesting to Laguerre's intense concern for collective man alongside the individual are his story drawn from one nation's history, characters described in terms of Greek mythology, and the presence of archetypes of human behavior inherited from remotest antiquity. In an age in which so many writers lead us into a labyrinth of despair, Laguerre maintains a realistic view of man's weaknesses and strengths and an optimistic view of his capacity to discover the good that lies within him.

Estelle Irizarry
Georgetown University

NOTES

1 The first was Alejandro Tapia y Rivera's *Enardo and Rosael, an Allegorical Novella,* translated by Alejandro Tapia, Jr. (New York: Philosophical Library, 1952).

2 Novels which had previously treated the theme were Guillermo Cotto-Thorner's *Trópico en Manhattan* (1951) and Laguerre's *La ceiba en el tiesto* (1956).

3 The only critics to explicitly identify the fictional Republic were Carrasco, Cartey, and Friedenberg (see bibliography). In his book of essays *Polos de la cultura iberoamericana* (Boston: Florentia Publishers, 1977, p. 164), Laguerre mentions that the Mexican critic and professor Andrés Iduarte advised him to change his temporary New York address because his life might be in danger, a warning he says was "well founded."

4 Antonio S. Pedreira, *Insularismo* (San Juan: Edil, 1968), p. 62.

5 *The Economist* (London), December 10–16, 1983, p. 13.

6 *The New York Times,* October 4, 1952, p. 3, col. 8.

7 See Russell R. Fitzgibbon's "Editor's Preface" to Jesús de Galíndez, *The Era of Trujillo* (Tucson: University of Arizona, 1973), pp. xi-xviii, and Robert D. Crassweller, *Trujillo: The Life and Times of a Caribbean Dictator* (New York: Macmillan, 1966).

8 Crassweller, p. x.

9 Germán E. Ornes, *Trujillo: Little Caesar of the Caribbean* (New York: Thomas Nelson, 1958).

10 Arturo R. Espaillat, *Trujillo: The Last Caesar* (Chicago: Henry Regnery, 1963), p. ix.

11 Page 161 in this edition; subsequent pages are given in parentheses.

12 Crassweller, p. 126.

13 Ibid., pp. 433–39; other details and names from Ornes.

14 Vladimir Nabokov, *Lectures on Don Quixote* (New York: Harcourt Brace Jovanovich, 1983), p. 1.

15 Richardson, Lewis, "A Love of Life and People: *The Labyrinth,*" *The San Juan Star,* September 16, 1960.

16 S. I. Hayakawa, *Language in Thought and Action* (New York: Harcourt Brace, 1949), p. 148.

17 Thomas Bulfinch, *Bulfinch's Mythology* (New York: Avenel, 1968), p. 152.

18 Edith Hamilton, *Mythology* (New York: New American Library, 1969), p. 156.

19 Carl G. Jung, *Modern Man in Search of a Soul* (New York: Harcourt Brace & World, 1933), p. 164.

20 An exception, however, is the narrator's explanation that Uribe had developed "what the psychoanalysts would call an evasive anxiety complex" (9).

21 Further descriptions of archetypes may be found in Jung, *Man and His Symbols* (New York: Doubleday, 1969), *The Archetypes and the Collective Unconscious* (Princeton: Princeton University, 1980) and Calvin S. Hall and Vernon J. Nordby, *A Primer of Jungian Psychology* (New York: New American Library, 1973).

22 M.-L. von Franz, "The Process of Individuation," in Jung, *Man and His Symbols*, pp. 175–76.

23 Jung, *The Archetypes and the Collective Unconscious*, p. 216.

24 Ibid., p. 222

25 Ibid., p. 220.

26 Ibid.

27 Ibid., p. 182.

28 Ibid., pp. 234–35.

29 Tom Chetwynd, *A Dictionary of Symbols* (London: Granada, 1982), p. 323.

30 Galíndez, p. 202.

31 Chetwynd, p. 169.

32 Ornes, p. 179.

Bibliography

Novels, in order of publication (first edition cited):

La llamarada (The blaze). Aguadilla, P. R.: Tipografía Fidel Ruiz, 1935.

Solar Montoya (Montoya Plantation). San Juan: Imprenta Venezuela, 1941.

El 30 de febrero (The 30th of February). San Juan: Biblioteca de Autores Puertorriqueños, 1943.

La resaca (The undertow). San Juan: Biblioteca de Autores Puertorriqueños, 1949.

Los dedos de la mano (The fingers of the hand). San Juan: Biblioteca de Autores Puertorriqueños, 1951.

La ceiba en el tiesto (The ceiba tree in the flower pot). San Juan: Biblioteca de Autores Puertorriqueños, 1956.

El laberinto (The labyrinth). New York: Las Américas, 1959. (Latest edition: 4th ed., Río Piedras: Editorial Cultural, 1974).

The Labyrinth. New York: Las Américas, 1960. Translation by William Rose.

Cauce sin río (River bed without a river). Madrid: Nuevas Editoriales Unidas, 1962.

El fuego y su aire (Fire and its Air). Buenos Aires: Losada, 1970.

Los amos benévolos (Benevolent masters). Río Piedras: Universidad de Puerto Rico, Editorial Universitaria, 1976.

Benevolent Masters. Maplewood, N.J.: Waterfront Press, 1984. Translation by Gino Parisi. Annotated edition by Estelle Irizarry.

Complete Works:

Obras completas. San Juan: Instituto de Cultura Puertorriqueña, 1974. Volume I: *La llamarada, Solar Montoya, El 30 de febrero.* Volume II: *La resaca, Los dedos de la mano, La ceiba en el tiesto.*

Books about Enrique A. Laguerre in English:

Irizarry, Estelle. *Enrique A. Laguerre,* Boston: G. K. Hall (Twayne's World Authors Series), 1982 (pp. 84–92 treat *The Labyrinth*).

Books about Laguerre in Spanish (with some treatment of *El laberinto*):

Beauchamp, José Juan, *Imagen del puertorriqueño en la novela* (*En Alejandro Tapia y Rivera, Manuel Zeno Gandía y Enrique A. Laguerre*). Río Piedras: Editorial Universitaria, Universidad de Puerto Rico, 1976.

Casanova Sánchez, Olga. *La crítica social en la obra novelística de Enrique A. Laguerre.* Río Piedras: Editorial Cultural, 1975.

García Cabrera, Manuel. *Laguerre y sus polos de la cultura iberoamericana.* San Juan: Biblioteca de Autores Puertorriqueños, 1978.

Morfi, Angelina. *Enrique A. Laguerre y su obra "La resaca," cumbre en su arte de novelar.* San Juan: Instituto de Cultura Puertorriqueña, 1964.

Zayas Micheli, Luis O. *Lo universal en Enrique A. Laguerre* (*Estudio conjunto de su obra*). Río Piedras: Editorial Edil, 1974.

Annotated Bibliography of Announcements, Reviews, and Articles on *El laberinto* or *The Labyrinth*:

Anonymous. "*The Labyrinth.*" *La Voz* (New York), October 1960, p. 3. Announcement of the English version and its value for an understanding of "recent events in Latin America" and of life in New York for Puerto Ricans.

Anonymous. "Quien habla: *El laberinto* (*The Labyrinth*)" *The Island Times* (San Juan), October 30, 1959. Brief announcement of the selection of the novel as book-of-the-month by London's International Book Club.

Basdekis, Demetrios. "Revista de libros: 'The Labyrinth'." *La Voz*, November 1960. Praises the translation and the novel as outspoken indictment of forces that molded the protagonist's sense of futility in New York and as a condemnation of Latin American tyrants.

Braschi, Wilfredo. "*El laberinto* de Laguerre; trasciende escenario puertorriqueño." *El Mundo* (San Juan), January 2, 1960, p. 7. Observations on the book's importance, noting careful characterization. General information on Laguerre and some of his own comments.

Carrasco, Sanson. "Men and Books." *La Voz*, May 1961, p. 16. Recommends the novel to English-speaking readers to familiarize themselves with Caribbean affairs and the roots of power in countries like the Dominican Republic.

Cartey, Wilfred O. "Libros nuevos: *El laberinto*, *Revista Hispánica Moderna* (New York), XXVII; 3–4 (1961), 353. Brief identification of symbols and discussion of corresponding reality, citing the central theme as the labyrinth that devours all characters.

Cruz Igartua, Gilberto. "Dos novelas puertorriqueñas: *Víspera del hombre* y *El laberinto*." *Educación*, IX: 76 (December 1959). General review of René Marqués's 1959 novel and Laguerre's.

Díaz Alfaro, Abelardo. "*El laberinto*, obra de Laguerre se incorpora a la literatura universal." *El Mundo*, November 21, 1959, p. 2. Notes use of suggestive mythological allusions, allegories, and names to disguise bitter reality and finds characters well developed.

Escribano, Luis M. "*The Labyrinth*. Circulará este mes versión en inglés obra de Laguerre." *El Mundo*, September 6, 1960. Information on the translation, book jacket, and publishing company.

Friedenberg, Daniel M. "Caribbean Labyrinth: Our Creature in Ciudad Trujillo." *The New Republic*, CXLIV: 3 (January 16, 1961), 18–19. Focuses on the novel as a study of the effects of power based on the Trujillo reality and calls the novel "a medieval Passion Play" for this century about "ordinary man," like Uribe, capable of redemption.

González, José Emilio. "*El laberinto*." *Asomante* (San Juan), XVI: 4 (1960), 70–76. Lengthy summary of plot. Cites interesting characters, exciting narrative, the condemnation of a mediocre, routine and material lifestyle, and lack of "local color".

Jiménez Lugo, A. "*El laberinto:* Publicarán en inglés novela de Laguerre." *El Mundo,* July 17, 1959, p. 12. Announcement of forthcoming publication of the novel in English translation with general information on Laguerre and some of his quotes about the Uribe characterization from different perspectives and about future plans for writing.

Maslow, Vera. "Enrique A. Laguerre: *El laberinto.*" *La Voz,* November 1959, pp. 17–18. Finds the novel valuable in providing varied insights into Puerto Rican reality—"*lo puertorriqueño*"—in New York and in Uribe's discovery of other people. Describes the personality of characters, plot, and moral and spiritual implications.

Parrilla, Arturo. "Nueva novela de Laguerre, *El laberinto.*" *El Mundo,* July 25, 1959, p. 29. Recounts plot and praises the reproduction of psychological, universal, and Puerto Rican reality, with emphasis on transmitting thought and feeling of the times authentically.

Richardson, Lewis. "A Love of Life and People: *The Labyrinth.*" *The San Juan Star,* September 16, 1960. Cites the novel's skillful handling of setting, plot, and character development. Notes Laguerre's "enlightened social and moral outlook" and respect and love for the good in people. Finds the novel "a pretty reasonable facsimile of life."

Valenzuela, Víctor M. "Enrique A. Laguerre: *El laberinto.*" *Revista la Nueva Democracia* (New York), October 1960, pp. 119–20 and *La Voz,* April 1961, p. 21. Summarizes plot and cites merits in the clear, concise prose, convincing characters and settings, and reflection of social concern and of man's anxiety to find a reason for living.

Part I

THE MAZE

CHAPTER

I

Night was already falling as he entered the building. Strange, he thought, that they hadn't yet turned on the lights. He paused for a moment before going farther in the darkness. But his heart was light, he was filled with an indefinable joy, as if for the first time in his life he fully realized that there was, after all, a place for him in the world. In a few seconds he would unhurriedly climb the stairs, counting them one by one as he climbed. He would call out to Rosana, he would let her give him a kiss before he invited her to go out with him for the evening.

Suddenly he saw a man coming down the stairs just as he noticed two other men coming out from under the staircase. Inevitably he would encounter all three men at the same point. Then two shots flashed, and a third. After which there was a brief silence, deep as a pit, and the man who was descending the stairs collapsed without a cry, without a murmur. Another shot flashed, and the two men ran into the street. He tried to follow, but stood rooted to the spot, unable to move. His left temple smarted as if burnt. There was a sharp pain in his right foot.

He retained one vivid impression: the slightly irregular movements of one of the fleeing men, an almost imperceptible detail which had become more remarkable as the man passed from the darkness of the hallway into the light of the street. The fugitive, in all probability, had one leg slightly shorter than the other. In his shocked state he had noticed only that one detail, so small, yet so vivid. He now became aware that the gunfire had deafened him. He was perhaps seriously wounded; it was said that people sometimes don't at first realize how badly hurt they are. But more tormenting than anything else were the questions crowding his mind. Who were the killers? Why did this have to happen to me? To *me*? He felt like screaming that question at the top of his lungs.

He managed to move one of his feet, but in doing so stumbled over the body. Once again he tried to pursue the fugitives, or flee after them, he was not sure which. But he could not force himself to act. Besides, it was too late. They would already be lost in the crowds of factory hands and office workers returning home at the end of the day.

As if by magic the hall was flooded with light. People were rushing downstairs, shouting and commenting on what had happened. Accusing fingers were pointed at him as he stood beside the fallen body, unable to speak, dumbfounded at what was taking place around him.

"Murderer! Murderer!" shouted someone. And from the head of the stairs sounded a maternal voice that he recognized: "Did you do it, Porfirio?"

It was Doña Isabel. He boarded with her, and the man on the floor, Adrián Martín, an exile from Santiago, had also been her boarder.

Porfirio Uribe did not reply, but continued to stare at the people around him, without seeing or understanding, without knowing what to say. He was completely bewildered. Why had he collided with the other men at the bottom of the stairs as the shots were fired? How had those two killers managed to escape? Why were these accusing fingers being thrust in his face?

4

"Look! He's splattered with blood!"

Ah yes, now he remembered. When Adrián Martín had collapsed—how incredible it all seemed—he had fallen against Porfirio and almost knocked him down. Porfirio looked at the bloodstains as though it were all a bad dream. But the burn on his temple was painfully real, and there was no doubt that his right foot had been wounded by the last shot fired toward the floor where Adrián's body had fallen.

"Here's the revolver!" said someone.

"Don't touch it! Wait for the police!" said someone else, running off to telephone in the room opening out into the hallway. His excited voice could be heard by everyone as he informed the police. "A Spic's been killed. Another Spic did it!"

Porfirio realized that the other "Spic" was himself, still alive, by a miracle.

"Say something, Porfirio," begged Doña Isabel; then, addressing the others: "This man is incapable of killing! I know him very well."

But as he still said nothing, Doña Isabel drew back, bewildered at his silence.

And everyone continued to stare at Porfirio, who remained dumbfounded, standing there in the midst of the circle of curious unlookers, as if he were a caged animal in a zoo, the only specimen of a species which had been thought to be extinct.

Adrián Martín's body lay at Porfirio's feet. Oh, if only the corpse could speak and explain everything!

But suddenly he remembered that he and Adrián had quarreled bitterly a few days before because the Santiagan, who occupied the room next to his, insisted on typing late in the night. The argument had become so heated that Doña Isabel, Rosana, and two boarders had come out into the corridor, and Doña Isabel had had to calm them down. Adrián Martín and Porfirio hadn't spoken to each other since.

5

And now Doña Isabel felt impelled to supply some information. "Yesterday afternoon," she was saying, "someone called Adrián on the phone. There was something mysterious about the answers."

Very few even deigned to look at Doña Isabel, and those who did regarded her with mistrust, as though they suspected her of being an accomplice. Her desire for justice evaporated. Just then, too, there was a distraction, as Doña Isabel's daughter, Rosana, came in from the street. She stood on tiptoe to look over the shoulders of the bystanders.

"Has something happened?" she asked.

"Not much," jeered one of the women. "Only a murder!"

"Adrián's been killed," said Doña Isabel.

"Who could have...?" Rosana stopped, her face pale. Terrified, she looked inquiringly at Porfirio, then exclaimed, "No! It's impossible!"

Two policemen shoved their way through the crowd. While one of them bent down to examine the man on the floor and pronounce him dead, the other questioned Porfirio.

"What happened? I want to know!"

Porfirio wanted to shout, "I want to know, too!" But not a word would come, and he continued to stand there, strangely silent.

"Portorican, eh?" said the policeman. "Why did you kill this man? Speak up!"

"Who witnessed the murder?" asked the other cop.

No one answered immediately.

"It must have been him," said someone at last. "Can't you see he's Puerto Rican? The Sanitation Department should sweep them out of the city!"

Porfirio listened without protest, stupefied that they could assume he was a criminal merely because he was a Puerto Rican. And it seemed even more unbelievable that no one sympathized with him, or realized what sacrifices he had made to become a lawyer. Why, only that morning he had been given his diploma!

6

The diploma and his ticket to Puerto Rico were in his coat pocket. He had planned to leave New York in three days. Why did this misfortune have to happen to him almost on the eve of his departure? All those sacrifices he had made, all those long hours of studying law, and all that trouble he had had to obtain a travel permit and a passage on a ship, in wartime, only to have this happen!

As these thoughts went through his mind, he made a frustrated gesture towards the pocket where his ticket and diploma were. No doubt believing that he was reaching for a weapon, the policeman seized and searched him. The policemen examined all his papers, then one of them put the papers into his own pocket. Porfirio, trembling, and still dazed, stood there, holding out his hand, until the two cops began shoving back the onlookers, with shouts of "Break it up, break it up!"

The crowd began to disperse. The ambulance would soon arrive. One of the policemen wrapped the revolver in a handkerchief and carefully stowed it away in his pocket. Then he fixed his attention upon Rosana, with the air of one who has discovered the key to a great mystery.

"Ah, now I get it! You're the woman."

"What woman?"

"The one they fought over. There must have been a woman in it. Oh, you Latins!" And he looked around complacently, as though he were Sherlock Holmes himself.

"At least, try to be original," said Rosana, shortly.

"You're the woman. Confess, you're the one they fought over."

"She's my daughter, and a well-bred young lady," said Doña Isabel. "I'd have you know that one of my ancestors was a governor of Puerto Rico!"

"You don't say!" exclaimed the policeman, in an exaggerated tone of mock astonishment. Then he asked: "Where do these men live?"

"In my house," replied Doña Isabel.

7

"In the same apartment with this girl, oh yeh?" And the policeman once more centered his attention on Rosana, almost strutting over his brilliant detective work.

"Oh yes," jeered Rosana, "and of course they fought over me!"

"Be careful how you talk! Anything you say, I warn you, will be held against you!"

"You and your mother, come along with us and this man," ordered the other cop, as the ambulance drew up at the door.

"This is the woman, ain't it?" Sherlock Holmes said to Porfirio, continuing his investigation.

The same coarse woman's voice that had spoken before now called down the stairs:

"That's how it must have been. That fellow never talked to anyone. I knew he had something up his sleeve."

Porfirio felt a weird change come over him. It seemed to him that with their prejudices they were inventing a new personality for him. He contemplated the woman on the stairs with an air of complete detachment, surprised that he could have lived in the same city with her for twelve years. And what had he achieved in those twelve years? But when you came right down to it, what had twenty centuries of Christian civilization achieved?

But why protest? Any protestation would have been in vain. Nothing hurts more than to be judged without having a chance to defend oneself. But after all, he had nothing to say! *God on high, All-Highest, how painful is life here below!*

Doña Isabel, sitting beside Porfirio in the patrol wagon, began to berate him because she, a respectable woman, had to ride in such a shameful vehicle. His only response was a look of sadness. He started to explain, then stopped, not knowing where to begin.

He turned to contemplate the city through the car's little window and felt such bitter disillusionment that the strength ebbed from his body. Yet only that morning he had felt so strong, had felt that he had himself in hand, for the first time in his life. After eight years of struggle, he had received his law degree. He had gone to the park with his friend Alfredo Laza in the afternoon to share the good news with him. And then, at the very moment when he returned to the boarding house to invite Rosana to celebrate with him, by coincidence he had converged with three other men at the scene of the crime. He was obsessed by the thought, and could only recall those last steps he had taken, over and over again.

From the window of the police wagon he saw ghostlike figures pass silently by. Who would come forward in his defense? Even Doña Isabel now regretted the friendly words she had said in his favor.

A tale from Greek mythology flashed through his mind, like a symbol of his martyrdom. It was the legend of the labyrinth of Crete. *He who entered the labyrinth could never escape, but would be a sure victim of the man-eating monster.* The hero Theseus, as famous as Hercules himself, ventured into that miniature hell from which there was no escape. But it was his good fortune to be aided by Ariadne, the daughter of the king, who gave him the guiding thread which enabled him to slay the monster and find his way out of the labyrinth.

He had heard the story told by his godmother, Catalina, who had raised him down there in Coamo, Puerto Rico, and now it came to mind like a dream. Indeed, he had always associated the events in his life with that distant legend, for despite his calm appearance, he had developed what the psychoanalysts would call an evasive anxiety complex. During the first four of his years in this labyrinth of New York, he had been on the verge of utter moral ruin. Later on, while employed in the Dead Letters Section of the Postal Service, he had withdrawn from the world to study law, with the intention of returning triumphantly to his native town. He had believed that education would put the thread of

9

Ariadne within his reach. But now he was almost in the monster's jaws, and he wondered if he would ever be able to escape the labyrinth. And he was bewildered, was convinced that no one would come to his rescue. Everyone around him was deaf and blind. Doña Isabel had turned against him. Even Rosana was silent and had given him not one encouraging glance.

He leaned against the door of the cage, swayed by a confused impulse to throw himself into the street and end his suffering, ground to a pulp of blood and flesh beneath the wheels of the passing cars, those roaring robots.

It would occur to no one to ask, "What kind of life did you lead in New York during the past eight years?" Instead, they called him a "Portorican", as if being a Puerto Rican were illegal, a crime. No one wanted to know about his spider's existence in the Dead Letters Section of the Postal Service and in the furnished room which was his only home, without diversions, without a wife or family, alone, alone, lost among dead letters and college text books, as though he himself were a dead letter.

Neither Doña Isabel nor Rosana even talked about what had happened. Perhaps they already regarded him as a criminal, having witnessed the bitter dispute he had unfortunately had with Adrián Martín the night before.

He stared persitently through the little window, seeing only the heartless indifference of the passersby, only the tormenting anguish of the grim labyrinth. Now and then the policemen looked askance at him, and one of them muttered, "Portorican! And I bet that's the woman!" The officer was obsessed with the idea; he would be terribly upset if his brilliant deduction proved false.

As Porfirio Uribe thought of the resolute efforts he had made to be a decent person, and how all this was now disregarded, his soul revolted. Oh, pitiful world which had evolved through so many millions of years yet could still be irremediably destroyed by mankind's evil passions! He had resolved to maintain a rational viewpoint; but in spite of all efforts he was submerged in a strange aberration which made the people around him seem almost unreal. All were trying to regard as acceptable a state of affairs in which he, Porfirio Uribe, was the victim. Surely, he told himself, this can't be Doña Isabel Cortines, who was once on the point of becoming a nun, a woman who prays every night and goes unfailingly to Mass, and who dreams of a nun's life for her daughter. Surely, this can't be Rosana, a slightly unpredictable girl, but nevertheless a talented artist, according to those who know about such things. And these two policemen are surely nothing but robots, they can't be human beings...

Doña Isabel was lamenting under her breath. "To think that I, Cortines' widow, should find myself in this mess! Oh, I deserve this punishment for having run away from the convent to marry a detestable man! I can only hope, now, that my daughter will dedicate her life to God!"

"What are you saying, Mamma?"

"Just thinking aloud, child. What's to become of you? When will you leave that wicked profession and dedicate yourself to God? When this happened"—she shot a glance at Porfirio—"I was waiting to talk this over with you."

"Mamma, how many times do I have to tell you there's nothing wicked in commercial art? It's my way of earning a living."

"But the indecent things you paint! God knows what will happen to you!"

"Art isn't indecent."

"But look at us, in this police car! I'm scared."

"What are you jabbering away about?" asked Sherlock Holmes, who did not understand Spanish.

"You certainly do your best to show us that liberty is just a myth in this country," Rosana shot back.

The other policeman laughed. The women fell silent.

Then Rosana turned towards Porfirio, with a sudden desire to console him. She wanted to say to him, "When you

11

get out of this, we'll be close, very close, so that you can tell me your troubles." And she decided she would be "generous" with him. Perhaps he could give her a little of what her life lacked, give her back some illusions. Never before had she thought of Porfirio Uribe in this way. Although they had lived in the same house for more than three years, she scarcely knew him. He had always seemed not to notice her, and she hadn't liked the stupid life he led, the life of a mole, shut up in his room, always studying, never going to Coney Island or the movies. A mole. He just went through the tunnel to his other cave, the place where he worked. He never even walked around Times Square at night, where you can sometimes see the moon hanging in the sky like a sad Japanese lantern. When he did go out, about once a month, it was always with Alfredo Laza. Sometimes she saw them together, saw them laugh, heard them laugh, while she waited impatiently for Alfredo to say something to thrill her. But he always treated her like the nine-year-old girl she had been when he had come to board at Doña Isabel's for a while.

Rosana's hidden love for Alfredo—whom she saw only occasionally and then when she went to his room with the pretext of showing him some of her paintings—expressed itself in a violent dislike for Alfredo's friend, the withdrawn and uncommunicative Porfirio Uribe, who spied upon her. It was when she had realized that he was spying on her that she had begun to flirt with Adrián Martín, the only other male boarder, simply in the hope that Porfirio would tell Alfredo Laza about it. That was to be her revenge! But there had been no response from Alfredo; her heart burned in vain for him. And so, she had decided to quench that fire with other men...Strange, the attraction she felt towards Alfredo. He was cold and unresponsive, and was much older than she. Far from being handsome, he was if anything rather ugly. A sociable and restless man. She herself could not explain it. He had left the boarding house when she was not yet thirteen, and she remembered the occasion. Actually he had been thrown out by Doña Isabel after he had fought with another boarder, a man more than fifty years old of whom Doña Isabel thought highly. Yet the fact remained, during all these years Alfredo Laza had been Rosana's dream-man.

Rosana had no faint idea that Porfirio Uribe had hoped to marry her when he should have finished his studies and become a lawyer. Yet that very afternoon, after his triumph, he had been on his way to her, had already framed the words he would say to her. "Let's go to a movie," he had intended to say, adding, "I have something important to tell you." The thought of it now caused him to rest his eyes upon her momentarily. She smiled—a generous smile of surrender—and he lowered his eyes. It was the first time she had ever smiled at him like that. Why had she not noticed him before? He knew he was no matinée idol, but she could surely see that he was sacrificing everything to his future career. But she could see no one but Adrián! Which perhaps explained why Porfirio had never been able to stand him. When she spoke to Adrián an almost feline note of pleading crept into her voice, her half-opened lips became moist, her eyes darkened to indigo blue. Porfirio did not understand her, had never understood her, but he had considered her as the logical reward for his triumph. He felt he deserved her! He had been attracted to her from his very arrival at the boarding house, years ago, while she was still studying in a downtown university.

Why, he wondered, had she ignored his existence and sought out Adrián instead? He now realized why Adrián's typewriter had so irritated him. She had never said to him what she had said to Adrián: "Be careful. Your life's in danger."

For Rosana liked to talk about the future of certain people, especially if they were men "marked by destiny," as she said with a mysterious laugh. Had she been attracted

13

to Adrián only because she had sensed what was going to happen? Her only premonitions seemed to be of misfortunes, especially if she felt herself "linked" to someone. Well, thought Porfirio, either she had no interest in him at all or he wasn't "marked." But look at what had happened to him today! Ah, but now she was smiling at him mysteriously, and her eyes had darkened to that strange shade of indigo blue...

After they had treated the slight wound in his foot and the abrasion on his temple, he began to consider his absurd situation. For it was absurd that he should be accused of the murder of Adrián Martín. Absurd—but he reeled at the thought. It was as though he had dived head first into space. He recalled having read somewhere that the blood in the human body travels more than two hundred kilometers a day, as though it were on a never-ending merry-go-round. Around and around on a merry-go-round of blood for more than two hundred kilometers! While one's heart throbs out the same two old organ notes, again and again...

He had let them take him to the police station without a struggle, without a sign of protest, because he felt already condemned by the mere fact of belonging to a despised and forsaken minority, and also because, even though Rosana had never told him so in a choked voice, he felt that he was a "marked" man. Just as he had thought he was about to emerge from the labyrinth, Ariadne had forgotten to give him her thread. And now here he was, lost, face to face with the monster.

An old fear returned; he had had this sensation before of being on the verge of madness. He kept repeating to himself, "Be calm, be calm." But his mind was skipping back and forth over the mental rope that divides sanity from madness. Once before he had been on the verge of ending up in an insane asylum, and he had taken hold of himself in time. But now he did not know what would happen. He decided not to talk, for he did not want to get excited. The same idea

14

hammered incessantly in his brain: "I was buried alive in the Dead Letters Section for eight years, without dreaming that one day I would be set in the stocks for all to stare at." Those eight years of seclusion and silence had not been a normal existence. Could that in itself be a sign of madness?

In moments of danger or triumph he had always turned to his friend, Alfredo Laza. Alfredo had warded off trouble in the old days; and that very afternoon he had gone to celebrate his brand-new law diploma with Alfredo, they had walked together in the park, talking about it. This was, perhaps, something he should tell the police. Why hadn't he thought of this before?

"Alfredo Laza was with me this afternoon," he said.

"Shall I go for him?" Rosana eagerly asked.

"Let's go," said one of the cops.

"Before we go," Rosana added, "I ought to tell you that yesterday afternoon Adrián received a telephone call, and when he had hung up he told me he would have to go out for a while after dark today, but that he would be back soon. He had invited me to go to the movies with him tonight."

Doña Isabel was obviously displeased.

"And it's for this sort of thing," she exclaimed, "that you don't want to take the veil!"

"It wasn't the first time they'd telephoned him," said Rosana, ignoring her mother's comments. "Adrián told me that those friends of his came from the same part of the country that he did."

"What were their names?"

"I don't know."

"Didn't you ever see them?"

"Never."

"Well, now, let's go find this fellow's friend."

When Rosana and one of the officers had gone, Porfirio was questioned further.

"Where did you go this afternoon with your friend?"

"To a restaurant in the park. He invited me to celebrate

with him. I received my diploma today..." Automatically his hand went to his pocket. "You have it, you have my papers. You took them, back there in the hallway."

"Here they are."

The sergeant picked up the papers and examined them.

"It's true. But why were you going back to Puerto Rico?"

"I wanted to be a lawyer in my home town," said Porfirio impulsively adding: "I wanted to be a leader in the majority party, marry, have children, and find a little happiness."

Suddenly he was able to talk and felt like confiding in the man who was questioning him. He told how he had studied while working in the Dead Letters Section of the Post Office; then he described the murder.

"When I entered the hallway it was dark and I didn't notice anything until I saw the flash of gunfire. I was stunned and deafened by the shots."

"So you didn't see anyone well enough to identify him?"

"They were only shadows at first, but when Adrián crumpled up and the two men ran off after firing the last shot, I caught a glimpse of them as they ran into the street. I believe I might recognize one of them if I saw him again."

"Had you seen the man before?"

"No, but he ran in a strange way, as if slightly lame. If I saw him again in the same circumstances I believe I'd know him."

The sergeant was unable to repress a laugh and the policemen standing by joined in the laughter.

"They're sure dumb, these Portoricans," said one of them.

Doña Isabel was then questioned as to Porfirio Uribe's past conduct. She assured them that he had always behaved himself well. Oh yes, he had had a little argument with Martín several times, when he was preparing for his exams. The Santiagan typed late at night.

"Did both men like your daughter?"

"I gave my daughter a Christian upbringing and I hope that she will become a nun..."

"She'll be some nun, I bet!"

While this was going on, someone entered the room with a file of papers. Yes, sir, Porfirio Uribe had been in jail, once, about ten years ago. He had been caught selling chances in the numbers game. He had also been in a number of bar-room brawls and street fights.

"You were a sort of bouncer, eh?"

He admitted it all. But that was his old way of life, which he had abandoned completely. He had paid his debt to society. Weren't his eight years of seclusion, hard work and study enough to prove this?

"I was an orphan," he said, trying now to be more explicit. "I was raised by my godparents, Estefano and Catalina. My godfather was good to me, but he was jealous because a neighbor was making eyes at my godmother, and so he..."

He went on talking about his childhood, as if he believed his hardships then could plead for him now. His godfather, Estefano, had a baritone horn, something like a tuba, he explained, and Estefano played it all the time while keeping an eye on his wife. Even her quick laughter made him jealous. And when he was bursting with anger, he would give short, loud, off-key puffs on his horn. Porfirio had been in his third year of high school when the tragedy had happened. He had heard the clang of the horn as it fell to the floor after a series of those loud, off-key blasts. Then his godmother had run out of the patio, trying to stifle her screams, and Estefano had run after her. Porfirio had tried to stop him, but reached his side too late. Estefano caught and stabbed his wife until she fell down in the street. Then he had dropped his knife and thrown himself on her body crying and sobbing. The street soon filled with people who came running to stare in horror at what had happened. The sobs of his godfather Estefano had sounded like a broken baritone horn...

17

Porfirio stopped talking to look at the policemen. Some were laughing, some were grinning, and all were saying more or less the same thing: "They're a funny lot, these Portoricans!"

Yes, those cops were definitely robots, not men. How could this story which made him tremble with fear and grief seem funny to any man? He remembered his god-mother Catalina, and how wonderful she had been to him; she had raised him as if he had been her own son. And his godfather Estefano hadn't been a bad man, just ugly-tempered and jealous. He had killed his wife in a moment of madness.

"After that," he went on, "I was completely alone in the world. When I couldn't find work in Puerto Rico, I came to New York. I was still young then, and I gradually drifted into bad ways. I was completely lost, then."

It was all true, so why deny it? He had reached New York in the years of the great depression, so was unable to find work anywhere. Sell apples? No, there was too much competition. Besides, he hadn't been able to speak English. The first thing he learned to say was a phrase very common in those days: "Can you spare me a dime?" Then he got into the numbers racket and this led to bar-room brawls and street fights. Why deny it? He had served a short jail sentence, after one of those fights, but he had committed no crime. And then he had reformed, he had left those friends who had such a bad influence on him, and he had started to learn. Education would be his Ariadne, and with her thread...

"Call my superiors and my fellow workers at the Post Office," Porfirio said, suddenly noticing the blank look on the sergeant's face. "Call my friends and teachers at the College. They'll tell you..."

The telephone calls were put through. A Post Office official was the first to arrive. He assured the officers that Mr. Porfirio Uribe was a studious and hard working man, that

18

he had become a lawyer, that he had resigned his job with the intention of returning to Puerto Rico.

"But of course, as a matter of fact," this Post Office official added, rubbing his chin doubtfully, "you never know what these Puerto Ricans will do."

The policeman who had previously expressed the same sentiment scratched his head, then let out a loud laugh.

Indeed, the phrase had been spoken so often that it was beginning to sound like a joke even to Porfirio. But a sad joke. Only the day before, on Porfirio's last day of work, his boss at the Post Office had looked at him in astonishment when he had announced he was giving up the job and hoped soon to be practicing law.

"Well, Uribe, I didn't think you'd ever make it. I didn't think you were capable of becoming a lawyer."

The boss had said that as he stared at Porfirio in his postal employee's uniform, as though he thought Porfirio could never shed it, the uniform was as much a part of him as a turtle's shell. And what would become of this turtle without his shell? Indeed, he seemed unable to forgive this postal employee for having studied to improve himself. And he had repeated several times, "Well, I never! A Portorican lawyer!"

All the fellows at the Post Office had seemed to have this same weird thought, and even Porfirio had smiled. As he had left the office he had felt like thumbing his nose at the lot of them, but repressed the impulse, as being unworthy. Instead, he went out smiling—smiling at the idea of his boss deprived of *his* turtle shell of officialdom.

CHAPTER

II

How was it possible, Porfirio asked himself, for so many things to happen in a day? That morning, when he had received his diploma, his heart had so throbbed with joy that he had almost fallen. And then immediately afterwards he had felt his loneliness keenly, for it was sad not to have anyone in the world to share his triumph. Even God seemed to have lost sight of him, and he thought whimsically that God was perhaps asking himself that very moment, "What ever became of that little boy in Puerto Rico whose parents died before he had a chance to know them and who was brought up by a baker called Estefano who was also a circus musician and a woman called Catalina who was a spiritualist and had such ready laughter?"

Yes, as he pocketed the diploma, he tried to summon up in his memory those parents of his, those third-rate circus acrobats who had died together in an ill-fated trapeze act, but in the faint memory he had of them, they were faceless. His father had been a Mexican; his mother had hailed from Santiago. Porfirio had been born in Coamo, Estefano's native town. And so it was that Estefano, who played the baritone horn in the brass band had adopted the orphaned child and taken him back to Coamo with him; in that town, between

20

seasons on the road, he worked as a baker. It was after this return that Estefano had married Catalina.

His childhood spent with them had been not too unhappy; but then, in his boyhood occurred the terrible tragedy, with his godmother murdered and carried away to the cemetery, and his godfather arrested and put into prison. Now, only that morning, he had resolved to banish those unhappy memories; the diploma was his, and would open up a brighter future. Yes, the day had started out well. But here he was, at the end of the day, recalling those unhappy times. His mind still in a daze, he thought of himself as falling, endlessly falling, as in a nightmare.

The sergeant had to repeat his question three times, so far away had Porfirio's mind wandered. It was Doña Isabel who at last secured his attention.

"Porfirio! Porfirio! What's the matter with you?"

He was about to answer when two of his college teachers entered the room. Their testimony impressed the police.

"His work was so brilliant that we saw no reason why we should not give him his diploma ahead of time," said one. "He had obtained a ticket to go home and we did not want him to lose his passage. It's not easy to travel in wartime."

The other teacher gave more or less the same testimony, and exclaimed, "It doesn't seem possible that he's got himself into a mess like this!"

It was good to hear these favorable words, but he still felt alone—alone and wounded by the mental image these police officers had of him. He realized that he existed only in the ill will and contempt of most people. "And to think," he reflected, "this morning I thought I had invented the sun!"

No one in the world remembered him with special affection. No one! He was a man without parents or wife or brothers or sisters. Therefore he was no one, because no one remembered him, since we truly exist only in the affections

21

of others. Why was there always this vacuum around him? Had he not just heard the friendly testimony of his teachers? Besides, he was sure that Alfredo Laza wouldn't forsake him. He looked inquiringly at Rosana when she returned from her errand. She drew near and spoke in an undertone.

"I've seen Alfredo," she said. "He's gone to look for a lawyer."

Someone pushed him almost roughly towards the sergeant's desk. He allowed it without resentment, filled with joy at existing in the affections of Alfredo Laza, even though he, Porfirio Uribe, had been unwilling to live the life of his friend, a voluntary exile, a nationalist just released from prison, a strike agitator.

That very afternoon Alfredo had tried to persuade him to participate in a conspiracy. Porfirio had not listened very closely, but he did remember something Alfredo had said: "If a person never does anything generous, what's the use of living? I wouldn't let my heart die wheezing like a punctured bellows."

Porfirio was interested in Alfredo Laza's opinions, but thought they were too wild to be much swayed by them. He himself had studied with only one purpose in mind: to live in the protective shadow of the majority party. "You, Alfredo, are a bohemian," he had said, "and there's no profit in that sort of life."

"True, but I'm enjoying myself," was Alfredo's reply. "The person who can't find time to enjoy himself will find time to get sick. Do you think I should envy your spiderish life? You know, we're still on this side of the tomb. That's what Adrián always tells me, at least. All right, so I'm crazy, but I don't envy your life of sanity."

"And you've spent your life behind banners," he had retorted. "You've spent your life on picket lines and in strikes. Do you think I studied for that?"

Why had he felt like insulting his friend? But Alfredo had merely smiled, although he was obviously hurt. And now Alfredo was running about, hunting a lawyer for him. He would find one, too; probably that Congressman with radical ideas, the one who was a personal friend of Alfredo Laza.

Porfirio now had to undergo the questioning of an antagonistic Italian detective, who uttered nothing but insults. The Italian was wearing an anemic necktie, a clear cream-colored tie, the same color as his pasty face, and Porfirio fixed his attention on that, reflecting whimsically that it made him look as though his face had melted and run down over his chest. He almost laughed outright as the thought struck him.

The questioning continued, as fatigue gradually overcame him. A distant foghorn on the river swept him with a wave of nostalgia.

In the taxi that was taking Doña Isabel Cortines and her daughter home from the police station, Doña Isabel began by assuming the silence appropriate to an offended mother. Rosana paid no attention as her mother dabbed her eyes from time to time with a handkerchief. She would wait till her mother spoke first.

"How did you find Alfredo so soon?" her mother finally asked, in an explosion of wrath.

"I know where he usually hangs out."

"Don't tell me that you go to those places!"

"It wouldn't be surprising if I did. But for your peace of mind, I know where he goes because his friends told me."

"And you asked?"

"Probably."

"A decent girl wouldn't do that."

"A friend would."

"I don't like you to be his friend. He has a bad background."

"I don't think I should argue that point with you."

"And with whom, then? Am I not your mother?"

23

"My mother, but not my conscience."

"Rosana!"

"Yes, Mamma?"

"You're not showing me the proper respect!"

"Forgive me, Mamma."

Rosana suddenly realized that it was preferable to take refuge in such mechanical little phrases, her only way of dissenting, of repressing her own feelings before a person to whom she really owed respect.

"Now you're putting on that infuriating air of condescension," Doña Isabel exclaimed, exasperated. "Anything, so you can have your own way!"

They said nothing more for the rest of the trip. But Rosana had something to say, and as soon as she had closed the door behind her, she went up to Doña Isabel and spoke.

"Look, Mamma. I'm twenty-four years old now and I think I'm able to express my thoughts. Today I want to speak out clearly. Before this, I've expressed myself indirectly, without being able to make you understand. Listen to me, please!"

"Go ahead."

"Ever since I've been conscious of what's going on, I've known that you try to imagine me as you would like me to be, rather than accepting me as I am. Well, if I can't be what you want me to be, imagine I'm someone else and tolerate me. I don't want to make you angry. Don't make me argue with you. I swore to you once that I wasn't born to serve God, so why do you keep insisting on it? And here is something I never told you before, but why do you think Alfredo quarreled with that gentleman who lived in our house? You made Alfredo leave, but he only wanted to defend me. That so-called gentleman went to church with you, but sometimes he said he was not feeling well and stayed at home. In your eyes he was a respectable person. I was then hardly an adolescent. Well, you've no idea what I learned from him! Ever since then, ever since I was a little girl,

24

I've felt as though I were engaged to Alfredo, but he still sees in me the innocent little girl he knew when he first came here to room. No, don't say anything, Mamma! I tremble every time I see him, and I don't want to meet him. I don't want to, Mamma! Now, do you understand?"

She broke off and began to cry. Doña Isabel started to say something, but Rosana interrupted her.

"I know what you're going to ask me. You want to know what that gentleman taught me. When I think of it, I look at my hands and wonder if I shouldn't cut them off. Now do you know why I sometimes run to wash my hands, and why I always keep that bottle of rubbing alcohol near me? After what happened, nothing seems to help. When I can't stand it any longer, I try to forget with other men...Why am I telling this to you! I don't know what's the matter with me. But to whom can I tell it if not to my own mother?"

"I'm at a loss what to say!"

"I don't mean to hurt you, but I had to tell you. Why do you think I took up painting? I imagined it would bring me closer to Alfredo, but I'm afraid he'll think I'm chasing him, and so I avoid him. I try to find consolation with other men...Three times in a row I've been left almost at the altar. It's always been my own fault! Sometimes I unconsciously called them Alfredo, and sometimes I began to cry without knowing why I was crying. Do you remember when Alfredo married? I thought I was surely going to die. Since then I've been a little crazy, but I can't help it. His marriage didn't last long, but instead of going after him, I stayed away. It was as though I were asking to be tortured. If you only knew how I cringe when you say, 'I brought you up to serve God. I brought you up to serve God.'"

Actually, Doña Isabel did not understand her daughter's anxiety, nor how the obsession for sanctity which overshadowed their home was overwhelming the girl. That was why Rosana wanted to work away from home, why she tried to spend as little time as possible there. She could not help

25

running after men. She was drawn to Adrián Martín almost involuntarily, because she noted a vein of sadness and discontent in him, and because he had thrown himself into the struggle against tyranny in his country. She disliked Porfirio Uribe because he had said he could not endure the sound of Adrián's typewriter. That Dead Letters Office mole could not realize that Adrián was a man of ideas, an exile, a valiant newspaperman who had dedicated his life to denouncing the desperate plight of his countrymen, a fighter who had conspired against the dictator and who would have been the first to take up arms against the monster! What could a mole burrowing in dead letters know about such things!

Feeling as she did, her dislike of Uribe increased when in sheer exasperation he tried to stop Adrián Martín from typing at night. What a nerve! And what was Uribe studying for, anyway? Evidently, to go on being a slave!

Nevertheless, she felt sorry for him when she caught that hunted animal's look on his face. And she decided that she could well afford to give him any consolation that he desired from her, no matter how generous he might want her to be.

But Doña Isabel had no place in Rosana's strange world, as was obvious from her prosaic reactions to what she had just heard.

"My dear," she said, "try to control yourself. You're acquainted with my family background, and you know how, in spite of it, I've even done servant's work, to give you an education. Think how I've sacrificed for you! Isn't running this horrible boarding house a sufficient sacrifice?"

Rosana started to reply, but checked herself. Why try to make herself understood? It wasn't worth the effort! And she was helpless; she was a worm trampled underfoot, a leaf crushed in the hand. She stood there, panting, her heart constricted as though all the lifeblood was being squeezed out of it. Oh yes, people were always saying, 'I wish I had a mother like yours, who thinks the sun rises and sets with her daughter!' And what kind of daughter, except a dastardly one, would hurt such a mother? Oh, but when a girl wasn't what others thought she should be, then she was condemned and on the way to hell, with other people's consciences pointing the way! It never occurred to them that each heart beats with its own particular rhythm.

"My heart's my own!" Rosana almost shouted. "My own, my own!"

Quite beside herself, she glanced into Porfirio's room on her way to her bedroom. There was the baritone horn, and there the guitar, those instruments Uribe had had with him ever since coming to the boarding house. The baritone had been Estefano's, the guitar had been bought in New York, he had earned money playing it during the hard times. Alfredo had baptized the horn Estefano, the guitar Catalina. Rosana laughed at the recollection of the tales Alfredo had made up about the baritone horn, which in his stories lived a life of its own, like a person. It was associated, too, with the popular music of Puerto Rico, for how could a real *danza* be played without a baritone horn?

Giving in to a wild whim, she took the horn and blew into it, shattering the silence of the room with off-key blasts. Then she ran from room to room, with Doña Isabel after her, imploring her to stop.

"Child, child! Put down that horn for the love of God!"

She was always asking things to be done for the love of God. God must be tired of the constant requests she made in His name!

"Let God hear me, if only with the voice of a baritone horn!"

"Daughter! What new madness is this?"

Tired at last, she returned the instrument to its place. Then she went into Adrián's room. Who knows? she thought. They may have killed Adrián because I associated with him. Something evil followed in her wake. At last her overwrought nerves demanded release, and she collapsed on

27

Adrián's bed to weep. Only a few days before she had been there with him.

She recalled how she had been drawn to him by the air of mystery that hovered round the Santiagan, and how he had talked in veiled language of an oath he had sworn which put his life in danger. He had revealed nothing, but smiled in silence. Rosana had peered into his life as into an abyss; indeed, she experienced a kind of vertigo whenever he approached her. He had no family, had nothing to cling to except an undeviating resolve.

After that telephone call the day before his death, he had muttered an odd phrase: "I'd meet the devil himself, if need be!" And she had merely said, "Don't talk like that! Mamma might hear you."

Then he had laughed. His laughter was a torch lit to guide him back from paths of darkness.

"We can still go to the movies," he had said. I'll come back to pick you up here. Okay?"

But he had entered the dark paths from which there was no return. Down there in the hallway, they had smashed the whirligig of his blood. Truly, that was an impenetrable mystery!

Rosana was half asleep when the telephone rang, and she heard Doña Isabel saying, "Hello...Yes. Who wants to speak to her?"

She rushed to the telephone and flung herself upon it. "Alfredo?...Yes, it's Rosana..."

Doña Isabel, who had remained at her daugther's side, still surprised at the way the telephone had been torn from her hand, listened to what Alfredo Laza said.

"It's just as I told you. Porfirio couldn't possibly have killed Adrián. They've discovered that his fingerprints aren't on the revolver. I went with Cayoctavio—you know, the lawyer—and we brought him back to my house."

"How badly wounded is he?"

"Nothing serious. It was painful because the bullet grazed a tendon."

"And how does he feel?"

"Quieter, even though he won't be able to go to Puerto Rico until they give him permission...God knows, he may have to stay here for weeks."

"Have they got it out of their heads that I'm the woman in the case?"

Laza gave a hearty laugh, but Doña Isabel was furious, and went off with her hand on her bosom, a gesture she always made when disturbed, murmuring, "My heart..." It was the final argument she used against her daughter ever since she had learned that she had high blood pressure.

"Listen," Rosana whispered, "I'd like to be with you two for a while, even if it's only for half an hour. Do you mind?"

"But...your mother?"

"I'll manage it."

"I'd like you to come very much."

"Is Porfirio in the room with you?"

"No, he went to my bedroom. I'm calling from downstairs."

"I'll take a taxi."

"Did you write down the address I gave you tonight?"

"Yes. Will you bring me home afterwards?"

"Do you think anything could stop me?"

Rosana's conversation had brought Doña Isabel back, still with her hand on her bosom. She was looking at her daughter, wild-eyed.

"Now what are you going to do?" she protested.

"You already heard, Mamma."

"A decent girl..."

"Oh, yes...I know, a decent girl never meets men, especially at this hour of night, and much less men like Alfredo Laza, who has a low-class background and is a bohemian and an outlaw—even though he became one through defending ideals in which he believes. I know it all by heart!"

29

"You'll be the death of me!"

"Either you've forgotten all too soon what I told you just now or you didn't understand a word I said."

Without saying more, Rosana went to her room. A half hour later, she went to take leave of her mother, who had thrown herself on her bed, her hand still pressed to her heart. It was a tense moment, even though Rosana forced herself to appear natural. Doña Isabel let her kiss her cheek, but did not look at her daughter, continuing to stare at the wall, her eyes wet with tears.

"Be reasonable, Mamma," begged Rosana, and, without waiting for an answer, she tiptoed out of the room.

"I bought fish for the three of us," Alfredo said, when she arrived. "Want some?"

"I'm hungry to know how you cook, at least."

"It's just about ready to come out of the oven."

"One of these days I'll show you what a good cook I am."

"It's probably the best way to reach a man's heart," said Alfredo, lightly.

Porfirio looked at them without speaking.

"How do you feel?" asked Rosana.

"Hard to say. I don't yet know whether they're going to put me on trial or not. The circumstances. . ."

"Cayoctavio says they have no grounds for action; but on the other hand you're their main witness, if the murderers are caught."

Porfirio was gloomy at the thought that he would now not be able, within the next week or so, to enjoy the soft violet dusk of his native town, that time of day when the distant mountains seem to dissolve in the sky.

"The most painful way to die is without a friend," he murmured, "as I realized tonight. I did the right thing this morning when I called Alfredo to share my triumph with me. For the last few years I've been living on the future, with the hope of returning to my home town. . ."

"I've always told him that," Alfredo said, speaking to Rosana. "Porfirio has to broaden his life. He's been hibernating for the last eight years. He studied just to tie himself down to the tyranny of everyday necessities."

Rosana paid almost no attention to what the two men were saying, thrilled and incredulous at being in the same room with Alfredo. Under other conditions, she would have considered Uribe's presence a nuisance.

They tried to avoid talking about the murder, but Laza finally said, "Porfirio and I are going to scour all the Latin neighborhoods in the next few days. There's a chance we might find the killers."

"Won't that be dangerous?" asked Rosana.

"You can't imagine the kind of life we once led in those sections of town. Four years of it! That experience will serve us now, for we know who sells numbers and marihuana, who are the criminals...Among them are paid gunmen. Well, some day we'll make the dictator pay for this!"

When they had finished supper, Alfredo took Rosana home, Porfirio preferring to stay, resting, in Laza's apartment. Doña Isabel was waiting for her daughter, seated by the door. Before going in, Rosana still had time to say something in a whisper to Alfredo.

"We're going to die together, whether you want or not."

He should have replied, "Why not live together? Wouldn't it be better?" But he said nothing at all.

CHAPTER

III

Alfredo Laza felt the time was ripe to awaken Uribe's conscience.

"I can't imagine," he said, "how you've been able to live such a hermit's existence for eight years. And what for? They'll always step on you when you least expect it. Besides, look how we ourselves behave. You and I have never been able to understand each other. And look at you and Adrián. You scarcely talked to each other, and yet you should have been great friends."

"You think so?"

"Our persecutors and tormentors take advantage of situations like that. You yourself did not conspire against the dictator, yet you were almost killed with Adrián, who did conspire. That bullet-burn on your temple might have been fatal. But who could have told you! You think you can live and die like an elephant. They say when elephants know they're about to die they go straight to a certain place to leave their bones. You want to go to your home town to leave your bones—or bury your moral faculties, it comes to the same thing with you."

"And what do you gain by opposing the powers that be?"

"Nothing, perhaps. But at least I have the illusion that I'm not wasting my life."

Porfirio said nothing. He was listening to the distant foghorn of a ship.

Even Laza stopped to listen, with an expression of nostalgia on his face. He remembered the voyages he had made back and forth between Puerto Rico and New York, always with the poor emigrants. The last time he had not come to New York of his own free will. In Puerto Rico he had participated in a political riot, and after the trial they had sent him to a prison in the United States. At length released, he had stayed on in New York.

It was on one of his first trips that he had met Porfirio Uribe; that was now twelve years ago. From the first day on board he had noticed that Porfirio carried the baritone horn around with him constantly, not parting from it even to eat. The boy's very consciousness seemed to be linked with the *bombardino*, it was a part of him, Laza decided. They struck up a friendship, and Laza heard how the boy had inherited the instrument from his godfather, Estefano. Porfirio told him how he had left his home and town alone, on foot, because he had no money, and very early in the morning, so no one would see him go. He had already heard of his godfather's suicide in prison, and was on his way to give him a Christian burial, then emigrate to another country, far from Puerto Rico. On the outskirts of town, some stray dogs began to follow him, winding round his legs and wagging their tails, hoping they had found a master. Porfirio had felt like crying; he hesitated, and almost turned back. However, he had no relatives in the town, and could not face all the gossip about the tragedy. Only three days before this, his godfather had asked to see him in jail, to bequeath him that horn! It was his only possession, aside from some ragged shirts and a few worthless souvenirs he had packed into a small cardboard suitcase, already bursting at the seams. Porfirio was never able to explain why he hadn't thrown the horn away. Perhaps it was because Estefano's voice, when he cried over Catalina's fallen body, had sounded like the broken old baritone horn. Or perhaps he thought he might earn his living with it: he was almost a musician.

At any rate, Porfirio had not turned back. It was dawn when he was overtaken by an old truck, its asthmatic engine laboring under a load of charcoal. The driver stopped.

"I'm on my way to Ponce," he said to the boy. "When I drive alone I'm afraid of going to sleep. So, come along with me."

He waited while the boy put the *bombardino* into the truck and climbed up beside it. They left the dog behind, the one that had persistently followed. With compunction Porfirio watched the poor creature moving its limp tail, its face uplifted, its eyes full of sorrow, for its canine dream of having a master was only a dream. Porfirio continued to watch the dog until it was lost in a cloud of dust. Then he had leaned on the horn and let his tears flow. He would never forget that poor dog that had wound itself around his legs, begging for affection.

He reached Ponce in time to see the terrible result of the autopsy on Estefano's body. His organs had been removed and his skull was stuffed full of newspapers. Porfirio stayed long enough to accompany all that remained of Estefano to the cemetery.

All this was strange, for the boy had never been sure whether he loved his godfather. Probably not, at least not from the time when he was six years old and set off to school for the first time. His godmother had said, "May your guardian angel accompany you." And Estefano had laughed and said, "That boy was born without a guardian angel!"

From the moment he first heard this story, Alfredo Laza had felt a deep affection for Porfirio.

As the boat approached New York, Porfirio, who was wearing a suit of coarse cotton drill, without either an overcoat or even a sweater, began to suffer in the November cold.

"It's clear you don't know what cold is!" said Laza.

34

"Here, take my overcoat."

Porfirio protested in vain. Laza swore he had another overcoat in New York—Porfirio later learned this was not the case—and besides, his heavy woolen jacket was enough for the moment. Okay? Then take it. Alfredo tried to minimize his generosity.

The first person who saw Porfirio wearing Laza's overcoat asked: "Who died?" In effect, the garment was too big for him; Alfredo was well built and at that time Porfirio was skinny. It was after this encounter that he noticed how little the overcoat favored him. It was impossible to button it with such enormous buttonholes, or even to determine from which mail-order house it had been bought, it was so faded. Porfirio decided to remain in the cabin below and not go on deck.

The poor emigrants gathered together to talk. There was a strong smell of medicinal herbs about them, for they were all taking herbs as gifts to relatives and friends in New York. The predominating aromas were of rue, Cuban grass, costmary, and lemon verbena. They assembled for parties, too, where there was singing and music, the musical accompaniment being furnished by some of them who played the *cuatro* (*) and the guitar. No one, not even Laza, could persuade Porfirio to take his *bombardino* from its case.

The emigrants formed a "pool" to see who could guess most accurately the arrival time of the ship. Porfirio did not gamble in this because he had nothing to gamble with. Laza, painter and guitarist, passed the time playing sentimental tunes and making caricatures of his friends. He was the most popular person aboard.

The ship entered port a little after midnight, but the passengers were not allowed to go ashore until after dawn. The cold was intense, but Porfirio, who never left Laza's side, was more doubled up with timidity than with the cold. Almost none of the immigrants spoke English, and so were

(*) The *cuatro* is a Puerto Rican instrument resembling a mandolin.

unable to explain the purpose of the strange herbs they were bringing in. The customs officials accumulated a large pile of these herbs, but nothing surprised them, they were used to the spectacle. They were not even surprised at Porfirio's battered suitcase which had to be tied together with a peeling strap, because it was too old and worn to stay shut of itself. But they did laugh at the *bombardino*. They took it out of its case and examined the little pieces of soap which sealed the holes in it. Was this some new kind of tuba? No? It was a baritone horn? What the...? Their faces were red with suppressed laughter. Using Alfredo as interpreter, they ordered Porfirio to play something. Thinking this was part of his duty as an immigrant, not realizing it was a joke, the boy pretended to play the accompaniment to an imaginary *danza*. Very soon some of the Puerto Ricans who were standing by began to hum the tune.

A crowd of compatriots who resided in the city waited on the dock for the immigrants to disembark. Some of them were there to welcome relatives, others had come merely to satisfy their curiosity. Among them was a fat, red-faced individual wearing a derby hat and a very shaggy coat. He and Alfredo greeted each other with loud shouts:

"Luis!"

"Alfredo!" Then, joking, "I've never seen a more useless bit of flotsam in my life"—his eyes were upon Porfirio. After which he looked at the boy mockingly, proceeded to button the overcoat with exaggerated care, then asked him, "Where's the funeral?"

Apparently Porfirio was tired of jokes, because without a word he dropped his woebegone suitcase and hit Luis over the head with the *bombardino*.

Infuriated, taken by surprise, Luis tried to ward off the attack. Others joined in, and there was almost a riot. Alfredo and some of his friends were unable to make peace before the police arrived.

They ended up in a police station, Precinct Number 27.

36

On the way to the station, Luis kept taking off his derby, more grieved over the damage done to his hat than by the blow on his head. But by the time they reached the station he had forgotten that he had ever been angry and broke out laughing whenever he looked at the baritone horn that had struck him.

After an admonition, the police finally had to let them go.

When they were in the street again, the man with the derby hat introduced himself properly.

"Luis Pororico," he said with ironic pride, "at your service. My God, what a bad temper you have! But I'll take the blame, since you are a friend of Alfredo."

They went to a bar to celebrate. There Porfirio had his first sight of a mass-circulation tabloid, with the single word SLAIN! in big letters on the front page. That memory remained with him always.

They left Luis soon afterwards because Alfredo was anxious to return to his room. Porfirio would live with him for the time being. When they got on the subway Porfirio noticed that someone gave him his seat. He thought such courtesy was very unusual in the city and said so. Alfredo merely laughed. Later on he explained that the person who had moved obviously had mistaken him for a Bowery bum.

Porfirio also learned afterwards that Luis Pororico had a police record, that he lived from some "racket" or other and kept a "stable" of women. At the time Porfirio was incapable of understanding such things. And he was convinced that only a miracle had saved him from a beating.

Alfredo lived in Harlem. Porfirio noticed a strange odor on the ground floor and in some of the rooms of the building. Alfredo told him it was marihuana: later on, he learned what that meant.

Twelve years later, Porfirio still remembered, as if it had been only yesterday, the trifling incidents that occurred during those first days in New York. Laza was given a rough reception in the house where he roomed. He was either to pay his back rent or move instantly. And did he have the gall to bring another person to his room? Porfirio didn't understand what they were saying, but knew they were talking about him by the gestures the superintendent was making. She was a fat Jewish woman who was not very convincing in her role of a hard-hearted person, and she ended by giving in to Laza's flattery. After this bout, Alfredo went almost immediately to look for work, leaving Porfirio alone and giving him instructions.

"I'm going to look for work for both of us, but you'll stay here. Walking around the streets for hours on end, cold and hungry, makes a person who's not used to it sick."

Porfirio agreed. No, he wouldn't leave the room. Was he hungry? What Puerto Rican immigrant wasn't used to hunger?

"Don't worry about me," said Porfirio.

"If someone knocks, don't open the door. If they keep on knocking, make sure the little chain on the door is fastened."

"Who do you think you're leaving in this room?" asked Porfirio, rather offended. "A girl who needs to be protected?"

"It's not that," said Laza with a laugh, "but you don't know the way things are here. There are a lot of unemployed on the streets who think there's something to steal in every room. And everything is so cheap, even though no one has enough money to buy things, that human life isn't worth much. If you want to take chances, that's your privilege."

Porfirio understood. Here in New York doors couldn't be left wide open as they were in his town in the south of Puerto Rico.

"Oh yes, I almost forgot," added Laza. "Be careful with the gas valve. Here it is. This is the way you open it, and this is the way to close it. Don't ever leave it open. Never forget that."

"Why?"

"Don't do it if you enjoy living a little...even though you don't have anything to eat. It's very dangerous."

"All right."

"I let my life-insurance policy with the Prudential lapse when I went to Puerto Rico. I'll have to pay it up to date immediately. If someone comes to sell you a policy, don't refuse point blank but tell him you intend to take one out as soon as you begin to work."

"What if I don't want a life insurance policy?"

"That's up to you. But would you like to be buried here if you died?"

"I don't know...Why think about dying when you're only twenty years old?"

"With people hungry and no work to be found and so many thugs on the streets, death doesn't respect youth. You could be killed at any time and, if you want to be buried in Puerto Rico, don't wait for us to take up a collection around the neighborhood."

"I'd be so ashamed I'd blush in my coffin."

"Think of your friends, your relatives..."

"I don't have any relatives."

"But you do have friends. I'd be ashamed to have to take up a collection to send you to Puerto Rico. You don't live for yourself alone; you live in the memory of others. If it wasn't that way, what would be the use of living?"

"And who told you I wanted to be taken to Puerto Rico if something happened to me? What difference does it make if you're buried here or there?"

"It makes a difference to me. A person is more than just this," he said, looking disdainfully at his body..."Besides, I'd be very cold if they buried me here. There's no wake here, no prayers, no wreaths. I won't accept that. They'll have to hold a wake and pray for me, and someone will have to accompany me to the cemetery....Sometimes they tell such funny stories at funerals that the corpse must double up laughing in his box."

That was what Porfirio liked in Alfredo. He had never had a friend like this before, to tell him these things. And

Alfredo reeled them off as if he felt what he said was both absurd and logical at the same time.

"All right," Porfirio agreed, "I'll take out a policy with the Prudential."

Alfredo went off and Porfirio was left alone in the narrow room which was barely large enough for the few pieces of furniture it contained. There was a rickety bed covered with tattered sheets and a bedspread, there was a folded army cot in one corner, a curtain of sorts, a small table, and a guitar lying on a chair. In the tiny alcove which served as kitchen there was a gas stove.

The city could not be seen from the window because it overlooked a court, but Porfirio tried to identify the sounds he could hear. He did not as yet know that the dull roar from below came from a subway, but he did recognize the constant flow of automobiles, the whistles of factories and trains, and the distant blasts of boat horns.

Porfirio felt trapped. He wanted to go out into the street for a breath of air, but he was afraid he would get lost or meet the woman who had come to collect the rent. He hadn't a cent in his pockets, and there was nothing to eat in the room. At first he leafed through some old magazines to kill time. But time passed all too slowly. He had to put on his overcoat again, for the room was cold.

Some packages were under the table. He examined them to see what they contained. He found artist's supplies and some paintings. Most of them were nudes. The landscapes had two predominant themes. Either they showed sunlight on virgin snow, seen from above, or they were southern scenes with poinciana trees flaming red. He rewrapped the canvases, sat down on the bed, took up the guitar and strummed a few chords. He was fond of the guitar; it always called to mind his godmother Catalina, who liked to play on it the old waltzes and *danzas* of the tropics. Afterwards he fell into a reverie, aimlessly twanging one of the strings, his gaze lost on the ceiling.

Finally he took the *bombardino* out of its case, with the idea of trying out some tunes, but then he remembered that this would disturb the neighbors. He contemplated with a smile the tremendous dent which Luis Pororico's head had left in the instrument. Then he remembered Estefano, and could almost hear his godfather's despairing moans. He pressed in three of four pieces of blue soap, useful for stopping the holes. Then he vainly tried to straighten out the dent. After that, he rubbed a cloth over the tarnished places on the metal and put the horn away again in its case, as one draws a shroud over a corpse.

Porfirio remembered every last detail of that day for the rest of his life, perhaps because he called them often to mind.

In those days he kept some yellowed old photographs of his parents in the dilapidated suitcase with the frayed strap around it. They showed the Mexican Lazaro Uribe and the Santiagan Juanita Moya dressed in their acrobatic costumes, as shabby as the circus they worked in. Porfirio always felt sad when he remembered those traveling circuses that announced their arrival with a scandalous brass band which paraded through the streets of the neighboring villages after they had set up their tents in a vacant lot. Now, seated in a tiny room during his first day in New York, Porfirio intently contemplated the portraits of his parents, whom he only remembered in dreams. He put them on the table and looked at them for a long while. They were so yellow and faded that it was difficult to make out the faces clearly, but he could still see the Indian features of his father and the tropical beauty of his mother.

He remembered that when the circus came to his town the waltzes which the band played had always made him sad. Once, when he was fifteen years old, he had fallen in love with a puppet-show girl with far-away eyes. Through a blur of tears he had watched her disappear with the circus caravan down the dusty road leading away from town. The sky was greenish with yellow and orange streaks that day, and she had seemed to disappear into nothingness. He had never seen her again.

As he thought of all this, a more recent memory was revived, the melancholy recollection of the dog that had rubbed against his legs...

Finally he lay down on the sagging bed and stared at the spots on the ceiling, trying to see identifiable forms in their haphazard convolutions. Time passed so slowly that the air of the room seemed to solidify and weigh down upon him.

He was hungry and cold, and the memories, the narrowness of the room, the solitude and silence and the lack of human warmth, made him feel very lonely. But little by little he began to fall asleep.

It was late at night when Alfredo Laza returned, bringing some canned meat and a large loaf of bread. Luis Pororico had given him enough work for several days, painting scenery. He had found the food in the house of a friend, who was using the cans as supports for a shelf. This canned meat was being handed out to the unemployed, but his friend, even though without work, refused to eat the contents because he suspected that the meat was cat meat.

"You know, it turns a person's stomach."

Porfirio made a gesture of disgust, but his hunger won out over the suspicions of Alfredo's friend.

"I might be able to get some work for you painting toilets," said Alfredo. "It's flat-brush work. Do you want the job?"

"Of course I do!"

"We'll go to work early in the morning. The only thing that could go wrong is if they happen to ask you for a union card. If that happens, I think Luis Pororico can fix it up. He works for a big shot."

When they left the house early next morning, it was snowing, but the thick flakes melted as soon as they touched the street. Porfirio felt ashamed to be wearing Alfredo's

42

overcoat, but Alfredo insisted that he could do without it.

"Don't worry," he said, "you'll buy a guitar with your first pay check, and Luis says there's a good chance they'll hire us as guitarists at the new club. I don't think Estefano will be much use to you."

Thenceforth they always referred to the *bombardino* as Estefano.

"What good is Estefano if they don't want us to play *danzas?*" said Alfredo.

This was the beginning of the precarious life Porfirio led during his first four years in New York. Sometimes he and Alfredo Laza spent hours racking their brains in an effort to think of ways of earning a living.

They did not remain for long in Harlem, but soon moved to James Street in Greenwich Village, since the outlaw organization to which Luis Pororico belonged controlled prostitution and the numbers racket in the downtown area. The room they took was an old garret near the docks, where their neighbors were Swedes, Danes and Norwegians, almost all of them longshoremen and truck drivers who had savage fist fights over the most trivial matters. During the first few days the noise of the elevated trains disturbed them, but they soon grew accustomed to it.

They had little actual trouble with the Nordic longshoremen, but the mute hostility in their eyes made life uncomfortable. However, the rent was low and they had nowhere else to go.

As musicians, they were more often unemployed than employed. At times they found work as painters. Their irregular life led them into the bohemian and artistic circles in Greenwich Village.

Although he was somewhat retiring, Porfirio had several passing love affairs with poor actresses and usherettes in the cheaper theaters. Alfredo was luckier, because the artists and bohemians accepted him as an equal. This led him to become a prominent member of a cooperative restaurant where for a small sum they were able to eat. Sometimes Porfirio played his guitar there, while at other times he paid for his meal by washing dishes.

At times the economic situation worsened, and there was nothing to eat, even at the co-op. Their little room was unheated, but occasionally they collected enough boxes to make a fire in the stove. When there were no boxes they went to restaurants to spend the night talking over a cup of coffee or napping, their heads resting on the back of their chairs or on the table.

Once when he was very cold and there was nothing to make a fire with, Porfirio took a hot bath. When Laza returned that night he found Porfirio sick abed with pneumonia; for several days he took care of the sick boy with admirable devotion.

This constant uncertainty, this being deprived of the most elemental necessities of life, set Porfirio on the downward path of vice. He became an "employee" of Luis Pororico, who was at that time quarreling with the chief of a rival gang. Thus began his life as a numbers peddler and a bouncer at a taxi dance hall. But he managed to stop just short of the bottom. On two or three occasions he fell into police dragnets, but he was lucky. They were never able to prove anything serious against him. He was usually charged only with vagrancy or disturbing the peace, and this always under an assumed name.

This life separated him from Laza, who continued to associate with bohemian artists and exalted political refugees, avoiding when possible men such as Luis Pororico. But although he saw less of his friend, he and Laza remained friends.

Finally, and just in time, Porfirio broke away from Pororico and found a steady job in the Post Office. Buried in his narrow office, he became another person, self-absorbed, unsocial, almost misanthropic.

Porfirio would never have admitted it but, in the last analysis, he had always had to depend on Alfredo Laza, from his first day in New York. Laza had oriented him during those early days, had found a job for him, had weaned him away from Luis Pororico's influence, had taken him to Doña Isabel Cortines' boarding house... And now he was clearing him of a murder charge. No one but Laza had thought of finding a lawyer for him. It was Laza who had brought Cayoctavio to the police station and to Porfirio's rescue. Now, as Laza accompanied Rosana home, Porfirio, left alone, paced the floor, asking himself why he was so dependent upon this friend. Why did he always have to turn to Alfredo Laza at every crucial moment in his life?

When he thought of all Laza had done for him, he was grateful, yet at the same time he felt angry and ashamed. His feelings were a confused mixture of anger and fear, of resentment and gratitude. Surprising how Alfredo was always able to solve his, Porfirio's problems so easily, although their points of view were so opposite?

Suddenly he clearly realized why he had prolonged his retreat from the world for eight years, why he had studied so intensely. He had fled from Alfredo Laza, not from the conspirator, but from the man who knew how to solve the most difficult problems of others; he was horrified at the thought, for he knew that Laza did not intend to humiliate him with his aid. Yes, he had studied so hard in order to pay off humiliation with humiliation. He had wanted to prove his capabilities, show that he could become an important person in Puerto Rico, while Laza would never be more than a bohemian and a conspirator.

Porfirio began to pace the floor, tortured by a new suspicion. Had he invited Laza to celebrate his triumph with him just to throw it in his face? At the thought, his body broke out in a cold sweat. But whom else could he have invited? Laza was more than a brother, he was almost a father, in spite of the few years of difference in their ages. *Like a brother. Like a father.* Nevertheless, Alfredo Laza's great passion for politics had cost him five years in prison. No, such a position was hard to understand. While Alfredo had served out his sentence, he, Porfirio, had studied, cutting himself off from the world, choosing to live in isolation rather than to run into any conflicts. In the beginning he had visited his friend in prison, but little by little the intervals between visits lengthened until they finally ceased completely. Then suddenly, when he least expected it, Alfredo, but recently released from prison, came to see him. When Porfirio made an effort to excuse himself for not having visited him of late, Alfredo changed the subject and praised his friend's devotion to his studies. This had made Porfirio feel very bad, but now his cup of bitterness was running over. His world caved in beneath his feet when Laza appeared with Cayoctavio, who presented some papers to the presiding judge and ended the matter.

"You can go," they had told him.

He had become a lawyer only to have a bohemian save him from the clutches of the law! He had studied ceaselessly for eight long years, only to have this happen! But wasn't Alfredo Laza his closest friend? He was his only friend!

But then, that very night, Alfredo had called up Rosana and had her over in order, clearly, to make fun of him. At times they had talked to each other as though he were not there, exchanging meaningful looks and smiles before his very eyes. Alfredo had saved Porfirio from the law, then had brought some fish, cooked it and served it up, chatting casually, as though he had the situation completely in hand, almost as though he were congratulating himself for a private victory. Rosana had completed it by decorating him with verbal medals. From time to time they had remembered that Porfirio existed and had said, "Isn't that so, Porfirio?" or "What do you think, Porfirio?" When it came time for Rosana to leave, Porfirio had been in a state of complete depression, having no desire to accompany them to Doña

46

Isabel's house, but preferring to remain alone. Anyway, he wanted to spend the night as far as possible away from the boarding house where perhaps his sleep would be disturbed by the sound of Adrián's typewriter.

And now that he was alone he felt even worse. In vain he told himself, "I am wrong to feel like this; I should feel grateful to Alfredo." In a sweat, he looked out of the window and felt overwhelmed by the labyrinthian presence of the city. He had an impulse which he immediately checked to leave without waiting for Alfredo, to avoid facing that man who had such natural and persuasive ways.

What were they doing at that very moment? In the taxi she would lean against him and let herself be kissed. Perhaps she would even want to be "generous" (as she said) with him. When she went into the house, she would say goodbye with her dark blue eyes fixed on him. Perhaps she would even warn him: "Watch out, Porfirio's jealous."

He became aware that Laza was opening the door, entering the room, and he gave a start as though he had been caught in the act of stealing something. When they began to talk he immediately realized that his friend was now speaking in his role of political propagandist, and at first he replied only in monosyllables. Then, suddenly exasperated, he took the offensive.

"It can't be helped!" he exclaimed. "I'm going to get something out of my law studies, I'm going to have a career! Is there anything wrong in that? I've already told you: that decision is as much a part of me as my shadow, and a person can't jump over his own shadow. Ever since I can remember, I've had this ambition. You know Juan Lorenzi. I know him extremely well because we're both from the same town. He always had everything and I had nothing. When I was a half-grown boy, I was always seeing him drive by in his convertible, showing off his dark glasses and his gloves. When he wasn't in his car he was driving a noisy motorcycle. All the women were after him, but he never took any of them

47

seriously..."

"Do you mean to say that you studied law because you envied Juan Lorenzi?"

"Probably. The situation is too common to be surprising."

"I admire your frankness, but your idea of life isn't what I call living."

"I'm not talking about your life, but about mine."

"You're not talking about Lorenzi's, either."

"I don't like to fawn on people. I don't like having to rub against anyone's legs, like that stray dog did against mine."

"And you can think like that in a world full of dictators and superstition?"

"You can only live once!"

"But living doesn't mean tolerating a rotten state of affairs. You don't live just to accumulate possessions."

"Do you live in order not to accumulate them?"

"You're so civilized, and yet you think like the Eskimos who have to spend their lives worrying about mere subsistence."

"The Eskimos aren't the only ones."

"Probably. But I refuse to wear a silver collar."

"You've always been fond of fables."

Since the conversation was beginning to take a disagreeable turn, Alfredo laughed. But Porfirio kept at him.

"Some day in the future they'll put up a sign on the house where you were born, which will say..."

Alfredo laughed again, disregarding his friend's words as they were harshly meant and completing the thought jokingly:

"I know. The sign will read, 'Danger. Ruined house.' "

This time it was Porfirio who laughed, mollified.

"I'm sure you don't take my stupid remarks seriously. Forgive me," he added.

But it was time to go to bed. Somewhere nearby a party

was going on, and, dominating all the other sounds was the hurt-animal wail of a saxophone.

Late one afternoon a few days later, Alfredo Laza arrived at Porfirio's boarding house to discuss with him the search for the killers which they had decided to begin without delay. It was almost dusk, but Rosana had not yet come home and Doña Isabel answered the door. She greeted Laza with cordial sarcasm and escorted him to Porfirio's room.

Laza had a piece of news. "Do you know who wrote me that he's coming to New York?" he asked. "You give up? Juan Lorenzi!"

"You couldn't have told me anything to make me happier!" said Porfirio, sarcastically.

"You're wrong to be so prejudiced. Lorenzi is having a hard time just now. Even though they haven't been able to catch him doing anything illegal, they're keeping after him and he's lost a lot of money. It's no secret that he's a smuggler. He intends to spend a few days in New York until things cool off. You know he's been a friend of mine ever since I lived in Ponce. He was a patient in the hospital where I had a job as a male nurse."

"But that he should come at a time like this!"

"I know. You would have preferred him to see you as an influential lawyer in your home town, right? But you would have liked even better to have had him come to you asking for a favor. Don't think I'm interfering in your private affairs, but your attitude isn't a healthy one. You said your determination to rise in the world was as much a part of you as your shadow. Well then, perform the miracle: jump over your shadow!"

Porfirio said nothing. His anxious wish to be a respected and prosperous man in Coamo, conforming to the accepted idea of what constitutes respectability, was like an incurable disease. Quixotic deeds and unattainable ideals were not for him. He must rise above his origin as the son of cheap circus

49

acrobats and the godchild of a couple just as poor and unfortunate. Juan Lorenzi would probably not even notice him, might not even recognize him. But for Porfirio, Juan Lorenzi was the symbol of the man who does as he likes and possesses everything. And he recalled with rancor Lorenzi's gloves and dark glasses, his red and ivory convertible, his raucous motorcycle, his ease in society, his amorous adventures, his irresistible audacity . . .

Oh, how he longed to return to his town to challenge the painful past and overcome it, so that once proud people but now poor would have to come to him to ask for some menial little job. Porfirio Uribe, attorney-at-law, would receive them magnanimously, as befitted the local leader of the majority party—for he had devised a plan which would make him a representative or a senator . . .

But he said nothing further on the subject, for he had learned how to be silent, to swallow his wrath, until he should be in a position to smile condescendingly.

Unexpectedly, Laza dropped the subject and spoke of something else. His eyes had wandered to the *bombardino* and the guitar—or to Estefano and Catalina, as he called them. He picked up the horn and examined it, smiling.

"Why don't you throw it away?" he asked.

"I want them to bury it with me," replied Porfirio, half in jest, half seriously.

"You know, Porfirio, when I compare myself with you I feel I'm the sanest of men."

"You think I'm crazy because I 'communicate' with my godmother Catalina?"

"That's not the only reason."

"Don't you believe she advises me?"

"Did she advise you to keep the *bombardino*?"

Porfirio smiled enigmatically. He was recalling Catalina's mockingly sad laughter when her husband was in a rage. Her flirtations with other men were innocent. Who could hold it against her that she had attractive and easy-going ways?

50

Sometimes Estefano had begun to quarrel as soon as he came home; obviously he had an urge to kill that smile on her face, a smile that injured his tragic feelings which the voice of the baritone horn so well suited. And Catalina would laugh it off; she laughed, it would seem, to forget something. She passed the time strumming the guitar. Her father had not let her marry the man she loved. No one ever knew why she had married the glum Estefano: some said it was so she could care for the dead acrobats' little boy. She never talked about her parents or anyone else in her past. In the village she was reputed to be a clairvoyant; but if she was able to foresee her own tragedy, she never said so. In the month that had preceded the tragedy, Estefano had been almost constantly drunk, and then there were quarrels, when he beat her. "Leave me alone and forgive me, spirit that I harmed in another life," Catalina would cry as she saw him coming home. She was always saying that she had to "pay the debts" she had incurred in another life.

In that atmosphere of accusation and repentance for evil deeds lost in the mists of time, Porfirio had grown from childhood to boyhood. He was deep in these thoughts when Rosana came in and asked him how he was feeling.

Rosana and Laza scarcely spoke to each other, but between them Porfirio sensed an unspoken understanding.

Doña Isabel came into the room after Rosana, trying desperately to separate her daughter from Laza. But Laza made it clear that he had come for Porfirio. They were going to visit the neighborhoods where Santiagans lived, counting on Luis Pororico and his henchmen for clues in their search. Every day they would visit a different section always at dusk, which was the time of day when Porfirio was sure he would recognize one of the killers.

So, taking advantage of Doña Isabel's presence to say goodbye to Rosana, they left the boarding house and went out into the streets.

CHAPTER

IV

Three days passed without Alfredo Laza's putting in an appearance. Porfirio spent hours on end alone in his room, reading and rereading the same books or lying on his back in bed, stupidly staring at the same objects, thinking over the same incidents, listening to the same noises from the street. And any little repetitious noise, such as a leaking faucet or the refrigerator motor infuriated him. He left the room, he bathed, he went back to his room, he tried again and again to write poems to Rosana; a train went by, a boat's horn wailed, another train went by. Rosana, Catalina, Catalina, Rosana, Alfredo, Coamo, Lorenzi, Adrián. Was Adrián able to write in the other world? Coamo. Did life go on just the same there, between the church and the cemetery? He would like to return. That wailing of the boat's horn was torture.

Why did not Alfredo come to see him? Surely he would forgive him for what he had said? Why did he have to stay in New York, where his very race was against him? *"Funny guys, these Portoricans."*

He talked to no one in the house. It was as though Doña Isabel and Rosana didn't exist.

But now, after three days of waiting fruitlessly, he tried to imagine, by the smells and sounds, what Doña Isabel and Rosana were doing, what attitudes they were assuming. In his years of seclusion and study, his senses of hearing and smell had become keener. From the odor of soap and the sound of the shower as the water fell on their bodies, he knew who was taking a bath. He tried to shut off his senses if it was Doña Isabel who was bathing. If it was Rosana, he tried to see her in imagination. That sweet smell now was Rosana's. The water from the shower formed little streams tickling her body, running between her breasts—a river flowing between hills—and down over her abdomen. Her hands, covered with soap, stroked her body. . .She opened her lips, closed her eyes. . .On the whiteness of her body, the blackness of her hair. And those little squeals of pleasure. Water, fresh water over her body. Porfirio felt strangely dizzy. The odor when she left the shower was different. Then, if she were getting ready to go out, new odors, and the soft rustling of clothes. He sensed, by the clicking of her high heels against the floor, when she put on each garment. Now the bracelet. Now the chain. Now one garter, then the other. And minutes afterwards, her voice.

"I'm leaving, Mamma."

"Why do you have to go out so often?"

The noise of the door shutting. And an overwhelming feeling of loneliness. . .

Rosana returned before ten o'clock, when Doña Isabel was already in bed. She placed the bracelet and the watch here, a shoe there, the other one over there. One garment, another and another. Her house slippers. Her housecoat.

Suddenly some light taps on the door of his room. He opened the door. It was Rosana.

"Can I come in?"

"Do."

She closed the door behind her and sat down on the edge of his bed. He looked at her, without saying anything.

"Do you know what's become of Alfredo?" she asked.

53

"No. Did you come to talk to me about him?"

"I came to be with you for a while. I want to talk to you. Why do you shut yourself up in your room without ever going out?"

"I don't know."

"What do you do, all day long, alone?"

"I listen to you bathe and come and go."

She laughed. There was a brief silence. Then she spoke, impulsively.

"I don't know what's the matter with me. Probably God has lost sight of me—didn't you say something like that once about yourself? Mamma has lost all hope as far as I am concerned."

He resolved to speak his thoughts.

"*I* haven't lost sight of you," he said.

"You're not God."

"Luckily! I'm made of flesh and blood, like you."

He approached her to kiss her, but she eluded him.

"Do you think I'm so easy?" she scoffed.

"I would like to make you my wife. What do you think I've studied so hard for?"

She was silent. Then, in a murmur: "I don't want that. What else do you have to offer?"

"My love."

"Are you capable...?" She immediately regretted the words and put her hand out to touch his. "Let me go to see if Mamma is asleep," she said, and left the room.

He waited anxiously. She returned, on tiptoe.

"She's asleep. Tell me, what illusions can you sow in me?"

They embraced. She could not suppress her tears.

Next day there was the same fruitless waiting until nightfall and the same trifling events repeated themselves. Night came, and Doña Isabel could be heard moving about briskly. What was she doing? He perceived the smell of the perfume she used when she went out. But he did not hear Rosana dressing or smell the perfume she used when she left the house. He was sure she was still at home. After supper she had shut herself in her room. Perhaps she was lying down. Then he heard Doña Isabel's footsteps again, and her voice calling out to Rosana.

"I'll be back early. You should come with me."

And Rosana's voice, from her room: "You know I don't like to go to those séances. Besides, I'm not feeling well." Then, a note of protest: "I tell you, those séances frighten me!"

The door slammed. What would Rosana do now? He heard her get up and walk back and forth in her room. He knew she hadn't dressed after her shower. She had eaten her meal with her house coat on. It kept coming open; she had had to close it several times. Then she had gone to her room to lie down. There, alone, she need not close her house coat over her breasts or knees. . .

Rosana was leaving her room. Porfirio held his breath. Yes, again the light raps sounded on his door. A few minutes afterwards she was sitting on the edge of his bed, but at a distance. She would not let him kiss her.

"Did you hear Mamma? She's always going to séances in the house of a neighbor. Her prayers to the Virgin didn't do me any good, so now she's trying to find out from "beyond the grave" what's the matter with me. They've told her that "a being" is pursuing me. What I wouldn't give to have a real human being pursue me!"

Seized with jealous rage, Porfirio almost attacked her then and there, but he was a civilized man, so restrained himself. She smiled placatingly, provocatively.

"I'm a soul in torment," he said, adopting her metaphorical style. "End my martyrdom! Pray for me with your love. Your prayer last night relieved me and other prayers of the same kind would help me tonight. . . ."

She laughed, delighted with his sally. When she laughed, she wrinkled her nose in such a provocative way that he

55

again tried to embrace her, but again she pushed him away.

"Rosana," he said, looking directly into her eyes, "I'm going to repeat what I told you last night: I would like to marry you. Will you marry me? If I could go back to my home town with a woman like you I'd be the happiest man on earth. We'd buy a car and you'd pick me up at work each day at lunchtime. I'm going to leave as soon as this matter is cleared up. Marry me. This is not a sudden impulse. For more than a year now I've been obsessed with this idea, and it hurts me now like a thorn..."

"Why, Porfirio, I didn't think you were capable of talking like this. I like you to talk this way."

She said nothing more, but her silence seemed to hold out a promise and she was smiling the way young girls smile at their first sweetheart. If Porfirio had only known, she was thinking, "Oh, if only Alfredo would talk to me like this!" Aloud she said, "Let's go to the movies."

At the movies she was tenderly melancholy. A good sign, Porfirio reflected, since women always become melancholy when they face their future. He was already imagining how they would live out that future together. But his torturing doubts were revived upon their return home. Just as he was about to whisper some poetic words to her, she yawned.

"I'm absolutely exhausted," she said.

Porfirio went to his room, flung himself on the bed, and gave vent to his frustration in an angry dialogue with himself. Why that sudden compliance of Rosana, and then why her indifference when we returned home? I know: she went out with me in the hope of seeing Alfredo. That was why she wanted to see "that picture" in the neighborhood cinema, a picture whose title she could not even recall. She may already have seen it. Yes, she had hoped to run into Alfredo...

Shortly after lunch next day there was a telephone call from Alfredo Laza. Doña Isabel answered the telephone, and had already hung up by the time Rosana reached it, with

56

her house coat half on, angry because her mother hadn't called her.

"I had something to say to Alfredo!"

"He only wanted to leave a message for Porfirio. He's coming this afternoon at five and wants Porfirio to go out with him again on that search."

Afterwards Rosana was very affectionate with Porfirio, spending almost the entire afternoon with him, talking about poetry. But he realized that she was trying out a smile that was not meant for him. She had bathed at four, put on her most elegant and provocative house coat, her most seductive perfume, and she seemed to be counting the minutes by the drops from the leaky faucet. She started nervously at the least sound outside the door. As the afternoon dragged on, and still no sign of Alfredo, he sensed that she was talking to him absent-mindedly; when he talked, it was as though he were talking to himself, and when she talked, he had the impression that she was shoveling words at him, no matter what words, anything to overwhelm him and silence him. Her mind was on Alfredo, and Porfirio felt hopelessly defeated by that man who was his friend. Her heart, he reflected, as he watched her, has become metamorphosed into the pendulum of the clock. And his own heart began to throb like a broken machine.

Even so, he kept on trying to carry on a conversation, but realized it was impossible when, as he was about to tell her "the funniest joke in the world," she interrupted with, "Do you think he's going to come?"

"How should I know!" he snapped, completely put out.

Just then the clock struck five, leaving her holding her breath. But another half hour of waiting followed.

"What were you saying?" she asked.

Completely exasperated, he was about to get up and go, leaving her alone, just as there was a knock on the door. Making a visible effort at self control, she walked rather stiffly towards the door. Porfirio could see that she must be

57

praying in her heart that her knees would sustain her. A strong smell of food being cooked for the evening meal penetrated the room. With a sensation of nausea Porfirio waited for her to open the door.

It was Laza. Barely giving the girl a glance, he greeted her casually.

"How are you?"

"What happened to you these past few days?" she asked.

Disregarding her, he walked over to Porfirio, shook hands warmly. Meekly, Rosana stood to one side. Her attitude was one of sorrowful repentance for having put on that house coat.

"I'll be right back," she said. "I'm going to get dressed." And she left them.

Porfirio was bewildered at this, and would have given anything to know what the two of them were thinking—not about him, but about each other.

"Where have you been, fellow?" Porfirio finally asked.

"If I told you, you wouldn't believe me, so it's better for me not to tell you."

"Are we going out today?"

"Yes."

"Where?"

"In a minute. Listen. I heard about some Santiagans, newcomers, not seen before."

"Where?"

"On Third Avenue."

"That's where we're going?"

"What do you think?"

"Let's go."

Laza began to talk about the political situation in the Caribbean, but Uribe made it apparent that he neither understood nor wanted to understand anything about it. He remained silent.

"You're wise," murmured Laza.

"Why do you say that?"

"It could harm you. An excess of wisdom makes a person surprisingly useless. But someone, I forget who, said that a man who lives without ever doing anything unwise is not as intelligent as he thinks."

"What are you talking about?"

"You know."

"No, I don't."

Laza changed the subject.

"It's all settled," he said, "Juan Lorenzi will be here any minute. Is Doña Isabel in?"

"Yes."

"I'll go speak to her."

What he had to tell her was that Juan Lorenzi wanted to room in her house. Shortly afterwards he returned, with Rosana. When she was with Alfredo she did not have to make an effort to look modest, but acquired a strange purity which transfigured her.

Actually, Porfirio disliked Alfredo's attitude of letting himself be loved. His indifference was annoying. "Don't throw yourself at him," he wanted to say to Rosana. But he disguised his feelings and said nothing.

That night the two men returned from a fruitless search, discouraged, still without the least notion of who could have killed Adrián Martín.

Next morning Porfirio went out alone in the downtown streets, feeling more than ever trapped in the labyrinth, more than ever convinced that there was no Ariadne to provide him with a thread, and that he was hopelessly at the mercy of the dread monster. He passed through the crowds without discovering any kind smile, any indication of human solidarity. No one even looked at him; it was as though he were nothing but a conglomerate of chemical elements, not a human being on the verge of despair. Fundamentally, although he would not admit it, he admired Alfredo Laza, who refused to submit to fate. But why revolt? Why tire oneself uselessly, why live in agony, why,

why, why? And what, indeed, was he but a conglomerate of memories? And why did he so persistently recall the innocent laughter of his godmother Catalina, and her last moan as she died, staring up at the dark beamed ceiling? What did they think of Estefano and his voice of a broken *bombardino*, there in the dark underworld? And did it matter? Those lives had been so small. And yet they had so much influenced his own life!

Alone, he reached for something to cling to, without finding it. From the depths of his being there welled up a cry of incorruptible rebellion, but he stifled it with silence and apparent insensibility. No, he did not want to suffer the hardships that Alfredo Laza endured.

It was Saturday, one of those terrible Saturdays in New York when people wander about without knowing what to do, each person reflecting the boredom of another. The benches in the downtown parks were filled with old men, draped on them like bundles of old clothes. Many of them were speaking to each other in foreign languages, and their words dribbled into the air like bubbles of blood from an open wound. Those mouths opening in so many somber faces somehow resembled open wounds. They were the early and later immigrants from every corner of the earth. Perhaps they were talking about a life which now seemed to them like a distant dream. Porfirio reflected that some of them gave the impression of being uprooted plants thrown there to be planted and then forgotten, their roots drying up in the sun and wind.

As he walked through the crowds, he saw nothing but "displaced" persons; yes, that adjective was very applicable to the people of this contemporary civilization, this glittering civilization in which so many people can see no purpose in life. Wandering aimlessly through this crowd, he felt more than ever the desire to escape the misery of the have-nots and to possess some of this world's goods.

It was almost five o'clock in the afternoon when he ran

into Laza. Upon catching sight of him, the thought came that perhaps all day long this seemingly aimless wandering had had a purpose: to meet Laza, "After all," thought Porfirio, "I know he lives in this neighborhood, and it is possible that I came here to find him and prevent him from going to see Rosana! Yes, that's exactly what I have done."

But though he was surprised at himself and upset at his own behavior, which seemed to indicate disloyalty to a true friend, it still pleased him to think of Rosana waiting in vain for Alfredo, starting at every little sound at the door, tearful and feverish . . .

Now he was greeting Alfredo and almost excusing himself for not having waited for him at the boarding house.

"It looks to me," said Alfredo with a laugh, "as though you came here in the hope of finding me."

"That's impossible."

"Man, I know you did. And by doing so, you're doing me a favor. The truth is that I'd just as leave not see Rosana today. She and I have different points of view as to what we mean to each other. To me, she's just a child, in spite of her close to twenty-four years. I knew her when she was a little girl, and I've always regarded her as a sister. I've done nothing to make Doña Isabel so afraid of me. But there's more to it than that. You see, Doña Isabel belongs to an old family, aristocratic landowners, while I was the son of a blacksmith in their town. My father shod her family's horses." He laughed, paused, then said: "Come, let's go indoors. I told Balalu I'd meet him at my place. He's coming at six. Then we'll go with him to see Luis Pororico."

This casual way Laza had was soothing, as always, to Porfirio, who reflected, with admiration, "Here's someone who doesn't avoid difficulties."

Balalu listened attentively to Porfirio's description of the two faceless individuals he had seen: one of them tall and thin, the other of normal height. The tall man was the one who limped a little, and it would be necessary to see him

61

run in twilight to be able to identify him.

"Well, it's hard to say, but they tell me two new Santiagans who work for one of the enemy gang live somewhere around the James Street neighborhood. But do the killers of Martín have to be Santiagans? They could be any hired gunmen."

Balalu ought to know: he was one of Luis Pororico's strong-arm men, and a hefty fellow with fair hair and skin.

"Perhaps you're right," said Laza, "but you don't know Leader Augusto's reasons for using Santiagans who have relatives down there in the Republic."

They all three went on to Luis Pororico's establishment near Chinatown where he kept his "stable" of women. Among his clients were several Chinese who paid well for the services he offered. As soon as they arrived, Balalu took his stand at one side of the room, peering through a slit in the wall: he and Luis were constantly changing guard there, always on the alert for a possible visit from the *jara*—as they referred to the police.

Most of the women pretended to be employees of the house, which included a bar, a small restaurant, and a manicuring salon. The men met the women in one or the other of these three places, and then could be seen casually going out together.

Luis greeted Porfirio respectfully but effusively, not neglecting, however, to remind him of the days when Porfirio had worked for him. Things had changed for both of them since then.

"The guys who used to insult me," said Luis, "now tremble when they hear my name. I'm not the greenhorn I used to be, when I wore cotton drill in the middle of a New York winter."

He still affected the peculiar attire he had worn when Porfirio first saw him, a derby hat and a shaggy overcoat. But his suit was an expensive English tweed, and plastic surgery had almost erased the tremendous scar he had had on his face. He had not lost his good humor or his bubbling laughter. He laughed, now, as he recalled with Alfredo and Porfirio various incidents from his adventurous life, as well as from their own early struggles.

"Remember how sentimental I used to be about Puerto Rico?" he said. "Well, that's a thing of the past. Remember when you two took your guitars out into the middle of a snowstorm to sing Christmas carols? Man, them were the days!"

They shared some pleasant memories as well, recalling dances they used to organize almost every Saturday night, with music furnished by a pianola. The woman who had been with Balalu at that time made *pasteles* wrapped in wax paper and tied with string, instead of the banana leaves that they lacked. And all four men laughed when they recalled how Balalu, every time he went out, made his wife go to bed and then sprinkled talcum powder on the floor around it to enable him later to detect any footprints that might be left there. . .

And there were grim memories that made them stop laughing, for instance the case of Charles Ortiz, whom they had all known. Ortiz had been accused of being a stool-pigeon for the boss of the rival gang. He had been found groaning in an alley-way. Luis and Balalu had taken him to the hospital as quickly as possible, but he had died on the way. The autopsy showed that he had drunk a deadly poison.

Dusk found them in the vicinity of James Street, where they entered a night club that was being remodeled. Some workmen were busy painting stage scenery. Laza knew one of the painters and began to talk to him. A group of men in a corner of the room were playing a casual card game. At another table two other men were leaning back on their chairs, discussing matters of their "trade". It was obvious that one of them knew Balalu, for he kept looking at him on the sly, and then directed a meaningful glance at his partner.

"He's from the other gang," Balalu warned Laza and Uribe. Then, to avoid involving the two in a ruckus, he left the room.

The men continued to talk, almost indifferently, but from the way they talked out of the corners of their mouths, they seemed to be giving each other veiled warnings, in cryptic language.

"Do you think this will be ready by next week?" asked one of them.

"It's got to be ready," said the other.

"Man, did you hear about Jack Gardello?"

"Yes, I heard the rumor."

"They knocked him off this afternoon, but it's still not in the papers. I looked through all of them."

"Two cops are hanging around here."

"They're probably waiting for their pay-off."

The men all seemed to be Italians. Presently, a big fair-haired and mean-looking man, apparently Irish, walked in. He approached the painter Laza knew.

"Your union card," he said, shortly.

Apparently the painter had no union card, for he stopped painting and began to pick up his brushes and boxes. One of the men talking in the corner stood up.

"Who told you to ask for his card?" he called out.

"Joe Chiento."

"What a pile of..."

He went to the telephone and called someone, talking almost in code. Then he shoved the receiver into the Irishman's hands.

"They want to talk to you," he said.

The Irishman hesitated for a few seconds, then put the receiver against his ear.

"Hello!"

The person on the other end of the line was obviously a

big shot, because the Irishman, visibly disturbed, only answered: "Yes, sir. Sorry, sir. Don't worry, sir. I'll tell him. I won't forget. . .Yes, sir!"

He dropped the receiver and ran out of the room. The men roared with laughter. The painter had laid his brushes and boxes out on the floor again as fast as he had picked them up, and went back to painting without a word. The Irishman's first "Yes, sir!" was enough to convince him that he could go on working.

After looking at the painter's work with an expert eye, Laza left, followed by Uribe. Balalu had vanished. They walked for a while aimlessly through the narrow downtown streets, then decided to give it up for the day. Then, just as they were going into a subway station, they saw two men walking down the street.

"They look like the two we're after," said Uribe.

And off they went in pursuit. But the men, realizing they were followed, began to walk very fast and were soon lost to view.

"You know what?" said Uribe. "I don't believe after all, that I'd be able to recognize the man who killed Martín. Those men might be the killers, and then again they might not be. The other day I saw a pair like that and was tempted to have them arrested. But I wasn't sure enough. I think we'd better stop the search, because it's useless."

He felt drained of strength with discouragement and longed only to sit down somewhere. Now he was sure he was caught in the labyrinth and would never escape. He would have to remain in New York as long as the police wanted to keep him there. What a waste of time those eight years of study and of work in the Dead Letters Section had been!

"I for one will not go out again to look for them," he said.

"It would be better to make one more effort," said Laza. "Then we'll go to the police and tell them we've looked but been unable to find the killers. Cayoctavio will accom-

65

pany us to the police station. Don't give up. There's always the chance that we might run into them."

"Do you think I'll ever be allowed to go to Puerto Rico?"

"You're innocent. What proof is there against you?"

"The fact that I'm the only witness and a 'Portorican'."

"Cayoctavio is sure they won't be able to involve you in the case. No charges have even been brought as yet."

Once again they were walking towards the subway. Darkness had fallen and the street was ill-lit. Absorbed in their conversation, they had not noticed the two men who were following them, almost at their heels—the two men they had lost a few minutes before. Suddenly the men pounced upon them, knocking Uribe down with the first blow. Laza stood his ground and began to slug it out. Suddenly one of the men gave a joyful yell.

"Laza! It's Alfredo Laza, Rafael!" then, as Laza stared, "Don't you remember me?"

"You look familiar," said Laza, brushing himself off.

"Sure I do. You saw me the other night at a meeting of Santiagan exiles. I'm Ruiz Corujo. Just a humble foot-soldier, so to speak!"

They shook hands, then turned to help Uribe to his feet.

"We're sorry, fella. We took you for agents of Leader Augusto, thought you were following us. We just came up from Mexico a month ago. What are you two doing here?"

They explained, and both Rafael and Ruiz Corujo promised to help in the search. They had heard of the crime, and felt it should not go unpunished.

In a Latin-American restaurant to which all four now went, Laza and the two Santiagans were soon discussing politics, and even alluding openly to a possible invasion of Santiago.

"What's happening in the Santiagan Republic is too horrible for words," said Ruiz Corujo. "The dictator has got to be ousted. I don't know how or with what. But it will be done."

66

Porfirio Uribe remained silent. He was not interested in anything the others were talking about and refused to be. He was irritated that he should find himself in the midst of political conspiracies which did not interest him in the least. Why had he mistaken these two conspirators for Adrián Martín's killers? The same thing would probably happen again. From the beginning, it was stupid of him to have told the police he would be able to recognize the killers. His evidence was too fragile. If the hallway had been lighted when the killing occurred, it wouldn't be difficult. As it was, there didn't exist the least possibility of identifying them.

Before they parted, Ruiz Corujo, noticing Uribe's silence, took Laza aside to tell him of a very important meeting being organized among Santiagan exiles. At the meeting, plans were to be drawn up for the expected invasion of the Republic.

Porfiirio was waiting in his room for Alfredo, when he heard the knock on the front door. It must be his friend, he thought, and was about to go out to meet him, when he heard another male voice and Doña Isabel's. Then he heard Alfredo's voice, and again reached for his overcoat. But after what he heard, he stood still.

"Doña Isabel, this is the man I spoke to you about. He wants to room here."

"Juan Lorenzi, at your service, Madam," said the person alluded to.

Yes, that was very typical of Juan Lorenzi, that "At your service, Madam." Porfirio could well imagine Doña Isabel's smile of satisfaction; she was always complaining of the lack of courtesy shown by the younger generation. Lorenzi's formula was old-fashioned now, but it still worked, still made him seem distinguished. Porfirio recalled Lorenzi's reputation for gallantry in Coamo, where he made a big impression upon his return from France, after several years

67

there, studying medicine. True, he returned without finishing his studies, but full of talk about the marvels of life in Paris.

His father was a very prosperous coffee grower and also the owner of a bakery and a large trading establishment in Ponce. Juan spent a great deal of time at his villa in Asomante and liked to visit Coamo, which was nearby.

It was then that he had made such a lasting impression upon Porfirio, who still recalled with bitterness the carefree Lorenzi racing about in his convertible or roaring along on his motorcycle, always showing off with sudden starts and daring stops, and flaunting his gray gloves, his dark glasses, before the adoring eyes of "females", as Lorenzi always referred to women. He had escaped from several spectacular road accidents, without injury; nothing serious ever happened to him although he was always flirting with death. That first year after his return from Paris, the life of the town had seemed to revolve around him. And Porfirio, a mere boy then, had scarcely been able to endure the sight of him. He knew Luis Lorenzi personally because Estefano had worked in the bakery for Lorenzi's father. Lorenzi liked to drop in and joke with Porfirio's godmother Catalina, whom he called Gypsy. And Catalina's face always lit up with pleasure when he thrust out his hand and said, "Gypsy, tell me my fortune!" He knew her fame as a clairvoyant, and took it for granted that she could also read the lines in the palm of the hand. To please him, she pretended she could, would take his hand in hers, close her eyes in a comical way and say: "Death fears you, but be careful, don't challenge death too much. And look for a woman who will make you happy." The scene was repeated every time they met. And sometimes Lorenzi, who really had a great affection for Catalina, kissed her on the forehead when she closed her eyes.

Porfirio recalled how jealous this made Estefano, although she was much older than Lorenzi and her affection for him was purely maternal. She would soothe Estefano, saying, "That boy's like my own son. His grandmother and my father were like brothers. And can you imagine him paying attention to an old woman like me, with all those young chicks surrounding him?"

But even Estefano was indulgent with Lorenzi, enjoyed his pranks, and laughed at the way all the "females" sighed over him, while he gave no sign of intending to marry.

One day—Porfirio still vividly remembered it—he had been particularly furious with Juan Lorenzi. Porfirio was in secondary school and had come home with a little girl friend. Lorenzi was calling on Estefano and Catalina, and the little girl stared in open-mouthed admiration at him. Porfirio was sorry not to have the *bombardino* within reach—he would have blown a loud and inharmonious blast on it, then banged Lorenzi over the head. Then, to add insult to injury, as Lorenzi started up his motorcycle, he almost ran down Porfirio. And he didn't stop to excuse himself, but just roared off as though nothing had happened.

And now there he was, talking to Doña Isabel, and the light footsteps of Rosana could be heard, and her voice: "So this is the famous Juan Lorenzi!" She was laying it on thick. "I can see, now, why he's so famous!" And Doña Isabel was saying, very pleased: "Don't pay any attention to my daughter, she's still just a child." Porfirio wished he could leave the house without seeing Lorenzi, but the only way out, besides the front door, was through the window...

"Take me to Porfirio's room. I want to see him. Imagine Porfirio Uribe here! You'll never know how much I loved his godparents, especially Catalina. Tell me, how are things going with him?"

"He's just finished his law studies."

"A lawyer—he's going to be a lawyer? Who'd ever believe it?"

"Come with me, I'll show you the way."

Porfirio heard their voices in the corridor, now.

69

Lorenzi, in high spirits, kept repeating, "A lawyer, just imagine." And he added, "He'll have to perform acrobatic feats there, for sure."

No doubt he said this without malice, but it was obviously an allusion to Porfirio's parents, acrobats in a cheap circus.

"Even though I'm the son of tight-rope walkers, I did finish my law studies," Porfirio muttered. "I haven't sunk so low as to become a smuggler."

As Laza had told him, Lorenzi's fortune had considerably declined since his father's death, after a storm destroyed the coffee crop and following some bad business deals. Then prohibition and Juan's natural desire for adventure had turned him into an audacious smuggler.

Now, Juan Lorenzi was knocking at the door, entering the room, holding out his hand to Porfirio and saying, "After these twelve years it's as though you'd risen from the dead!"

Juan Lorenzi was no longer the dashing young fellow he had been, he was now in his forties, but still good looking and vigorous. Porfirio muttered something by way of greeting. Juan, very much at ease, was looking about the room, and his eye fell upon the *bombardino*.

"Is that Estefano's baritone horn?" he asked. "Yes? And are you going to stay on in New York or...?"

"I was going back to Coamo, had already bought my passage, when..."

"Alfredo's told me about it. Too bad. I hope everything will be cleared up for you soon. If I can help you in any way..."

"Thank you."

"Well, aren't you surprised to see me here, Porfirio? I'll confess, I'm in a mess. But I wouldn't be what I am without being in trouble, would I? Probably the people back there think I'm dead—I left without saying a word to anyone, disappeared, and came here. They're saying, I'll bet, 'That fellow's shark bait by now!' But I mustn't think about that, for when I do I sometimes almost believe it myself, feel I am dead. And I may be dead for them now, but in a few weeks I'll perform the miracle of resurrection, just wait."

"Or you might dedicate yourself instead to defending a just cause?" inquired Laza very seriously. He had effaced himself, smiling at the encounter between Juan and Porfirio.

"I'd envy you, Alfredo," said Lorenzi, "if I was sure you're defending a just cause. It's horrible to have to live according to the dictates of others. They caught me up in their schemes, it's true, but I'll not accept their opinion of me."

As Lorenzi talked, he was watching every movement Rosana made. No one would have believed that he was taking what he said seriously.

"Is that child an orphan?" he asked. "I mean, is she single?"

"Ask Porfirio," suggested Laza maliciously.

"She's single," Porfirio managed to say.

That same night the three of them went out, but Porfirio was silent most of the time and when he did speak, it was with restraint and a veiled hostility. He was burning to ask, "What became of the convertible and the motorbike, the gloves and the glasses?" But he contained himself. And while the others kept up a brisk conversation, he pretended indifference, as though he were not in the least interested in what was said. Aware of this, Lorenzi began to talk jestingly.

"Uribe, you should really set up your practice in Puerto Rico," he said, "because I'll need a lawyer, at the rate things are going. You know what happened? A rival took some pot-shots at me, and now they'll not rest till they get me. They're all at my heels! It's one of the few times in my life that I've felt really important. I'm going to show them what Juan Lorenzi is capable of!"

"Too bad, using up all that energy in smuggling. It's a dead loss."

71

"Dead loss, you've said it! I've lost everything. But I've still got some energy left."

"So then," said Laza, "we're going to hunt down the monster?"

They looked at each other understandingly, but Porfirio was completely mystified. Obviously they were talking about something important and Laza was trying to persuade Lorenzi to do something. They were talking in symbols, as if they did not trust him.

"Speak out," said Lorenzi. "What candle are you carrying in the procession?"

"I'd be glad to carry a candle to set at the head of the dead monster. Frankly, I hate the idea of wasting my life when there's so much to be done, so many bloodthirsty monsters on the loose. . . ."

"You're talking about Greek mythology, of course?" Porfirio interrupted sarcastically, annoyed at not understanding a word they said. "About the feats of Theseus, of course?"

Lorenzi and Laza took their friend's irony in good humor. Porfirio was not stirred by Laza's epic outbursts or by Lorenzi's defiance of the established order. He knew they were talking politics, the one topic that fascinated Alfredo Laza. But as for him, he wanted to go on living, free of all political ties. Had he been asked to describe the forms of government of the American nations, he would not have known what to say. And he was always surprised that Alfredo Laza thought of himself as a political exile. The fact was that Alfredo had been imprisoned for aggressive nationalistic acts, and should have foreseen and accepted the consequences. No, the unending political revolt of Laza and his friends was senseless. During his eight years of seclusion from the world, Porfirio had lost track of these things. And anyway, he knew exactly what his future was to be: he would be a prominent member of the majority party. Why become involved in other people's affairs?

In the depths of his consciousness, Porfirio blamed those professional conspirators for getting him involved in the murder of Adrián Martín. Laza had brought Adrián to room at Doña Isabel's in the first place. And so, because of those conspirators, here he was, still in the labyrinth, just when he was on the point of escaping to a normal life. In an upsurge of resentment, Porfirio decided that, if the opportunity offered and the pay was good enough, he would even serve "the monster" Lorenzi and Laza were talking about. It would be a kind of personal revenge for him to do the opposite of what they thought he should do.

Laza, with a knowing wink, appropriated for himself Uribe's favorite figure of speech. "The only labyrinth we're caught in, that I can see, is that of dictatorial powers which set unjust restraints upon our liberty. We must win the love of Ariadne, kill the monster, and escape from the labyrinth!"

Porfirio said nothing. Let them mock him. He was still free to think his own thoughts.

CHAPTER

V

One afternoon, as Porfirio was waiting for a bus in his neighborhood to take him to Greenwich Village, where he was to meet Laza, he saw Rosana crossing the street towards the subway station. From the other side, she waved at him. He returned the greeting and, delighted, was about to join her when someone behind him let out a shout of recognition, which held him back, disagreeably surprised, for it was Lorenzi.

"Hi, there, Porfirio!" he shouted, "Where are you off to?"

"I'm on my way to meet Laza," said Porfirio, a bit glumly.

"Good. I'm going in the same direction. But come with us in the subway. It's faster, I like it better. Every time I get into that train my animal instincts awaken, I forget my human worries, and I relax a little."

Unable to make up his mind, Porfirio looked at Rosana who was waiting—there was no doubt about it—for Lorenzi. She was very pretty.

"Come on," said Lorenzi. "A lady is waiting."

Porfirio's feelings were a mixture of anger, jealousy, an urge to kill, and shame. What a fool he had been to respond with such enthusiasm to a greeting Rosana directed at another man! He had not noticed Juan Lorenzi walking be-

74

hind him. And now this "enemy" of his was no doubt taking Rosana out for the evening. He blushed at the thought of what they would say about him. But perhaps they hadn't seen him wave back at her? She was surrounded by a crowd of people waiting for an uptown bus. But the arm he had raised burned with shame.

And how irritating Lorenzi was, with his improbable explanation about riding in the subway! Why should a man's animal instincts awaken in the subway? Because riding underground turned one into a mole, running from one cavern to another, farther and farther away from the sun? He himself knew what a mole's life was, during those eight years of seclusion, when he left the cave of his room to enter the cave of the subway and pass through it to the cave of the Dead Letters Section of the Postal Service, and then back again at the end of the day, by the same route. Yes, sir, many times he had felt like a mole, wilfully deaf and blind to the call of the man within him. He had sealed that man off from the world and deadened his senses. Sometimes, as he passed under Times Square, he had been tempted to go up there for a little fun, but he had always ruthlessly stamped out the impulse. For eight years he had followed that mole's itinerary, but always seeing ahead that exit to the light by way of the College of Law. Yes, sir, he had been a bewildered mole, but always with the hope of becoming some day a respectable person, a man at last! He had visualized that man as driving alone in a solemn limousine, perhaps with a chauffeur—his dream went far beyond convertible roadsters or raucous motorcycles! Oh, that Lorenzi, and his affectations!

And there was Rosana, as much of an animal as this "enemy", waiting on the other side of the street for Lorenzi, ready to be "generous as the earth which lets itself be sown" —as she had said, once, in a breaking voice. Would her voice break when she spoke to Lorenzi? Wrathfully, Porfirio remembered the indulgent smiles of the women in Coamo,

75

when Lorenzi returned from Paris with an unfinished medical career... Why did he now have to come to New York and stay in the very boarding house where Porfirio was? In a city of seven million inhabitants and almost countless hotels and rooming houses, Lorenzi had had to pick on Doña Isabel's house! But Alfredo Laza was to be blamed there, he reflected.

The main question, however, was in regard to Rosana. How had Juan Lorenzi been able to charm her so soon? For obviously their affair was running ahead of schedule. No great feat with a woman of her sort, but still, the affair had got off to a quick start. And Doña Isabel was only too glad to accept the situation. Perhaps a soul in the other world had told her that Juan Lorenzi was the man destined for her daughter. At any rate, Rosana's mother had stopped talking about a convent life for the girl. Apparently she was devoting all her mind to thinking up special dishes to cook for Lorenzi...Porfirio had even heard her say, "He's of good family, has no debts, is a fine man. He needs to get married and settle down. That kind of man makes a good husband, strange as it may seem. Look at what happened to me with my little dead fly of a husband! And to think I left the convent for him! Well, thank heaven, we have a chance to make amends for the mistakes we make in this life. The medium tells me I have to live out this life as a test run, and then I'll return to the world to live the kind of life suited to me. My husband was only a test..." Yes, clearly, Doña Isabel thought Lorenzi a "good catch" for her daughter. She was always suggesting this or that place to which Lorenzi could accompany Rosana. The periodic absences of Alfredo Laza played into her hands. And Rosana, nowadays, rarely mentioned Alfredo. What kind of girl was that disturbed little creature?

All these thoughts went through Porfirio's mind in a flash.

"Thanks," he said crossly to Lorenzi. "I prefer the bus."

"Too bad. We're going to have a good time. I say, Uribe: is there anything between you and Rosana?"

"No, nothing."

"Do you know if she and Alfredo...?"

"I can speak for myself, not for Alfredo."

"She tells me she's completely free."

Free, yes, the girl was certainly free, Porfirio reflected, and almost spoke the thought. It would be a foul thing to do. But he remembered her "generous" impulses, remembered how she turned off the light—so that she could imagine the man she was with was Alfredo, no doubt! However, Rosana had once told him, "Porfirio, there's something about you, I don't know what, that appeals to me. And I've been thinking a lot about what you said, that you'd like me to go back with you to your town in Puerto Rico, where you lived as a child, a poor little orphan!" How false all that was! God, how false!

He watched them disappear into the subway station. She was clinging to his arm, and had gone off without even turning to look at Porfirio, that orphan she pitied! Lorenzi had tossed off a gay parting remark: "Oh, if the people who think I'm dead could only see me now! What a beautiful soul is accompanying me through purgatory!"

This encounter was a turning-point; thenceforth, Porfirio expressed his hostility towards Lorenzi in thorny silences.

Laza did all he could to change this attitude and became the self-appointed chronicler of Lorenzi's good deeds.

"There are few men of his caliber," said Laza that same day, "Juan is one of the few who take friendship seriously. I could tell you several stories...Take that one when he was still carrying on commercial fishing, before he went in for smuggling. And you know he intends to go back to fishing as soon as they've forgotten the smuggling. Listen to this. A comrade of his once fell into shark-infested water. A shark caught him, and Lorenzi and the others watched him sink, screaming, into the blue sea, without being able to do anything to help him. For weeks Lorenzi was unable to sleep or work in peace. For weeks he fished at that site, using big chunks of meat for bait and a very strong hook and line. For days it was without result. Then one evening Lorenzi felt a strike, and a big struggle began. Lorenzi fought the shark alone until he landed it. Later, when it was cut open, they found human remains. A terrible coincidence, perhaps, but it happened just as I'm telling you. One of the fishermen who worked for Juan told me the story, right here in New York. I tell you, he's a great guy!"

"Better than a fairy tale!" commented Porfirio.

"You ought to try to overcome your prejudice against him," was Alfredo's concluding remark, that day.

Not long after, Porfirio overheard an interesting conversation between Rosana and her mother. Rosana was taking a shower. Her mother was nearby, and when Rosana shut off the water she called out to her.

"Mamma, I've brought you a medallion."

"Where is it?"

"Wait till I come out, I'll show you."

"No, tell me where it is."

"In my pocketbook."

After a pause, he heard the shower running again. Suddenly there was a knocking on the bathroom door. The water again stopped falling.

"What is it"

"Is it possible . . .?"

"Is what possible"

"This."

"What?"

"Open the door."

Porfirio heard the door open, then Rosana's voice.

"Let's see."

"This."

"Oh! That! Well, Mamma, would you rather have me become pregnant?" Then, after a pause, "Sorry, Mamma,

78

I don't like to hurt you. Forgive me."

The door closed again, and the shower was turned on once more. Porfirio in his room visualized her, with the little streams of water running over her fine skin, her lips open, her eyes closed...*If she would come to see me again, I would still ask her to marry me.*

But she did not come to his room again. Nor did she appear to be particularly upset when Doña Isabel shut herself in her room for two days. Then, at the end of the third day, Porfirio overheard another conversation between mother and daughter.

"Rosana: does that man *owe* you anything?"

"Who?"

"Lorenzi."

"No, nothing."

"If he does, I'll see to it that he marries you."

"I don't want to marry him! Why, I'd just as leave jump head first from the top of the Empire State Building."

"Then who...?"

"Alfredo Laza is the only one who 'owes' me anything, even though he's never so much as touched my little finger."

"You'll be the death of me! Such madness!"

"What I'm saying isn't madness. Alfredo *must* love me, must rescue me from my illusions. Loving him is like sowing seeds on stone and expecting them to grow! He's everything to me! With him, I'd be a good woman."

"God will punish you!"

"God is just and He knows what I'm going through. He knows what I don't know myself. I'm like a blind person, going I don't know where. If I don't kill myself, it's because I love life and don't want to throw it away. I'd be willing to die after having done just one worthwhile thing, as Alfredo says!"

"But that man..."

"I know, you've told me so many times! He's the son of my parents' blacksmith, possibly he's 'a mongrel' as he himself boasts, like an American. Besides, he's a nationalist, a conspirator, an ex-convict. All right! But he's generous, he doesn't poison himself with hatred, he has a fresh, healthy attitude, he has no mercenary ambitions, he's brave and determined, he paints, he writes poetry, he's a good public speaker. What do I care if he's ugly! I'd gladly die with him, defending a just cause! Perhaps that will come, in time."

Doña Isabel's only reply was to burst into tears. Then she embraced her daughter.

"My child, I don't know what to think!"

Rosana also broke down and wept.

"Mamma! I love him so much. I can't help it."

"And do you think that your way of loving him is right?"

"No, Mamma, but I'm all mixed up. He's the only man in the world who can save me, I swear it, and I hope he'll save me before it's too late."

"Do you want me to speak to him?"

"No. I just don't want you to be rude to him?"

"I won't be rude to him. I promise you."

"Make him feel at home in this house. If I can get him to take an interest in me, I'll not look at any other man."

But Laza did not show the least interest in her. Instead, he seemed to be avoiding her, even giving signs of contempt. Meanwhile, she continued to go out with Lorenzi. It was one way, probably, of flinging herself head first into the abyss.

Doña Isabel continued to seek an answer to the problem by consulting an intangible and mysterious world beyond the grave; indeed, the actual, physical world in which she moved had become even more mysterious to her. She could find no logical explanation anywhere for her daughter's behavior, that daughter she had educated in the best private schools and brought up in the fear of God, the God she knew or thought she knew.

Little by little Rosana became increasingly involved with Lorenzi. She imagined that he would eventually take her to the altar, believed he vaguely thought of her as his future wife but was unable to make up his mind. One day, in front of Porfirio, Lorenzi was questioned by Alfredo Laza.

"Where were you? Didn't we agree to meet at three?"

"Rosana delayed me," said Lorenzi. "Italian food's my weakness."

"I see. The way to the heart is through the stomach," said Laza indifferently.

"The road to my heart is long and winding," said Juan, with a careless laugh.

Porfirio was indignant, but said nothing. How could Rosana so lower herself? That evening he hinted something of this to her, but she only smiled, as if to say, "How silly you are!" And when he grew angry, she gave him the best sedative she knew of: a view of a magnificent pair of crossed legs, uncovered to a little above the knees. He surrendered completely when she said, "I've realized that I shouldn't hope for anything from Juan Lorenzi."

As a matter of fact, Lorenzi was preparing to leave the boarding house. He was spending most of his time with Laza, while carefully avoiding the group of exiled Santiagans in whose society Laza frequently moved. This had been agreed upon between the two men, since Lorenzi enjoyed the confidence and friendship of Leader Augusto, whom he had visited in the National Palace and at the Leader's country residences. He had also accompanied him occasionally on the presidential yacht. Their friendship had flourished because they had two interests in common: horses and cars. And Lorenzi possessed great mechanical skill and a vast knowledge of automobiles, boats, and ships. He had used his smuggling experience to satisfy the Leader's whims in cars and wine, helping him to stock the presidential wine cellars, and so on. When he did encounter the exiled Santiagans who were Laza's friends, he was regarded by them with obvious suspicion. Lorenzi did not conceal his admiration for the man who imposed his will upon millions of people, and

81

without hesitation he said that many of the Leader's adversaries were "hurt pigeons", that other men, if given the opportunity, would do the same or worse than the Leader. He had nothing but scorn for the rotten tropical politicians who spent their time preaching freedom while denying it in practice. In private conversations with Alfredo Laza he expressed his absolutely independent viewpoint.

"Augusto is a pleasant man and a good friend," he said, "but he's the product of two situations. He was sufficiently intelligent to create a myth about himself, and it's easy to exploit the superstition of the ignorant masses. The ex-overseer of big plantations, Ursulino A. Cachola, has been turned into the all-powerful Leader Augusto. He's known how to take advantage of his opportunities. Frankly, I admire him. He hasn't yet been able to establish his myth firmly, but when he does, no one will be able to overthrow him."

"To my mind," burst out Laza, "General Cachola is nothing but a plain conglomeration of perversities. He's too monstrous to be able to create a benevolent myth about himself. However, he has been able to exploit the superstitions of the ignorant, I agree with you there."

"You don't know him personally, Laza! I'd say he's a progressive chief of state with paternalistic ideas. Life is just a puff of air—yours, mine, Leader Augusto's. But he's been able to do something with his life that we haven't. Even so, I'm sorry for him. He must get bored at having everything turn out his way. And at times I feel tempted to challenge his omnipotence."

"You'll have the opportunity. You have a good boat and you can enter and leave the Republic without hindrance."

"I need the boat to carry mahogany. I forgot to tell you: Augusto's given me the exclusive contract on mahogany for Puerto Rico. Do you think I should throw away that gold mine, above all now that smuggling doesn't pay? I prefer to deal with the leader rather than defend the cause of some little down-and-out politicians."

"I'm not thinking about those politicians you're referring to, but of the right to a better life for thousands of people."

"Who's going to give them that better life? The politicians? Many of the Leader's enemies are actually just bosses and overseers who've had less luck and been more stupid than he. Their only aim—you call it a cause—is to remove him from power so they can take his place. That doctrine doesn't appear very sound to me. Some of them, once in power, would be more monstrous than the Leader himself."

"Up to now," said Laza tolerantly, "you've only received favors from Augusto, so it's only natural that you should talk this way. But I don't think you'd feel the same if they'd taken your father or a brother as hostage, or if they'd violated your sister, not if you clearly realized that everything depends upon the favor or disfavor of a single man; and I don't think you'd talk this way if you had to talk in whispers in the streets, or if you were thrown into a filthy prison just because you dissented...But you have the Leader's friendship, you talk to him about cars and horses, you accompany him in his yacht, you see him in his home, you have exclusive rights on the sale of mahogany."

"Perhaps both of us, Laza, go to extremes. Perhaps you're right, but I don't like the little politicians who are out of office. I prefer to spend my time with women, even though I may sometimes fall on all fours in front of them, thinking I'm on my knees. It's a better way to spend time..."

"I'm also conscious of my animal nature, but I defy it with an ideal."

"Well, I don't want to commit myself. If Augusto wanted something more from me than talk about cars and horses, I wouldn't keep his friendship. On my boat I'm the absolute master of my own destiny; at least that's how I feel. I don't belong to any party, I flee from marriage, and all I'm interested in is my own individual freedom. I won't fight for any cause that I don't want to fight for."

83

They talked no more on the subject. Once more, probably, Laza was disillusioned.

Sometimes Lorenzi accompanied Alfredo and Porfirio in their excursions through the Spanish-speaking neighborhoods. It was a fruitless search, which always ended in a cabaret or a bar.

One night, as they were leaving a rather unsavory bar, Lorenzi stumbled against a big, ugly individual who did not accept his apology but roughly shoved him away.

"Do you know who I am?" said the aggressive individual.

"Yes, I know who you are," replied Lorenzi at once.

"Then, who am I?"

"Who could you be if not a son of a bitch?"

And saying this, Lorenzi flung himself on the man with lightning swiftness, giving him no time to repel the attack. Someone called the police. Before they could arrive, the three friends took to their heels.

Although Lorenzi did not mention it, he was clearly trying to avoid Rosana. The remote possibility of becoming involved with her had filled him with fear. Sensing this, Doña Isabel lost no time in urging her daughter to shorten the road between Juan's stomach and his heart. And in spite of everything, Rosana could have been glad to accept the prosaic role of a housewife.

More and more, Juan Lorenzi and Alfredo Laza went out together, leaving Porfirio behind, giving him a tormenting feeling of being abandoned by people who had formerly felt some affection for him. Porfirio's loneliness was like a veritable poison flowing through his veins and constricting his heart. Again, he shut himself in his room, listening to Rosana's footsteps, Rosana's voice. Her withdrawal from him made him feel as though he were now living in a vacuum. For Rosana was nursing her wounded pride, was staying more and more in her room, often not even leaving it to eat. Doña Isabel, all solicitude, brought up trays of food to

84

the girl in her cloistered retreat.

Rosana realized that she had thrown herself at Juan Lorenzi's head, and was bewildered at herself. Why did she have to give herself to a man who had attracted her only momentarily? Why did she feel the need to be "generous" with men? There was no doubt that she had become involved with Juan while merely trying to provoke Alfredo's jealousy. It was absurd, more than absurd, that she couldn't stop herself from going from one man to another! Rosana had wanted to reform herself, to conquer and kill her promiscuous impulses. For this reason she had shut herself in, not wanting to see any men. At times she felt like talking to Porfirio Uribe, but her unexpected determination to isolate herself from men always won out. She stayed in her room, was seen nowhere in the house. An invincible need for renunciation had overwhelmed her, and she would gladly have taken refuge in a convent, but for that feeling of guilt which obsessed her. She imagined she would be able to rehabilitate herself by self torture. Her conscience began to hurt like an open wound. How gladly would she have gone to some uncivilized country as a missionary, to make amends for her sins! Oh, if only it were possible to undo what had been done, to free herself once and for all from her urge to be "generous"!

She dared not talk about it to Doña Isabel. This present repentance might be merely a feverish delusion. She was probably depressed, she told herself, because she had no real vocation for the religious life which Doña Isabel so wanted for her. Or perhaps, she reflected, she was depressed because she was not capable of holding one man's affections...But would she finally overcome her sinful impulses? Even now, she wondered if she would be strong enough to resist him, if Alfredo ever asked her to live with him. Would Alfredo be capable of making such a proposal? And if he did...She shivered. But supposing he made the suggestion, just when she least expected it, would she have the courage to say No?

She continued to torture herself with these conflicting thoughts. When she heard the sound of Lorenzi's voice, Lorenzi's footsteps, she blushed with shame at what he must be thinking about her, and imagined him saying to himself, "I don't like easy women."

In her own isolation, she thought with pity of the loneliness and isolation of Porfirio, and remembered how he had said, "I'd marry you and take you back to my town to live." What a pity he had said that to a flighty woman such as she was! She knew that Porfirio listened to every movement she made, and she now waited until he had gone out before bathing or undressing. She was afraid he was still seeing her in imagination, and she did not want to torment him with visions of her under the shower, for she had a great and sudden yearning for sanctity. . .

As for Porfirio, he was ready to discontinue the search for Adrián's assassins and ask the authorities to permit him to leave the United States. Within a few days the *San Jacinto* would sail, and Cayoctavio had given him to understand that he could have a passage on that ship. Oh, that he might be sure of it!

"Have you resolved to renounce the sins of the flesh and dedicate yourself to the life of a mystic?" Juan Lorenzi put the question ironically to Alfredo Laza.

"I don't understand."

"Well, I see that you have a religion: your nationalism. And it would also seem that you have renounced the flesh-pots."

"What are you talking about?"

"Don't play dumb. I'm talking about Rosana."

"Did she say anything to you?"

"What do you mean, did she say anything? You must know she lives only for you."

"But you told me that she and Doña Isabel wanted to trap you."

"There are signs of it. But Rosana would be capable of committing suicide if she thought it would attract your attention. She'd marry me and God knows whom else. For the first time in my life I've failed in a love affair. I assure you, if she married me, you could go to her on the very night of the wedding, reproach her for it, and she'd leave me for you. Such a thing never happened to me before. Either I'm failing or it's a case of mental fixation with her. That this should happen to me in the very prime of my life! Imagine! Several times she's called me—me!—by your name. At the most inconceivable moments, she's talked to me about you! What have you given her, a love potion?"

"A rather strange thing happens to me when I'm with her. I only want to think of her as a sister. I met her when she was ten or eleven years old and I always wanted to have a sister. I've always felt that if I touched her it would be like committing incest. Besides, Doña Isabel never liked me. I was surprised at her changed attitude the last time I went there. Perhaps because I'm your friend and she wants her daughter to marry you...I'm sure I don't know. But you've seen how things are. Doña Isabel was mortified over Rosana's friendship with me."

"Well, you're going to have to forget all that. Go to see her. Did you know that for the last few days she hasn't gone anywhere, and has even been taking her meals in her room?"

Go to see Rosana? No, Alfredo Laza's conscience would not permit him to do that. More than ever, now, he felt that it was best for them to remain apart. Rosana stirred very strange emotions in him. Actually, Doña Isabel's objections to him and his wilful big-brother attitude towards the girl were only part of the truth, mere excuses for his flight from her. There were other reasons which he would not even admit to himself. When he examined his most intimate feelings, he had to admit that he was dominated by the myth of class differences. Rosana had been brought up in the tradition of landowners, her family belonged to a privileged class of rural aristocracy. This led him to imagine that they could not live together harmoniously under the same roof all their lives. He confessed, a little ingenuously, that he had not been able to free himself from his past as a blacksmith's son. He felt no humiliation; rather, he accepted an inevitable fact, which still made a difference. Lorenzi, the son of a landowner, admired his friend's serene frankness.

And there was something else. One day he had been surprised to discover that another reason made him think he could never link his fate with Rosana's. That was what Doña Isabel referred to as her daughter's clairvoyance. And he recalled what Rosana had once said to him: "I'm not interested in you on account of your brilliant future, as they say in the graduation exercises. I like to be with you, as you are, and I am ready to be submerged in the maelstrom of your life."

That day, and later on, Laza had scoffed at her clairvoyance and called her "a Cassandra." She was not offended, but merely smiled enigmatically, as if to say, "Time will tell." And often when they were together he saw that same smile on her face, the smile of a woman who sees into the future. She never said "Marry me," for that would have given him a chance to repeat his veiled excuse, "I don't belong to myself, for I have dedicated myself to a cause, the struggle of my people and all oppressed peoples for freedom. From experience I know I can't make the kind of home for a woman that all women want. Oh yes, it's very easy for sweethearts to say 'I'd live happily with you under a tree.' But after the honeymoon is over, the least shower of rain makes them long for a better shelter. I know myself, and I know I couldn't make any woman happy."

He had said all that to her once, and she had promised herself never again to mention marriage to him. But she was ready to follow him in any fashion, if he wanted her, even though she could not be his wife. All he had to say was

"Come with me," and she would obey, even though it might cause her mother's death. She had made her decision and would abide by it.

Strangely enough, her "clairvoyance" did not enable her to foretell whether or not she would ever live with Alfredo. This uncertainty impelled her to go after any man who caught her fancy momentarily—a confused state of mind that would finally be her ruin. Lacking will-power to resist temptation, she was doomed to alcoholism or another vice. Try as she would, she could find no explanation for her behavior. Surely it would have been more dignified to let herself be consumed by a hopeless love and resign herself to a life of sacrifice behind the walls of a convent, or even merely choose to face the anguished existence of a spinster in her own home? Or why not look for an honorable man and establish a home with him? No, she could neither face entering a convent nor resign herself to a spinster's penitential life; to have done either would have pleased her mother and, though she prayed God to forgive her, she had a deep hostility towards that mother, that woman who had abandoned a religious vocation, while still a novice, to marry a man whom she later repudiated. She had never forgiven Doña Isabel for this or for letting that man, her father, die in a mysterious accident before she was old enough to know him. She was convinced that had her father still been alive, her life would be very different. Rosana had heard from Doña Isabel's relatives that he had been a good man who had given his wife no apparent reason for turning against him. Then, too, in the beginning, Doña Isabel had even looked upon the child as the fruit of sin. Only later, when she had formed the fixed idea that her daughter should become "a servant of God," did her attitude change.

Rosana's suppressed hostility towards her mother had partially deranged her. She said "Yes, Mamma," or "No, Mamma," whichever was called for, and then as a challenge, often did exactly the opposite of what her mother had advised. Perhaps it was because her mother demanded purity that she reacted in the opposite direction. She felt bewildered and lost. Then, to make matters worse, she had given her heart to a man who could not make her happy in the normal and conventional way, through marriage. Very well, she would go to live with him, would follow him wherever he wished. Many times she tried to visualize such a thing, or to think of alternatives. So that he might not have to work for her, she imagined herself merely receiving him in her own apartment. They would take walks together, talk to each other, visit art galleries and museums...But for that kind of life she needed to be a "free woman" without conventional ties, in order not to be affected by what others would think.

But Alfredo insisted on regarding her as a very sheltered and over-nice girl, the product of a private school education, the daughter of Doña Isabel Cortines!

Her present retreat from the world was an effort to overcome her confusion, to examine the past and reflect upon the path Doña Isabel wanted her to follow. It was also perhaps a sincere effort to become again a "decent girl". Yet Doña Isabel's advice, far from soothing her, actually increased her exasperation. She remained silent, but it was a silence of frowning wrath.

Did she regret her past promiscuity because of her love for Alfredo, because she did not want him to have anything to reproach her for later? She did not know. Her clairvoyance was of no help at this point. Merely, she felt that she was testing herself.

Then one late afternoon, at nightfall, shortly after Doña Isabel had left the house for her séance, Laza came to see Rosana. And without any preliminaries he told her why he had come.

"I've discovered that I'm running away from you because I love you," he said. "I came to tell you so."

She reacted as any woman would. Instead of showing enthusiasm, she replied quite conventionally: "You surprise me."

She even considered for a moment getting even with him by telling him she had only been infatuated like any inexperienced young girl, but was over it now. She opened her lips to say this, but instead burst into tears. Disarmed, she poured out her heart in reproaches. But finally her despair was dissolved in eager surrender. Deeply affected, Alfredo listened to her, until she asked a question from the conventional viewpoint of a well-bred young lady.

"Would you marry me? Mamma knows that I love you."

"Can you ask such a thing? I'm afraid you won't be happy with me, but we'll try. If for your love I have to renounce..."

"Don't say that! I don't want you to make promises you cannot keep." She paused, then spoke in a lowered voice, fearful that he would not understand. "From now on you'll be my only love. I understand your ideals and dreams, and I don't want to be a burden to you. All I ask is that we postpone our marriage for a few months...Do you understand?"

He was about to protest, but she closed his mouth with a kiss. His face was wet with her tears.

In the solitude of his room, Porfirio Uribe resolved to make arrangements for his trip to Puerto Rico at once. On the 18th, only four days away, the *San Jacinto* was due to sail.

CHAPTER

VI

Porfirio was fortunate enough to obtain passage for April 18th. Still more fortunately, he was cleared of all guilt in Adrián Martín's death. Everyone now believed that it had been a political assassination and the newspapers were again giving it great attention. Porfirio spoke to no one about his departure, not even to Alfredo. Staying away from the boarding house, he walked aimlessly in the streets of New York, his own loneliness increased by the loneliness of the crowds that surrounded him. Three horrible days were spent like this, still caught in the labyrinth.

Now and then he entered a subway, with no other purpose than to kill time and sit down. Round and round the subway train went beneath the great city. He read newspapers found on the seats. Their big headlines recalled the headline he had seen on his first day in New York: SLAIN! It occurred to him that the same headline might have stood over his name, had the police extracted a false confession from him.

He tried to remain insensible to the city, so that he might not smell its disagreeable odors, not see the robots, not notice so keenly the prevailing indifference. Never before in his life, not even when he had left his godparents' home, had he felt so abandoned, so moved by the impulse to shed tears. Intermittently he almost succeeded in shutting off his senses and passing the shadowy borderline of consciousness. He imagined that he did not exist, because no one remembered him. Several times he seemed to hear an inner voice admonishing him: *Careful! Careful! Who will claim this body if it is found crushed on the street? Who will offer up a prayer? And then, of what avail will those years of seclusion, hard work, and study have been?*

The day before he was to leave New York, he suddenly realized the danger of embarking upon a ship in the midst of a ferocious war. The teletype news bulletins flashed in Times Square told of ships being sunk every day. To die in mid-ocean would be terrible; his heart was gripped with fear. Hundreds of people would go down with him, hundreds of lives would be snuffed out with his. Ingenuously he rebelled at the idea of all those incomplete lives. Incomplete. He had not lived out his life yet, had not achieved his dream. No, he could not die! And with this resolve he drew a breath of hope in the midst of his fear and loneliness.

He had been lost in the labyrinth, but now he glimpsed the way out. And he began to reflect upon the attraction of life in a small town. "As soon as I'm settled in Coamo," he told himself, "I'll be a part of the fabric of its everyday life, I'll be a dignified citizen, I'll go to Mass, I'll find a nice girl and I'll create the home I've never had and always wanted. I refuse to die one day in a cheap hotel bedroom surrounded by a jumble of rags and old shoes. I'll be useful and respected. I'll accept the past and rise above it. The townspeople will come to ask me to represent them in the House. And I'll accept, overjoyed. As the years pass and I grow old I'll spend the time listening to the pendulum of time which marks the hours between baptism and burial with no fear. And a multitude of people will mourn my passing."

Surrounded by the crude reality of the labyrinthian city, he imagined the tranquil life of that little town. Even the hot dry season along the southern coast of the island which had once seemed intolerable now returned to mind clothed in romantic mists; he could hear the sound of the waves breaking on the reefs, of the birds singing in the mangrove trees, could see above the trees flocks of herons flying, and on the sea white sails...*The poincianas and the live-oaks are beginning to bloom now.* He would sit down in a field of fragrant grasses and flowers, would watch the world come alive, follow with his eyes the flight of a bee, locate the nesting place of the wild pigeons, hear their song in the opalescent evening sky. He would wait for nightfall, gazing at the ever-changing shades of sky and earth. In the west it would be violet-colored one evening, another it would be yellow with saffron streaks, or greenish there, over the distant mountains.

He had almost forgotten the reasons that had made him stay in New York so long...

His thoughts turned to Rosana. At first, when she had withdrawn from him, he had believed that it was only a temporary abandonment, and he had thought her devotion to Alfredo completely senseless. But now, events had taken another turn...What would Doña Isabel do when she learned what was happening? Would she shed tears and begin to talk about her illustrious forebears? Would the spirit world console her? Recently she seemed to be trying to explain events in this world with the logic of that intangible world. Recently she had seemed to accept more readily the inevitable.

Twelve hours before the time set for departure, he went down to the docks to see if the *San Jacinto* had berthed. Yes, there she was. Next day she would already have launched out into the solitude of the sea. Porfirio watched the sailors working on deck and became so absorbed that he was a little startled when he felt a hand laid on his shoulder. Not really startled, for intuitively he knew it to be a friendly hand.

He turned round. Juan Lorenzi, visibly affected by this un-expected encounter, was standing there.

"What have you been doing with yourself for the past few days?" he asked.

Porfirio forgot his loneliness.

"Oh, wandering about," he said. "I sail tomorrow."

"I know. I just found out. That's why I'm here, I came here hoping to find you. We were all surprised at your dis-appearing like that without a word." Lorenzi, who could not resist a joke, added with a twinkle, "Believe it or not, I even looked in the papers to see if...?"

Porfirio surprised Lorenzi by laughing.

"I wanted to go off by myself to think about Coamo," he said.

"Do you know that Alfredo has decided to marry Rosana?"

"Yes. And Doña Isabel?"

"She hasn't said a word. We began to look for you be-cause of her. She thinks that in another life you...But why talk about that? Doña Isabel is a little off her head!"

"I understand. The great dream of her life has gone up in smoke."

"Did you know that I wanted to leave on the *San Jacinto,* too? But I hadn't your luck, couldn't book passage. Look at her lying there so peacefully at the dock! Yet tragedy could occur any minute when she enters a sea infested with Ger-man submarines."

"We only live once," said Porfirio, rather shaken. "Our whole life is a risk. Even so, I hope to reach Coamo and put my plans for the future into effect. You mean to say you wanted to sail on the *San Jacinto* because there might be a catastrophe?"

"Yes. But nothing ever happens to me. Do you want me to tell you something? Do you know why I'm in New York? I was approaching the coast in a launch with the lights out, expecting the police might be waiting for us and wanting to be on the safe side before unloading the contraband. Another launch came out from the mangroves and ordered us to halt. I told the two men who were with me to get ready to fire. They turned a searchlight on us, and we exchanged shots. One of my men jumped into the water when he saw that he was wounded, and the other man followed him. I turned the boat towards the open sea and made them follow me through a channel between the reefs—I know those waters well. Next day they found the other launch run aground. She belonged to an enemy of mine who's also a smuggler. He was trying to trap me by making me think the police were after me."

"What happened to your men?"

"It seems the wounded man's blood had attracted the sharks," Lorenzi went on, after a short pause. "He was never found, but we discovered the body of my other man among the mangroves, horribly mutilated. His relatives helped me bury him. I left the boat and the launch with my partners —and came here. The police were unable to clear up the situation and had to accept my explanations, and my rival kept himself hidden. I know he's having me watched, though. But what does it matter? We'll meet, one of these days. For the moment I'm finished with smuggling. From now on I intend to go in for fishing and the mahogany trade with the Republic."

"How can you go on living like that?"

"You mean, smuggling? The history of Puerto Rico is filled with stories of smuggling. Surely you're not so innocent as to believe that governments are just? No, my friend, governments impose themselves by force, by crooked deals. They make laws which benefit themselves, and trample on the individual—on you, on me. Just a moment ago you told me all life is a risk. It certainly is! Does the government protect you, clothe you, feed you, care what happens to you? I refuse to let governments impose their will on me. I'll keep on defying them until the high sea is no longer

96

able to afford me protection. I never feel happier than when I break a chain and slip through their nets."

"I don't believe in courting danger."

"Well, I'd rather meet a violent death than go out in slow agony. I should have been born during the conquest of America. I'd have explored the land for myself, and not for Charles V or Philip II of Spain. And the empire would have been mine!"

"Too bad there's nothing left to discover."

"Nothing left to discover? Who's yet discovered the world we came from and the world where we're going? I challenge the great mystery! And until the last moment of my life I'll refuse to be regimented. Yes, I know, you think I'm decadent. Perhaps I am. It's a feature of my generation. To think I was on the point of letting Rosana's husky voice get the better of me! I was almost ready to marry her. Thank God, my instinct protected me. Anyway, it was humiliating not being able to dominate a woman who was crazy about another man . . ."

Lorenzi's confession astounded Porfirio. Why was he unburdening himself like this? Porfirio suddenly found this man with his contradictory attitudes rather likeable.

"So you were fond of Rosana?"

"As a woman, yes. But as a wife? Could I have been happy with her? You can be happy with any woman when you're not in love with her. But she's got to love you! And she wasn't in love with me. She was trying to forget Alfredo. I pity Alfredo if he falls in love with her! He'll cease to be what he is. And at his age, I doubt that he can turn himself into something else. He'll have to leave Rosana, and then what will happen to her?"

"I was ready to marry her."

"Yes, I know. But you wouldn't have been happy with her. You were too infatuated with her. I'll admit, she's attractive. Those eyes. . .there's something strange in her eyes. They reminded me of the sea on a calm evening under

97

a dark blue sky. They attracted me. The tragedy of the girl
is that she's an incomplete being. She'll always be 'the other
half,' an 'extra rib,' she'll always be a perpetual question
to answer."

"Isn't it possible that the answer to the question is in a
well established family?"

"Perhaps. But my temperament doesn't allow for that.
I prefer to steal love for a day or for several days, as long
as I can keep my foot in the door. It's great to steal a kiss!
And perhaps later on, when I'm old, I won't have the money
even to pay for one."

"Do you call that love? Love isn't just a matter of giving
in to animal instincts."

"You talk like a priest."

"Love is a fuller life."

"Come on, fellow!" laughed Lorenzi. "Are you trying
to tell me—me!—what love is? Teach a fish to swim! Go on!"
He laughed again, then continued in a friendly tone: "You're
the kind of person who needs a quiet and conventional life.
But you also need to have a little more aggressiveness. Instead of running away from your difficulties you should face
them and challenge them. Now we're going to look for
Alfredo and Rosana so you can say goodbye to them. I think
Alfredo is more than a big brother to you. He's been looking for you everywhere. We agreed to meet in his apartment
at eight. Come, let's go. From there we can pick up Rosana
and Doña Isabel too, if she wants to come along with us."

Surprisingly "cured", Porfirio agreed to the idea.

"Let's go," he said. But he lingered for a few minutes to
listen to the melancholy wail of a fog horn, which sounded
like the lament of a wounded prehistoric beast.

That night Doña Isabel had an appointment with spirits
from the other world, so could not join the little farewell
party. They went to a small Spanish restaurant in Greenwich
Village.

Rosana was as if transfigured by her new-found peace, but

98

Laza seemed to be a little restless. Secretly he was worried about whether he could give Rosana the happiness she deserved. With her by his side, he would not be able to go on bemusing himself with dreams of incredible deeds. He realized that his audacity put him outside the pale of conventions, and that the average family is steeped in conventions. Rosana herself had but a confused idea of what constituted happiness for her. She only knew that Alfredo was the one man in the world for her. They had already made their plans: they would establish a commercial art studio, and they would live in a Greenwich Village apartment, which would be small and have a stone fireplace. In the early winter mornings they would look out at the snow on the streets, the sidewalks, the lampposts, and then they would go out for a walk, taking singular pleasure in treading on the virginal whiteness of the snow. But, though Rosana was happy, she was assailed by occasional pangs of uncertainty. Doña Isabel had adopted an attitude of sorrowful acceptance of the inevitable. All the saintly aspirations she had had for her daughter were things of the past. But she was resigned, and now that everything had been settled, she would no longer even oppose Alfredo's political ideas, no matter what happened.

Porfirio behaved admirably, and it was altogether a memorable farewell party. He had no way of knowing that twice in the course of the evening Laza had to fight off the temptation to ask Rosana, "Why don't you marry Porfirio?" But of course that would hurt her, and besides, he loved her. Had he been younger, no doubt it would have been less painful to alter his way of life. But now the roots were deep. . .

Porfirio did not want them to see him off at the dock, preferring to leave without last minute goodbyes. The boat was delayed for a few minutes, the departure being postponed in order to wait for the arrival of some diplomats, according to one of the officers. The diplomats arrived, and turned out to be two young men who had flown in from Washington. They looked tired, their clothes were wrinkled, and they went straight to their cabins.

As soon as the ship cast off, while most of the passengers were at the stern watching the New York skyline, Porfirio went to the bow to contemplate the immense ocean which lay before him. Because of war hazards, the ship would sail without lights.

There was an ominous silence among the passengers, and the crew went about their tasks like shadows. When they talked it was in low voices, and their eyes scanned the sea anxiously. They all seemed to hold their breaths as the *San Jacinto* set its course towards the open sea, outside the harbor. The passengers were informed that the coast would be kept in sight at all times. Lifeboat drills were carried out almost immediately. An attack might occur at any moment, everyone realized, and the slightest roll or jolt was a cause for fear.

During the first night Porfirio hardly slept. Now and then he peered out into the night, but could see nothing but a thick fog. Lying there in his bunk, he tried to review his past life. It was too late now to regret having boarded the *San Jacinto,* but there in the solitude of his cabin (which had fallen to him only because the passenger who had originally been assigned to it had taken fright and cancelled his passage), his forebodings and anguish became more acute.

During the first long and anxious days, Porfirio found himself killing time on deck by looking for the two diplomats, and when he did not see them, he was oddly disappointed. They were young men, and perhaps subconsciously he had hoped to meet them, become friends with them, learn what country they represented and to what country they were going. They remained invisible.

By the third day at sea, the passengers had become slightly more optimistic, the tension sensibly decreased.

Then, just as everyone was feeling most confident, at half past eight o'clock on the third night out, they heard an explosion and felt the ship tremble. Porfirio, who was dozing in his cabin, got to his feet in a daze, then ran towards the deck. The screams and cries of women and children filled the air as the crowd ran in all directions, without knowing what to do. Muffled noises came up from the hold of the vessel, and pieces of broken glass rolled along the deck. The frantic and useless flight of the passengers brought them face to face with the night and the heaving, immense void of the dark sea. Lifeboats were lowered. They would flee from the wounded ship only to confront a worse danger.

Loud-speakers announced that the enemy submarine would give the passengers twenty minutes to abandon ship. As the lifeboats were lowered, many people threw themselves into the water, without waiting. Porfirio waited his turn, and the twenty minutes passed rapidly. The cries grew louder as people looked vainly for a son, a mother, a wife. It was slow agony. Apparently there was no hope of escape. No one could remain on board, and yet the black waves moving over the depths might hold greater danger.

Again the submarine attacked. The vessel shook violently, and Porfirio jumped blindly overboard, falling into one of the lifeboats and on top of a fat man, who yelled at the top of his lungs. The boat was overloaded with women and children and wounded persons, and at every minute was in danger of capsizing.

When the boat had regained its balance, Porfirio tried to find a comfortable position and felt a sharp pain in his right shoulder. An unexpected roll threw him into the bottom of the boat with the seriously wounded, among them a seven-year-old boy with both legs broken. He was calling frantically for his mother, but gradually his voice became weaker.

As the ship sank, the lifeboat rolled dangerously from side to side. The fat man, who was seated in the stern, lost his balance, fell into the water, and disappeared in the darkness. His voice could be heard, shouting for help; then it, too, was swallowed by the dark sea.

The lifeboat drifted under the stars. When they realized that the child with the broken legs was dead, they threw him into the sea. The explosions of the depth charges from the destroyers that were pursuing the submarine could be heard. At dawn, one of the destroyers picked up the survivors to take them to a port in Virginia. They entered the hospital almost blind, and exhausted by their sufferings.

Although his shoulder was seriously dislocated, Porfirio's mind was sufficiently lucid that very day to realize that he was in a long ward with two lines of beds. Many of the survivors of the torpedoed ship were in the same room.

The wounded man in the bed beside his was delirious. He kept mentioning characters from Greek mythology, particularly Orpheus. Two days later the fever dropped and he regained consciousness. Half sitting up in his bed he looked at Uribe.

"Where are we?" he asked.

"Somewhere in Virginia."

"What a hell we went through!"

He was one of the two diplomats for whom the ship had delayed at New York. Apparently he had an enormous wound in his chest, judging by the gauze that covered it.

"Where is Dr. Jaramillo?" he inquired.

"Jaramillo? I don't know who he is."

"He's my companion. My name is Jacinto Brache. He and I are Santiagan diplomats."

While they were talking, a nurse approached them and admonished Brache not to talk but to rest quietly. When she left, Brache, without sitting up or looking directly at Porfirio, asked a question.

"You're Puerto Rican, aren't you?"

"Yes, Puerto Rican. Porfirio Uribe."

"Are you badly hurt?

102

"Very slightly."

"I must have been unconscious in the lifeboat because I don't remember a thing."

Porfirio was wondering how this man had known he was Puerto Rican, when Brache was impelled to explain.

"Dr. Jaramillo and I were the only Santiagans on board. I imagined that all the other passengers must be Puerto Ricans." He gave Porfirio an inquisitive look, and added: "Uribe, I'll never forget that experience." Then, with obvious anxiety: "What could have become of Luis? Luis is Dr. Jaramillo, my brother-in-law. Have you lived in the States long?"

"For twelve years."

"I once studied music in Boston. Violin." He held up his left hand, on which a finger had been amputated. "When I lost this finger, that ended my hopes of becoming a concert artist. I conduct a small orchestra in the capital when I'm at home. Music is my passion."

The information Brache gave was of unusual interest to Porfirio. "One of them is a doctor, the other a musician," he ruminated, and concluded, "It's impossible to think of them killing anyone." To his surprise he realized that when he had first seen them on deck, he had suspected they might be the killers of Adrián Martín. But a doctor couldn't be a murderer, and it was even less conceivable of a musician. And now he felt ashamed of his earlier suspicion, which had made him almost unconsciously watch their cabin and look for them in the dining-room and game-room. Even in the most dangerous moments, when the fear-maddened crowd was milling about the deck, caught between the fearful depths and the dense blackness of the night, he had instinctively searched for them. Even when he was in imminent danger of losing his own life, his chief thought had been that they must not escape him. Apparently his experience in the hallway in New York had been terribly lacerating. Yes, even when he was almost out of his mind with the pain in his

103

shoulder after falling into the lifeboat, he had tried to locate those two men among the other survivors! How was such conduct possible at so desperate a moment?

He was almost tempted to confess all this to Jacinto Brache, but conquered the impulse. His new friend would think ill of him, and that would be another cause for shame. He would not even mention the subject. It could only offend such an agreeable person as this young musician seemed to be. Actually, Porfirio was hungry for friendship. Suddenly he remembered that his mother had been a Santiagan, and mentioned this to Brache, with timid satisfaction. Brache seemed pleased to hear it. Their friendship was soon firmly established, and from that moment on they conversed frequently. Brache talked mainly about classical music, but he listened with interest to what Porfirio had to say about popular music.

The young diplomat laughed gaily when Porfirio told him about the baritone horn, how he had inherited it, and how it not only stayed with him always in his room in New York but had been a part of his baggage for the return to Puerto Rico. Alas, it had been left in the cabin when the ship was torpedoed.

"Poor *bombardino!*" exclaimed Porfirio with wry humor. "It's full of water now, at the bottom of the sea, the soap plugs have melted by this time. Perhaps it's better so. I don't know why I went around with that horn, as if it was a part of me. High time I abandoned it!" *¡Adiós, bombardino! Hasta siempre, Estefano. Farewell forever.* But parting with it gave him a sense of relief, as though he had been born again. He had not fully realized until he mentioned it to Jacinto Brache that the baritone horn had drowned in the dark depths of the sea.

"Yes, I could have been a good concert violinist," Brache was saying. "But at least I can still conduct my orchestra, the "Orpheus." As he looked again at the stump of his finger, his face clouded over.

104

Two days after Porfirio had made the acquaintance of Jacinto Brache, they learned what had happened to Luis Jaramillo. He had been taken to a private room, due to the seriousness of his condition. He had been unconscious for more than three days, but was now asking about his brother-in-law. The doctors, though they believed he was out of danger, felt it better for him to wait until he was stronger to see Brache. He had had a severe hemorrhage, they learned from the doctor who attended him and who was interested to hear from Brache that Jaramillo was also a physician.

From then on, Jaramillo frequently asked to see Brache in his room, and Brache became his interpreter in the conversations with doctor and nurse.

Finally, one afternoon, Brache told Porfirio that the doctors would now allow others to see Jaramillo, and they went together to the private room. They found the wounded man lying on his back, with eyes closed. He appeared to be asleep, but Porfirio felt that he was pretending, although Brache had to call him several times before he would open his eyes. Just then the nurse came in, and Jaramillo looked at her like a love-smitten Don Juan. She smiled with the satisfaction of a woman who knows she has attracted the admiring gaze and flattering smiles of a handsome man, and as she touched his forehead, her blushes seemed to indicate that she knew he would have grasped her hand if they had been alone. Jaramillo's voice broke slightly when he explained to her that he was still not feeling well.

"These Latins!" murmured the nurse.

She was not pretty, but was wholesome and pleasant, exactly what was needed to cure a Latin-American Don Juan's loneliness. Either Brache did not see the exchange of glances and smiles, or he pretended not to notice, being perhaps used to this sort of thing.

In speaking to his new acquaintance, Porfirio Uribe, Dr. Jaramillo assumed the attitude of a person who, because of his health, does not feel strong enough to be cordial. With the nurse, it was different. But perhaps he was forcing himself to maintain the tradition of Latin-American courtesy for her.

"So you're the Puerto Rican?" remarked the patient, in a low voice, as if trying to conserve his energy.

Porfirio nodded in affirmation, truly astonished that they referred to him as *the* Puerto Rican, and named himself: "Porfirio Uribe."

"Luis Jaramillo," the other said, completing the introduction. "My brother-in-law talked to me about you. Did he tell you I'm a Puerto Rican by birth?"

"No, I didn't know that."

Jaramillo resumed his attitude of a man who closes his eyes in order to give his enormous personality some rest. Brache and Uribe remained silent. The ticking of the small bedside clock sounded louder. If a stranger had entered the room, he would have concluded that the patient was in critical condition and that Brache and Uribe were waiting for the end.

Brache finally became convinced that Jaramillo really needed to rest, and motioned for Uribe to leave with him.

"So, Dr. Jaramillo is Puerto Rican...? Porfirio inquired when they were outside the room.

"Well, yes, he was born in Puerto Rico. Nothing strange in that. Didn't you say your mother was Santiagan?"

"No, it doesn't seem strange to me. It's just that..."

"Luis Jaramillo comes from a very distinguished family in the history of the Republic," interrupted Brache. "In his family there have been a president, two ambassadors, several ministers...His father was a minister in the government of General Beniquez. With the fall of that government, he went into exile in Puerto Rico where, being a widower without children, he married the woman who became Luis's mother. They returned to the Republic when Luis was a little over two years old. He and the man with whom he works in the Republic, Don Joaquín Valverde, are descendents of our founding fathers."

He paused, clenched his teeth, then spoke in a different tone of voice. "Don Joaquín Valverde happens to be the father of my fiancée, Hortensia." He forced a laugh. I'm not the son of a founding father, even though my sister is married to Luis Jaramillo and I'm betrothed to Hortensia Valverde—without Don Joaquín's approval." He turned to look smilingly at Porfirio. "I imagine you're saying to yourself, 'What's this to me?' Well, it's been so long since I talked to anyone about these things. You see, we've been traveling for quite a while. The Leader entrusted to us an inspection tour of our embassies and consulates in Mexico, Central America, and the United States. And Luis is reserved, he doesn't talk to me about such matters."

Brache remained pensive for a moment, then, restored to good humor, apparently, exclaimed: "Eurydice! Eurydice!"

"That's what you often said when you were delirious," said Porfirio, somewhat astounded.

"I call Hortensia by this name, 'Eurydice.' She likes it, and calls me 'Orpheus.' That happens to be the name of my orchestra. I've always liked the stories from Greek mythology."

"I do too. They have a great deal of wisdom in them."

On their next visit to Jaramillo's room, the patient repeated to Porfirio what Brache had already told him as to his Puerto Rican origin, and Porfirio acted as though he were hearing it for the first time.

"I wanted to live in a free country, apparently even when I was a baby!" Jaramillo said, jestingly. "And so I returned to the Republic. But I still have a regard for Puerto Rico on account of my mother."

"And for my mother's sake," said Porfirio, "I'm bound to love the Republic."

They all laughed, and Porfirio was glad to see that he had broken down Jaramillo's reserve. He began to feel that he had two good friends in these men. And indeed, from then on, they talked together like three old comrades.

Porfirio noticed that Jaramillo seized every opportunity to praise Leader Augusto as a man of many merits. He also noticed that Brache merely agreed on this subject, but without saying anything laudatory himself.

Jaramillo knew how to make the nurse give him splendid service. He staged a veritable comedy, meticulously smoothing his moustache, pretending to be asleep so that she would have to wake him up, complaining of a pain here, a pain there, so that she would touch him and he would have the opportunity to hold her hand. Or he would drape the sheet over his shoulder in the manner of a Roman Proconsul, or he would pretend to be jealous...It went on and on, unending. She was obviously impressed; perhaps she had never seen anything like this before. In this way he got what he wanted.

"She is like a young mare," he said to Porfirio one day, after she had left. "Just notice what clumsy movements she has."

"Then why are you upsetting her?" asked Porfirio, unable to keep back a laugh.

Jaramillo replied with another question: "And what don't we do to get what we want? I don't like to ask for anything directly. This is the way I like to get things I want."

Brache merely looked on with a smile. He only spoke when he was asked a question, and then he always tried to give his friend the desired answer.

"Jacinto, here, understands," Jaramillo explained. "No one could have a better brother-in-law."

In order to impress the nurse, Jaramillo occasionally lamented the loss of his diplomatic papers more than was really necessary. On these occasions she looked at him as though he were a little god. She had probably read many novels about young diplomats who go to foreign lands in order to charm romantic girls.

Apparently Jacinto Brache took Luis Jaramillo very seriously, because he never joked with him directly, in spite of their close friendship. He only exceeded the limits a little when they gave each other names from Greek mythology. Anyone who knew more about politics than Porfirio did would have noticed that the mythical deeds the two men attributed to each other were merely a way of disguising reality. It was a delightful game, and clearly both of them, especially Brache, were easing their consciences.

"My brother-in-law, Orpheus Brache," said Luis, with a malicious wink, "never thinks about anything but going down into hell to rescue his Eurydice. He's counting on his magic music to hypnotize the infernal deities."

"And my brother-in-law, Bellerophon Jaramillo, only dreams of conquering the Amazons and the Chimera," said Jacinto. Then his thoughts ran away with him as he added, "He's a horseman on a spirited charger who will reach the doors of Olympus. May the gods not bar his entrance!"

Jaramillo gave a nervous laugh and commented, "The gods protect me."

Visibly upset at what they might be revealing, Jacinto tried to cover up his error and shift attention from himself to Porfirio, since it was too late to turn back.

"I say, Uribe," he said in the same joking tone, "Do you want to be a member of this mythological fraternity? Whom do you choose to be?"

Porfirio could not bring himself to admit that his favorite myth was that of Theseus. How was he going to identify himself with the renowned hero of the labyrinth of Crete, when he looked more like an antihero than a hero?

"We're acting like children," he murmured.

Suddenly, trying to make his concern seem natural, Luis said: "Not to change the subject, Uribe, do you realize that you'd have a great future in the Republic? We need lawyers there who are well acquainted with United States law. What phase of the law attracts you most?"

"Commercial law."

"Magnificent! We need people with your training. Would you like to work in the Republic?"

"I've already made plans for my future."

"I know, you're going to open a law office in your home town and go into politics. I know the situation in Puerto Rico, so I can tell you, there are few opportunities there."

It was true. Porfirio had thought about it more than once.

"Your people are going to emigrate *en masse*," Jaramillo added. "Our country is much less densely populated, and we have more land and more natural resources."

True again. And Porfirio, who had intended to say that he did not want to go to Santiago, found himself replying instead: "I'd like to try my luck in any foreign country."

"Make up your mind," advised Brache, "and as soon as we get out of here we can arrange your papers for you in Washington."

Who would have thought that Porfirio Uribe would have seriously considered such a proposal? He was as if taken by surprise. However, when he thought the matter over, he decided that it wouldn't be a bad idea to try his luck in a country with many more opportunities than Puerto Rico.

Part II

THE MONSTER

CHAPTER

VII

From then on, they frequently talked to Porfirio about the great achievements of Leader Augusto in Santiago.

"He took a backward country," said Luis Jaramillo, "infested with bandits, and transformed it into a prosperous, industrious country, without a single external debt."

"It was like magic," added Jacinto Brache. "What my brother-in-law says is true. The only debt the nation has is to Leader Augusto. The Republic of Santiago never had so many hospitals, so many..."

"That's right. His public works are marvelous."

"Win the Leader's friendship," advised Brache. He's a grateful person and he helps his friends. More than one Puerto Rican has become a general or a minister."

"And you don't think it will be difficult for me to enter the Republic?"

"Here in the United States the ambassador will help me," promised Jaramillo. "In the Republic we'll put your case in the Leader's hands. You'll see. The development of the country requires skilled people. You come along at the right time: a lawyer who has specialized in commercial law, who was educated in the United States, who had a Santiagan mother..."

Porfirio was pleased. He almost considered the disaster of the *San Jacinto* as an act of Providence. It looked as though he would end up by becoming a permanent part of life in the Republic. He would be able to go farther than in Puerto Rico. "What the devil!" he said to himself. "I'm alone in the world, without parents or brothers and sisters or a family of my own. I don't know why my relatives are in Mexico and the Republic. My mother had a brother in the Republic, a Florito Moya, who almost became a general once."

He dared not mention this uncle to his friends. In spite of Brache's and Jaramillo's open faces, in spite of their eagerness to obtain his services for their country, there was always an indefinable zone of mysterious secrets between them. Without doubt he trusted Jacinto Brache more, although during the past few days Luis Jaramillo had been very courteous and friendly. He understood that Jaramillo liked small flatteries, and so he prepared to flatter him. It was now a necessity for Porfirio to procure some degree of conventional security, whether it be in Coamo or the Republic. He must somehow accomplish the miracle. His urge to satisfy his daily needs led him to accept security wherever he found it.

As soon as he was able to have confidence in his friends, he felt that a road had opened for him. He remembered that Juan Lorenzi frequently visited the Republic. Juan would keep him informed of what was happening in Puerto Rico, and if for any reason he had to leave the Republic, Juan would certainly be able to help him. He decided to write to him as soon as he arrived in the Republic. It wouldn't be a bad idea to let his Puerto Rican friends know about it also. Had they heard about the sinking of the *San Jacinto*? Probably not, because of the wartime censorship.

He started a letter to Laza, then thought better of it. As long as he was still in Virginia, he did not want Alfredo to deplore his having accepted the two young diplomats' invitation. "Am I forgetting the case of Adrián Martín?" he asked himself. But...who was Adrián Martín? Surely he must have committed a serious crime to have had to flee his country. Perhaps he was a "desperado". On the other hand, how friendly and sensible and distinguished were Jaramillo and Brache! Above all, what fine connections they had in the Republic! How spontaneously they said, "Come to the embassy and we'll arrange everything!" No, he would not write to anyone before leaving Virginia; once he was in the Republic, then he would write. It would be a bad idea to stir up Laza's prejudices. To do so would be to fling himself into the whirlpool of political plots. All he wanted was to get some good out of those years of study. He would sell his professional services without sticking his nose into things that were no concern of his. According to Jaramillo and Brache, Leader Augusto had brought peace and tranquillity to the country. It was only natural that agitators in the Republic should be persecuted. The agitator is persecuted everywhere. Why should the Republic be the agitator's paradise?

He was not exactly sure why he had accepted without the least hesitation the invitation to work in the Republic. Perhaps he had secretly believed that Coamo was not far enough in the past for people to have forgotten that Porfirio Uribe was the son of poor circus acrobats. More important still, only twelve years had passed since Estefano's baritone horn had been silenced and Catalina had fallen bleeding in the street. Only twelve years! The memory would be even more vivid in such a small town because of the disappearance immediately afterwards of the acrobat's son. During his childhood and adolescence people had always stared at him. As though it weren't enough to be the adopted child of a clairvoyant woman and a jealous baker-musician, he had left the town almost before the rosary had been recited over the body of the dead woman. Actually no one had known when he left the town or where he had gone. His return

115

as a lawyer would cause a commotion. Nevertheless, what pleasure it would be to shove his law diploma into the faces of those curious people!

Yes, he would postpone his return to Coamo. The opportunity to try his luck in the Republic was too good to be wasted. No one was waiting for him in Puerto Rico, he had no home, no parents or friends...His mole-like existence in New York had been a living death. He had willed it. And now he willed his resurrection. Since no one was waiting for him and no one worrying about him, then it was almost as though he existed only for himself and things. His great ambition was to conquer the tyranny of his daily necessities, to cease being the victim of his daily needs! And he wanted to put all those years of loneliness and privation behind him, wanted to forget those dead letters, official orders, tedious books and papers, the smell of cheap food cooking in boarding houses, the people who doubted his honesty merely because he was a Puerto Rican. And he wanted friendship. He believed he had found it in Jaramillo and Brache, in the latter, particularly. All this inclined him to accept their invitation to the Republic. A man has to take some risks, even when he's looking for security.

As for his lingering doubts of Jaramillo's sincerity, Brache had put an end to them, surely, when he said, "Luis is more than a brother to me," and had gone on to tell how Luis Jaramillo had given him medical care so successfully and devotedly. "After I lost my finger," said Brache, "I was in great pain and suffered strange delusions. He cured me with a prescription of his. He's also the favorite doctor of the Leader's father, who was suffering from a malignant tumor. Since Luis was able to end his pain, he can get whatever he likes out of him."

And so he made up his mind. When released from the hospital, he remained in the town to wait for his friends, whom he visited every day.

One afternoon, when paying them a visit at the hospital,

116

he accidentaly heard Brache and Jaramillo discussing an article they had read in a local newspaper about the murder of a noted Santiagan journalist, Adrián Martín. Porfirio was scared. But they seemed to consider the affair unimportant.

"The most astonishing part of the case," exclaimed Jaramillo, "is that they're blaming the government of my country for his death. The general's political enemies take advantage of everything. In the consulate they showed me the payroll which proves that Adrián Martín was working for the General. Why, then, would he have him killed? The Leader's enemy wasn't Adrián Martín. His enemies were those who killed the journalist with the sinister aim of creating international complications."

Now, more than on any other occasion, Porfirio proved that he knew when to be silent. Fortunately his name was not mentioned in the newspaper reports of the investigation of Adrián Martín's murder. They had cleared him before the newspapers found out about it. He therefore accepted Jaramillo's explanation. What would Alfredo Laza have said to that? His inner voice gave him the answer. *Alfredo would say that the payroll in the consulate was faked. He would say that Adrián Martín had not worked for the Leader.* "But Alfredo is blinded by political passion," Porfirio told himself.

Jaramillo was stressing his point.

"Judge by my own case," he said. "My father was a minister in the government headed by one of the Leader's bitterest enemies. Do you think that he treats me like an enemy, when he gives me the opportunity to represent him abroad? My family was ruined in bad business deals, not by any political opposition. Then, take the case of Don Joaquín Valverde. Some of Valverde's relatives are still fighting against the Leader, within the Republic. Has the Leader taken any action against Don Joaquín, who happens also to be his friend and godfather?"

These proofs more than satisfied Porfirio Uribe.

When the plane took off for the Republic, Porfirio noticed that Jaramillo became even more authoritarian while Brache withdrew into a painful silence, merely agreeing with everything his companion said. The two hardly spoke to each other. Naturally, Jacinto Brache was only the official aide of Dr. Luis Jaramillo, who was inspector of consulates and special envoy of Leader Augusto. But when they were over the Republic, Jacinto, who was sitting next to Porfirio, did say an odd thing. "How pretty it is from here!" he exclaimed, adding, with a laugh, "It makes one want to stay up here! I'm something of a poet, and I do admire my country's scenery."

Certain details had impressed Porfirio. The government of the Republic had chartered a plane merely to take its diplomats home. In the embassy they had treated Jaramillo with great respect, and they had cleared Porfirio's papers without difficulty. The pilot treated Jaramillo with the respect reserved for important personages...Porfirio could not help but feel an almost superstitious regard for Jaramillo. Watching him, as they approached the capital, he noticed that the young diplomat's pale, angular face became tense. Indeed, the change had begun to be apparent as soon as Jaramillo was released from the hospital. Porfirio recalled how rude he had been to the nurse. "What good is she to me now?" he had said. She had watched him go with her eyes full of tears. He had not mentioned her again. In Washington he had maintained a strictly official attittude, either saying nothing at all or responding in monosyllables. The cordial friend had become the arrogant official.

And now in the sky over his country, Jaramillo's tension visibly increased. As for Brache, as the plane prepared to land, a look of suffering appeared on his face. Even so, he was still able to crack a joke.

"Orpheus still hasn't descended into hell," he murmured to Porfirio. "No doubt Luis is thinking, 'I'm approaching the Olympus of the gods.' Do you see his face? It's the face

118

of a conqueror."

Porfirio's heart gave a sudden throb. He felt faint, and asked himself, "Am I entering the depths of the labyrinth?"

"Now you'll see," Brache exclaimed, "you'll see the marvelous works of the Leader, that never-setting sun, that glorious dawn, that greatest hero of all time. . . ."

Jaramillo turned around, wrathfully, but Jacinto had spoken with absolute seriousness.

However, the tension between the two men was frightening. Porfirio had an almost irresistible impulse to succumb to nervous laughter. "What have I got myself into?" he wondered.

The afternoon was beautiful, sky and sea were a deep blue and the landscape was luxuriously green. It was unthinkable that a monster was running loose in this paradise. . .

Porfirio went to live in the boarding house were Jacinto roomed, an old mansion that was the property of one of the first families of the country, whose last survivors, two pale spinsters perpetually dressed in black, had filled the house with solemn portraits, the most prominent being that of Leader Augusto. Even though the two ladies benefited by a generous pension, they took in boarders, in order, no doubt, not to be alone. The family would disappear with them, and they were already descending the far slope of their lives. . . The house reeked with incense. Garbed in mourning, the owners rarely spoke, and when they did it was in barely audible whispers.

That same night Porfirio accompanied Jacinto Brache to the home of his sister Paulina, Dr. Jaramillo's wife. There he met Lieutenant Sebastián Brache, Jacinto's brother and a member of the Leader's personal guard, a man of few words. But even Sebastián repeated the words on everyone's lips: "You'll see, the Leader is forging a new fatherland. The country isn't in the chaotic state it was before, when it

119

was notorious for its lawlessness, as you must have heard in Puerto Rico."

Very soon Jaramillo arrived, and when Paulina spoke to him, her faltering words, spoken in a crystalline voice, sounded like the tinkling of glasses in clumsy and shaking hands. Following this, there were a few instants of cold silence, which Porfirio tried to dissipate by contemplating the prominently displayed portrait of the Leader, a sign of distinction in that home. He noticed that Jaramillo, Brache, and Paulina all had their eyes fixed on the same portrait. But Paulina, obviously disturbed, lowered her eyes and reached for Jaramillo's inert arm; she looked as though she were making an effort to keep back her tears.

"How did you feel today?" her husband asked, almost courteously.

"Better."

"Don't wait until the last minute to go to the hospital."

"I prefer, I beg of you, for you to attend me right here, in this house."

"She insists on having the baby here," explained Luis.

"She would be better off in a hospital," Jacinto added.

Porfirio was rather embarrassed at overhearing this matter discussed. He noticed strange inflections in the tone of their voices, and above all, in Paulina's frightened voice.

In spite of her somewhat pale and emaciated face, the young woman was beautiful. Jacinto had already told Porfirio that she had been the queen of one of the carnivals.

"Were you ill while we were away?" asked Jacinto.

"A little."

"You're not the first woman nor the last to have a child," interrupted Jaramillo, slightly irritated.

"How was the trip?" she asked, trying to change the conversation.

"Good," said Jacinto.

"It must be nice to travel in other countries, see other lands."

120

"Luis has probably told you about the *San Jacinto* incident?"

They talked about the torpedoing for a few minutes. And Porfirio had the impression that the four people gathered there were drifting over echoing depths. Paulina left the room presently to supervise the preparation of the supper, and Luis Jaramillo once more assumed the attitude of a man weighed down with responsibilities. Porfirio prepared to take his leave, but Luis, suddenly very attentive, begged him not to go, saying, "I want to talk to you."

What Dr. Jaramillo had to say was that he had spoken with Don Ursulino, the Leader's father, about Porfirio, who was promised a job by the following week. The speed with which Jaramillo was coming to his aid deeply affected Porfirio, and he very sincerely expressed his gratitude. Jaramillo was so pleased with this response that he embraced Porfirio as they parted: their friendship was sealed.

Walking back to the boarding house with Brache, Porfirio noticed something very peculiar in his behavior: whenever he made a remark bearing on politics, he spoke in a very low voice if no one were nearby to overhear, but if they had to pass close to a wall he raised his voice and changed the conversation, exalting the country's progress. A strange silence, a dark fear, seemed to hover round those walls. He also noticed that Brache greeted some people with exaggerated effusiveness while he merely nodded curtly to others or pretended not to see them at all.

The situation was a prolongation of the zone of mystery, reticence, and reserve which Porfirio had noticed in the relations between himself and his two friends ever since they had boarded the airplane. Perhaps his eight years of seclusion and withdrawal from the world had made him more sensitive to such things, he told himself, as he made an effort to overcome the feeling. But whenever he opened his mouth to say something, he shut it again without speaking, for fear of expressing something imprudent. And his own

121

silence thickened still more that already opaque fog covering the mystery.

He was made acutely uncomfortable by the inevitable lack of communications which was growing up around him, and he would have returned to Puerto Rico, except that he felt his experiences here were still insufficient to warrant his judging the situation fairly. Perhaps he was misinterpreting the things he saw. And to the nagging question, "Have I entered the worst labyrinth of all?" he countered, "Do I have the right to prejudge?" He had always detested the much-touted intuitions, those superstitious attitudes which allow nothing to be settled or attended to rationally. Besides, was he not perhaps influenced, deep down, by the constant carping of his friend Alfredo Laza against the Leader? On the other hand, this attitude of reserve and irritability that he had noticed in the Santiagans, in Jacinto, Paulina, even in Adrián Martín, in the people he saw on the street, in the two spinsters at his boarding house—might it not merely be an innate national characteristic? Why should he expect Santiagans to behave like Puerto Ricans?

And besides, the Jaramillos and the Braches were one single family, really; perhaps they had intimate problems about which he knew nothing. All families have their private affairs which only reach the public through peculiar attitudes adopted. After all, why should he, Porfirio Uribe, be so sensitive to these situations? He could not recall the faces of his own parents; he had been brought up by his godparents Estefano and Catalina; his life in New York had been divided into two completely different periods, one of scandal, the other of withdrawal and study. Hadn't he felt as though a whole life had been sunk when the *bombardino* was engulfed by the sea? He had even imagined that as the ship began to sink, the abandoned instrument had begged to be rescued in its deep, broken voice. During the first night spent in the Virginia hospital, the sunken baritone horn had played the main role in his nightmares. When we are isolated for years on end, we become more conscious of the objects which accompany us. He had let the sorrowful old soul of the poor *bombardino* influence him! In short, he of all people should be the last to identify an individual's conduct with a possible political situation. He decided to wait, to reserve his opinions, to listen merely and, at times, perhaps, not even to listen.

But now, as they reached the center of an almost deserted plaza, Brache stood still to say something. "Don't doubt my good intentions, Uribe!" he exclaimed. "Ever since we were neighbors in hospital beds, I've valued your friendship." He smiled a deeply melancholy smile. "From the very beginning, I let you into a secret of mine: Eurydice." He glanced discreetly behind him, then said, "If someone comes up behind me, warn me."

Porfirio nodded assent, again uncomfortable.

"You must also not doubt my affection for Luis," Brache continued, "not only because he's my sister's husband, but also because he was more than a doctor to me when I had my accident, and it was he who made the Orpheus orchestra possible. I will always unreservedly serve him, just as I suffer certain family matters with him..." He was speaking with such intensity that his voice broke. Again he looked discreetly around him before saying anything more. "Luis has trouble with his superior, Don Joaquín Valverde, even though it seems that Luis is favored by the Leader. After all, Luis serves the Leader unconditionally and in addition he has gained the respect of Don Ursulino. You should be grateful that he took the trouble to get work for you so soon..."

He was evidently finding it more and more difficult to express what he wanted to say.

"Luis is ambitious," he went on finally. "But that's not a defect. He's young, has a future. Even the Leader respects the old line of the Jaramillos. But Luis wants to rise too quickly, and you're not too well informed about our national life..."

Brache walked on a few steps, and Porfirio followed. They stopped again in front of an enormous portrait of the Leader which loomed suddenly from behind the trees. It bore these words: CREATOR OF THE NEW ORDER. Brache again spoke, this time almost in a whisper.

"Luis is looking frantically for proselytes who will help him reach the position he desires. Of course he's intelligent and clever, but I'm telling you again, you're new here. I noticed his affectionate goodbye to you just now; it's clear he's counting on you. Go slowly, and don't feel that you're completely obligated. Do you understand? Go slowly. Be grateful for Luis's help, but don't hand yourself over to him. Between us, Luis is jealous of Valverde. But Don Joaquín is not beaten yet. He's the Leader's friend and godfather. The best thing for you to do would be to make friends gradually with all of these people. By dropping hints I'll try to make Luis see that you're a foreigner here and..."

A couple of soldiers were approaching. Jacinto Brache interrupted what he was saying and began to talk enthusiastically about the "new order". The soldiers saluted him with the respect due to an influential person.

That night they did not discuss the matter further, but—why not admit it to himself?—Porfirio began to fear Jacinto's company. What if all his talk was merely a way of feeling him out? Just in case, he would be careful to say nothing. Nevertheless, there was nothing wrong in his advice. He, Porfirio, would try not to feel "completely obligated" to anyone, no, not to anyone! And when he began work, he would quietly try to change to another boarding house. For the moment he would study the country's history and laws; above all, he would study the Leader's biographies. His decision to study made a good impression on Jacinto Brache and all those who were beginning to know him. Studying also gave him an excellent excuse not to make awkward visits.

Even so, he wished Jacinto would invite him to Don

124

Joaquín's house. He refrained from mentioning it, for he wanted to train himself to be cautious. But he did not have long to wait for the invitation to the Valverdes'. It came three days after his arrival in the Republic.

Don Joaquín was alone in his study to receive them. He remained seated behind his desk, not getting up as Jacinto introduced him to Porfirio, because he had only one leg. His crutches were resting against the desk beside him. On the wall in front of him was the inevitable portrait of the Leader.

"Uribe," he said, "you've been recommended for a job in the legal section of the Police Department. Jaramillo spoke to Don Ursulino about you and he wants to meet you. Don Ursulino was a friend of Juanita Moya's father and he still remembers how the old man grieved when she fell in love with the Mexican acrobat."

"When do you think it would be convenient to...?"

"Jaramillo can accompany you. I ought to tell you that I resigned today as head of the legal section of the Police Department. I've just been honored with another appointment as a representative in congress. I serve the Leader wherever he wishes me to serve." He looked gravely at the portrait facing him, then said, "Come, meet my family."

Jacinto had meanwhile remained merely an interested bystander. But Porfirio had observed the quick glances the old gentleman shot at that quiet bystander: indeed, they were more than quick, they were fleeting. The younger man waited respectfully for the other to speak.

In the living room Don Joaquín called out to his wife.

"Rosa! Rosa!"

Doña Rosa came in and greeted Jacinto Brache quite cordially. They all sat down. The talk became trivial. Porfirio was asked the inevitable questions: "How do you like our country? How long do you expect to be with us?" He restricted himself to simple answers or pretended to be unsure. The conversation lagged. He saw that Doña Rosa was directing anxious glances at Jacinto, but without daring to

125

ask him anything.

"We have two children, the Niño..." she said finally, breaking off when Don Joaquín reproached her with a look and a gesture. "...who is away on a trip," she went on, "and Hortensia, who is studying in the university."

Tears had filled her eyes. She stood up, blinking away the tears, and went to the door at the far end of the room where she called out to her daughter.

"Hortensia! Come here, child!"

The girl, who was quite attractive, came without delay. She greeted Porfirio graciously and maintained a modest, dignified attitude towards Jacinto, her fiancée. She tried to be natural, but she had an air of stifled rebellion whenever she said anything, and before speaking she always consulted her father with a look. She kept up a dialogue of smiles with Jacinto, which illuminated her golden face and brought gleams of happiness to her large greenish-grey eyes.

Don Joaquín tried to ignore Jacinto as he talked, as though his words were passing over the young man's head towards where Uribe and Doña Rosa were sitting. It was an uncomfortable situation. Jacinto assumed an attitude of silent defiance to begin with, but finally moved over to sit beside Hortensia, who was slightly outside the group, to the left of Don Joaquín. There the two talked in low voices for a while before joining in the general conversation. The brief silences became longer, and it was obvious that only courtesy kept a slight and inexpressive smile on Don Joaquín's lips. But the old gentleman was very cordial with Porfirio, whom he invited to call whenever he liked.

When they were in the street again, Jacinto made some explanatory remarks.

"It seems the Leader is put out with his friend and god-father Don Joaquín Valverde. Some months ago he was a justice in the supreme court. When we left to visit the consulates he was head of the Police Department's legal section, and today he's only a congressman. This constant shifting is not normal."

Porfirio would have liked to ask some questions, but refrained. He would have liked to know what had really happened to Niño Valverde and why even his own parents avoided discussing the matter. He was secretly glad to hear Jacinto's spontaneous explanation.

"Niño Valverde was a newspaperman who gave signs of wanting to challenge the Leader's authority. . . ."

The story was this: the police came to call him to account, but he had vanished, had managed to flee the country. No one knew where he was.

"Don Joaquín is a fox," Jacinto added. "But these shifts could eventually land him in jail."

"He seemed like a good sort to me."

"How good can you be! He doesn't even eat meat, because he says eating meat turns us into brute beasts. But the brave bulls are also vegetarians! They say he even tried to persuade the Leader not to eat meat."

"Was he successful?"

"No. The Leader likes to eat meat. Doves are his favorite dish. A refined taste, isn't it? Perhaps he thinks that he may thus acquire the innocence of a dove."

This was too much! Porfirio began to suspect that Jacinto was hopelessly unbalanced mentally, to talk like this in the street. Jacinto laughed at his own joke, while Porfirio remained ominously silent.

"The falcon feeds on the flesh of doves," Jacinto went on.

Porfirio said to himself: "If he's waiting for me to say something, he's out of luck." And again he resolved to move to another boarding house. Without realizing why, he began to whistle a Puerto Rican tune.

"Are you one of those who whistle at night along the road?" Brache commented. "You do well not to say anything," he continued, recovering his judgment. "I won't talk to you any more about these things. It's just that every time I think about my amputated finger, I go a little crazy." And

127

again, in a nostalgic tone: "I could have been a famous violinist. A musician harms no one. My life has been ruined."

A few days afterwards, Luis Jaramillo came to the boarding house to see them, arriving in high good humor.

"I bring great news," he announced. "I invite you to come with me to Don Joaquín's house."

Jacinto, who knew his brother-in-law well, prepared to obey, saying merely, "I'll be ready at once."

As for Porfirio, he stifled his curiosity. He had begun to regard Jaramillo as a superior; with good reason, now that he was Jaramillo's subordinate in the Police Department.

"What I don't get...," Luis began, in a blustering voice, then checking himself immediately, he talked about other things, about trifles, perhaps merely to exasperate his friends. He seemed to enjoy provoking curiosity.

As a matter of fact, Jaramillo had an announcement to make to Don Joaquín Valverde which took the old gentleman by surprise.

"Don Joaquín," he said, "the Leader has given me the privilege of notifying you that you have been appointed Rector of the University. Where is Doña Rosa?"

Not knowing whether to be happy or sad, Valverde forced himself to appear overjoyed, and summoned his wife and daughter.

"Rosa! Rosa! Hortensia! Come here!"

They were pale when they came in. Jaramillo, bursting with self-satisfaction, proclaimed the news.

"I bear a special message from the Leader! I congratulate Don Joaquín! They have named him Rector of the University."

"It's the fourth position he's held in the last few months," Hortensia could not refrain from saying. The reproachful look which Don Joaquín directed at her made her add: "My father should feel very pleased at such a sign of generous confidence shown him by my godfather."

"Exactly," replied Jaramillo. "And there are those who say that women can't express themselves well! In Don Joaquín's case, it's a reward for his diligence and unfailing loyalty. It's just as I've always said: the Leader is wise and just, even when he punishes." He thrust out his chin and gave them a quizzical look. "You'll feel at home in the University, with your father as Rector," he said to Hortensia, who seemed to be very nervous. And he laid a soothing hand on her shoulder, as though he were addressing a younger sister.

Turning to the others, he took an exaggeratedly deep breath, and added: "And you don't know the other piece of news!"

He lowered his head, pretending to be afraid they would think him boastful, and, in a hushed voice, as if pronouncing something sinful, he said, "The Leader has named me assistant to the Rector, Don Joaquín."

For a minute, no one said a word. Then, a little tardily, there were the usual embraces and handshakes. Hortensia was obviously nervous and was actually not in command of herself as she said, "They've told me that the Niño is in the United States. Did either of you see him while you were there? I heard this only today."

There followed one of those paralyzing silences. Doña Rosa retreated to her room, taking Hortensia with her, and Don Joaquín, who accepted the inevitable, repeated her question.

"Did you see him?"

"We could not see a person who had offended the Leader!" Jaramillo replied very stiffly.

"But the Niño is a friend of both of you!" Don Joaquín exclaimed, unable to contain himself.

"Loyalty to the Leader is very much above personal friendship! You know that."

"And so it should be," admitted Don Joaquín, swallowing his pride and conquering his paternal love.

129

When his visitors had left, Don Joaquín had a talk with Hortensia, reminding her that she must use more self-restraint. He cautioned her to be especially careful what she said in front of the servants. Nor did he trust Jacinto...

The girl began to cry, but Don Joaquín tried to stamp out any sign of emotional weakness.

"Now you know! Not another word!"

Having said this, he went to his office and began to examine the family albums. The Valverdes had always governed in the Republic, until a ranch foreman named Ursulino Cachola had felt the prick of his invincible personal ambition. A member of the Valverde family was president when Cachola was promoted from the rank of colonel to general, which put him in command of the troops. From there to the presidency was but a step: a statement from the General, denouncing the President as a traitor who had jeopardized the national economy with foreign loans.

It hurt to be ordered about by his one-time godson Ursulino Cachola, now also his friend. At one time the Jaramillos and the Valverdes had held the whip, taking turns in power. Now the Jaramillo or the Valverde who did not serve the Leader was either dead or exiled and living in poverty. Whenever Don Joaquín leafed through his family album in the solitude of his office, he looked with deep animosity at the large portrait of the Leader.

Meanwhile, strolling along the avenue facing the sea, Jacinto Brache was holding forth to Porfirio Uribe.

"The Leader saved us from a disastrous situation. He's a man of the people, strong and vigorous. He shines with his own light, like one of the fixed stars. Do you imagine that Don Joaquín would have allowed me even to speak to his daughter if he still had the whip hand, as before?"

Within a few days there was to be an officers' dance at the barracks, and Jacinto would be there directing his orchestra. Since Hortensia was sure to attend the dance, for

130

Don Joaquín had received a personal invitation from the Leader, Jaramillo was going to manage to use his influence with Don Ursulino, to get him to ask, on behalf of Jacinto, for Hortensia's hand in marriage. Hortensia knew about this and, in the event of a request from the Leader's father, Don Joaquín could not refuse.

"And if this isn't soon settled," said Jacinto, "I'm going to go out of my mind." He lowered his voice: "Which will give me the opportunity to see from within one of the finest of the asylums built by the Leader."

On this occasion he would have to conduct the most beautiful music in the world, in order to hypnotize the infernal deities and rescue his Eurydice. Moreover, he counted on the valuable assistance of Bellerophon.

This constant shifting to a mythical world in which he acted out the real events of his life put a tremor of uncertainty in Brache's existence, as though he were perpetually crossing a dangerous frontier. Whenever he entered upon this line of thought he talked for hours on end in symbols. Hortensia was a prisoner in a hell of insecurity, waiting for him, Jacinto Brache, to descend to her rescue. It was inevitable that he would have to face the evil deities.

"Do you know how I lost this finger?" he asked. "After I'd spent a year in Boston studying music, I came back for a vacation. I was asked to do a favor for the Leader, and when I went to comply with the order, our enemies were waiting for us. They killed a friend of mine and wounded another and myself. In the fight I lost this finger. And I had to abandon my study of the violin."

Porfirio had already persuaded Brache that it would be best for him, Porfirio, to move to another boarding house nearer the office where he would be working. Now he said he was sorry to have to leave his friend's side, but explained that he was in the midst of an intense study of the history and laws of the Republic and needed time and isolation to finish. Brache understood.

131

"But we'll see each other occasionally," he said.

"Of course!"

In reality, Porfirio had sensed that Jacinto Brache's company was full of danger. And he felt no desire to accompany him to the underworld.

CHAPTER

VIII

More than three weeks passed without an encounter between Brache and Uribe. Porfirio was therefore surprised one day when Brache came to seek him out.

"I was passing by on my way to visit my sister," he said, "and I thought you might like to go with me. Nothing important, I just want to talk to somebody. Paulina is in a very bad condition."

His conversation wandered a little. He seemed to have had one drink too many. But obviously he was worried about his sister.

"She was always so pretty and gay," he said, on the way to the Jaramillo house, "until that Carnival. How could the poor girl know what a Carnival could do to her!"

When they arrived, Porfirio was horrified to realize that he had been brought to a house where a woman was in labor: Paulina's groans could be heard as they entered the door. Jacinto said she had been suffering the pains of a difficult labor for now more than ten hours.

They were not the only visitors. Other friends and relatives of the family were milling about in the sitting-room downstairs and on the terrace outside. They withdrew to the terrace, where Paulina's groans were less audible. Out there Brache made a confession.

"You know, Uribe," he said, "I'm tight. I had to get tight to stick this thing out, when I heard of Paulina's serious condition. And I'm thinking of Hortensia; she's fond of my sister, and she'd be horribly shocked and grieved if anything happened to Paulina..."

In the bedroom, pale and sweating, the suffering Paulina was attended by a nurse and Dr. Jaramillo. She would let no one else come near her, had insisted that her husband himself must deliver her of the child. All three people, at the end of ten dreadful hours, were haggard.

"Come nearer, Luis," she begged.

Pale and frowning, Jaramillo obeyed, sitting down on the edge of the bed and leaning over towards Paulina, who was speaking in a very weak voice.

"Luis!" she murmured. "It's dreadful to think of this child's coming into this world. He's not your child, nor is he mine, really. You know that! I'm going to bear a child to whom I feel painfully foreign. I want to die! You needn't have married me when *he* told you to. But you gave in to his will. You and I are victims of *his* power. Oh, why was I Queen of the Carnival! If I'd not been, *he* might never have noticed me! Luis, I want to die!"

Jaramillo remained silent for a few minutes. "Come," he said then, "you must make an effort."

Again her labor pains were excruciating. The nurse and the doctor worked feverishly. But the child was born dead.

"Oh God, forgive me," moaned Paulina, when she heard. "But it's better so. Who knows what that breath of life might have brought!"

Jaramillo explained to the nurse: "The child was strangled by the umbilical cord."

The nurse immediately went about her duties...

The murmur of voices of the people who were milling about in the living room and on the balcony entered the room of suffering. Perspiring and exhausted, Paulina buried

134

her face in the pillow and wept.

Meanwhile the news spread in whispers through the crowd on the terrace and in the sitting room. Porfirio was overwhelmed with a feeling of anguish. *We are all born to die. But that child died to be born.*

"You know what?" said the drunken Jacinto Brache.

"I'll bet it was a suicide. The child may have known what kind of world he would have to live in. But Luis is a doctor, he'll know."

The misplaced sense of humor was shocking.

"For God's sake, Jacinto!" Porfirio implored. "Hush! Don't say such things."

"It could be," the drunken man went on, "that the child didn't realize that we live in the most fortunate country in the world!"

Jaramillo had appeared on the terrace. His brother-in-law questioned him.

"What happened, Luis?"

One could see that Jaramillo would prefer to say nothing, but the tipsy Jacinto was insistent.

"Please, what happened? How is my sister?"

Jaramillo replied, his eyes averted: "Paulina is well, thank God. The umbilical cord was very short. During the pains of labor it displaced the placenta and twisted around the infant's neck. That's all. A misfortune."

Sebastián Brache had joined them. The other visitors quickly dispersed. It was late at night when the two Brache brothers gave the signal to leave, and Porfirio went with them. They walked for a while in silence, and when Sebastián parted from them, to go to the barracks of the palace guard, he could scarcely say goodbye, so big was the lump in his throat. They watched him move off in the darkness, walking stiffly, like an automaton.

Jacinto had sobered up. When Porfirio indicated that he wanted to go in the opposite direction, Jacinto took offense and begged him to stay. Not wanting to appear discourteous, Porfirio yielded.

"If I don't talk to someone tonight," said Jacinto, "I'll go completely crazy. I'm longing to talk, to hear someone else talking. Please go with me to the beach. The roar of the sea at night makes me feel so small that human suffering almost doesn't count. I think about the depths of the sea and lose all idea of my own."

"Let's go, then."

Jacinto was talkative. Porfirio had to say almost nothing.

"I remember the night we boarded the *San Jacinto*," Jacinto began, "and how I could think only of the fragility of the ship and the dephts of the ocean where the submarines were waiting. I'm not afraid of death, but I am afraid of depths. When I talk to someone who understands me, it's as though I were pulling out my monsters from the depths and could then steer my course with less danger."

For several weeks, now, Porfirio had noticed that his friend was trying to tell him something, but he had not been able to discover what was hidden beneath the strange symbols he employed. What "infernal deities" separated him from Hortensia? What "monsters" filled his "depths" with danger?

"Those three nights on the *San Jacinto* were horrible. Luis snored, but as for me, sleep was impossible. I felt I was losing my mind. I felt that there were more frightful monsters in my own depths than any monsters in the sea. When the explosion came and Luis went wild with fear, I felt a great relief. I controlled him. 'Come on,' I said, and led him up to the deck. It was as though I had an appointment in the depths of the sea. I thought perhaps we should remain in our cabin and sink with the ship. But they swept us out and took care of us, because we represented the government."

Now, facing the sea, Jacinto was less tragic. When he spoke again, it was in a voice much less tense.

136

"I know that I'm gradually being left alone, that people are giving me a wide berth because of the things I say. I shouldn't have pressed you to come to this country, but Luis and I were afraid..."

He interrupted himself. And Porfirio dared not ask him of what they had been afraid. Suddenly Jacinto changed the subject.

"How old are you?"

"Thirty-two. Why?"

"Almost the same age as Christ! And you haven't saved anyone yet?"

"Do you want me to save you from one of those monsters you're always talking about?" asked Porfirio, taking it jokingly. "I haven't even saved myself, just imagine!"

"The only way I could save myself, Uribe, would be to live peacefully with Hortensia. Then perhaps I could forget that accident in which I lost my finger."

"You have another road open: after all, you're the conductor of an orchestra."

"That's only to entertain the courtiers. Luis has failed me as much as Don Ursulino did. They can't overcome Don Joaquín's stubbornness. Why do you suppose he's against my betrothal to Hortensia? If I were a concert violinist of international renown, he would consider it an honor for me to ask for his daughter's hand in marriage."

It was getting very late.

"Wouldn't you like to return to your apartment now?" asked Porfirio.

Jacinto disregarded the question, absorbed in his own thoughts.

"You, Uribe, haven't yet seen a man, a friend or brother of yours, hanging from a tree in the public plaza. The police of course decide that it's suicide. And since he was a dear friend, the Leader sends him a wreath. You haven't seen anything yet! My nephew committed a truly ingenious suicide..."

Porfirio was finally obliged to leave Brache standing there on the seashore and return to his lodgings.

But Jacinto Brache pursued Porfirio like a nightmare. Instead of dedicating his free time to rehearsing his orchestral group, he spent hours on end with his violin on his shoulder trying to overcome the handicap of the missing finger. And when he found this impossible, he sought out Porfirio.

Jacinto had left the routine work in his office when the Leader, feeling that culture needed to be stimulated, suggested that he devote himself entirely to his music. The newspapers of the nation praised the exalted understanding of the Leader, who, they said, had an infinite knowledge, knew "the beginning and end of all things." Jacinto Brache was placed in charge of the musical programs with which the Leader regaled the international celebrities who were his guests.

A Hungarian refugee and a Spanish refugee were in the orchestra. It was noted that the Leader was surrounding himself with talented "displaced persons", to whom he gave asylum in the Republic, thus creating good will for himself internationally. The Leader's private secretary and counselor was Jacinto Martínez, a man who had fled from "the bloody dictatorship" in Spain to enjoy the benefits of the excellent democracy presided over by Leader Augusto.

Jacinto Brache was well acquainted with his illustrious namesake, Jacinto Martínez, who was in charge of social functions and protocol in the Palace, since the "Orpheus" orchestra necessarily participated in most of these demonstrations of culture and refinement. The courtly suavity of Martínez disgusted Brache. Martínez, a Doctor of Political Science, influenced even the internal policies of the Republic, commanded the Santiagan bureaucrats with the same authority Pizarro must have used with the Incas, yet behaved towards the Leader with groveling servility.

"When I talk to Martínez," Jacinto explained, "I realize we're still savages here in America, mere apprentices in civilization—and I'm fed up with his sickening adulation."

It was one more reason to be uneasy, and now he hardly saw his brother-in-law since Dr. Jaramillo had become assistant to Don Joaquín Valverde in the university administration.

"Luis has gone completely into politics now," said Jacinto. "He's decided not to practice medicine any more. He'll most probably become an ambassador or a minister. But he won't go any farther than that!"

"I haven't seen Don Joaquín since he became Rector of the University."

"Watch what happens. You'll see, my brother-in-law won't mark time. He'll not find it very easy, though, to take over Don Joaquín's job, because Don Joaquín is still respected, not only because he's the Leader's friend and godfather, but also because he was once upon a time Ursulino Cachola's boss. I imagine Cachola is planning a prolonged torture for his former employer. To carry it out, he'll use Luis's services. It's a shame he's decided to go in for politics when he could have been a good independent physician."

"I only hear the Leader's full name when you refer to him. How does he like the name he had when he was only the son of a foreman?" asked Porfirio timidly.

"You mean Ursulino Cachola?"

"That's it."

"No. The name Cachola is only present in the 'C' of his official name, Augusto C. Luna del Valle. It won't surprise me if one day he changes that 'C' to Caesar."

"Then you shouldn't talk about it."

"That's true, but I know you won't turn me in."

Porfirio wanted to leave his new boarding house. He had found a countryman of his who lived at the other end of the city, and he was thinking of going there, if he could find lodgings. He no longer talked about his uncle Florito Moya, who had almost become a general in the army of the Republic, for he had run up against a wall of silence when he had first inquired about him. Not even in the Dead Letters Section of the New York Post Office had he felt as perturbed as he now did in this labyrinth of conjectures, collective silence, fears. The case of Jacinto Martínez had impressed him; he would have liked to make friends with the man and learn what methods he had employed to reach the post he now occupied.

For he had decided to serve the Leader, obtain a good position, make money, and then leave the country. And he could not wait, his worldly ambitions must be satisfied without delay, the sooner the better.

One day, to his surprise, Don Joaquín sent for him. It was to take him to meet the Leader's father, who promised to introduce him to his august son. Very soon thereafter, Porfirio was given an important legal position in Foreign Relations. The Republic wanted to expand its commercial relations with the United States, and in this Porfirio Uribe, attorney-at-law, could be very useful. So he was told by the Leader's private secretary, Jacinto Martínez in person.

"The General wants to meet you," announced Martínez.

From the very moment that he took the post in Foreign Relations, he felt that he was being watched. Now, more than ever, he must be careful in his private conduct, and now, more than ever, he would strive to penetrate the vacuum of silence that surrounded everyone, a silence that gave him the impression of falling from abyss to abyss, sinking ever deeper, a sensation of living on an unstable terrain, where the ground was constantly shifting beneath one's feet.

His new position again attracted the valuable friendship of Jaramillo, upon whom Porfirio fawned in countless ways. Jaramillo had warned him that he had best not become involved in a friendship with Don Joaquín.

"He's not bad as a person," said Jaramillo, "but he knows too much. He's very clever at getting out of tight

140

places. He leaves the others caught under the ruins and continues merrily on his way. I never lose sight of him. Just two or three months ago I thought he was done for, and now, as you can see, he's my superior."

As usual Porfirio let Jaramillo talk.

"Since he's lame, he always remains seated in his armchair or at his desk. This gives him an advantage, he can study people, and he's become an expert at it. He watches them come and go and just sits there. Be careful. He might be saying to himself, when he sees you, 'Here comes a fool. I'll use him to my advantage.' He's capable of selling his own mother to stay in power. Well, he'd better not lose Don Ursulino's friendship. . ."

Jaramillo did not mention a plan he was concocting to drive Don Joaquín insane. He was afraid the plan might fail, as others had already failed, to defeat this silent and observant man, who noticed and never forgot the smallest details in anyone's conduct. But Don Joaquín had two weaknesses: first, the hidden anger of the deposed boss who is obliged to obey the orders of the former foreman of his ranch hands, and secondly, his unfailing paternal devotion. These details had not escaped Luis Jaramillo's assiduous observation.

Brache assured Porfirio that Jaramillo would eventually supplant Don Joaquín.

"Mark my words," he said.

At first Valverde had tried to use Jaramillo to his own ends, but Jaramillo proved to be the more audacious and ambitious of the two. And since Jaramillo was young and had a whole lifetime ahead of him, besides being from as distinguished a family as Valverde's, he would no doubt survive to be a very contrite mourner at the old man's funeral.

"It will come to that, I assure you," insisted Brache. "You know that Don Ursulino is very fond of Joaquín, but Don Joaquín is not a doctor, and Luis is. Luis is Don Ursulino's private physician, and he can't live without his prescriptions. The same thing has happened to me."

Horrified, Porfirio asked himself, "What kind of drug is Jaramillo using to obtain such effects?" He remembered that he had seen similar cases when he was working for Luis Pororico in New York. He hoped that he would never be tempted to ask such a question, even in his sleep. After all, it was none of his business, and he really didn't care.

"Luis will succeed in pulling out the old fellow's tail feathers—you know the old saying, 'A plucked chicken can't stay on its roost.' By the way, I have to see Luis tomorrow, I'm going to his office."

When Jacinto Brache entered Dr. Luis Jaramillo's office without being announced, he caught the doctor in the act of kissing his secretary. Apparently Jacinto was used to these situations, for he remained cool and collected as Luis introduced them.

"My secretary, Señorita...My brother-in-law, Jacinto Brache."

"Delightful work, yours," said Brache to Jaramillo, flatteringly, as the girl left the room, covered with blushes.

"Don't say anything to Paulina," Luis requested, almost absent-mindedly. "You'd do the same, wouldn't you, if you had the chance?"

"Quite probably. I haven't seen Paulina for some time. How is she?"

"Much better, but she's disinclined to go out, no matter where."

"With the pretext of bringing you a message, I came in the hope of seeing Hortensia. Do you often see her?"

"And who doesn't? I have to see her whether I want to or not. And I ought to tell you...Mind you, I don't meddle in other people's affairs, but I have the feeling that Don Joaquín would like to have our friend Porfirio Uribe as a son-in-law."

142

Jacinto made no immediate comment, but went on with what he had to say.

"Yesterday afternoon I met Don Ursulino. He wants you to go to see him today. He said he's run out of his prescription."

"Don Ursulino shouldn't get so used to..." Dr. Jaramillo began, then cut himself short. "I'll go at once. Would you like to go with me?"

"I can't. I must talk to Hortensia. Does she attend classes in the afternoon?"

When Jacinto met Hortensia shortly afterwards, he gathered from the girl's reticence that what Luis had told him was true.

"Father encourages my friendship with Porfirio," she said, "and often praises him."

"Does Uribe realize what's up?"

"I don't know. But I believe, Jacinto, that he loves you like a brother."

"We'll have to act fast. Are you willing?"

"Have you consulted Luis about it?"

"Yes. He promised to have Don Ursulino or the Leader himself speak to Don Joaquín about us. That's the only way...I've noticed that he's very evasive with me, of late."

"Luis is very good."

"Do you see him often?"

"Yes. At times he seems very sad. It must be the death of his child."

"Why do you say that?"

"I don't know. Suppositions."

"And how does he seem to be getting along here in his new post?"

"I wish you could see him! The students are crazy about him. He intends to organize a Student Guard. You know he plays the guitar and sings and recites. The girls adore him."

Jacinto was surprised by Hortensia's enthusiasm for

143

Jaramillo, and was even more surprised to hear that his brother-in-law had dusted off his skills as guitarist and reciter of verse, as attractions for the students. And why was he going to organize a Student Guard?

"Don Joaquín won't last long in the University," muttered Jacinto.

"What did you say?"

"Nothing, nothing. Can I come to see you tonight?"

"Yes."

Then he spoke in the symbolic language he often used.

"And don't forget that Orpheus will go down into the underworld for his Eurydice."

He said it jokingly, as they parted. They both smiled.

Don Joaquín was an obstacle in Jaramillo's path to power, and the ambitious young man was doing everything he could to destroy the old man's peace and compromise him. Since he had become a bureaucrat, Luis Jaramillo found it intolerable to be tied to Don Joaquín. He had been with him in the Police Department, and now they sent him to direct the University with him. It was Don Joaquín who had suggested that Jaramillo be sent on the inspection tour of the consulates and to carry out a certain very delicate mission.

Obviously the Leader was bringing into play the arts he had learned as an omnipotent ruler to destroy these two old families, before whom he had to humble himself in the past. It could be no mere coincidence that he always put them together politically. Jaramillo's suspicions were aroused, and he resolved to be the winner in the contest.

He understood that he had to surmount some very difficult obstacles. When Augusto had come to power, Don Joaquín had been close to being head of the government, and he still conserved some of his former influence. He was the friend and godfather of the Leader, and he maintained an unalterable and fruitless friendship with old Don Ursu-

144

lino. Don Joaquín concealed his wrath very cleverly, as no one could better appreciate than Jaramillo, since he, too, belonged to an old ruling family. But Don Joaquín had the advantage over him in his imperturbable calm and in his age. But after all, was age an advantage? Jaramillo hoped to turn it into a weak point, which he would attack and smash through.

Already he had begun to challenge the old man's authority. Ominously, in subtle ways, he was gradually building up his case with trifling details, from day to day, seeking to win over the students and the lesser employees of the University. He missed no opportunity to damage his superior's reputation, always operating in such a way that no one could accuse him of insubordination. And Don Joaquín never knew where to attack his young rival.

Jaramillo's strongest method of offense consisted in praising Valverde to the skies, while interjecting veiled criticisms, asking his listeners to bear with and aid a man who was getting on in years...

"It's only natural," he said at every opportunity, "that Don Joaquín can't understand young people. He has no ill will towards anyone, though, and he never hurts anyone deliberately. I'm fond of him, he's like a father to me. I try to persuade him to change his attitude, to make him see that times have changed since he was young. Only think how different life is today! Our beloved Leader had good reason to found a new order."

Don Joaquín committed his first serious mistake when he relieved Jaramillo of most of his duties, to show the others on his staff that he no longer had confidence in the young Doctor. With less work to do, Jaramillo had more time to undermine his superior's position.

He wore a peevish expression when he came to the office and, in the presence of the other members of the staff, directed sly glances and smiles at Don Joaquín's office. In spite of having less to do, he came to work earlier than usual, in order to palaver with the numerous sympathizers he had attracted. When he left late, it was to let the same clique accompany him a part of the way.

If Don Joaquín or a friend of Don Joaquín entered the room while he was having a lively conversation with the staff—among whom women predominated—a meaningful silence fell over the group, or they walked away. At times he directed a pointed question at the old man or informally put some problem to him. It was almost always some trivial affair which the others had asked him to take care of.

"You understand, Don Joaquín, how we have always had faith in your vast ability," he would begin.

Since Jaramillo was head of an administrative division, whenever a disciplinary case was submitted to him, he always managed to pass judgment on Don Joaquín Valverde along with the accused. He used his unwillingness to work as a bureaucratic weapon, to create a vacuum around Don Joaquín. Don Joaquín's physical handicap, which obliged him to remain seated whenever possible, had made him an expert in human nature, but he was helpless before his intrepid young rival's well dissimulated machinations.

The situation transcended student and governmental circles and was soon the talk of the town.

"I told you so, Uribe," said Jacinto Brache. "Things look bad for Don Joaquín. It seems as though Luis is breaking through his armor. And he's too old now to die little by little from slow torture."

The Leader must have heard of the situation, but he said nothing.

Jaramillo was highly praised when his newly-formed Student Guard performed a solemn oath of loyalty to the Leader. He had not excluded the girls from the organization, but on the contrary allowed them to take an active part. The students were completely on his side, and the girls were among his most fervent propagandists. Among the girls was Hortensia, Don Joaquín's own daughter . . .

146

It was only natural that she should feel as she did, since everything was done in the name of her father, the Honorable Rector. Jaramillo had Don Joaquín leave his office on several occasions to address the Student Guard. Jaramillo had proclaimed that he had placed "the Guard under the leadership of Don Joaquín, without whose wisdom we would not be able to continue." He called him "an illustrious educator" and ended up by recalling that the Fatherland and the Leader were one and indivisible.

If some office girl was slow in backing Jaramillo's ideas, he sat down beside her with pencil and paper to sketch her portrait, which would be flattering, while conserving the basic likeness.

Perhaps his most enthusiastic follower was Hortensia, who was placed very close to him in the hierarchy of the organization. For fear of being misinterpreted, Don Joaquín did not venture to suggest to Hortensia that she keep away from the group. After all, everything was being done for the greater glory of the Leader, who had already given his blessing to the Student Guard.

Jaramillo's credit was so high and the press harped so much on the subject that the delicate bureaucratic situation was forgotten. That is, the public no longer talked about it, but the attitude of Jaramillo and his followers was the same, and had perhaps become even more serious than ever. And since it was too late to retreat, Don Joaquín stood his ground. Now Don Joaquín's only hope was that his friend and godson would support him.

With great protestations of love towards his superior, Jaramillo proceeded with his plans to eliminate the Chimera. Never before had he wielded such a collection of pat phrases and hyperbolical statements about the Fatherland of the Leader. These words were repeated by his followers and the members of the Student Guard; indeed, many of his phrases began to appear in the official communiqués from the Palace, while most of them were printed by the daily newspapers.

Jaramillo found himself so much in demand and so admired that he scarcely ever put in an appearance at home. He was almost always surrounded by young people of both sexes, particularly on the University campus, which now revolved about him. The Leader himself addressed the students more than once. On these occasions Don Joaquín expended himself in compliments and courtesies. . .

The loneliness of Paulina became intensified; she was a recluse in her own home. When others were present Luis treated her courteously, but in private he rejected her. Paulina knew about the admiring young women who surrounded her husband, but she never mentioned it.

She became very thin and was easily frightened. She silently worshiped her husband, and blamed only herself for her abominable sin. She tried to anticipate his wishes, but he almost always met her advances with scorn. The most curious part of it was that her brother Sebastián stopped visiting her and seemed by his attitude to condemn her. Only Jacinto brought her consolation. But Jacinto, in her eyes, had lost his vital orientation and was now unable to give her the spiritual support she needed.

Paulina was not seen anywhere outside of her house, within which she had immured herself since her terrible ordeal. She avoided entering the living-room, even, in order not to have to face the portrait of the Leader. At times she gave the day off to her maid and the cook, so that she could bar the door and take down that detested portrait. Then she placed it face down on the floor and would have trampled it with pleasure, but at the least sound she hastened to restore it to its place of honor before opening the door. Usually she stayed in the back of the house, knitting things which she dedicated in silent homage to her husband, or else she shut herself in her room to pray or read.

She remembered that she hadn't even wanted to look at the lifeless body of her tiny son. And she remembered the

148

unforgettable night when, accompanied by her fiancé, the young Dr. Luis Jaramillo, she had been, as Carnival Queen, the guest of honor in the Leader's beautiful country house. Her reign as Carnival Queen had been magnificent, and Leader Augusto had often complimented her. At that country house party, they had made her drink more wine than she was used to. Feeling ill, she had wanted to withdraw, and since her fiancé was not in the room, she had let some ladies take her somewhere to rest. The next thing she knew, she was being helped into an automobile...Just before daybreak, she had found herself in a luxurious bedroom, with *him*, with...

When she reached this phase of her recollections she always became extremely disturbed. She was deeply in love with Luis and was grateful to him for having taken charge of the situation. She forgave him for the way he had abandoned her lately, and she would gladly have died for him...

One day Don Joaquín, in exasperation, recriminated Jaramillo. It all happened in the large room where most of the staff had their desks.

"You can't judge me," exclaimed Jaramillo. "But I can judge your son as a traitor!"

Don Joaquín leaned against the door-jamb, trembling. Then, pale with rage, he shouted: "The person who says that lies!"

"You all heard that!" said Jaramillo to his unexpected audience. "He called our judges liars. Oh, he knows who he's calling a liar!"

It was too late for Don Joaquín to take back his words. He stood dumb with terror, his face drawn. Jaramillo thought, irreverently, that he looked like a sad old horse.

Someone approached to try to smooth the matter over, but Jaramillo merely made another accusation.

"Haven't I always said so? He's never been devoted to our Leader."

149

This time, with a weak voice, clinging to the wall, as if otherwise unable to stand, Don Joaquín said, "That's a false accusation."

Tears fell from his eyes. One of the employees drew near to assist him back to his chair, but he drew back in sudden fear, as though he were coming into contact with a contagious disease. The others lowered their heads.

Jaramillo finally went to his office, muttering in a loud voice: "Can Don Joaquín have forgotten that the Leader is unique and unrelenting?"

Next day he went to Don Joaquín's office as though nothing had happened and, in private, asked forgiveness.

"I don't hold grudges," Jaramillo assured Don Joaquín. The apologies were accepted. Don Joaquín even tried to stand up to shake hands, but was unable to do so.

Since he knew who his borderline friends were, Jaramillo said to one of them later, "I flew off the handle, but he shouldn't have said what he did. I've always loved him like a father."

However, from that day on Don Joaquín found himself even more alone and surrounded by silence more than ever before. At Jaramillo's generous suggestion, they filled his desk on his birthday with flowers, as though it were a tombstone. Some approached him to offer the usual congratulations, and talked to him in low voices, as though they were praying for a dead man. Only one old colleage from his days as judge, now in disgrace although he still conserved some influence, admonished him.

"You shouldn't have argued with a man like Dr. Jaramillo." this person said. "Don't make mistakes like that again."

Just then Jaramillo approached Don Joaquín to wish him a happy birthday, and the old judge became so flustered that he could hardly find the way out of the room.

Don Andrés Martínez, one of those old professors who have never sold their conscience, came in while Jaramillo was present. He greeted Valverde ceremoniously and then, facing Jaramillo, he explained, "Don't be in such a hurry. It's not worth it." And, without waiting for an answer, he left with the majesty of one who has nothing to lose.

Jacinto was surprised to find that Hortensia was more on Jaramillo's side than on that of her own father.

"According to Mamma, Papa hoped that I would be a boy, and he's never forgiven me for being a girl."

"You shouldn't say that. He loves you, and even more, now that the Niño...." He stopped, suddenly pale.

"What were you going to say?"

"The Niño is out of the country and Don Joaquín needs you."

"Luis is well liked by almost everyone."

"Don't count yourself among them, without being reasonable with your father."

Jacinto would not admit it even to himself, but it looked to him as though Hortensia was in love with Luis. When it was time for the next class, Hortensia went off, and Brache went back to see his brother-in-law.

"For Hortensia's sake, Luis, stop fighting with Don Joaquín!"

"You know I'm fond of Don Joaquín, why, he's like a father to me!"

"You don't treat a father like that. You've confused Don Joaquín with the Chimera. Whatever he is, he's not that bad."

"I have nothing particular against Don Joaquín. Now that you mention it, I'll try not to fight him. Although the truth is that sometimes even Hortensia says that I'm right. By the way, what's the matter with you two?"

"Why do you ask?"

"She doesn't talk about you to me as she did before."

Jacinto felt a strange pang. From that moment on, he sensed that no one could save him. He no longer had a

151

Eurydice who would be faithful to him.

Porfirio noticed the change in his friend. It was something like a horrible mutation. Jacinto no longer even talked about the mythical world in which he had used to take refuge, but wandered from place to place, like an automaton. At times he wanted to be with Porfirio, not to protest, as before, but to let himself be swallowed up by the silence, like a boat sinking in the high sea. But he shattered the silence, once, with some mysterious words.

"I have a secret that's tearing me apart inside."

But he said no more.

Don Joaquín Valverde at last made a decision. He summoned his daughter and spoke to her about his situation.

"You must do me a favor. You're perhaps all I have left. God knows what's happened to the Niño. I beg of you, stay away from Jaramillo."

"What reason should I give him?" she asked, rather defiantly.

"None. Just put a distance between you, little by little."

"That's impossible now!"

The argument between father and daughter became bitter and ended with his slapping her face. Then he left to ask Jaramillo for an explanation. When he reached Jaramillo's house the doctor received him with the frank smile of a virtuous man, and Valverde had to swallow his wrath. To himself he said, "It's all right, he's an archangel!"

Uncertain as to what decision to make, Hortensia made a surprising discovery about herself. Her love for Jacinto Brache had merely been a way of fleeing the temptation to become Paulina's rival.

At any rate, Jaramillo had understood the situation, and he did not stop until he had turned the daughter utterly against her father. By playing on the girl's feelings, he played his best card against Valverde. But he kept her in reserve for a better occasion. And so, while continuing to

152

excite her feelings, he pretended that he was protecting her for Jacinto's sake, thus creating a confusion of emotions in her. His deliberate flirtation with the other girls, Hortensia's companions, and with the university secretaries, complicated the situation still more.

All this being so, it was not strange to see him brushing up on the artistic skills he had cultivated in his youth—his facility in interpreting romantic songs to his own guitar accompaniment, his gift for reciting lyric poetry (recitations almost always held in semi-darkness, deliberately directing the poems at some of the girls present), his talent as an actor which enabled him to play the role of a misunderstood man who nevertheless could rise above petty jealousies as few others could...

The students competed for his attentions, his verses, his songs. He presented himself to them as a sentimental prize to be fought over, and more than once he gave Hortensia the idea that she, of them all, was the favorite. When she discovered that she was hopelessly in love with him, she had real reason to challenge her father's authority.

And Don Joaquín found himself facing a dilemma: either he risked having the sanctity of his home violated or he openly made an enemy of the Leader. Indeed, perhaps he would suffer dishonor and political persecution simultaneously. However, the only thing that Jaramillo was really interested in was political victory, the definitive elimination of the man who was standing in the way of his rise to power. He would withhold the other card, Hortensia's love, to smash Valverde's pride as a moral man, devoted to the sanctity of his home. Then, after he had finally eliminated the old man from the political scene, he would go to him and say, "My dear Don Joaquín, your daughter has always been like a sister to me."

CHAPTER

IX

Since it was a holiday, Porfirio accepted the invitation of a Puerto Rican who lived in the country to visit him. By now he felt an irresistible desire to talk freely to someone, to learn the answers to questions which were choking him. He thought that perhaps the silence and tension only existed in the capital, and he longed to refresh himself, if only for a day, in the provincial life.

There were other passengers in the car, but at first no one spoke a word. By about ten o'clock in the morning the heat became unbearable, a blistering sun beat down, and the bumping of the vehicle over the bad roads and the tremendous cloud of dust added to their discomfort. The driver entertained himself watching the faces of his passengers in the rear view mirror.

The sweating passengers were glad whenever someone thought up some trivial topic of conversation which could not be interpreted as an allusion to the government. When one of the passengers whose upset stomach was suffering more from the jolts said, "These roads are unbearable," there was a dead silence as the others looked at him reproachfully, and the whites of the driver's eyes became enormous in the mirror. The individual who had spoken, terrified, put his

154

hands over the stomach as if to say, "I wasn't the one that spoke, it was my stomach." They had to stop so that the little man could run into the brush, and he reappeared more relieved a few minutes later. He did not open his lips again. When another passenger, who was dying to say something, murmured, "The drought is terrible," his companions' faces were so disapproving that he was afraid they thought he had blamed the Leader for the lack of rain.

The silence grew so heavy that Porfirio felt as though he were smothering and he put his head partly out of the window. He jumped guiltily when he heard the driver shout, "Do you want your block knocked off?" He touched his head and felt like looking in the mirror to see if the head, which he had always thought so worthy of the fertile brains it contained, really looked like a block. In other circumstances —had he lived in any country but this!—he would have answered the man as he deserved, for no one made fun of him and got away with it. To regain some of his self-respect, he now recalled with satisfaction his first four years in New York.

With an effort he managed to keep quiet. The driver might well be one of the Leader's anonymous informers. And if not the driver, then any one of the passengers could be. He glanced at those he was able to observe without arousing suspicion and saw only expressionless faces. One of the passengers, however, was desperately clenching his teeth—his jaws must have hurt—in order not to let a single word escape him! He was probably one of those talkative individuals who find it a great deprivation not to talk. Porfirio understood. It was the little man who had made the unwise comment about the road and didn't want to make the mistake again.

Seeing the man's attitude and associating it with his hurried little run into the brush, Porfirio could hardly keep back a hearty laugh. He felt he either had to laugh or burst, even if he had to explain to the police afterwards, but he

155

held in the laughter until his face turned red. He tried to put the hapless cause of amusement out of his mind, shifted in his seat so as not to see the little man out of the corner of his eye. The man looked like a lizard hunting flies as he searched the others' faces, trying to detect even the smallest desire to talk, so he could release his unpleasant mouthful of silence. But everyone ignored him, perhaps thinking it was dangerous to talk to a person who had dared to doubt that the roads here were the best in the world.

Porfirio's face was now scarlet from repressed laughter and he felt a pain in his chest. He finally had to succumb. The rear-view mirror filled with the whites of the driver's eyes, but almost everyone else joined in the laughter. Even the little man laughed, slapping his thighs, as if he understood why Porfirio was laughing. But suddenly Porfirio was struck dumb and turned pale when he saw the driver contemplating an enormous portrait of the Leader by the side of the road, as big and spectacular as the Coca-Cola signs he had seen on the roadsides in the United States.

The dense silence gathered again and Porfirio tried to cut through it with his voice. He made up a funny incident which he said had happened to him in New York, and in passing he praised the country which was fortunate enough to have a chief like Leader Augusto. This satisfied the driver and everyone admired Porfirio for being the only traveled man among the passengers in the car.

As noon approached the suffocating heat increased and Porfirio felt sweat running down his back. They must have been nearing their destination, judging by the signs the driver was making to him, when the unexpected occurred.

A detachment of soldiers stopped the car and asked for identification papers. Everyone but Porfirio had theirs. He had left his at home, unaccustomed to carrying them. The soldiers paid no attention to his explanations.

The gaze of several people converged on the little man, who was dumb with terror, but he looked so inoffensive that no one had the heart to tell the soldiers what he had said about the roads of the Republic.

The car continued on its way, minus one passenger—Porfirio—and no one in the car dared look back for fear of being accused of sympathizing with the strange individual who hailed from New York.

Porfirio spent the rest of the day and the following night in jail. There was no place to lie down, so he sat on the floor with his back against the wall. All night long he listened to the guards' foot-steps. He spoke to no one and did not want to talk to anyone. He was waiting for them to tell him the results of a call they had put through to the capital. They had telephoned to inquire if a certain attorney named Porfirio Uribe, who lived at such and such address, was employed in Foreign Relations. Next morning they told him that they had been able to talk to Dr. Jaramillo, who would come in person for his friend Mr. Uribe.

The commanding officer of the detachment begged Mr. Uribe a thousand pardons and treated him as well as possible in the circumstances.

"We have orders to arrest anyone who looks suspicious, no matter who he is," said the officer, taking him aside. "You see, sir, a person who doesn't have his papers on him is suspicious. Do you understand now why we had to arrest you? I hope you'll excuse me. I'll explain to the doctor, he'll understand. Will you help me explain to him?"

"Count on me."

Porfirio did understand. It could have happened to Dr. Jaramillo himself if they hadn't recognized him. Perhaps Leader Augusto was even capable of disguising himself and provoking his own arrest. No one knew. It was imperative to remain on the alert. Those were the orders given by the commander-in-chief of the army.

Jaramillo's arrival was spectacular. The officer fell over himself in solicitous attentions, and Porfirio's ego was considerably inflated at seeing himself in the company of such an important personage. He would even have held it against the officer if the latter hadn't persistently wagged his tail. But he knew that these demonstrations of courtesy were not addressed to him, but to Jaramillo, and through him to the Leader.

Dr. Jaramillo made it very pointed that he had come for Mr. Uribe in his double capacity of friend and a representative of Foreign Relations. This made Porfirio feel even more important and increased the officer's dismay.

Meanwhile, Porfirio was thinking, "Why did Jaramillo distinguish me by coming personally to obtain my release, when he could have done it just as well by telephone or messenger?" There was no doubt that his stock was going up, perhaps because of the personal interest taken in him by Don Ursulino, that staunch friend of Don Joaquín. Or perhaps the Leader himself had fixed his august gaze upon an individual who, having a specialized knowledge, could be extremely useful to him.

He almost felt like preening himself. If what he suspected was true, there was indeed reason to feel self-satisfied. However, he had to admit that his first conjecture was more reasonable: possibly Don Joaquín wanted him as his son-in-law. But he would have to proceed with caution. The silent struggle between Don Joaquín and Jaramillo was becoming fierce. The Leader said nothing, but he was doubtless pleased to see a Valverde and a Jaramillo destroying each other.

Jaramillo was driving his own car.

"Where were you going to, in this direction?" he asked, as he took the wheel.

"I was on my way to see a Puerto Rican friend, who had invited me."

"Did you know that Don Ursulino is interested in your career? He knew your grandfather."

Even though his heart turned over, Porfirio remained calm.

158

"I didn't know that."

Now more than ever Porfirio realized that something unfortunate must have happened to his uncle Florito Moya for these people never to mention him. But he made no effort to find out more.

"Don Ursulino has a great deal of influence with his illustrious son," continued Jaramillo. "If it weren't for him, God knows what would have become of Don Joaquín. Fortunately Don Ursulino is also my friend. But the truth is that the chief has never forgiven him for Joaquincito."

Porfirio looked at him questioningly, and Jaramillo explained.

"Joaquincito is the son of Don Joaquín, the one they refer to as the Niño. The Leader favored him with a responsible post on the official newspaper and he repaid the Leader by conspiring against him. It's believed that Don Joaquín helped him leave the country, because he was in the Police Department at that time. After Joaquincito fled, Don Joaquín spent three nights in jail. And look at him now, he's Rector of the University. But I want to ask you a question."

"Go ahead."

"Are you fond of Hortensia?"

"Why deny it? Hortensia is very attractive. But I understand that she's Jacinto's fiancée."

"The old man doesn't approve of him, but I suspect that he does approve of you."

"Why?"

"I've noticed that he'd like to have you as a son-in-law. Perhaps because you're a foreigner and you can...

He did not finish.

"I can what?"

"You can leave the country at any time."

"I don't know why I should leave, unless they threw me out. I like this country and I haven't even considered leaving. I can be as Santiagan as you; I just need time."

159

"I am glad to hear you say that. You can help us a great deal."

Porfirio fell silent. He knew that he had lied when he had said he had never considered leaving the country. In reality he would have liked to leave, if he could do so without awakening suspicion. He had heard that some foreigners had disappeared without leaving a trace. He didn't want to take that chance, and even less at a moment like this with the armed forces on the alert.

"However, I ought to tell you," Porfirio said, "that Don Joaquín has never even suggested such a thing to me, and I've always treated Hortensia as the fiancée of my friend Jacinto."

"Jacinto is not quite in his head. I pity him. It has got Paulina very worried, because she's very fond of him."

Porfirio was used to the way Jaramillo talked and made no comment. But he suspected that his friend was concocting a plan. Was he going to use Hortensia in some way to smash Don Joaquín? Why did he no longer encourage Jacinto and Hortensia to get married? Formerly he had been their best champion, but now he almost admitted that Jacinto was on his way to the insane asylum. Very probably it was already being said that Jacinto talked more than he should. Perhaps Jaramillo was thinking of committing his brother-in-law to an asylum in order to protect him. Perhaps. Porfirio arrived at these conclusions after analyzing Jaramillo's evasive words and also what he left unsaid.

That afternoon there were clear signs in the streets of the capital that an uprising was expected. The number of arrests multiplied, and the passersby were searched. Soldiers patrolled the streets with their cartridge belts crossed over their chests. At times groups of prisoners passed on their way to forced labor for not carrying their identification papers. Porfirio promised himself not to become involved in anything.

There were a number of "accidents" in which the victims

160

died mysteriously. The people shut themselves up in their homes. Leader Augusto declared in the barracks, "I'm going to make the conspirators come out of the sewer!"

It was a magnificent opportunity for Jaramillo to demonstrate his zeal and unconditional loyalty. In a harangue to the Student Guard he screamed: "I'm not ashamed to proclaim myself an idolater of Augustoism! Let us defend it to the death! Let us swear loyalty to the Leader! Leader! Leader! Leader!"

Augusto liked the term, and from then on "Augustoism" became a synonym of patriotism in the press and in speeches. Everyone insisted on the necessity of building the cult of Augustoism.

This consecrated Jaramillo. Whenever he suspected that anyone was not sufficiently devoted to Augustoism, he said: "The fellow's already fighting off flies, he'd better look out or he'll be full of maggots." He said this, for example, of Professor Andrés Martínez, the man who had taken Valverde's side in the University and who went about cloaked in scornful silence. The professor even dared to break out with a peculiar little cough every time the Leader was praised in his presence, and then he would leave the group with his head held high.

One day Andrés Martínez disappeared. Everyone said that he had fled to join the conspirators. This gave Jaramillo an excuse to say, in a harangue to his Student Guard: "We must close our ranks to defend Augustoism!"

Soldiers mounted on horseback continued to patrol the deserted streets. Suspicion grew to such an extent that friends informed on friends if they made an imprudent remark. Who knows? The perpetrator of the remark might have been testing the other's loyalty.

Finally, two weeks after his disappearance, Andrés Martínez was seen again, at least, his dead body was seen, hanging from a tree in the park. Suicide? Or. . .? At the funeral, the Leader's private secretary Jacinto Martínez, exalted the

161

many civic virtues of the deceased, saying, "Leader Augusto favored him with his friendship."

Meanwhile government offices were filled with outside counselors. Jacinto Martínez's personal power had grown considerably. He used his vast knowledge of the social sciences to improve "democratic" practices in the Republic.

One afternoon at dusk Porfirio received an urgent message from Jacinto Brache, asking him to his house. Porfirio was afraid that Jacinto was confined to his house by some illness, because he had not been seen for some time. Before going to see his friend, Porfirio stopped by to ask Jaramillo to accompany him, but the high priest of Augustoism was not in.

Then something occurred which Porfirio could never have imagined. Just as he entered the hallway of Jacinto's lodgings, he saw Luis Jaramillo coming down the stairs. They met in the middle of the hallway and there, almost in the dark, they greeted each other and stopped to talk for a few minutes.

"Poor Jacinto is ill," said Luis in a tragic tone. "If he keeps up like this, he'll have to be sent to a sanatorium. If he's left loose, they're going to think he's a malcontent and he'll suffer the consequences. I'm going to consult Paulina about it and I'm also going to ask Don Ursulino for advice."

Porfirio dared not express an opinion, but let Luis go on talking.

"It seems that Hortensia's indifference towards him has affected him strongly. He doesn't even talk about Orpheus and Eurydice any more. It seems to me that he's accepted a reality which for him is horrible. Formerly, he at least enjoyed living in the world he had invented for himself." He paused, then added, "I have to leave right away. An important matter. They're waiting for me."

They said goodbye, but as Porfirio began to climb the stairs, a fleeting curiosity made him look back towards the street door. At that moment Jaramillo was stepping out on the sidewalk and hurrying across the street towards his automobile. For the first time Porfirio noticed that Jaramillo walked with a slight limp...Porfirio rejected the evidence before his eyes. But there was little doubt of it: the killer of Adrián Martín was Dr. Luis Jaramillo!

"And Jaramillo's companion," he said to himself, almost uttering the words aloud, "was Jacinto Brache..."

His heart sank, and for a moment he hesitated whether to go to the door to call Jaramillo back or to continue up the stairs. He recalled the scene in the New York hallway vividly. What a time, though, to discover that Jaramillo not only ordered others to kill but was also a killer himself!

For a few seconds he remained undecided, with his foot on the first step. Painfully surprised, he watched Luis enter his car. As the car lunged forward and then vanished down the street his distress was overwhelming. More keenly than ever before he felt he was caught in the labyrinth.

He seemed to hear Doña Isabel's voice again: "Say something, Porfirio!" And the voice of the New York policeman: "Portorican, eh?" And there was Adrián Martín, lying at his feet. Suddenly he wanted to return to New York, wanted to know what had become of Rosana and Alfredo. And he felt the inevitable pangs of remorse. Why had he agreed to come to the Republic? Why had Jaramillo invited him to come here? In order to watch him? Had Jaramillo thought, back there in the United States, that he, Porfirio, had recognized him and his companion?

"The imperious desire to possess brought me here!" he thought. "My glutton's desire for material things!" Thus he reproached himself. But at once he reacted against this self-accusation. "After all, I'm not the only one who wants to get ahead," he reflected. "Jacinto Martínez could give me lessons." He smiled. This time the lights in the hallway were not turned on. He went up the stairs in the darkness.

After greeting Brache, he waited tensely for his friend

163

to confess. But Brache only talked about the man who had hung himself in the park. Andrés Martínez had been one of his most intimate friends.

"Luis assured me," he said contritely, "that he wasn't responsible for Andrés' suicide. I had to hear him say it himself. That's why I asked him to come here."

Porfirio discovered that he wasn't interested in Brache's qualms of conscience. Secretly he reflected, "Before the night's over, he's going to tell me what happened in New York. Why did I accept their invitation to come to the Republic? The truth is, I was frightened at the squalor of poverty."

These thoughts had barely flashed through his mind when he realized that Brache, in commenting on the death of Andrés Martínez, was saying much the same thing about himself.

"I feel guilty of that suicide," said Brache, almost as if talking to himself. "Guilty, guilty, guilty! I sold my soul to the devil. And why? I was a coward. I was afraid of poverty. I can't stand the smell of rags. I still seem to smell the stink of the urinated rags I wore when I was a child."

IIis eyes had been averted. Now, looking up at Porfirio, he spoke in another tone of voice.

"Don't sit down. I want you to go to the beach with me. We're safe, nothing will happen to us. My brother Sebastián is in command of the patrols in those streets. Let's go."

In the street the guards flashed lights into their faces, letting them pass when they were recognized.

When they were alone Brache again began talking about the death of his friend.

"I can't sleep for thinking about Andrés' death," he exclaimed. "It's time I made a confession to you. Do you want to know the truth about Adrián Martín?"

Porfirio was sorry for Jacinto Brache, and almost felt impelled to say, "No, it's better not to say anything." But he remained silent, and Brache continued.

164

"I helped kill Adrián Martín. We watched his movements for almost a week. We saw you go in and out of that house where he lived several times. It was a horrible coincidence when the four of us met in that hallway. Once our mission was accomplished, we returned immediately to Washington."

"Did you kill just like that, in cold blood?"

"They tell us that it's our duty to carry out the will of the Leader, that it's our duty to risk our lives for him. No father, mother, or brother can stand in our way."

"Incredible!"

Porfirio then told Jacinto that he had not seen the killer's face, and that the only clue he had to the identity of one of the men was his slight limp when he hurried out of the shadows into the light of the street.

"The strangest part of it is that only tonight I noticed the same limp in Jaramillo, as he was going towards his car. How could a situation like that repeat itself? When I arrived in your room I didn't say anything, and I didn't ask you for any explanation. Now, without my asking, you have answered all the questions that were seething in my mind."

"What else could I do? I noticed your attitude. And anyway, I've always had to be sincere with someone. I saw the face of the hanged man unexpectedly. Ever since, I've been fighting to keep my balance. Now and then I tell myself, 'Remember where you are, don't do anything foolish.' I can't be sincere with Luis. I've been his accomplice. I lost this finger in the first 'job' we did together. And he always says the same thing: 'Don't open your mouth to anyone.' I know that by speaking out to you I'm putting myself in your hands. But I don't know how I could go on living if I didn't tell you these things. I believe I'd begin running through the streets and shouting the facts at the top of my lungs. That would be horrible."

Jacinto Brache was still aware of reality and still remembered that he was living in the Republic, for after a brief silence he added: "If you repeat what I've told you, neither you nor I will ever tell the story again." Then, in a friendlier voice, he said, "I know you've been avoiding me for several weeks, but all the same, I trust you."

"But you've 'worked' with Jaramillo voluntarily?"

"I suppose so. The first time, we were told to watch the movements of a possible enemy, Luis didn't want me to go with him, but I couldn't let my brother-in-law go alone."

"And he naturally gave in, under protest."

"Exactly," said Brache ingenuously.

"An excellent friend and brother-in-law!"

Brache did not understand. His eyes held a lost look as he continued his confession.

"The 'enemy' was accompanied by others, and he attacked. They fired on us and we threw ourselves to the ground. You know what happened to me. From then on I've never been the same person. I only found relief in Luis' medical treatments. He was more than a doctor and more than a friend to me; he was like a brother. I felt even more attached to him when he married my sister, in spite of what had happened. He didn't want me to go with him to the United States, but I was the one who offered to accompany him."

"Aha! He begged you not to go, even though no one could accompany him better than you, right?"

"Well, yes. Who better than his brother-in-law?"

"I see."

"I made him take me along. Luis had already told me that our superiors wanted me to go. I didn't want to get him into trouble. What would have become of me after the accident in which I lost my finger if it hadn't been for him? What would have become of my sister if he hadn't hurried to give her his name? And what would have happened to Sebastián? We Braches don't have presidents or ministers among our ancestors. Do you understand? So I went. We inspected the consulates and then we remained in

166

New York for a few days in order to accomplish our last mission. We were there more than a week, sleeping in a different hotel every night. In the best hotels, because we were diplomats, distinguished persons. Only Luis was armed. I accompanied him to help, in case our 'enemy' should resist. I wouldn't have been able to use a gun. I hardly know how to shoot. Besides, I couldn't have brought myself to do it!"

"I know how you were going to help him!"

"What did you say?"

"Nothing."

Again the lost look in Brache's eyes, as though he were stunned. He began to weep, sobbing.

"Take it easy. Take it easy," said Porfirio, drawing near.

Brache sat down on the sand. His feeling of helplessness increased as he contemplated the sea which was heaving in deep ground swells. The waters were a mass of rolling shadows.

"Take it easy, Jacinto, take it easy."

"When I knew who Adrián Martín was," Brache said, after a while, when he could control his voice, "it was too late to turn back. I never imagined that it could be him! How could I? It was Don Joaquín himself who had urged us most to accomplish that mission!"

"I don't understand. Or...is what I think possible?"

Porfirio peered into Jacinto Brache's face questioningly.

"Is it possible that Adrián Martín...?"

"...was the Niño Valverde?" Brache completed the sentence.

"Yes, it isn't possible?"

"Adrián Martín was Joaquincito Valverde, Hortensia's brother. I didn't know it, and neither did Luis, but we knew when we saw him in New York. By then it was too late to turn back!"

"And he told you that no brothers or parents should stand in your way when you served...No, it was too late to

167

turn back."

They looked at each other, frightened.

"Did Don Joaquín know?" asked Porfirio.

"No, he didn't know, and I don't think he knows now. But just imagine! It was Don Joaquín himself who commissioned us to silence a desperado named Adrián Martín, who was sending tremendous articles to the press of all America, in which he proposed 'hunting down the monster'! Can a man be more unfortunate?"

Porfirio let himself succumb to the superstitious fear which any reference to the Leader inspired, and remained silent. Why was he listening to Brache? But Brache was now talking as if to himself, as if Porfirio Uribe were not standing there in front of him.

"Luis is right," he muttered. "I ought to take a rest in a sanatorium. I need a rest. Every time I remember that I could have been a concert artist and wasn't, I feel as though I began to die when I lost my finger. Do you realize how I've lived? Only my love for Hortensia and the Orpheus group have kept me going. But the power of the infernal deities..."

He stopped short. Then he got to his feet and began pacing up and down by the sea.

"Why think about all this?" he asked at length, almost wrathfully, turning towards Porfirio. "Luis has assured me that Don Joaquín would be very pleased to have me as his son-in-law."

It was incredible that Jaramillo had said that to Brache. Porfirio could not help but feel afraid. Had Brache brought him down here to the beach to ask for an accounting? What could he expect from a man who admitted that he ought to be in an asylum? And what if he pulled out some kind of weapon with which to attack him? Or what if he suddenly began to run through the streets of the city in the dead of night shouting "The Puerto Rican, Porfirio Uribe, is a spy!"?

168

Instinctively Porfirio put himself on his guard and summoned all his strength to speak calmly.

"I don't know if what Jaramillo says is true, but even if it is, everything would depend on Hortensia and myself. I know she has no particular liking for me, that perhaps she does not like me at all. I've never said anything to her, for I have always regarded her as the fiancée of a friend."

Jacinto's eyes were shining with gratitude.

"I know that," he said, "and that's why I've talked to you. I always suspected that Hortensia was not really in love with me, but used my affection for her to bring her closer to Luis. Perhaps to kill her real love for him she accepted me, in order to show my sister that she didn't want to betray her. She would have married me and would even have come to love me, because she is a kind-hearted girl. However, I've recently noticed that she seems hostile towards her own father. She's very close to Luis in the Student Guard. Can Luis help letting himself be loved? He's always treated her like a sister."

Porfirio was surprised that Brache persisted in justifying Jaramillo's conduct. How could he have fallen so low? Again it occurred to him that Dr. Jaramillo's prescriptions were certainly suspicious. He would have liked to take one of those pills to the laboratory and be able to proclaim: "Dr. Jaramillo has enslaved Don Ursulino and Jacinto Brache with drugs." But it was too great a risk to take. He wished he might open Brache's eyes to the truth. Jaramillo was not only deceiving his friend and brother-in-law, but he had also made him an accomplice. Nevertheless, why didn't Jaramillo kill his accomplice, potentially so dangerous to him? Perhaps his decision to send him to a sanatorium was a good idea, after all.

However, Jacinto's seclusion would mean an even greater solitude for Paulina. It was hard to explain why he was so concerned with what happened to that sad and silent woman. He would have been very glad to be able to serve her, to contribute in some way to her happiness. Surprised at his own thoughts, he asked himself, "Am I in love with Paulina? Is that why I let myself be overcome with animosity towards Jaramillo?"

"I feel better," said Brache, breaking into his thoughts. "Now I'll not run shouting through the streets. I really don't want to get Luis into trouble. The disappearance and death of Andrés had made me desperate. I felt that nothing mattered to me any more. Luckily I unburdened myself to you and Luis. Perhaps a few days in the sanatorium will do me good."

Now it was Porfirio who began to rave.

"Jacinto," he exclaimed, "I still don't get it! Why did you and Luis insist on bringing me here?"

"When we saw you on board the *San Jacinto,* we were scared and expected the worst. We were on the point of forcing our way into your cabin, one day. We thought you had recognized us and that you would turn us in. To tell the truth, I threatened to throw myself into the sea if the chain of deaths continued. Later on, when we were hospitalized in Virginia, I was convinced you hadn't recognized us. But Luis wasn't sure, and so he offered to find a job for you in the Republic. He wanted to make sure of you. At the embassy in Washington, they agreed to the plan. When Luis was finally convinced that I was right, he really did use his influence to get you a job. They'll take advantage of your professional services here, but don't get mixed up in anything like I did. After all, though, it wouldn't be so easy for you to get mixed up, since you're a foreigner. And, for the love of God, don't tell anyone, much less Luis, what we've talked about tonight. If something leaked out about the death of Joaquincito Valverde, even Luis wouldn't be safe, and if they knew that you know, then you wouldn't be safe either. The Leader would have to avenge the death of Niño Valverde, the son of his beloved friend and godfather."

His lips curved in a bitter smile. "Perhaps we shouldn't
170

see each other again for a few days," he said, then. "It's better for you not to come to see me alone, but if Paulina asks you to accompany her when she comes to see me, do so, for her sake."

He held out both hands, surveying them. "These hands," he said, "could have been noble on the strings of a violin."

Now, more cautious than ever, Porfirio resolved to be on his guard. He would wait for the most propitious moment to leave the country without arousing suspicion. What he had only vaguely suspected had now been confirmed as a horrible fact. He was even afraid he might betray himself by talking in his sleep. Henceforth he would avoid Jaramillo; he would stay out of Bellerophon's way.

Of one thing he was sure. He had studied for a profession that would earn him a living and so free him from the tyranny of fear as regarded basic necessities. In doing so, he had followed a Puerto Rican tradition. But this was not enough. He had still not made a name for himself. Nostalgically he thought of the small town life of Coamo, centered round the church and the cemetery. Would he have found satisfaction and peace in Puerto Rico? Perhaps. Who could ever know! But the newspapers in New York never tired of expatiating on the desperate poverty in Puerto Rico... What had he done in his thirty-two years of life? Nothing worthwhile. He was suddenly assailed by an unbearable anxiety.

They were now walking silently through the streets of the city. Occasionally a soldier turned to look at them, but they were allowed to go on without any hindrance. There were few passersby. From time to time they saw someone being searched for arms. Then Sebastián Brache barred their way, and they all stopped to exchange a few words.

"How are you, Counselor?" asked Sebastián, addressing Porfirio ceremoniously.

"Very well, thank you."

"I like to see Jacinto in your company," said Sebastián

warmly, looking almost paternally at his brother. "Only the other day I was telling Jacinto to be more careful. He has an artistic temperament, I understand that, but...well, you know."

"You're quite right, Lieutenant."

"Why do you call me Lieutenant, so formally?"

"Because you called me Counselor."

"Oh, that!" said Sebastián, with a friendly laugh. "But now, sincerely, I'm glad to see you two together. You see, I was the eldest in our family and when our parents died this fellow here listened to me as though I were his father. He ought to come to live with me, I've asked him to, but haven't been able to persuade him. Perhaps you'll be able to."

"God knows, you'd never be able to stand me," commented Jacinto jokingly.

"I can see you're worried, Jacinto. If you don't want to live with me, why not go stay with Paulina? She'd be glad to have you, I'm sure. She's too much alone now that Luis is so busy..."

"I know they'd be glad to have me, but it's better that I live alone. If ever I should change my mind, I'll move into your house without any warning."

"This is no time to be walking through the streets. There are plenty of desperados..."

Since he was a man of few words, he said no more, but his definite loyalty to the Leader was obvious. Even though he commanded a detachment of the Palace Guard, the Leader, who trusted him completely and had honored him with his personal friendship, had put him in charge of the street patrols during this period of tension. The two brothers were rarely seen together: Jacinto had decided that it was better for Sebastián not to be seen too much in his company. He knew that Sebastián had a strict sense of duty, and he did not want to disturb him with arguments. The taciturn Sebastián had risen from the ranks and would go far; eventually he would be a general, for he always obeyed the orders of his superiors, although he never went beyond what was asked of him.

When Sebastián had left them, Porfirio noticed that Jacinto was hesitating, as if on the point of saying goodbye.

"I must go see Paulina," he suddenly said, and went on to explain that he was very troubled about her, living so withdrawn from the world, so starved for affection. "When I see Paulina nowadays I'm reminded of those fish who have lost their sight from living in the dark caverns deep under the sea. I grieve when I see her all alone there, knitting or sewing..."

Porfirio dared not discuss the matter with his friend, but he felt like saying, "Luis Jaramillo is the one person responsible for this situation. He's abandoning her, little by little. He's made her believe that she and only she is a shamefully sinful being. She's accepted the bad opinion he has of her, because she's given herself to him utterly and does whatever he wants her to do." Oh, how he would have liked to make a home for such a woman! He remembered the last time he had gone to see Luis Jaramillo, and how Paulina's questions, put in that thin little voice, were ignored. Since he spent almost all of his time away from home, she tried to surround him with affection when he did return, but he acted as though she did not exist.

Jacinto would not admit it, but inwardly he must surely condemn his brother-in-law's behavior. He showed his brotherly solidarity by visiting Paulina often, talking to her while she kept on sewing, trying to interest her in a number of subjects. But she was obsessed by one only: Jaramillo. And the more Luis stayed away from home, the more she stayed in. Many times late at night she longed for the warmth of his body. But how could she tell him so? She stifled her sobs in her pillow.

At times Porfirio felt like protesting aloud against Luis Jaramillo's conduct. But what would that accomplish? Neither Jacinto nor Paulina would forgive him for intervening. He must keep his thoughts to himself. Life, he thought, as he parted from Brache, is a constant series of frustrations.

He walked on alone, still thinking of Paulina.

An anonymous telephone call had recently informed Paulina that Hortensia was following Luis Jaramillo about like a shadow. She had been unable to eat for several days afterwards. However, when her brother Jacinto came to see her, she asked no questions and made no comment. But whenever she mentioned her husband, her voice broke...

CHAPTER

X

His Excellency, Augusto C. Luna del Valle, President of the Republic, had designated Dr. Luis Jaramillo to represent him at an international conference in Brazil.

"I've already spoken to your brother Sebastián," Luis said to Paulina, "to arrange for you to stay in his house while I'm away."

"I'd rather not leave here," she said imploringly. "Jacinto would be glad to come stay with me."

"I should have told you at once that Jacinto voluntarily entered a sanatorium this morning. It's the best thing he could have done. When he leaves there he'll be well. I've put him under the care of my friend, Dr. Olalla."

"Does Sebastián know about it?"

"Yes. He approved your brother's decision."

"It's God's will. I'll go to live with my brother Sebastián."

Paulina hadn't suspected that Jacinto's condition was so bad. Only three days before, he had spent a few hours with her and had talked quite normally.

But she knew nothing of what had happened the previous night. Jaramillo had visited Jacinto in his apartment and had found him slightly delirious.

"Don't stir from here, wait till I bring my medical kit,

175

you need an injection," he had told Jacinto. "At the same time I'll try to find your brother Sebastián."

He left, and when he returned, accompanied by Lt. Brache, Jacinto's eyes were quite wild, and from time to time he was ejaculating, "I'm going to kill General Cachola!"

It was a very serious case. Not even a madman ought to say a thing like that, because it could get those who were not crazy into trouble. Jaramillo put him to sleep with a sedative. Then, without commenting on what Jacinto had said, he asked Sebastián's advice, but Sebastián, also without commenting, asked for Jaramillo's advice. He didn't dare to propose anything very mild for a man who had announced his intention to kill the Leader. The unsaid words put barriers between them.

"He's just raving," Sebastián said, at last.

"I'll see if there's anyone in the house," proposed Jaramillo.

He left, returning a few minutes later.

"There's only one person here and he's in his room. The ladies have gone to church."

"What do you, as a doctor, advise?"

"Don't you think it would be a good idea to commit him to a sanatorium?"

"It's the only solution, for the moment."

"However, you should warn the directors so they won't think his place is in a prison and not in an asylum..."

"No, wait a minute. I'll go see Don Ursulino. He'll help us."

Don Ursulino went with them to the sanatorium, a luxurious new building with a large sign across the front: WE OWE EVERYTHING TO LEADER AUGUSTO.

Jacinto Brache would remain there under Dr. Olalla's personal care. Don Ursulino acted as though the matter were of little importance, and outdid himself reassuring Dr. Jaramillo and Lt. Brache.

Dr. Jaramillo was already on his way to Brazil when

Porfirio received a message saying that Don Joaquín Valverde wanted to see him. Would he be so kind as to dine with him and his family in their home? Porfirio accepted.

During the course of the meal, various trivial topics came up for discussion, but the conversation died almost immediately. Although she was very friendly and courteous, Doña Rosa was obviously suffering from an ill-concealed case of nerves. Hortensia ate with her head bowed over her plate most of the time. Frequently, Don Joaquín praised their guest, Porfirio Uribe, mentioning his virtues as a man, his skill as a lawyer. Porfirio was slightly uncomfortable.

After dinner they listened to music for a while, then Don Joaquín invited Porfirio in to his study for a talk. When Porfirio noticed the old gentleman's anxious manner, he remembered Catalina's aspect when she put herself into a trance because "a soul that had passed on" wanted to communicate with her. And indeed, Don Joaquín's mind was disturbed by thoughts of someone in the other world.

"I want to talk to you," he began, "as I would talk to my son, the Niño, if he should still be alive. . . ."

He paused. Obviously he was feeling out Porfirio to see if he had some concrete information, but his efforts were in vain.

"Has something happened to your son?" asked Porfirio.

"I don't know anything for certain about him, and the worst of it is that I can do nothing!"

"Perhaps the Ambassador. . ." Porfirio suggested, knowing the futility of his suggestion before making it.

"Impossible!"

Porfirio involuntarily looked at the portrait of the Leader, and Don Joaquín hastened to say, "We can talk here without fear."

The young man felt ashamed.

"I wouldn't wish. . .well, you understand."

"I'm not even offended that you should think. . .Permit me to speak to you as to a friend! It's true. I don't have a

177

clean past. What's more, my hands are soaked with blood..."

"Surely you haven't..."

"Why hide it? Perhaps my son has paid for the things which my family and I have done. I should be ashamed to admit it, but we Valverdes governed with whip in hand. Now my protegé Augusto has taken it upon himself to humble our pride with his own whip. It hurts to admit it, but that's the way things are. We're paying a debt. The landowners, presidents and ministers of my family enjoyed crushing other people's pride."

He again paused, waiting for Porfirio's reaction. But the young man remained impassive.

"I wouldn't dare to talk of these matters with one of my own countrymen but, I don't know why, I trust you," old Don Joaquín went on. "I'm putting myself into your hands. Perhaps it's a last, desperate resort."

Porfirio was moved, but he commanded himself mentally, "Listen, and don't commit yourself." He let Don Joaquín continue talking.

"I know that Jaramillo's rapid rise is a bad sign for me. By destroying us, Augusto wants to liquidate two once-powerful families. I see another shake-up coming, and I don't know where they'll throw me this time. Do you know what worries me most? My daughter Hortensia. She's become too involved in Jaramillo's Student Guard. She's easily impressed. You can see for yourself, she suddenly lost interest in Jacinto—she hasn't even gone to the sanatorium to see him. Their engagement didn't have my approval, and her friendship with Jaramillo has it even less. I've tried to persuade her to leave the university, but the truth is, I'm afraid of reprisals."

It was a monologue, because Porfirio Uribe said nothing. The old man made an additional effort.

"What I'm going to say to you now," the old man added, "will surprise you. I'd like her to marry a man like you and then leave the country."

178

"And what does Hortensia think about all this?"

"She'll understand. Things are reaching a point which obliges us to express our feelings frankly, and above all to people we trust. I feel as though I've been relieved of a great weight by telling you this."

"Thank you very much for trusting me, Don Joaquín. I'd like to ask you one thing..."

"I'm listening."

"What do you think I should do, in these circumstances?"

"I wanted to warn you about that. We have to learn to seize the best opportunity. Rosa and I are old; we think about our children. I know I'm a selfish old man, but you understand. I myself don't know what's become of my son, but I suspect that something serious has happened to him. I don't like to think that Hortensia is going to suffer. Tell me frankly: wouldn't you like to leave the Republic if a good opportunity presented itself?"

The truth was that Porfirio didn't quite trust Don Joaquín. He stammered as he replied.

"Well, Don Joaquín, why deny it? Although I have nothing bad to say about..."

"You think that I might be able to get you into trouble. I've already told you what I am. Or rather, what I ought not to be. Do you see me here? I have the presumption to want my children to think of me as a man worthy of respect. It seems impossible, doesn't it?"

His eyes filled with tears, and if he hadn't been lame, he would have begun to walk about in order to dissipate his emotions. Porfirio was touched, but he still didn't give in. He kept searching for the old man's intentions.

"I beg you to reserve judgment," pleaded Don Joaquín. "I don't even ask you to trust me. Who can trust a man who sank so low just to maintain his rights as a landowner? Don't think about me. Think about Hortensia, who has her whole life ahead of her. I don't deceive myself. I don't deserve pity from anyone. Do you suppose I don't know

179

that my actions and those of the other Valverdes were in great part responsible for the government we have now? Yes, my grandfather oppressed the Cacholas and then, when the revolutionary crisis came, for fear of losing our properties, we backed the overseer of our lands, who had suddenly become a Colonel. We encouraged him, telling ourselves, 'He won't forget that we were his masters.' We were right, but in another sense. The Leader has never forgotten that we oppressed his family."

Porfirio nodded, but said nothing.

"I'm not talking to you," Valverde added, "in the name of the clean record of my family, in spite of the many blessings bishops have bestowed upon generations of domineering Valverdes. Nor do I even speak to you with the authority old age should have. My gray hair does not even command respect. If it hadn't been for my son, who rebelled, I would have become powerful in the service of the Leader. Nor do I speak to you in the name of that power, either. Rather, I appeal to your humanity. I ask you to consider Hortensia and to decide that it would be a dreadful thing for such a young and beautiful human being to be crushed."

Porfirio was unable to contain himself any longer.

"You're right, Don Joaquín! I'll do what I can."

Don Joaquín gave his friend a warm embrace. Then, losing his self-control, he laid his head on the young man's shoulder and wept. In any other circumstances, Don Joaquín would have made Porfirio think of a mollusk which had suddenly lost its protective shell. In spite of everything, he could not help but feel a certain filial affection for the old man.

"I promise that all this will remain between the two of us," he said.

"But, you know, my son," said Valverde, turning to survey the portrait of Leader Augusto covered with medals and wearing a showy plumed hat and gold braided uniform, "you know, Augusto has an extraordinary natural intel-

180

ligence in financial matters. He paid off the foreign debt for which other governments were responsible. And besides, to a certain degree he's progressive."

It was Valverde's bad conscience that impelled him to pronounce these words. But now Porfirio responded with coolness and aversion, privately wondering if his former attitude hadn't been imprudent.

"He ended the disorder and anarchy which reigned in the country," the old man continued. "He once told me that it was a wise person who said that government is the organization of idolatry. He's probably right in his own way, but excessive idolatry has turned him into a man without personal sentiments or consideration for others. That's why the slightest slip puts one in danger and why his supporters are converted into lackeys. As I was. But he's gradually losing confidence in his own countrymen and is surrounding himself with foreigners. Take, for instance, Jacinto Martínez, who began as a mere office clerk and has become a power behind the throne, arrogant and pretentious."

"It's easier to govern with persons who feel no moral responsibility towards the people," Porfirio ventured to say.

"True. I realized that, when we Valverdes were in power. Don't think that it will be easy for me to face the consequences if you're able to leave the country with Hortensia. You've seen what the Niño's flight has cost me."

Porfirio was on the verge of revealing what had happened to Niño Valverde, but he reflected that if he did so he would not only endanger Jaramillo and Brache but would also hopelessly imperil himself. There still existed a certain troublesome barrier between himself and Don Joaquín. God only knew how the old man would react if he found out that the young Puerto Rican standing before him had witnessed the murder of the Niño. But now Don Joaquín's mollusk-like soul would never again have a chance to retreat into its shell . . .

Don Joaquín, who had been a promising writer in his

181

youth and was now a frustrated one, proceeded to speak metaphorically.

"The important thing is for you two to leave. I'll stay and try to distract the bull with my cape. I'll be risking very little at that point. The only thing I can be proud of now is that I'm the father of a girl who merits my deepest love. She has the right to live and be the mistress of her own respectable home."

They left the study. Hortensia spoke to Porfirio, but kept her eyes averted, while Doña Rosa and Don Joaquín exchanged anxious glances.

After several days of political turmoil, searches, arrests, suicides and accidents, there came a period of ominous calm. Even the transparent air seemed to be full of watching eyes.

To his surprise, Porfirio received an invitation to attend a solemn official ceremony which would be held in the central army barracks, General Augusto Luna del Valle's favorite place. Porfirio could hardly sleep the night before the celebration. Obviously, he was already being talked about in the Palace. It was the sign of a rapid ascent.

When he entered the parade ground, Don Joaquín, who was accompanied by Don Ursulino, called to him from the grandstand, where a place had been reserved for him. Don Ursulino's cordiality so impressed him that he was already beginning to regret having wanted to leave the country. Probably he would go far here, perhaps even becoming a minister, if he took Santiagan citizenship. He hadn't forgotten, after all, his mother's nationality, and he now congratulated himself for not having made any inquiries as to the fate of his uncle, Florito Moya, the frustrated general. Porfirio Uribe y Moya, attorney-at-law, felt that destiny had great things in store for him.

For a few seconds, he inwardly blamed himself for his disloyalty to the pledge he had given Don Joaquín. But he immediately countered this thought with a question: Was

Don Joaquín himself loyal to his friends and family? Then suddenly other questions occurred to him: What would Alfredo Laza think if he could see him here? What would Juan Lorenzi think? What would the clairvoyant Rosana Cortines say to him? His whole life in New York seemed more dream-like than real. Was Porfirio Uribe y Moya, attorney-at-law, as it said on the invitation, the same person who had worked for Luis Pororico, the same Porfirio Uribe who had withdrawn from the world and led a mole-like existance in the Dead Letters Section and in his room at Doña Isabel's boarding house, was he the same as that man who had almost gone to jail accused of murder and who had afterwards been shipwrecked in the *San Jacinto*...? Was this Porfirio Uribe y Moya, attorney-at-law, that same Porfirio Uribe, the "Portorican" sneered at by the police and the postal employees? Possibly he might one day be sent to the United States to carry out some mission for the Santiagan government, and in Puerto Rico the press would acclaim the triumph of a Puerto Rican in the Republic, as it did when Rius Rivera or Mascaro triumphed in Cuba. And Estefano would remain forever buried with his baritone horn in the depths of the sea, and the hoarse, broken voice would cease to echo in his memory...

A horseman on a nervous roan stallion, General Luna del Valle, known as the Leader Augusto, General-in-Chief of the Army, Illustrious Patrician, Master of Generations, "Greatest of Titans", "Absolute as the Ocean Waves", was reviewing his troops. It was the first time that Porfirio had seen him near at hand, with so much pomp and circumstance. He wore a gold braided uniform with five stars on his epaulets, a plumed hat, and so many medals on his chest that there was room for no more.

The "monster" seemed very human—indeed, Porfirio had an inclination to laugh. But this was no place for laughter, and he tried to repress the impish thoughts that danced through his brain. Was it possible that His Excellency, the

President of the Republic, Don Augusto C. Luna del Valle, had once been known as the ranch-foreman, Ursulino Cachola? The most illustrious historians had invented the greatest battles and the most unforgettable feats of courage for him. Diplomats had announced triumphant proposals for international peace in his name. The most powerful nations had decorated him or allowed him to bestow decorations upon their chiefs of state. His biographers no longer knew what to call him. He even overshadowed nature itself.

Porfirio was now bursting with repressed laughter. Could it be that the fiction created by historians and biographers was actually this man of flesh and blood, with a face bloated as if he were blowing into an imaginary *bombardino*?

Now the troops were facing him at attention and he was holding forth to them on their patriotic responsibility. The soldiers, as rigid as robots, looked as though they had been mass-produced in some kind of factory. And no one laughed at the voice of the illustrious General-in-Chief of the National Army, which sounded like a baby's rattle.

After the parade, the most solemn part of the celebration took place in the patio under improvised canopies. First, the pen with which the Leader had signed an important international agreement was proclaimed a national memento of great worth. Then the decree was read which rechristened the Leader's native city Augusta, in his honor, and at the same time awarded it the title of City of Merit.

The magnanimity of the Leader was most clearly manifested when, not forgetting that he was above all things the Chief Agriculturist of the Republic, two beautiful young heifers from his herds were brought out to be presented to some peasant youths from his native city, an act calculated to stimulate the nation's husbandry.

Now seated in the presidential box, the Leader was beaming. At his side an exceedingly fat matron, his wife, exchanged occasional remarks with the ladies who accompanied her, the wives of high dignitaries, all of them imposing in their dimensions. "She probably tries to scare up women even fatter than she is," thought Porfirio, "in order to make herself feel better, and perhaps she thinks she looks younger by comparison with them." He could be malicious in thought, although he was afraid to show any slight disrespect on the surface. He tried to forget his absurd thoughts, but almost broke out laughing when Don Ursulino made a remark in line with them.

"My son's wife is going to asphyxiate!"

The old man had a keen sense of humor. At times he even made fun of his illustrious son's appearance, and those who overheard his remarks were uncertain how to react. Both Don Joaquín and Porfirio were obviously uneasy at the moment.

"Don't pay any attention to me," said Don Ursulino. "I like to be with my friends so I can say what I like. Over there with my family, I'd have to keep my mouth shut out of consideration for the President."

Don Ursulino had not lost his peasant simplicity. As he looked at the heifers that were going to be given away he said to Valverde, "Joaquín, I haven't forgotten country life. Look at those stupid heifers. They don't even know how to behave in the presence of Leader Augusto."

Don Joaquín and Porfirio remained silent.

"I know I shouldn't say such things in front of you," said Don Ursulino, aware of their silence. "Pardon me if I abuse your confidence." And, to change the subject, he gave Porfirio a friendly glance and addressed him. "They've spoken to me very highly of you, Uribe," he said. "I'm pleased that you're Santiagan on your mother's side. Juanita Moya was a woman of character; she followed the man she loved. You can make this country your own."

"Yes, sir."

"You have a future here. In your country there are too many people for too little land. I don't know if it's true,

185

but they tell me there are few opportunities in Puerto Rico for young men like you."

"I'm afraid it *is* true."

But now the ceremony of presenting the two heifers to the young rustics was beginning. The Leader was waiting in the middle of the platform, his august hands placed on the tousled heads of the boys, who didn't move a muscle, paralyzed by the Leader's almost mythical magic.

Those who were leading the animals by their halters tried, with the Leader's approval, to make them climb upon the platform, but one of the heifers resisted so stubbornly that her halter slipped off. The First Agriculturist of the Republic stepped forward to calm the animal, placing a gloved hand on her flank. But as Don Ursulino said, the heifer didn't know how to behave in the august presence. With a sudden lunge, she charged the Leader, sending him running to safety, making him fall on his knees in a most undignified fashion, while the spectators looked on in an anguished, tomb-like silence.

The Leader jumped up and looked around defiantly, *to see who dared*—but no one dared, not even his own illustrious father, Don Ursulino C. Luna del Valle.

An officer who was seated nearby exclaimed furiously: "The person who bred that heifer should be shot for not having taught her the proper respect!"

These words were no more absurd than those used to describe the Leader as "beneficent rain", and they caused no laughter. While the President recovered his dignity, the people in the grandstand averted their eyes and remained silent. The all-pervading silence was more than weighty, it was bone-crushing.

Some men cornered the animal and managed to put its halter back on. The ministers and aides-de-camp, solemnly garbed in frock coats, hastened to obey the orders of the Leader, who was determined now that the heifer should mount the platform. While two of them pulled on the halter, three or four pushed the animal's rump. The animal tried to raise her tail, with the very worst of intentions, and one of the dignitaries had to hold it between her legs. Strange sight, those men in frock coats engaged in such an operation! They finally succeeded in forcing the heifer to mount the platform, and thus ended a somewhat embarrassing situation.

Now the Leader was smiling and very sure of himself. He well knew who held the halter of the Republic.

It fell to Jacinto Martínez to close the ceremony with a judicious speech, in which he illustrated with documents—interspersed with opportune sociological observations—the Leader's providential intervention on behalf of better relations between the nations of the world.

Shortly before the reception which followed this ceremony, the Leader approached his father and exchanged a few cordial words with him and with Don Joaquín Valverde, his friend and godfather. Porfirio tried to efface himself, but Don Ursulino led him by the arm towards his illustrious son and exclaimed without further ado: "Augusto, this is Attorney Porfirio Uribe y Moya, the Puerto Rican who works in Foreign Relations."

The Leader responded with exquisite cordiality: "As a matter of fact, I've told my secretary that I want to see you."

Such a signal honor made Porfirio Uribe tremble from head to foot. Fortunately the Leader wanted to share his time with all of the guests and so left the group.

When the reception was over, Don Joaquín wanted Uribe to accompany him directly to his home. There they talked again in his study.

"I knew that we'd meet him there," said Don Joaquín, smiling mysteriously. "It's best to establish good relations; they must not see any reserve in your attitude towards them; one day you may be granted leave to visit Puerto Rico." He winked at Porfirio after saying this, then asked, "How did the Leader impress you?"

187

"He impressed me very much."

"That's to be expected. I'm going to tell you a secret. My godson is rather superstitious. Did you know that on the old family estate of the Valverdes there's a soothsayer who told the young overseer Ursulino Cachola that he would come to be the most powerful man in the Republic? It was he who advised Augusto to become a soldier. The old Valverde estate now belongs to the Luna del Valle holdings, and the old soothsayer still lives there. He's absolutely loyal to me, both because he was once in my service and also because I saved his life on two occasions. Well"—and he winked again—"my friend the soothsayer told my godson that his greatest misfortune would come from hurting his godfather, that is, me. Do you understand? And there's more. The same soothsayer has told the Leader that a young Puerto Rican named Porfirio Uribe will render him outstanding services."

Porfirio could hardly believe his ears. He asked himself if it was possible that Augusto's superstition could reach such a point, and if it wasn't an enormous risk to use such trickery.

"I assure you," Don Joaquín added, "that Augusto has not only regularly consulted the soothsayer since he told him about his rise to power, but that he believes in him implicitly. As you know, we all have our weaknesses. From my own experiences I know that Augusto is very superstitious, and when all of my other resources are exhausted, I take advantage of that weakness."

"But suppose the soothsayer tells him . . ."

"That I told him to say that? It's a dangerous card which we have to play. But I can assure you that it won't happen. For about two weeks my heart was in suspense, as if hanging from a thread, for fear my old servant would betray me. It would have been my end and perhaps yours as well. Forgive me for my egotism in using such a trick, but I only did it to protect my daughter."

"But the soothsayer can still betray you!"

"Not now. If he told the Leader now, he would be killed

even before I would be, for having deceived his master. I'm glad that one can still count on people like that. Not everything that the Valverdes did was bad. I assure you that I couldn't sleep during those first two weeks of waiting. Do you know how old the soothsayer is now? Almost a hundred years old."

"And he has kept his health?"

"He's as strong as an oak. His wife was my old nurse. I saw her the other day and she told me what had happened."

Porfirio remembered that in the past many kings and emperors had been influenced by magicians and soothsayers, and so found this present situation comprehensible. Even in his own life there had been several examples of this type of "clairvoyant" people: his godmother Catalina, Rosana, Doña Isabel. Apparently soothsayers are most commonly women, who are so fond of "reasoning" by magic, above all when they want to convince the people they love.

Jaramillo had still not returned from his mission to Brazil when he was named Rector of the University, to supersede Don Joaquín Valverde. The latter was to remain in office, without a shadow of authority, until Jaramillo's return. The old man spent most of his time sitting alone in his office, rooted like a cactus in his enormous chair, bristling with resentment and suspicion.

Hortensia pitied her father, but she was sure that Jaramillo would arrange everything. The Student Guard expressed its noisy approval and the members of the staff, even those who had been closer to Valverde than to Jaramillo, openly expressed their desire to welcome the new Rector in style. Don Joaquín's loneliness increased.

On his return, Jaramillo decided that he preferred not to have a reception of any kind, because "the Leader places men where in his wisdom he thinks best," he said, "and I am only a pawn which his wise hand moves on the chessboard." He announced that, with the President's approval,

Don Joaquín would be his advisor and counselor from that moment on.

But as the days passed no one consulted or paid the least attention to Don Joaquín Valverde. In spite of their frequent protestations of friendship and sympathy, Valverde's former followers subjected him to a constant series of small humiliations, while others, particularly members of the Student Guard, were singled out for marked privileges.

There was no public ceremony at which Jaramillo did not have his "beloved advisor and counselor" Don Joaquín Valverde at his side, but in the large general office where the ordinary employees had their desks, he made Don Joaquín sit at a desk in a corner. There the old man had to make himself deaf and blind in order not to notice the coldness, the double-edged phrases, the indifference and even the hostility of the others. Sometimes Jaramillo passed like a victor between the rows of desks to greet the "illustrious teacher". He sat down beside him and kept up a lively conversation, always inviting Don Joaquín to "give whatever orders you wish". However he actually paid no least attention even to Don Joaquín's most trifling requests or suggestions.

As time passed, the situation did not improve. The University became filled with political climbers, and Don Joaquín's position became more and more intolerable. He tried to find relief by unburdening himself to Porfirio.

"I'll not be able to endure this much longer," he said one day. "The University is full of cuckoos. I'm referring to the European type of cuckoo. You know, it lays its egg in another bird's nest, from which it steals another egg, so that the trick won't be noticed. Then, so as not to waste anything, it gobbles up the stolen egg. The young parasite hatched in a strange nest pushes his step-brothers out so that he alone will get all the food. He grows up strong and healthy at the expense of all the others."

"Haven't you taken up the matter with your influential

190

friends?"

"Yes. They tell me to be patient, that everything will work out."

"And what do you think?"

"God only knows where this new shakeup will take me. But it's best to get out of there as soon as possible. And the worst part of it is that in front of the rest Jaramillo treats me with the greatest respect and consideration. There are times when my blood boils. It did, yesterday, when he told me, 'My dear Don Joaquín, you can't imagine how I miss those days when I was only your assistant and all of the university decisions were made wisely. I feel overwhelmed, now, with my responsibilities, and that's why I appreciate your advice so much.' He said that in front of some congressmen and I felt like insulting him."

But, as Don Ursulino had foreseen, Don Joaquín's new appointment was not long in coming: he was made director of the legal department of Foreign Affairs, with the title of Vice-Minister.

Leader Augusto himself came to see him one day when passing through the university to receive the oath of allegiance from the Student Guard, and he expressed his personal satisfaction at the appointment. Dr. Jaramillo could not contain his joy. As he explained later, "The world is undergoing some very difficult times. It is always in danger of being victimized by atheism. In times such as these, the wise advice of this illustrious jurist and humanist is surely needed." This said, he gave Don Joaquín a warm embrace and took out his handkerchief to dry the tears—more imaginary than real—that presumably had started when he said, "he will leave a vacuum which will be difficult to fill in this House of Science and Letters." The President approved these expressions with his accustomed circumspection and dignity.

That very day Don Joaquín was on the verge of asking the Leader's permission to name the attorney Porfirio Uribe

191

y Moya as his assistant, but dared not. However, next day, as if he had read Valverde's mind, Leader Augusto sent him a personal note suggesting that Uribe be named personal secretary of the Vice-Minister.

Don Joaquín's situation changed very little. He was consulted only very occasionally. Now that he was in the same office with the grand old man, Porfirio could observe that the rumors of new arrests and shifts in the government disturbed Don Joaquín's seemingly imperturbable calm. Always seated, he hardly appeared to notice the coming and going of other people. However, he possessed an enormous ability for deciphering a frown, a smile, an open or shifty look, or the frank or cautious movements of one of his superiors or of some aide-de-camp. A brief glance of his hawk-like eyes discerned without fail the stool pigeon and he immediately sharpened his vigilance. Perhaps his many years of experience in the courts and the Police Department had given him his remarkable powers of perception. He had made an art of placing himself on the defensive, always on the alert for insidious or sudden attacks.

Porfirio admired Don Joaquín's skill. He had thought that after his own eight years of a hermit's life in New York no one could surpass him in observing and remaining silent, but now he took his hat off to this man whose senses had been sharpened by constant observation from the desk at which he sat. Besides, no one defended his traditional rights as a landowner with more obstinate patience than did this lame bureaucrat.

Working in such an atmosphere led Porfirio to fall in with Valverde's plans, without admitting it. When first thrust into this environment, he had felt, inevitably, a queasy disgust; but gradually he took it all as natural as breathing. It was an unforgettable school, with courses in observation, patience, and adulation.

In this peculiar situation he accepted the idea of rescuing Hortensia and began to visit the Valverdes quite often. How

192

did the girl behave towards him? She was friendly, at times coquettish, but almost always withdrawn, lost in thought, an absent look in her eyes. And she blushed whenever Jaramillo was mentioned.

Don Joaquín evidently knew more than he wanted to admit about the fate of his son. He was too sharp not to know it, but he tried to reject the truth.

Even though Porfirio liked helping Don Joaquín and even though he was fond of Hortensia, he was deeply troubled whenever he examined the most secret depths of his conscience. He found that he could not bring himself to renounce the clear possibility of climbing up the bureaucrat ladder. Perhaps he was deceiving Don Joaquín; perhaps he was deceiving himself. But for some reason or other he kept saying to himself: "My present position is just the beginning of my ascent." And he no longer knew what his next step would be.

CHAPTER

XI

Porfirio's new experiences wounded him almost physical-
ly. It was as though he were undergoing a terrible mutation,
for he had to become another kind of being in order to live
in this fear-charged atmosphere. Anxious to escape from poverty, unable to "jump over his own shadow", he now found
his desire for freedom was being frustrated.

How could those who wanted to destroy the peace and
order of the country ever succeed? The Leader would not
merely fold his arms and wait. Little by little, Porfirio became accustomed to the whispers, the silence, the absence of
laughter, the sight of armed soldiers and policemen patrol-
ling the streets.

He almost considered it an indiscretion when Don Joaquín took him into his study at home to warn him.

"What I'm going to tell you derives from my personal
experience," said Don Joaquín. "Don't misinterpret me. Go
slowly. Don't let what happened to me and what's happening to Jaramillo happen to you. They were careful to fatten
me like a pig before they sacrificed me. I'm scared at the idea
that the same thing could happen to you."

Porfirio studied the movements of the goldfish in a bowl
on the nearby table, so that Don Joaquín would not observe

the contradictory reaction his words had provoked.

"Pretty, aren't they?" observed Don Joaquín, playing along with Porfirio. "My daughter gave them to me on my birthday."

"They're beautiful," murmured Porfirio.

"Did what I say offend you?"

"How could I take offense?" said Porfirio, with compunction. "I listen to you with great respect, always."

"I was once sold to the idea that I had the right to enjoy every privilege. That was, just imagine, the tradition of the Valverdes! When Augusto came to power, I didn't adapt myself to the situation but simply handed myself over, body and soul. I thought that I'd be able to keep my property in that way. I kept my self-respect at first, but soon I was involved in an intrigue, not one of my choosing but one of Augusto's. Do you understand? From then on I ceased to be a respectable person in his eyes and became his accomplice. And as I told you before, it's not as though we Valverdes have clean hands; we committed whatever crimes we chose, without any outside interference. But for Augusto to choose my crimes for me...!"

Everything he said that night was like a mirror which he held up to Porfirio. Don Joaquín warned him about Jaramillo, his insatiable ambition, and the extremes to which he would go to satisfy it. He explained how his own downfall was initially brought about by Jaramillo.

"Rarely have I felt so helpless as when I gave him the chance to accuse me of disloyalty in front of the University office staff, I can't bear to recall it. The sad thing is that I let him exasperate me. He's the kind that knows how to 'manage' an intrigue. I must save my daughter from his influence, and you can help me. I would like to think she will remember me with kindness!"

What tortured Don Joaquín most when he considered the abominable life he had led was the idea of being an unpleasant memory in the minds of his victims. He could have been a good writer, for he had plenty of talent. But who could write with blood-stained hands?

"I remember, or rather I'm obsessed by the memory of what some poet once said: *I know that there's a beast in me; but if I kill the beast, I, too, will have to die.* As in the poem, the beast is challenging me, saying, 'Kill me! But you'll die with me.' "

He confessed that he felt very close to things. They comforted him in his loneliness, the loneliness of a man who has prostituted himself. For that reason he could not kill the beast, could not face dying with it, could not bear the idea of dying and leaving his possessions behind. The beast thrived on that love of things. And it challenged him, time and again: "Kill me, if you dare."

For the Valverdes, as for almost everyone else in this unbalanced civilization, the worst crime was illegal theft. Of course, one could rob within the law, but not against the laws which the tyranny of property had erected. There was the case of Augusto, for example, today an immensely rich man, respected and feared, a man who could be called generous, even. For Augusto, too, the worst crime was robbery; but as for the life of a man, it was of so little value, so cheap that any slight whim put it in danger.

Porfirio was surprised that a man of Don Joaquín's stamp should think like this, since he had always obeyed the urge to possess and was completely representative of this civilization based on an exhaustive and destructive drive to procure material possessions.

"From what you've said, Don Joaquín," he allowed himself to remark, "it would seem that you are now ready to kill yourself with your beast. Have I understood you correctly?"

"Very probably," replied Don Joaquín, understanding Porfirio's meaning. "But I imagine it's too late, now. Nevertheless, in a case of extreme necessity, I could perform the feat, if it meant that I would be saving young people by

196

doing so. That's why I'm telling you about my experiences and saying, 'Go slowly. If you want to, throw some scraps to the beast, amuse him, but don't let yourself be dominated by him!' "

He got up, very agitated. But as he reached for his crutches, he lost his balance, and in trying to grab something before Porfirio could spring to his rescue, knocked the fishbowl on the floor. It shattered, and the fish flipped desperately in the air.

The noise attracted Doña Rosa and Hortensia. Hortensia burst into tears when she saw the fish in their hopeless struggle against suffocation. Porfirio and Doña Rosa ran out of the room and returned with a washbowl full of water, but it was too late to revive the fish, which were now floating, their bodies inert, on the surface of the puddle of water that was spreading on the floor.

As if he understood that Hortensia was crying not merely over the fish but over many other unconfessed troubles, Don Joaquín drew her gently down on his knee and dried her tears with his handkerchief, as if she were a little girl.

"The only thing I regret in this accident," he said, "is that I've lost the present you gave me."

She seemed to interpret her father's words in another way, because she replied oddly.

"I won't oppose you any longer, Father," she said. And at his look of surprise, she added, "You know, you never wanted to have fishbowls or birdcages in the house."

"During these past few days they have entertained me a great deal."

"But I shouldn't have given them to you. I swear, I won't go against your wishes any more."

Porfirio was irresistibly impelled to visit Jacinto in the insane asylum. He found him calm, almost normal, except for the fact that he persisted in confusing Leader Augusto with the infernal deities. Nevertheless, he was sufficiently

197

rational to lower his voice whenever he referred to Augusto. Porfirio noticed that he never mentioned Hortensia, and that for the first time he spoke with reserve about Jaramillo.

As the time came for him to leave, Porfirio wondered why, after all, he had wanted to see Jacinto Brache. To become more involved than he already was? It was better to live without confronting one's conscience. The transmutation that was taking place could not be avoided, now.

"Only since I've been here," Jacinto was saying in a whisper, "have I fully realized what's going on. I'm ashamed of myself for everything I did. And all, just to please a man whose whole life is contained in his digestive tube! Just notice how that area is completely covered with medals and decorations..."

Porfirio felt it was definitely better to leave, and did so without further thought.

Once, when Jaramillo was paying a visit to his "illustrious teacher", as he put it to Don Joaquín's secretary, Porfirio noticed a look of such manifest hatred in the old man's eyes that he was intrigued. But Don Joaquín immediately forced himself to keep up appearances, and Luis acted as though he had noticed nothing.

Porfirio soon knew the reason for that flash of hatred: Don Joaquín now knew that Joaquincito had been murdered and also knew that the person directly responsible for the assassination was Jaramillo. If he said nothing on the subject, it was to keep his family from learning the facts. Besides, there was the dreadful realization that he himself had suggested that they "silence" Adrián Martín! Who would have thought that the author of those furious journalistic attacks was his own son? With infinite pain he remembered his own words: "General, we must silence a desperado named Adrián Martín." And at once Jaramillo's and Brache's trip had been arranged.

"The worst of it is," he said to Porfirio, "that they kept

me as hostage while they hunted down my own son. And
I was the one who pushed Jaramillo into his first good job!
Jacinto is just another of Jaramillo's victims. He'll tell you
about it some day: ambition dug that man's grave."

Porfirio waited for Don Joaquín to ask, "Why didn't you
tell me that you witnessed my son's death?" But the old man
asked no such question. Nor did he even inquire, "What
was the real reason for your coming to the Republic with
Jaramillo and Brache?" Don Joaquín asked no questions.
Why, then, should he, Porfirio, supply unwanted explanations?

Don Joaquín's problem was how to communicate the
terrible news to Joaquincito's mother and sister. He looked
at his hands in horror.

"Rosa doesn't know what these hands have been capable
of."

He took his crutches, left his chair, and began to limp
up and down in front of Porfirio, who was torn with pity.

"I implore you to help me," Don Joaquín said.

Porfirio found he still had the strength to remain silent.
But he averted his face.

Mass arrests and unexplained suicides again occurred.
The impending invasion of the conspirators was discussed in
whispers. Augusto gave manifest indications of alarm.

One morning after a night filled with cries of "Halt!"
when people in the streets were being searched for weapons,
the General appeared in Don Joaquín's office. He walked
slowly up to the old man's desk and greeted him kindly.

"How are you, Godfather? No, don't get up."

The General began to walk again slowly, this time
around the seated man.

"Ah, Godfather," he said at last, putting his hand on
Don Joaquín's shoulder and smiling in a flattering way.

Don Joaquín had a gripping sensation in his bowels,
followed by cold shudders, and the feeling that the contents

199

of his body were going to empty themselves in one horrible rush. But he had the strength to control himself and the courage to prevail over his hatred for the man who had so humiliated his family. To himself he said, "You think I don't know how my son died, but I do know. You'd better beware." But aloud he said nothing, merely sat there, fingering a letter-opener in the form of a small stiletto. If he had had two feet he would have jumped up, thrown himself on his enemy, and plunged the stiletto into his heart.

"Why don't you speak, Godfather? Say something!"

"General, I can't think of anything to say that would do justice to your merits."

"Ah, my beloved Don Joaquín Valverde, no one can equal you!"

Augusto's frank and almost jovial laughter relieved the tension. But Porfirio, whose desk was separated from Don Joaquín's only by a little swinging door, suddenly recalled the night when his ship had been torpedoed and the people had run in a panic across the deck, not knowing where to go. And a profane thought flashed through his mind: "Have I, for a soul, nothing but a digestive tract?" He felt as though the most incorruptible part of his being had been violated. At least he should have reared up on his hind legs like a spirited horse...But the question remained: *How to free oneself from the oppressive shadows of poverty?*

A few days later Don Joaquín's situation unexpectedly became more complicated. The Law College having invited him to speak on the Laws of the Indies, he gave a sober analysis of those statutes and nothing, in his closing speech, alluded to the Leader's wise legislation on human rights. Of course, he naturally praised the "broad knowledge" of his "illustrious teacher" as well...

Then, his brief speech over, Jaramillo found himself unexpectedly surrounded by newspapermen and let fall a spontaneous comment, which had far-reaching effects.

"I can't imagine," he said, "why Don Joaquín omitted

any mention of the great work of the Leader."

"You don't know why, Doctor?" one of the newspapermen exclaimed. "As though Valverde doesn't remember the days of General Beniquez! In those days he and his supporters were the power behind the throne. The Leader has handled him with kid gloves, and he's kept his place, but always grinding his own axe."

Jaramillo turned away from the group because he was without the least intention of provoking such a reaction. As for Don Joaquín, a vacuum had already been created around him, and now dumb with surprise, not knowing what to do, he sat still. He felt like rectifying what he had said; he might even have gone so far as to attribute the Laws of the Indies to Leader Augusto! But it was too late to turn back now. His crutches seemed to mourn at his side...

The newspapers made bitter comments on what they termed the "unpardonable omission" of the speaker. Don Joaquín replied with a public letter, filled with excuses.

That night Porfirio was unable to sleep. An unremitting rain drummed on the roof and on some tin cans below. Again and again he recalled that time when his godmother Catalina had screamed and run out into the rain. And he had an unspeakable feeling of helplessness.

When Jacinto Brache left the sanatorium, he went to live in the tower-room of his brother Sebastián's house, remaining shut in there, almost never going out except to visit Paulina.

Through consideration for Sebastián, a silent man who was, above all, a career army man, Jacinto avoided all contact with other people. His brother was really more of an empty uniform than anything else. There was thus no need to involve him in personal problems of a political nature.

The effort which he made to keep his personal problems from Sebastián turned Jacinto into a sealed fountain. Porfirio was astonished at the change he saw in Jacinto when he occasionally paid him a visit to inquire after his health. He was alarmingly thin, and Porfirio almost had to extract words from Jacinto's mouth. "He's burning up with the perpetual though repressed desire for revenge," Porfirio reflected.

Luis Jaramillo almost never visited Jacinto. Very occasionally he stopped by to excuse himself for not having paid a visit, and usually Jacinto's calls upon Paulina were made when Luis was not at home. Jacinto no longer liked to go into the streets at nightfall. With the vanishing of daylight he was assaulted by painful memories and it was then that he most lamented his cruelly mutilated artistic career and his lost love. As darkness gathered, he began to feel that his existence was a living hell. The sounds made by soldiers and policemen became louder as the shadows lengthened. Sometimes he spent the night in one long and tormenting vigil. In his ears sounded a constant succession of footsteps and voices raised in commands. Footsteps, voices, commands. Footsteps. . . .

Not wanting to upset them, Jacinto said nothing to Sebastián or to Sebastián's wife about these vigils. A dangerous concentration of ill will and frustrations began to build up in his consciousness, which became an inferno. And at the bottom of this inferno was Hortensia. Porfirio was afraid that Jacinto, driven by an irresistible compulsion, might suddenly decide to confront the infernal deities.

Paulina also noticed her brother's dangerous mental derangement. In order to counteract his state of mind, she gave him phonograph records of masterworks, thinking they might rescue him from the vortex of his unchecked hallucinations.

At times Porfirio was tempted to ask Hortensia what had happened between her and Jacinto, but she always avoided the subject. Indeed, she never mentioned her former fiancé. In addition, she had stopped seeing Paulina. And she tried to stay away from Jaramillo, although she continued to fulfill her political obligations.

This new state of things did not pass unnoticed by Jaramillo. He talked to her whenever he had an opportunity, in a fraternal way, as he said, speaking in a low, vibrant voice, looking into her eyes. Sometimes he gave her poems and sometimes even recited them, giving them clearly intimate implications. When the girl left his side it was to go somewhere to cry, alone, in silence.

Although she was never very explicit with him, Hortensia was obviously beginning timidly to seek refuge in Porfirio's friendship. She now went to welcome him at the door and stayed to talk with him, when he came to call upon her father. And Doña Rosa and Don Joaquín left them alone together. Porfirio was aware that he should not try to hurry up their engagement. She would first have to overcome certain painful emotions, would have to conquer her feeling of repressed animosity towards Paulina, and banish the thought that Luis Jaramillo could ever have loved her.

She was mutely determined to keep her promise not to oppose her father's wishes any more. The recent attacks of the press against Don Joaquín Valverde had unnerved the family, but the defamation campaign ended when the Leader extended a cordial invitation to Don Joaquín to visit him at the Palace.

As Porfirio left the office one afternoon he saw, to his great surprise, Juan Lorenzi standing in front of the National Palace. Overjoyed, Porfirio welcomed him warmly. At that moment Lorenzi represented freedom. Perhaps the adventurer could rescue him from the labyrinth in which he was caught. And, he reflected, "Who better than Juan Lorenzi could be best man at my wedding?"

"Well, well, how are you, brother?" asked Lorenzi, using Alfredo Laza's peculiar greeting.

"I'll tell you all about it."

He had learned to look about him discreetly to see if anyone were watching. Yes, there were soldiers and policemen nearby.

"They're watching us," he said in a low voice.

"Don't worry! On personal orders of the General, a guard of honor escorted me shortly after noon from my hotel to the Palace. They already know me."

"Not even an ambassador receives such treatment!"

"Well, that's what I thought I was when I received Augusto's cordial invitation this morning. At such moments I become solemn and imagine that I'm a special envoy from the President of my country."

"Since when is our country a Republic?"

"It's no crime to dream." He lowered his voice: "Not even here."

"All right, Mr. Ambassador, what did the President of the Republic want to see you about?"

"I told you in New York that he and I are old friends. Do you know how many quarts of good liquor I've brought him? And not long ago I got some caviar for him, right in the middle of the war."

"How do you dare to travel in wartime?"

"Many people ask me that. I like to challenge danger, but what I want to happen never does."

"What you want to happen!"

"Yes. I wish a submarine would come up suddenly from the bottom of the sea. Do you know what I'd do? I'd fire on it with my little deck cannon to see if it would retaliate and sink me. But as I said, the wished-for never happens. No matter how much I defy death, it always eludes me. How many times do you think I've been in danger from sharks both in and out of the water? But nothing ever happened, when I was working outside the law. Who knows, now that I'm working within the law, events may take another turn."

"I gather the smuggling affair worked out well."

"They couldn't prove anything. On account of the war there's a great need in Puerto Rico for mahogany, so I left to tempt danger with the blessing of the authorities. I also promised to take back any food stuffs I can pick up. We'll see."

"You haven't told me how things went in the Palace."

"It's hard for Augusto to obtain machines for his personal use on his ranches, and I think I can get some for him. He still has his old passion for good liquors, machines and cars. We talk about that and about the mahogany trade."

"He didn't allude to the situation...?"

"The political situation? No. The General never talks politics. He runs a country basking in order and peace. The only people who think they hear the rumble of revolution in this country are foreigners."

"Are you serious?"

"I'm only repeating what a brother of the General told me."

Discouraged at Lorenzi's disconcerting attitude, Porfirio tried to change the conversation by asking for news of his friends in New York.

"It's been some time since I saw Doña Isabel," said Lorenzi. "You knew that Rosana only lived with Alfredo a few months, didn't you? Then she took to drink and knocked herself out. She was hospitalized for a while. After her cure, she stayed on there, as a student nurse."

"It was bound to happen."

Yes, it was bound to happen; not because Alfredo Laza was a bad sort, but because he lived only for revolutionary causes. Rosana could never stand to be alone, and Laza's absences would convince her that he did not love her. She would tell no one of her unhappiness, not even her own mother. And so, alone, thinking she was abandoned, she would begin to drink.

According to Lorenzi, Laza gave up painting and neglected his meetings while she was in the hospital. He got a job. He visited her every day. But when she recovered her health Alfredo was unable to persuade her to go back to him. The sight of all those sick people in the hospital had

205

made her want to take up nursing.

"I'm surprised that Doña Isabel...You know, she always wanted Rosana to take the veil."

"We human beings change more than we like to admit."

Doña Isabel had changed a great deal. She no longer spoke bitterly of her husband, no longer referred to the former grandeur of her family, no longer tried to persuade her daughter to become a nun. She consoled herself for everything by believing that everything that had happened to herself and others was a punishment for misdeeds committed in another life, far beyond the point where memory begins. She no longer complained of having to do servant's work in her boarding house; she was eager to humble herself and was ready to wash the feet of the unfortunates, as did Jesus Christ. She was so sure that the end of her life was approaching that her one burning desire was to show a good record for this life and reduce to silence the complaining and misty figures beyond the grave. This unexpected dedication separated her a little from her daughter. "Let her live her life as she chooses," she had said. She now realized that she had been very mistaken in trying to force a religious life upon Rosana. She had worried and suffered over her daughter's behavior, over Laza's irresponsible neglect, but believed it was all fore-ordained. When she had visited her daughter in the hospital, however, she merely expressed the hope that the girl would turn away from a life of sin. And she approved Rosana's decision to become a nurse.

All this seemed very strange to Porfirio, because he had only known the "other" Doña Isabel. But, as Lorenzi had said, "We human beings change more than we like to admit."

They had been walking aimlessly through the town as Lorenzi talked, and the sea was now in sight.

"Let's go down to the beach," Porfirio suggested. "Afterward, I invite you to have supper with me."

"And I accept."

206

They continued their conversation on the beach. In spite of Porfirio's old grudge, he felt he could trust Lorenzi, could confess himself. And how he wanted to relieve his soul!

"In New York," he said, "I was caught in a labyrinth of poverty and non-conformity and tried to liberate myself with a formal education. That's what happens to us Puerto Ricans. We think we can find freedom by that road, even when the education we receive is foreign to us. In Puerto Rico we're stuck in a dead-end street. We don't know ourselves. We're tortured by the agony of not having any past or any future, by the awareness of our own smallness. We're cramped in a very narrow present. That's our great misfortune."

"I had no idea that you ever thought about such things."

"Here in the Republic I've done more thinking than ever before. Unable to talk aloud, one thinks more. Shall I confess something to you? The idea that I was escaping the labyrinth was sheer hallucination. You can't imagine how glad I am to see you, Lorenzi. I'm hoping you'll be able to help me leave this country."

"But I've told you I'm a personal friend of the Leader. I have exclusive rights to the mahogany trade, thanks to him. I can't do anything illegal."

Again Lorenzi's words were disconcerting. Porfirio regretted having spoken so frankly, and began to mistrust Lorenzi. Yes, he would have to proceed more cautiously in the future. The slightest indiscretion could cost him a lot. Was it possible that Lorenzi was a devotee of Leader Augusto?

"I ought to tell you," Lorenzi added, "that very soon I'll be going into the interior, on business."

Porfirio felt like asking Lorenzi to take him along, but refrained from expressing the wish. Secretly he admired this free man, captain and owner of a good schooner, a smuggler when he wanted to be, facing death calmly, always doing whatever he liked. Porfirio was no longer concerned with the

Lorenzi of the past, the young man with the motorcycle and the convertible, the cheeky individual in the adoration of women. Even so, he still felt like humiliating Lorenzi.

"Rosana turned me down," he said.

"You liked her, eh?"

"A lot. She also turned you down, though."

"That's true," said Lorenzi, irritated. "But why say it in that tone of voice? You never did like me much, did you?"

"For a long time I disliked you."

"Well, I'll admit, I was pretty stuck on myself," said Lorenzi. "I'd always had all the women I wanted, and no strings attached. I liked to play the field. That's why my pride was hurt when Rosana turned me down. You're right. For a while I thought I must be getting old, but I got over it. At first I wondered what special quality Alfredo had that I didn't have. Was it because he was an artist and a bohemian? 'I'm as much a man as he is,' I told myself. Then I finally understood that Rosana loved Alfredo the way he was, and you can't argue against that kind of thing."

"Yes, but women..."

"What about women? Generally speaking, a woman is what her man makes her. Since I haven't been the type of man who ties himself down to a home with a wife and children, I've never cultivated my women. Instead, I've appealed to their primal instincts. I've never talked to women about security and I've never liked to show them off, like an institution, to my friends. I don't discuss things with them, I don't introduce them to my relatives. I avoid becoming too involved. I like to see them as naked as when they came into the world, defenseless, trembling and panting in my grasp. Who remembers institutions or civilization at a time like that? I don't completely satisfy them, but I conquer them. While I desire them I just give them samples, whet their appetites, so they'll follow me. I never offer them anything that might tie me to them. 'Love me as I am,' I say to them. You don't know how surprised I was when Rosana

208

dropped me. I must have been failing in my old age, for I even proposed marriage to her! That's the lowest I've ever descended!"

Listening to Lorenzi talk, Porfirio felt very dissatisfied with himself because of his bad luck with women. He had never been the type of man who could treat women as Lorenzi did.

"In Coamo," recalled Juan Lorenzi, "I always had my way with my father. Getting things so easily did me a great deal of harm. That's why I didn't become a doctor and why I never appreciated anything, really. Later I wanted to do difficult things. I defied the law, I defied death. But everything always turned out well. It's a bore. And boredom is torture. I can imagine how bored the Leader must be, always getting everything he wants so easily." He lowered his voice and added, mysteriously, "Later on I'll tell you something very important. I'm tempted to relieve the Leader's boredom."

Porfirio looked at him in alarm. Lorenzi smiled and changed the subject.

"Come, let's talk about women," he said. "Wouldn't you like to know more about Rosana? In my opinion, she failed in her marriage because she played the role of a Cassandra too much and tried to keep Alfredo out of the streets. Having a witch for a wife must be pretty dreadful, and even more so when she tries to take her husband away from his friends. Alfredo is a man of the street, yet at the same time rather superstitious. He lives for his ideals. And on top of all that, he's an artist. She could neither follow him nor endure living alone. Easy to see why they broke up."

After a pause, Lorenzi again spoke mysteriously.

"Alfredo couldn't tie himself down to Rosana while he had a mission ahead of him. And now the time has come..." He checked himself.

These interruptions and veiled allusions were exasperating!

"I say, Uribe!" Lorenzi exclaimed, then. "Did you know they've dug up the Adrián Martín case again? He turned out to be a newspaperman whose real name was Joaquín Valverde. He was the son of a distinguished Santiagan family. I suspected as much. What do they say about it here?"

"Nothing," was all Porfirio would say.

"According to the latest reports, they've traced the crime to some consular agents. Their names aren't yet known."

"Who could the killer have been!" exclaimed Porfirio with assumed indifference.

"We'll soon know. What about going back to your room, now?"

"Let's go."

"But what about supper first?"

"As you like."

"Is it safe for us to talk here? asked Lorenzi, that night as they entered Porfirio's room.

"As long as you don't raise your voice..."

"Good. I've two commendations for you: a 'live letter' and a written message, both from Alfredo. Want to begin with the letter he wrote?"

"Yes. But first, let me lock the door."

The letter was short and cryptic:

> "My friend Julio Antonio Cruzado once told me that success is not to be measured by the way one ends up, but by the way one influences others. I got married, finally. I hope to influence you by my example. Or perhaps you're already married?
> The years pass. We should do something lasting. Life won't wait for us."

"But didn't you say that Rosana and Alfredo are separated?"

Lorenzi went to the door, tried the lock, returned.

"Are you sure we can't be overheard?"

210

"No if we speak in low voices like this."

"All right. Well, now, here's the 'live letter', the explanation of that message. Alfredo's real marriage was to the revolutionary idea of the invasion. Well, I, too, have got married. Very soon our plans will become a reality. The preparations are under way."

Porfirio was greatly alarmed. "They're abusing my friendship," he reflected. "They have no right to get me mixed up in this." He felt ready to faint, and threw himself on his bed. "Why do I have to sacrifice everything because of some crazy ideas of others?" he asked himself. "When they try to involve me in this, they're not treating me as a friend. What has Alfredo ever done except to conspire and live like a bohemian? While I was studying, he was in jail. And now that I'm on my way up, along comes this supposed friend to. . ."

Was he, Porfirio Uribe, such an idiot that they all took it into their heads to confide in him? As if he were incapable of informing on them to assure his own safety! Why should he be expected to act like a sealed repository for others' plots? First it was Jacinto Brache. Why? Then Don Joaquín. Why? And now Alfredo Laza and Juan Lorenzi. . . Oh no, he wouldn't sacrifice himself so cheaply! He'd show them he wasn't so stupid. He'd go to the authorities and reveal this plot against the Leader! No one need know of his denunciation. Neither Brache nor Valverde nor Laza nor Lorenzi. No one. The Leader would pay him well and have confidence in him. He would go far. That was why he had studied, needless to say. *A Minister*. Involuntarily he held up his hands and looked at them. By some strange mutation they were turning into claws. . . Terrified, he looked at Lorenzi. Then he sat up and put the letter in his pocket. Malevolently, he remained silent.

"Well, what do you say?" asked Lorenzi.

Again he looked at Lorenzi with mixed feelings of terror and wounded self-esteem.

211

"But what do you all take me for?" he asked. "Doesn't it occur to you that I could turn you in?"

"To anyone else, I'd say 'I'll kill you'. But not to you. You're not that kind of person. Right now you feel as though I'd pulled the ground out from under your feet. I understand. You want things you've never had. You've not wakened up to what's going on in this troubled world. I want to tell you...well, maybe I'm not quite awake, either. I've always been too much in love with myself to think about anything else. But I don't desire things. It was easy for Alfredo to persuade me because I like to take risks and it would give me a kick to relieve Augusto of the torture of his boredom. And also because I'm on the decline and I'd like to leave some good deed behind me. Or, I don't know..."

"But you haven't the right..."

"Yes, I do have the right. Remember your acrobat parents, remember Estefano and Catalina. Haven't you seen anything here that turns your stomach? You've seen nothing? No persecutions, no abuses, no searches in the middle of the street...? I've been here only one day and I've seen plenty. The people who live here must have seen hundreds of incidents. The monster is running loose in this beautiful country. He must he hunted down!"

The entire world Porfirio had dreamed of came tumbling in ruins about him. He sat up in bed again, dazed. And Lorenzi laughed as though nothing were happening!

"There's nothing better than challenging your own fear," Lorenzi exclaimed. "How many times have I been afraid! Do you remember the story of the shark's fin that followed me when I swam from my boat to the beach? I felt two kinds of fear. Fear of the bullets that would welcome me when I reached land, fear of the shark behind me. Brother, what emotion!"

Porfirio was in no mood to listen to Lorenzi's stories.

"I really don't understand..."

212

"Uribe, I had orders not to say anything to you, unless I noticed something in your behavior to indicate that you'd support us. Well, I noticed it. Weeks, perhaps months will pass before the final decision is made. I've got to travel through the Republic, meet groups of rebels. I've brought the codes with me. The mahogany trade will cover up my activities. We don't ask much from you, nothing that could get you in trouble. But what we ask is something important: we need certain information that you can give me."

Noticing Porfirio's reluctance, he added, "You don't have to accept at once. Think it over. Now you know what it's all about, burn that paper. I don't have to tell you, whether or not you agree to work with us, keep our secret. You were the first person we thought of."

For the first time a shining thought occurred to Porfirio: he existed in the memories of generous people.

CHAPTER

XII

Yes, he existed in the memories of Laza and Lorenzi, and it gave him satisfaction to know this. But on the other hand it was mortifying that they should take advantage of his generosity, as if disputing his right to live his life as he pleased. True, he was incapable of informing on anyone; but why did they have to settle this point for him? No, he was not an informer; but neither was he a conspirator.

Did he have to concede that the world's problems could be settled with the ideas of Alfredo Laza or Juan Lorenzi? Why did he have to support an invasion to overthrow the regime for which he worked? He had resolved to obtain some of this life's comforts by selling his professional services to the highest bidder, and he was determined to keep that resolution.

Besides, Lorenzi's attitude was irritating. He did not consider all the consequences of this political adventure, but instead plunged ahead as if merely engaged in another feat of smuggling. Tossing it all off as a joke, Juan Lorenzi was now referring to the charmed life he led:

"I have a personality which acts like a lightning rod, grounding all evil currents. They'll not get me with their thunder-bolts! The fact that I've decided to keep in with the Leader while the invasion is being prepared should show you that I have good sound sense, though I may appear to be mad. I have complete freedom to travel all over the Republic, which will give me the opportunity to contact all of the rebels by means of the codes we've set up. Your reports can be very useful to me."

Porfirio said nothing. Lorenzi winked knowingly and went on talking, this time about other things.

"I know you'll end up, Uribe, by marrying Hortensia. Whether you marry her tomorrow or next week, be sure you never tell her anything. Women may be able to keep a secret as well as men, but they have an inclination to share their secrets with quite a few other women! And by the way, I've also noticed that Don Joaquín acts scared. I believe he'd do anything to regain the Leader's favor. You'd think, from the way he acts, that he's forgotten all about the death of his son."

Next day Lorenzi left the capital for the interior of the Republic, with Augusto's personal safe-conduct pass. When he returned, a week later, he spoke with Porfirio again.

"Our agents all over the country are becoming impatient," he said. "We'll have to speed up the attack. The truth is that it's already getting difficult to keep it secret. And this puts the friendly country that's protecting us in a bad position."

He had extracted no promise from Porfirio, but apparently he considered it a foregone conclusion that his cooperation with the conspirators could be counted on...

Dr. Jaramillo was now in a key position: he had been made editor of the official newspaper, the government mouthpiece. Since former editors of that paper had gone on to occupy high positions in one or another of the ministries, everyone said that he was on the way up, that he would soon be an ambassador.

Again, he wanted Hortensia to work for him. Don Joaquín and Doña Rosa stubbornly opposed the idea, and at first Hortensia was far from eager, but after Jaramillo had urged her in an intimate tone, assuming the air of a man who was misunderstood, she agreed to his proposition. To avoid appearing in a suspicious light, her parents had no alternative but to yield to the inevitable.

Jacinto Martínez was now an inseparable friend of Jaramillo. Martínez wrote sociological articles containing enthusiastic appraisals of Augustoism, which were published in the official newspaper. "I arrived here, fleeing from tyranny," he affirmed, "and found peace in this admirable country."

Martínez, Jaramillo and other enthusiastic supporters of the Leader met almost every night in the Hotel Atlantico. Naturally, aside from rather frivolous topics of a more or less esthetic nature, they discussed ways and means of exalting the Leader's wise rule.

Invited by Jaramillo, Porfirio occasionally attended these reunions, which gave him his first opportunity to observe Jacinto Martínez at close range. Martínez was a pale, chubby individual with a large moustache. He spoke with deliberation, heavily sarcastic regarding any possible opponent, oozin flattery whenever he referred to the Leader, and was always ready to attack savagely anyone in a precarious political situation. Porfirio sized up Martínez as being a man who would delight in pushing anyone over a cliff, particularly anyone struggling frantically to keep his balance. But how prodigal he was with subtle and suave remarks, whenever the Leader was mentioned! Naturally, those who attended these reunions knew that Martínez was the personal friend and counselor of the President. And indeed, Martínez had a good nose for smelling out and anticipating the desires of his protector. Porfirio noticed immediately that Martínez was able to tolerate the abuses of powerful people, although punctilious on questions of honor when they concerned men of little influence.

Jacinto Martínez had in fact become an imposing personage, an expert in all the arts and sciences, a past master in the art of consent. Porfirio noted that Jaramillo was trying to discover Martínez's "Achilles' heel". Yes, it was obvious that the foreigner was fascinated by power. But above all things, the Leader's anger must not be provoked; that would be dangerous.

Luis Jaramillo resolved to use Martínez's influence, and in the pages of his newspaper he tried to hypnotize him. Nevertheless, he grew increasingly more jealous of the confidence which Augusto placed in Martínez. At times Porfirio was amused to observe the subtle wiles which Jaramillo employed in this silent struggle for influence.

Martínez often alluded to sexual episodes. When Jaramillo became aware of this he felt sure that sex was the Achilles' heel of his rival and at once began to sharpen his arrows.

Sometimes days and even weeks passed when Paulina had no opportunity to talk with her husband. He arrived at home late at night and had taken to sleeping in a room that had a private entrance.

As always, she occupied herself with prayers, sewing, and household tasks, while he was absent, presumably at his office. Occasionally she listened to good music on records with Jacinto. But throughout the night and throughout the next morning her anguished thoughts were concentrated upon one sole idea: how to win back her husband, how to manage things so that she might talk to him and hear him talk to her. But he always managed to elude her, and her anxiety increased. She now regarded herself as being what Luis obviously considered her: an abominable creature. She had ceased to think of herself as the victim of horrible circumstances; the sole guilty person was herself. Her solitude and isolation increased after Jaramillo became editor of the newspaper, for quite often he did not come home at night, but slept in a hotel room near his office, or went out with his friends, Martínez and others.

Jaramillo was, in fact, trying to make Paulina ask him

217

for a divorce. He was also trying to avoid Jacinto Brache, being worried over the publicity now being given the Adrián Martín case which was again filling the newspapers in the United States. His gallantries to Hortensia had initially been an element in the role he was playing, but gradually he had been actually drawn to her, as a result of her silent adoration.

Hortensia, for her part, had tried to fight her strong attraction to Luis, but had finally succumbed. However, there was no happiness for her in this love; she could never quite forget her conduct towards Jacinto or her betrayal of Paulina or the inevitable sorrow she caused Don Joaquín. And so she implored Jaramillo not to make their love public until he had obtained a legal separation from Paulina. The situation between them at the office was tense. When he approached her to give orders and she felt his breath on the nape of her neck, her hands turned cold.

In spite of Hortensia's efforts to keep up appearances in her relations with Porfirio, he immediately noticed what was happening. There were a number of trifling incidents which, added up, gave him the way to her real feelings, and he resolved to visit the Valverde home less frequently.

Finally the news was being whispered about. Even Paulina heard about it, in her isolation. From then on, after nightfall, she spent hour after hour by a shuttered window, always hoping to see Luis arrive, and although more often than not he did not put in an appearance, she did not lose hope.

Porfirio felt that the situation relieved him of his promises to Valverde. But now, even less than before, was he inclined to lend any aid to the conspiracy for a revolutionary invasion. Lorenzi's absence in Puerto Rico bolstered him in this attitude. Relations between Don Joaquín and Porfirio gradually became restricted to their contacts in the course of official duties.

One night when Hortensia had been escorted home by

218

Jaramillo, Don Joaquín, after that gentleman had left, begged his daughter to break off the friendship, which was putting her in a very bad light. Without answering her father, she walked on towards her room.

"Come here!" he shouted, exasperated.

She turned, defiant.

"I'm going to marry him!"

"He's already married, don't you realize that?"

"If I can't be his wife. . . ."

Her father, beside himself with rage, would not allow her to finish the phrase.

"He's your brother's murderer!" he shouted.

"What's that?" screamed Doña Rosa.

When the full revelation had been made, Don Joaquín sank into a chair, exhausted. Hortensia knelt before her father and in tears sought the comfort of his embrace, with the simplicity of a child. It was then, on her knees, that she made up her mind not to return to her work in the newspaper office but to consider the possibility of entering a convent.

Jaramillo, soon acquainted with all this, was enraged, but Don Ursulino, at Don Joaquín's suggestion, persuaded him to accept the situation without seeking revenge.

As always, he yielded to Don Ursulino's advice, but he never returned to Paulina.

It was in this period that Jacinto Martínez was given twenty-four hours to leave the country. His crime? He had been found in the house of a lady who happened to be the mistress of an important general, a brother of the Leader. Completely altered, trembling with fear, Martínez went to Jaramillo to ask him to intercede for him with the Leader.

"You introduced me to her, and you never warned me of her alliance with the General! Had I known she was his mistress. . . ."

"I didn't know it myself," replied Jaramillo, all in-

219

nocence, and seemingly deeply affected.

"It was a terrible mistake, Luis."

"It could have happened to me, Jacinto."

Martínez knew that his friend was lying, but it was no time to give way to anger. Jaramillo promised he would intervene personally in behalf of Martínez, and on this promise they parted.

Of course, Martínez would have to leave the country anyway, but Jaramillo felt that this affair gave him a magnificent opportunity to get closer to the Leader.

Now returned from his trip to Puerto Rico, Juan Lorenzi met and began to associate with Dr. Luis Jaramillo. Juan knew from the beginning that Luis objected to his presence but realized this was no time to acquire new enemies. In private talk with the Leader Juan praised Jaramillo warmly, and very soon afterwards casually acquainted him with what had been said in this conversation.

"Man, I didn't know the Leader regarded you so highly," he told Jaramillo. "I took occasion to tell him that in my opinion you would be a good servant of the Republic in no matter what position. Would you like to go to the General's country house one of these days? He's invited me, and told me I could bring along a good friend. I hope you can accompany me."

It was all true, although perhaps the Leader did not expect Lorenzi to show up with Jaramillo. But it was sufficient that the choice had been made by Juan Lorenzi, who was such an expert in horses and cars. It could immediately be seen that the General held Juan Lorenzi in high esteem. Augusto was attracted by the jovial and adventurous character of a man who was not interested in power. Lorenzi never asked him for anything. On the contrary, he disinterestedly offered his services. It had been Augusto himself who offered Lorenzi the exclusive rights to the mahogany trade. And Lorenzi had accepted it, he said, to please the

General. Yes, Augusto appreciated the spontaneous generosity of his friend, who offered whatever he had without asking for anything in return. Recently, for instance, Lorenzi had even told him that he would put his skills and his schooner at the service of the Republic during the present crisis, if need be.

"Aren't you afraid that something unpleasant might happen to you?" Augusto had asked.

"Nothing ever happens to me. You'll see, I never have an accident," Lorenzi had replied, quite naturally, without boasting.

Luis Jaramillo realized that the friendship of a man such as Juan Lorenzi could be of great help to him, and the invitation to the Leader's country home so pleased him that he could not thank Lorenzi enough.

"Be careful," Porfirio warned Lorenzi. "You don't know who you're associating with."

"I know very well who Jaramillo is. From this moment on he'll be watching for my weakness, to betray me. Didn't you see what he did to Jacinto Martínez? He's done the same to many others. I'm forewarned. I'll be under his closest observation. I'm quite aware of it. The minute he thinks that nothing lies between him and his goal, the General's confidence, he'll take advantage of my weakness to climb on up. I don't doubt that in the least. But I don't intend to give him the chance. I have no ambitions, I want nothing. Perhaps I'll give him the General's confidence in order to flatter him while at the same time fulfilling my mission. It may be that when he's almost reached his goal his own ambition will betray him."

"But that's very risky."

"So it is. Didn't you tell me that Brache calls him Bellerophon? Well, between us, the General knows him by that name. Do you know what Augusto told me after that day in the country? Get set for a surprise. He said, 'Friend Lorenzi, I never forget that Jaramillo belongs to a family that offended my family. Our little Doctor is clever. He always does whatever I ask him to, without hesitation. If he had to sacrifice his wife or his mother, if she were alive, he'd do it. That's the way he is. At times he impresses me, because he's intelligent. Besides, I like clever people, when they serve me without question. It's good for me to have a Jaramillo or a Valverde in my service...Don't laugh, it's true...But I can't forget that he should be called Bellerophon. They say he's pursued the Amazons and the Chimera and is now knocking on the gates of Olympus. Perhaps he'll reach the antechamber...He's a Jaramillo who would like to try to replace an old Cachola.' When I ventured to suggest to Augusto that he let Jaramillo into the antechamber, at least, he replied that such a thing would be Jaramillo's ruin. It wouldn't surprise anyone to see Dr. Luis Jaramillo enjoying the Leader's confidence at any time now."

Lorenzi had noticed that Jaramillo had a strange predilection for perfumes and rare liquors, so he brought him some from Saint Thomas and San Martín. More than once he feasted him like a prince on board his schooner, knowing that Luis Jaramillo liked to spend his time on soft cushions and being served by young men. That and his ambition were his great weaknesses. He let no others show, and he even knew how to dissimulate those that did show. But he had met more than his equal in Juan Lorenzi, who associated with anyone he cared to and who had no disproportionate love for material possessions. Lorenzi bedazzled him, and Jaramillo was soon caught in the web of flattery.

All this happened before the very eyes of Porfirio, who already had reason to believe that Lorenzi was an exceptional being. And the mere fact that Lorenzi so highly esteemed Porfirio Uribe was enough to enlist Jaramillo's respect for the silent little lawyer, who never seemed to become too involved with anyone.

Then came Luis Jaramillo's promotion to the post formerly occupied by Jacinto Martínez. Speaking of it to Lorenzi, Jaramillo let slip a confession.

"I'm honored with the post, and I owe it all to you," he said. "But I can't forget that Martínez went from here to exile, poor fellow. I realize I'll have to be careful, although I don't believe they'd exile me."

He bit his lip, immediately regretting having made these remarks.

"You're quite right," commented Lorenzi. "And if I can ever be of any service to you, count on me."

Jaramillo expressed his most fervent gratitude, but Lorenzi noticed that he was very ill at ease.

It was horrible, Porfirio reflected in one of his relapses into discouragement, having one's personal security depend upon the decision of one sole man. One moment he was riding on top of the world, the next moment in the depths of despair. It made his head swim.

He had learned to read the political situation in the expression and attitudes of the people around him, which reflected the jubilation or fears of the Leader; and these were days of recurrent fears. When Porfirio wanted some situation explained, he sought out certain people, not to question them—no one would talk—but to observe them. Don Joaquín had become a prickly cactus of silence in a parched wilderness of mind and soul. Jaramillo, dangerously deranged by this ambition for power, was already striking the first blows on the gates of Olympus, keeping a jealous eye on the incomprehensible friendship between Lorenzi and the Leader. The Leader was exerting himself to make everyone believe the myth he had created about himself. Hortensia was poised on the brink of disaster; Paulina had finally accepted her home as her tomb; Jacinto was a fuse already burning...

Porfirio tried in vain to establish contact with these beings, but only met with bitter defeat. What then could he do? What inner comfort did he derive from serving the

Leader? Must he forever be dominated by the tyrannous need to possess? Must he let his life be crushed under the weight of this world's goods which the monster threw at him?

For the first time he began to suspect that happiness lay elsewhere than in the satisfaction found in study, in occupying a good position, in showing off one's influence, in bemusing oneself with superstitious myths. He envied men like Alfredo Laza, who had pledged himself to a life of heroic action and scoffed at a civilization founded on the cult of property. Part gay bohemian, part madman, Alfredo Laza, instead of hunting lions in the depths of Africa, proposed to hunt a monster at large in a beautiful tropical land of the Caribbean. A feat worthy of the old heroes of Greek mythology! And this contemporary monster thought of himself as living in Olympus.

Porfirio also envied Juan Lorenzi, even though he had only come to the Republic to relieve the Leader of his great boredom. Because he did not aspire to possess anything and had nothing to lose or to gain, the impenitent adventurer had attacked Bellerophon himself at the very roots of his ambition. When Porfirio studied Juan Lorenzi closely and looked beneath the surface into his friend's mind and soul, he saw something worth seeing, and which made him feel like renouncing the scraps of paper he had earned while working in the Dead Letter Section, and becoming a humble assistant to Lorenzi on board *La Barracuda*.

Yet no, there was no reason why he should serve the conspiracy. Far better do nothing but sail the seas, catching big fish and trading in foods, having a woman in every port, laughing at the power-hungry, scoffing at the poor myths created by political superstition. That would suffice, that would really be living! Disconcerted, breathing an atmosphere of insecurity, he felt himself gradually emptied of life: the sap was running out through some unsuspected gash.

He said nothing of this and made no suggestion to Juan Lorenzi, but simply let himself be swayed by the Captain of *La Barracuda,* coming gradually to realize that he was ready to collaborate in the revolutionary invasion which was being organized. Lorenzi kept him informed.

"There are trusted agents in the interior," he said, "and other agents are frequently arriving at night. We must make contacts with them and provide them with the information they need."

Porfirio said nothing; he accepted the fact.

"We must obtain a wide range of useful information about troop movements, arrests, searches, the Leader's intentions," Lorenzi went on.

Porfirio said nothing; he merely accepted.

"We'll have to study Augusto's personal movements carefully and learn to recognize his spies. We want him alive. He arouses as much curiosity in people as the Abominable Snowman of Tibet. He's dangerous, is utterly unscrupulous, and pays his agents well."

Porfirio said nothing; he merely accepted.

"They're on the alert. We must split up their troops with false rumors and make the Leader look ridiculous. There's a sad, rotten heart under that armor plate of medals."

Porfirio said nothing: he merely accepted.

"Do you realize that fomenting strikes would help a great deal? If we can distract their attention it will allow us to distribute arms all over the Republic. And there will be just one cry. A secret government has already been formed, which will take over as soon as the signal is given. We'll have to start learning which of the key men and officers are discontented, but we'll have to move cautiously."

Was his little law degree any good to him? No? Then he should conspire, and thus save Alfredo Laza's life when he landed. Laza's experience as a soldier in the United States Army would be good for something—he had wanted to learn the use of weapons before going to jail.

225

"We must defy the devil right in his own hell and carry out a sudden, well coordinated *coup* both from within and without. We must divide the enemy, divide, divide! We must destroy myths, and overthrow Augusto! That's our job! Forward, march!"

Even though he had a safe-conduct pass from the Leader himself, Lorenzi, at Leader Augusto's own suggestion, was always accompanied on his travels. Wherever he went, some army officer, usually Sebastián Brache, was with him.

Lorenzi made no comments on what he saw, but was astounded at the terrible poverty of the countryside. It was even more surprising when contrasted with the fabulous appearance of the capital, a city of great buildings and palatial hotels.

At times, when Brache went to the barracks or to the home of a friend, Lorenzi had a chance to talk secretly with one or two of the agents of the conspiracy. The leaders of the movement had given him a list of names of persons who could be trusted. He memorized the names and addresses and after he had located them he communicated with them by code. Some were persons who had recently landed at various points on the island under the protection of night and friendly fishermen.

The revolt had to be organized hurriedly, which meant that Lorenzi had little time to spend in properly concealing his activities. He knew the risks he ran, but he held some strong cards: his personal friendship with the Leader, his above-board business affairs, his personal charm, his intelligence and, above all, his self-confidence and audacity.

Lorenzi also knew that he was accompanied by a man who had the Leader's complete confidence: Lieutenant Sebastián Brache of the Palace Guard, a man of few words, who never alluded to his sister Paulina's marital troubles or to his brother Jacinto's insanity. Only once did he mention Jacinto, and then merely to say, "Jacinto could have been a great musician, a concert artist. His mind became slightly unbalanced when he lost that finger." Nothing more. And nothing, absolutely nothing about Paulina.

Nor did Lorenzi ever try to draw him out. Their conversation usually consisted of laudatory remarks about features of the Leader's government. Lorenzi could see that Brache was repressing a great desire to communicate with someone. He pretended not to notice. He waited.

Juan Lorenzi had a pretty fair knowledge of Augusto's character. He knew that Augusto had developed a sixth sense for smelling out conspirators, with whom he was ruthless. Were he to discover that his friend Lorenzi was plotting against him, he would see to it that Lorenzi "disappeared". Lorenzi was aware that his very friendship with the Leader made him vulnerable, for Augusto trusted no one and even had his most intimate friends watched closely. Indeed, the Leader's intimate circle of friends was little more than a chain of spies spying upon one another. To counter this, one had to become a master of deception. The most trivial act or comment could be misinterpreted. Often an arrested man was sincerely unaware of the reason for his arrest. Everyone was vulnerable, for the unseen informer was everywhere, and a small personal grudge might well bring on a spate of terrible repressive measures.

There were many mirrors in which Lorenzi could see himself. Valverde's case was one. Don Joaquín Valverde had not only been trusted by the Leader, but had also helped plan crimes, among them, unknowingly, the assassination of his own son. Accused of having helped the Niño escape from the country, his prestige as a judge had not saved him from a short jail sentence. And from that time onward he had not had one moment of peace. He had become an invisible man; no one wanted to see him. People passed by him as if he were non-existent, and he had let himself be enclosed in a strange bubble of silence. Indeed, had it not been for Augusto's superstitious belief that their destinies were linked, Valverde would in fact have ceased to exist.

It was almost incredible to observe how the Leader's blessings inflated the worth of his favorites. Everyone talked about the genius and the wisdom of those men. However, when the Leader withdrew his blessing, the wise man and the genius disappeared as if by magic. Don Joaquín Valverde had been a wise man and a genius; now he was an invisible man. Even the traditional prestige of the Valverdes had gone up in smoke. Don Joaquín was still seated in his armchair at the Foreign Relations offices, but it was as though he were not there. A look of gratitude like that of a stray dog showed in his clouded eyes whenever Juan Lorenzi or Porfirio Uribe approached him out of courtesy. Jaramillo also visited him from time to time and called him "illustrious teacher"— which brought a flash of hatred to the old man's eyes.

Lorenzi was not a Santiagan citizen, which meant that if he were caught conspiring he might perhaps be able to leave the country. Perhaps. God only knew whether Sebastian Brache was spying on him. It had also not escaped Lorenzi's notice that ever since Dr. Jaramillo had secured the Leader's confidence the Doctor had begun in subtle ways to show his previously guarded jealousy. Lorenzi suspected that Jaramillo, on the pretext of protecting the Leader's "sacred person", was really against him. The insatiable ambition of Jaramillo astounded Lorenzi. Bellerophon was in a great hurry to enter Olympus. That sealed his fate...

Lorenzi began to feel desperately anxious when, on his last trip to Puerto Rico, he found the newspapers still filled with the Niño Valverde case and learned that the names of the suspected killers would soon be made public.

Besides all this, the Leader's diplomatic representatives had submitted formal protests to the government of a neighboring country because it was tolerating preparations for an invasion of the Republic.

There was no time to lose. They would probably have to move forward the date of the invasion. For the first time

Lorenzi felt the force of the whirlpool into which he had plunged. However, he said nothing to Porfirio Uribe.

The ominous silence in the Republic became intensified. The government gave no information to the public, but with every day that passed the vigilance of the troops was reinforced. Augusto was now spending more time in the barracks than in the Palace.

At the first sign of a threatened strike the army smashed it without hesitation. But new strikes surged up here and there throughout the country. Rumors circulated that warlike aggressions against the Republic were being prepared abroad. Public statues of the Leader were defaced, and irreverent jokes were being passed about in whispers. Official circles sponsored new solemn ceremonies to bestow upon the glorious head of state still more decorations to add to his innumerable ones.

Porfirio Uribe made a concrete proposal to Lorenzi, for the first time. "All that's needed," he said ironically, "is to cover the Leader's entire body with his medals and decorations then throw him into the water. No matter how well he swims, he'd go straight to the bottom."

One late afternoon Porfirio and Lorenzi were sauntering in the park while waiting to go somewhere to dine together. They had just sat down on a park bench when a drunk approached them. Looking in all directions to make sure no soldiers, policemen, or plain-clothesmen were nearby, the drunk addressed them.

"General Cachola won't escape this time! The whole country is going on strike."

"Talk of the Leader with respect!" said Porfirio, getting to his feet and putting on a show of anger.

"Why do you get drunk, friend?" Lorenzi put in.

"Water is no good for anyone, that's why I get drunk. Listen! General Cachola never leaves the barracks. Do you know what they're saying...?"

They did not let him finish but, holding the fellow tightly between them, they took him, struggling and shouting like a madman, and handed him over to two policemen.

When they were alone again, Porfirio said, "They're watching us."

"I've known that for some time."

"But we're suspects. Valverde told me about those so-called drunks, and I didn't believe him. That fellow wanted to find out what we think."

"No doubt of it. My suspicions were aroused when I saw no soldiers or police around. They sent him to us. That was why we had to turn him over to them. Now they'll send him far from here, on some other mission...that is, if we fooled them. If we didn't they'll arrest us and the 'drunk' will approach someone else."

But no one bothered Lorenzi or Uribe again, and in spite of the tension, the Leader found time to talk to Lorenzi on the eve of his departure to Puerto Rico to ask him to bring back a new motor for a boat, a motor he had already ordered.

CHAPTER

XIII

When Lorenzi returned from Puerto Rico to the Republic, he revealed to Uribe that the invasion would take place at any moment. He would soon be advised of the time and given the exact plans.

"Individuals like Augusto," he said, "could be kept on as figureheads, an extravagance, a useless luxury, like some modern monarchs, if they could be kept caged. But he's a monster on the loose, and very probably when he's eliminated the tyranny will cease."

"True, but why did we have to get ourselves mixed up in it?" commented Porfirio.

"I sometimes ask myself the same question: why did I get myself into this? But then I tell myself that a tyranny such as this cannot be accepted with indifference. You know me, I'm a rugged individualist, but I won't let my egotism turn me into a bottle with a captive genie inside. Nor is extreme caution reasonable in a time like this."

"Don't misunderstand me if I'm frank with you."

"Go ahead, say whatever you please."

"Do you know what I've been thinking? Alfredo plotted to involve me in this situation. And to have studied as I've studied, only to become a conspirator—it makes no sense."

"And what does make sense? Did becoming a lawyer just to try to be a representative from your district make sense? But there's still time to turn back."

But Porfirio could not turn back.

"I'll do what you want me to do, but let's suppose that the uprising fails. Is there any possibility of getting away in your boat?"

"Yes, there is."

"Good. Then I ought to tell you that I've made a promise to Don Joaquín."

"Have you talked to him about our plans?"

"Never. He can't be trusted."

"Exactly. What did you promise him?"

"To help Hortensia to get away. He's obsessed with the idea. But she wants to enter a convent."

"The struggle against the dictatorship is above our personal problems. But are you in love with Hortensia?"

"I'm afraid so."

"Does she love you?"

"I suspect not. But Don Joaquín would like to see us marry."

"Does he still insist on it?"

"Yes."

"What do you think you'll do?"

"If she loves me, we'll get married and, if possible, escape to Puerto Rico."

"Count on me."

"Of course, if Hortensia enters a convent, that relieves me of my promise. Then I'll devote myself completely to the cause. I'm afraid to die. Why should anyone accept this state of madness?"

"I'm glad to hear you talk like that."

"Even if Hortensia wants to flee with me, I'll do what I can for the cause. It won't be easy to escape without the Leader's approval."

"I understand. The important thing is that we can

count on you." And Lorenzi laughed, as he gave Porfirio a look of sincere admiration.

"Nothing is impossible," he went on after a pause. "Not even Augusto's fall. Suppose we don't accomplish everything we want to for the moment. At least, we'll give an example. We must attempt an audacious movement that will arouse those people who are still asleep. It's the least we can hope for. There are organized groups, there are arms. Strikes will be fomented. We have to divide and scatter the enemy, threaten to attack at several points, then attack violently at other points. Above all, we must hunt down the monster! Nothing is impossible. Look at you: haven't you succeeded in jumping over your own shadow?"

Porfirio, deeply moved, said nothing.

"To tell the truth," Lorenzi continued, "I was mistaken about you, I'm glad to admit. I hinted to Alfredo that we shouldn't count on you. I know what it's cost you to enter your profession. I didn't think ill of you, I just thought it was only reasonable for you to want to get something out of your studies now. Why not be honest with myself? It wasn't hard for me to join the movement, because I seek danger for its own sake. God knows, I may even have a secret admiration for Augusto! You know, sometimes I wonder if we're not merely fighting to create another Cachola, perhaps a worse one than this! I tremble when I look at some of Augusto's opponents. But if I've lived uselessly, Brother, then why not do something finally that Laza believes is useful? That's what I said to myself. And so I joined Alfredo Laza in his struggle for freedom."

"Alfredo influenced me, too. He has the luck to be able to help others. Here I find myself in the worst labyrinth of all, without any hope of salvation. Perhaps I'll escape from it by helping Alfredo."

"I'm not too sure what those ideals that torture Alfredo really are. I've almost never looked beyond myself, and the only thing I've ever worried about was my personal indepen-

233

dence. Above all, I wanted to do as I pleased. But Alfredo was able to show me that dangerous beasts shouldn't be allowed to run free. And here I am. I think we understand each other."

"It seems almost impossible that we're in agreement! Having a good opinion of others makes one feel better, doesn't it?"

Now it was Lorenzi who was moved.

"Go on!" he said, trying to make light of it. "You're not trying to make me believe we can't live without the esteem of others! You're trying to make me ashamed of my egotism."

Next day both Don Juan Lorenzi, a personal friend of the President, and the respected attorney, Porfirio Uribe y Moya were in the grandstand at a magnificent ceremony which was held in honor of the Leader. The nation was conferring its highest title, that of Field Marshal, upon General C. Luna del Valle in recognition of his many merits and his tireless efforts in behalf of the Fatherland. During the spectacular parade, the citizens would clearly demonstrate their "loyal allegiance to the Father of their Country."

And so it was. Rarely had a more solemn or important ceremony been seen in the Republic. There was Leader Augusto, mounted on a spirited sorrel, wearing his full-dress uniform, his chest covered with medals and decorations, his glorious head held high as befitted a Field Marshal, riding his horse so well that it looked as though he had been born there. His rigid, mechanical movements were reflected in his officers, who looked like reproductions of himself. The various parts of the program were announced on loud-speakers and every mention of the illustrious Marshal was accompanied by the most exalted adjectives. He heard them without changing his expression, as though he had been born with those attributes.

Such an attitude was an implicit tribute to the patriarchal figure of Don Ursulino, who was responsible for giving the Republic such a glorious statesman.

234

After the military parade came the parade of civil servants and then the tumultuous wave of citizens, with a marked percentage of women.

Lorenzi and Uribe were near Valverde, but Jaramillo no sooner recognized Lorenzi than he invited him over to a place next to the presidential box, which the Leader had reserved for his friend. While the long parade was reviewed with such solemnity by the Leader, now invested with the rank of Field Marshal, Jaramillo outdid himself in praise which Lorenzi, apparently impressed, seconded.

All of a sudden, just as the Leader, assisted by members of his Special Guard, dismounted from his steed to take his place in the presidential box, a man lunged out of the crowd, brandishing a revolver, and let out a yell.

"Down with the monster!"

It was Jacinto Brache, who was attempting to kill the Leader when his Guards were unprepared.

Lieutenant Brache rapidly threw himself between his brother and the Leader, taking the first bullet in his shoulder. Since everything happened in front of the presidential box, Jaramillo jumped down before the Guards could react, snatched a revolver from a soldier, and fired several times at his friend and brother-in-law. Sebastián Brache, blood oozing from his wounded shoulder, was protecting the Field Marshal who was now surrounded by his Guards, all of them on the alert and ready to use their guns.

Calmly, as if nothing had happened, the valiant General of more than one glorious battle turned his back and climbed into his box amid the cheers of the multitude.

Dr. Jaramillo verified Jacinto's death, then bent his head and murmured a brief prayer. He then handed the gun he had used to Lieutenant Brache and went up to sit near the Leader, who stretched out a generous hand to congratulate him for his opportune intervention.

All eyes were fixed on the two men who had saved the Leader's precious life: Sebastián Brache, who was looking down with obvious pain on the fallen body of his brother, and Dr. Jaramillo, who had so speedily come to the defense of his chief.

At the express orders of the Leader, the corpse was carried away and Jaramillo went to render, in person, first aid to the wounded man. A calm and dignified wave of the hand from Leader Augusto was sufficient to quiet the crowd, and another motion of the hand signaled for the ceremony to be resumed. He then turned with a smile towards Lorenzi.

"He was the conductor of the Palace orchestra," he said. "His mind had been unbalanced for some time."

During the following days many people were arrested and many houses in the city were searched. Augusto publicly commended the valor and loyalty of Lieutenant Sebastián Brache and Dr. Luis Jaramillo, awarding medals to both men. Lieutenant Brache said, with his usual economy of words, that he had only performed his duty as a soldier and that devotion to the Leader came first.

The Leader, as usual nobly and benevolently patriarchal, said that he blamed no one for what had happened, since no one is responsible for another man's madness. He said that he remembered Jacinto Brache with personal affection and that, besides, he had always admired his musical talent. He caused posthumous honors to be rendered him for having served in the National Palace until the very moment of madness. What other illustrious chief of state, no matter how glorious he might be, could compare his deeds with those of Leader Augusto?

Jacinto's death left Paulina in the most absolute solitude. Now she had no one with whom to listen to good music, no one to whom she could confide her most intimate thoughts. Sebastián hardly ever visited her and she now had no communication with her husband. She became increasingly listless, and the servants had to help her perform her smallest and most disagreeable necessities.

Jaramillo was opposed to having her committed to a sanatorium, and he arranged for a nurse to take care of her. Paulina submitted, like a well-bred little girl, to the care of the nurse. Never again would she leave her house, never again would she enter the living-room to confront the portrait of Leader Augusto. For the most part she remained in her bedroom or on the gallery above the patio. She complained of nothing and no one. Never speaking, living in the midst of a profound silence, she passed the time leafing through the family albums, except the one which contained the souvenirs of her reign as Queen of the Carnival. She ate only when the nurse besought her to. No longer did she take the initiative in anything. From sheer inanition, she would have let herself die. The only thing that seemed to cheer her was an occasional visit from Sebastián's wife, who brought her children to visit their aunt. Paulina always held the smallest of her little nephews in her lap and rocked him tenderly. She had determined so desperately to erase from her mind certain incidents of her past that it was as though she now lived an entirely new existence. She never mentioned the carnival, never referred to her stillborn son. However, at times, she still liked to watch her husband from a distance.

After Jacinto's death, Luis Jaramillo was depressed for several days.

"Poor fellow," he said, "I would rather have killed myself than harm him. It was a painful duty."

Nevertheless, in view of the fact that the assassination of Niño Valverde in New York was being whispered about everywhere, it was now said that Jacinto Brache was responsible for that death. It seemed there had been an old grudge between Jacinto and Niño Valverde, because the latter had opposed Brache's courtship of Hortensia. Dr. Jaramillo, it was said, had tried to prevent the encounter, but his generous effort to intervene had been futile...

All these recent events increased Don Joaquín's worries, and he talked almost desperately to Porfirio of the possibility of Hortensia's escape; indeed, he practically harassed him in an effort to speed things up.

"I'm no saint," he averred. "If I had the reins of power in my hands, who knows, I too might act like a despot. I'd probably think that you were not good enough for Hortensia. But don't imagine me as I could be; think of me as I am, a destitute old man with a daughter to protect. Deep down it hurts me not to be in power, as in other times. In those days the dishonor of others didn't affect me because it wasn't mine. Now it does hurt me, and it's what hurts me most. I know I'm asking too much when I want others to feel sorry for me, but it's no time to deceive myself. What can I gain with that? Already I have one foot in the grave!"

He heaved a great sigh. With an effort he reached his crutches, lifted himself up, and began pacing the room from one end to the other. It was impossible not to pity that mutilated human being, older than his years, who was trying to assure himself of Porfirio Uribe's aid in a desperate plan of escape.

"Will Hortensia want to go?" asked Porfirio.

"She has to go. She's my only child. To shut herself up in a convent would be to bury herself alive...And it would be a terrible ordeal for her, I know, because she has always wanted so much to have children."

"I don't think she loves me."

"I think she does. We can find someone who will marry you secretly and who will have horses ready. I've considered the possibility that, on his next trip, Lorenzi might...But I doubt that he would. He's very close to Augusto. But you'll find a way. Surely someone will do it."

"I don't know what to say."

"Quite possibly we could make a social event of it with the Leader himself as best man. In which case, he might give you a trip to the United States as a wedding present."

Of course, this was too much to expect.

"I would like to have grandchildren to teach them what

238

I never learned," Valverde added.

Porfirio ventured to say, "We almost always discover too late what we should have done and didn't."

"That's true, and it's even truer when one has been degraded after hundreds of nagging little humiliations that bend and wound one's spirit. Cachola appeared as an avenger of the oppressed, at the expense of the Valverdes. He then liquidated us by turning us into collaborators in his crimes. But, it's true, it's too late to undo things now." He paused, then went on in a broken voice: "It would be horrible if Hortensia has to pay for my sins. My acts have been so ignoble that I'll never again know a minute of peace."

Next day the Leader stopped by to greet his godfather as he was passing through Foreign Relations. He was obviously in a bad humor, for he was wearing dark glasses—a sure sign. Valverde tried to stand up, but he failed to reach his crutches and was almost on the point of falling when the Leader jumped forward to catch him.

"My dear Godfather! This isn't the first time that I've kept you from falling," he said, as everyone remained silent.

It was true. Something similar had occurred on another occasion. Don Joaquín, who was completely upset, was still able to utter the usual phrases of politeness.

"Sit down, Godfather," said Augusto. "Anyone who saw you trembling would say that you have something against me. As though I didn't know how loyally you serve me!"

At that moment Jaramillo, who had lagged behind to talk to a friend, entered the office to rejoin the Leader's retinue. Augusto suddenly became good natured.

"I think that my godfather is too old to have to work so hard, Doctor. Look for some position where he'll be more comfortable."

"Whatever you say, Your Excellency. How are you, Don Joaquín?"

"Goodbye, Godfather," said Augusto. "No, no, don't get up."

Porfirio, in the next room, was relieved to hear the Leader say goodbye, for he had been afraid lest he, too, would be visited. But...did the Leader even remember him? What presumption, to think that he was worthy of Augusto's attention! He felt like laughing aloud at his own vanity.

Don Joaquín was so shaken that Porfirio had to take him home.

"Jaramillo took very good advantage of my weakness," confessed Don Joaquín. "I know the worms will soon have me, now. My pricks of conscience should have forewarned me."

He would never be able to forget his former privileges as a landowner and would always regret their loss. What was most lamentable was to be destroyed by his traditional rival. Yes, it was intolerable that a Jaramillo was putting him to shame! How had he let the little doctor get the upper hand? It was sickening to have to admit defeat. But this was absurd, absurd! It was absurd to be unable to think of anything else. The obsession was in itself a sickness, he realized that. Indeed, it was so serious a malady that he had even ceased to worry about the fate of his own family. Yet try as he would to banish the thought, it kept on hammering away in his brain: "The little doctor is making a fool of me." And to be in such a situation in the declining years of his life! Why did the glories of the Valverde family have to end with him? His grandfather's and father's words had been law in the Republic.

And now there was another tormenting thought. Could it be true, as rumor had it, that Augusto's daughter was going to marry Jaramillo?

In effect, a rumor was circulating that, in view of Paulina's derangement, her marriage to Jaramillo would be annulled, leaving him free to marry Acté Luna del Valle. It would be an enormous triumph for Luis Jaramillo!

It would be hard to explain his suffering to Doña Rosa

240

and Hortensia, he reflected aloud. He was completely un-
done; his very bones seemed to have become disarticulated,
and his head swam as though he were staggering on the verge
of an abyss. These feelings were not mere figments of the
imagination, but an absolute physical reality. His whole
attitude, as he talked to Porfirio, was that of someone who
is saying goodbye. He was breathing with difficulty and he
had the stricken look of a mummy.

Porfirio's heart sank at the realization that there was no
one to whom he could appeal if he got into trouble. He
imagined himself attracting the jeers of people. He longed
for the invasion to occur soon, before the poisonous air became quite unbreathable. He was tempted to take refuge in
the United States Embassy, but immediately rejected the
thought. No, he did not want to die forever in the memories
of his friends; that would be too terrible a death.

Suicides, mysterious sicknesses and accidents continued
to occur. The tragic circle was closing every day more tightly around him as news reached him of the disappearance or
death of an acquaintance or friend. Then he realized how
desperate Jacinto Brache had felt when he saw the body of
Andrés Martínez hanging from a tree.

"I won't escape through the sewer," he promised himself. "I may not understand why I'm in this, but the most
beautiful things are those which can't be understood...I
no longer feel as though I'm just a pitiful patchwork of accidents and easy concepts of success."

He had discovered that a man's life encompasses more
than himself, since it is prolonged in the lives of others.
How painful it was to recall that he had once confused the
life of the mind and the life of the body by thinking at
times of himself as nothing but a digestive tract! The long
vigil had killed his appetite. He quivered with his incorruptible resolution to perform his duty as a man in these difficult
times.

241

The headlines of an official newspaper, announcing that Juan Lorenzi had offered to fight for the Leader, took him by surprise. Porfirio Uribe was unable to go to work that morning.

In the afternoon of that same day, news spread that invaders were landing in the north. Then other landings were reported. Some incipient strikes were crushed by the army.

The Leader's family went to a secret retreat to pray for the defenders of order and religion, those valiant men who were opposing the machinations of the devil. *Long live Leader Augusto, Crusader in a just cause!*

Porfirio was lost, caught in the center of the whirlpool of events. The newspaper headlines were incomprehensible. "Perhaps," Lorenzi had said, "perhaps we won't see each other again." He had said that when giving his final instructions. Porfirio was to remember the password—"Pleased to meet you! My brothers are waiting for me! Come and meet them." And he was to follow anyone who said that to him.

But no one appeared. At dusk, disinclined to eat anything, he went back to his boarding house. As he entered, he almost collided with the landlady, but she said nothing. And when he asked several questions in an effort to find out whether she was in the doorway by chance or design, she made no reply.

He went to his room and found that his bed was still unmade. Had they merely forgotten? He suddenly felt himself gasping for breath and unbuttoned his collar. He was prepared to await the worst. But nothing happened. Sick with anxiety, he lay down, without the least inclination to sleep.

As when he had lain on his bed in Doña Isabel Cortines's boarding house in New York, his sense of hearing became suddenly acute. A dead silence seemed to reign in the house, although several people were there, he was sure. Once he heard a low whispering outside the door of his room. From

242

the street came occasional sounds: an armed guard was tramping by, two by two. There was an occasional shouted command, then the hurried footsteps of someone running, a cry of "Halt!" followed by the crack of bullets...

What to do? He thought of leaving his room, of saying a few words to the landlady, inquiring discreetly...He checked the impulse. Even though he had eaten nothing all day, he was not hungry. What Ariadne would now offer him a guiding thread? He felt, with a sensation of an inward bleeding, betrayed by his friends. He reflected that he had brought his misfortune on himself. Lorenzi might actually be one of Augusto's spies. And then what? It was hard to conceive of such a thing, even; but if Lorenzi was not a false friend, then why had he left his compatriot to the mercy of the monster?

God only knew what was happening. When he had had that last talk with Lorenzi, he had been told that the plan was to divide the army with strikes and landings on various parts of the coast, thus making "Operation Hunt Down" possible. They were counting on the aid of a prominent officer in the National Palace. Victory would be at hand with the arrest or death of just one man.

He spent all night listening, starting up in a cold sweat every time he heard a noise or the sound of a voice. Oh, to sleep and not wake up until morning! Oh, to overcome the torture of this nightmarish vigil! But fear and loneliness made sleep impossible. Sometimes he imagined that they were about to break in his door; sometimes he fancied he heard his name pronounced on the other side of the wall.

It was truly horrible to accept a life planned by the Leader! He resolved that when morning came he would leave his room, go out into the street, and walk to his office without saying anything to anyone; he would see what was happening. Either he should contact the Embassy and try to leave this hell, or else he should accept whatever might come, including arrest and even death. But he could not

243

live the monstrous life offered here. He had made his decision: he could not go on like this.

He remembered Don Joaquín, Niño Valverde, Paulina and Jacinto Brache, and it was like seeing his own reflection in so many mirrors. Suddenly he thought about Jaramillo. Could Jaramillo help him? No, impossible! If he had no scruples in killing Niño Valverde and Paulina's baby and Jacinto Brache and God knew how many others, then he would have no scruples about killing him. Jaramillo would have even more reason to kill him now that they were investigating the Niño Valverde case in the United States. He, Porfirio Uribe, was known to have been an involuntary witness of the crime. They might already be after him, to get his testimony, which would be valuable to the investigation. He had never talked to Jaramillo on the subject, had talked to no one but Jacinto Brache. Did Jaramillo know that he knew who killed Niño Valverde? But perhaps Jacinto... Could a madman be held responsible for his acts?

According to Lorenzi, the murder of Niño Valverde was threatening to become an international incident. That frightened the Leader, even though no one talked about it in the Republic. *There's no doubt that they distrust me*, thought Porfirio. He would have to remain silent and be vigilant. No, he would not see Jaramillo; instead, he would go to call upon Don Joaquín. Perhaps Don Ursulino's intervention would save him...Perhaps! After he had talked to Valverde, he would go to the Embassy, if they let him reach it. At least he could communicate with someone there before they arrested him, before he "disappeared", never to return!

Next morning, earlier than usual, Porfirio started off towards his office, a half-conscious challenge to the authorities. He walked slowly and steadily, looking straight ahead, not even glancing at the soldiers or the police. But at every step his heart sank. It was as though he were being driven forward by his heartbeats, as though his steps were taken

244

independently of his will. Footsteps...heartbeats...Footsteps...heartbeats...

Twice he thought he was about to be called to a halt by some soldiers. Twice he thought, "They're going to arrest me, and I shall "disappear" and my acquaintances will say, 'What ever became of Porfirio Uribe?' when I'm already dead."

Propelled forward by his footsteps and heartbeats, he reached the office, arriving early. The watchmen and the lesser employees looked the other way as he walked by. No one spoke to him. He sat down at his desk and, without knowing why, began to look through the drawers, like someone taking an inventory before departure.

Don Joaquín was quietly cordial. When Porfirio told him that he would like to call that evening upon him, the old man agreed to it, then volunteered a remark in a whisper: "I imagine I'm renouncing the world, when actually it's the world that's abandoning me. I still keep the illusion that I determine my own acts. But this last shift is the final step towards retirement."

They said no more.

That evening after leaving the office, Porfirio heard, in the very middle of the park, these words: *Pleased to meet you! My brothers are waiting for me. Come and meet them.* It was an agent disguised as a peasant. Porfirio understood.

"Tonight? At the hour and place agreed upon?"

"Exactly."

He was on the point of asking about Lorenzi, Laza, and the others, about what was happening on the other side of this thick curtain of silence, but at the sight of a policeman, the peasant held out his hand, as if begging.

"I haven't got any money, friend. Could you give me something to travel on?" he said.

The policeman, in a protective way, asked Porfirio almost cordially. "Is he molesting you? In this country, people work for a living!"

"I had already offered him something to go to the country on," said Porfirio, "because he's lost his money."

He gave some coins to the 'peasant', who took them and left. This time Porfirio was sure he hadn't fallen into a trap. What the agent had told him was obviously a message from Alfredo Laza.

At nightfall, ignoring the police and the soldiers, he unhesitatingly entered Don Joaquín's house on the outskirts of town. It had formerly been the main house on a ranch. Below the old sugar cane mill, the agent who would take him through the mountains to Alfredo Laza's group would be waiting for him. Porfirio could hardly bear the weight of his own heart.

He was surprised by the news which Don Joaquín gave him.

"This very afternoon Hortensia entered the convent. She told her mother that she could not run away, leaving us here."

Never before had Porfirio felt such a painful desire to weep for the sons he had dreamed of having one day, for a home imagined, which dissolved like mist. The cry remained in his throat. He wanted to say goodbye to someone, some loved one, Hortensia or perhaps Paulina, who no longer knew what was going on around her, who was buried alive in a great tomb, sunken in a heartbreaking silence. He also suddenly thought of Catalina and her groans, and heard far-off echoes of Estefano's sobbing, which recalled the sound of the *bombardino*. It was as though he were beginning to retrace his steps, as they say dying people do...

Afterwards he told himself, "Hortensia did the wise thing." But at the time he thought, "Oh, to live in a world without fear! Oh, if only children were born into a less monstrous world!" And he felt that all around him and beneath his feet everything was failing him. Gone were the sweet dreams of a life shared by two people, a life containing things worth clinging to, a life in which he would hear the first cries of a newborn baby, a home in which he would smell the good odors of food cooked by beloved hands, and the sweet fragance of talcum powder. Oh, how irremediably that imagined life was being overwhelmed by an avalanche of monstrous events!

He wanted to delude himself with the idea that there was still someone who would help him escape, and so he imagined that he had found a father and mother in Don Joaquín and Doña Rosa.

"I'm sorry to have to abandon you," he said gently, "but I have to leave tonight. I shall go from here, from this very house, which I've come to think of as my home."

"My son," murmured Doña Rosa, "I pray God that everything will come out well."

"We now have little to lose," sighed Don Joaquín. "I know they suspect you, but if I had to protect you with my own life, I would be glad to do so. What else can I do to lessen my suffering over my past actions?"

In spite of the fear that at any moment the police might come in search of Porfirio, Don Joaquín and Doña Rosa made an effort to give him a good farewell supper. Then, almost at midnight, he slipped through the patio towards the place where he was to meet the agent, Purificación López.

CHAPTER

XIV

Augusto regretted having let his wrath get the better of him when he expelled Jacinto Martínez from the Republic. Martínez, who was clever and calculating, was always careful never to risk giving his opinion in public, and had therefore remained silent ever since he had left. In fact, Augusto missed the culture and guile of that man who was the product of many centuries of European civilization. The Leader needed Martínez' sociological and political wisdom, so useful in planning the Republic's international politics. Rarely had the Leader been favored with such an intelligent propagandist. Then, just when he was beginning to reap the benefits of Martínez' exertions, he had expelled the man from the country. Of course, the deep-seated moral convictions of the Leader, jealous Guardian of Decency, would not permit him to shut his eyes to an offense such as the one which Martínez had committed, but his expulsion had certainly been an unpardonably hasty action. At first the Leader had been satisfied with what he had done, but later on he had begun with regret to notice the absence of his zealous aide.

Jacinto Martínez had planned and created the myth of Leader Augusto. The General complacently recalled what Martínez had said the first time they had talked together.

"My dear General," he had exclaimed, "the people you govern should be made to believe that you have magical powers."

Augusto had laughed heartily at the notion. From the minute he laid eyes on this crafty doctor whom the European undercurrents had washed up on the shores of the Republic he had liked him.

"And how, Doctor?" he had asked. "Don't you people regard us as somewhat primitive?"

"You primitive, Mr. President? I've just met you and, believe me (I have no reason to flatter you), I've rarely seen among the European heads of government a figure so well endowed with authority as your Excellency."

"Ah, don't exaggerate, Doctor."

"You're being told this by a man bred in the atmosphere of many civilizations and with much political experience."

"You know," the General interrupted, "I'm going to need your services."

"I've already been engaged by a university in the United States."

"Forget that university, Doctor. As of today I've hired you. And you can name your own salary."

"But General...!"

"By the authority with which I am invested I order you to work with us," replied Augusto in a bantering but at the same time self-assured tone.

"In which case, I obey."

Thenceforward he had been one of the General's most confidential advisors. The Leader learned from him to plan his propaganda in such a way that the Republic would appear before the eyes of the world as a prodigy of wealth, liberty and progress. Through international refugee organizations he announced that the Republic would open its doors to the persecuted of the world.

Augusto had little to learn about hiding the realities of the domestic situation, since for some time the words "suicide" and "accident" had acquired in the Republic meanings rather more extensive than those usually ascribed to them, and dead men had learned to confess their crimes. The Leader also knew very well that lies, no matter how incredible they may seem in the beginning, end up by being accepted as truths after systematic repetition.

Until Martínez arrived in the Republic, General Augusto C. Luna del Valle had been merely another tyrant in the eyes of the world. Then Martínez, with his inexhaustible fantasy, stepped in and took care of the invention and repetition of those myths which created a favorable personality for his master. In domestic and foreign newspapers, well written reports began to appear, describing the enormous business ability of the First Citizen of the Republic and telling of his experiments in agriculture, husbandry, and industry, as well as describing his devotion to family and religion...In the interior a multitude of stories grew up about his institution, his ability to foresee events, the example he set for the country's workers by laboring fifteen hours a day.

His equestrian statues and full-dress portraits began to give way to others depicting the simple businessman, the worshiper kneeling in church, the loving father, the progressive farmer.

Augusto remembered the time when he had asked Martínez' opinion of Jaramillo.

"Regrettably, he's more foolish than bad," was all he had said.

"The boy is ambitious," was Augusto's own comment. And he had asked: "Do you think he'll go far?"

"Whatever you think, General," Jacinto Martínez had replied, and they had both laughed.

Martínez had been mistaken, however, in his estimate of Jaramillo, who turned out to be not as foolish as he thought. Only a few hours before he left the country, Martínez had realized his mistake. Although the Leader was fam-

250

iliar with Jaramillo's machinations, he had not hesitated to include him in the august inner circle of advisors. He had kept a close watch on him, all the same. As for Jaramillo, he had received his appointment with gratitude.

"General," he had said, "how can I fulfill such a tremendous responsibility? I must try to acquire a sixth sense which will enable me to anticipate your desires, which are laws for me."

"Your mission is to make them believe that I have an agreement with God," Augusto had said, half joking, half serious. "Can you carry out that task?"

"With the inspiration of Your Excellency..."

Augusto had liked Jaramillo's attitude.

"What are you going to do first?" he had asked.

"Mr. President, what would you think if we began with your birthday within a few weeks? Not only will it be a national holiday from one end of the country to the other, but..."

He stopped and it could be seen that he was somewhat fearful, but Augusto had encouraged him to go on.

"Speak frankly, I have the utmost confidence in you."

"What I'm going to say may seem like madness, but it's the best I can think of to show you how honored I am to enjoy your confidence."

"So?"

"Let's give the impression at your birthday celebration that you hold the terrestrial globe in your hands..."

Augusto, perplexed at first, roared with laughter.

"You mean I'm to treat the world globe as I would a painted balloon at one of those festivals of the patron saints?"

"Yes, Mr. President. We will invite representatives from all nations with whom we maintain diplomatic relations. It will be a magnificent day."

"Damn it, that's not a bad idea. To release the globe of the world in the celebration...Damn it, Doctor, I like your ideas!"

251

Although he was bursting with satisfaction, Jaramillo kept surprisingly calm and did everything he could to show the President that whatever he could say to exalt him as Leader would always be too little, so great were his merits.

"General," he said with sincere humility, "you can always consider me your most devoted servant."

The Leader then did something very unusual. Approaching Jaramillo, he placed his hands on his shoulders and looking him straight in the eyes, he declared, "Luis, I think we understand each other very well."

More exactly, Jaramillo did everything he could to understand the Leader. Nevertheless, the Leader missed the suave sublety of Martínez. He had above all been sure that Martínez could never aspire to the presidency. That had kept Martínez in line. Things were different with Jaramillo. No matter how intelligent and cautious Jaramillo might be, Augusto could never completely trust him. For one thing, the Jaramillos had done their share in making the history of the Republic, and a former Cachola could never forget that, even though that Cachola now called himself Augusto C. Luna del Valle. Given the slightest opportunity, Jaramillo would not for long be able to contain his bitter hatred of the Cacholas. Augusto was powerful. But privately Jaramillo was convinced that he himself was the only representative of the old ruling families, and he worked ceaselessly to discover the weak point that surely existed in the usurper.

To achieve his aim, Jaramillo was ready to resort to any means, including the temporary betrayal of his own class. All his actions were guided by one painful reality: Augusto's power. Jaramillo's first step had been to get as close as possible to the monster in order to know him better. He had succeeded in that and now he was on the alert, ready to act with sudden violence to attain his other great objective, which was to avenge the humiliation which filled him to the point of suffocation. The humiliations suffered by the

Jaramillos were painfully mortifying. He must remain on the alert, hour by hour, without respite. And he was expending all his effort not merely to topple Augusto from power, to replace him with no matter what other Leader, but to supplant him and become himself the next Leader.

At times his desperate intentions showed all too clearly. This, as he knew, could be his ruin. And so he tried to dominate his ambition, a hard thing to do. Whenever he tried to anticipate the movements of the Leader or of any other influential person, he watched their steps like a wild beast stalking its prey, concealing his constant vigil beneath a pose of most studied indifference. At night he spent long hours analyzing the observations he had made during the day.

For the past few weeks, Don Ursulino had been in very poor health and had clamored for Dr. Jaramillo's attentions. Jaramillo, in fact, did not need to be summoned, for he practically lived in the old man's house. This gave him a chance to feel out his patient's opinions surreptitiously. There was no doubt that Leader Augusto was worried over the domestic situation, especially by the reports that were again being published in foreign newspapers in regard to the death of Niño Valverde, and Don Ursulino obviously shared these worries.

Jaramillo himself was terrified, although he was careful not to show it. His name was dropped more than once in the newspaper accounts of the famous case. True, he had only been obeying orders from higher up, but Augusto was always Augusto. If the matter became critical, the Leader would not hesitate to sacrifice his aide. Jaramillo already observed an obvious withdrawal, a certain ominous coolness in the President.

He had confidence, nevertheless, in his lucky star. He believed that he was destined to accomplish feats of great national importance. He had promised himself to restore public decency. By "public decency" he understood the restitution of political power to the Jaramillos, some of whom were in exile, others in prison, and most of them impoverished and forgotten. At no moment of his official life had he been in greater danger. He sensed it even in the Leader's looks and reticences. He also noticed it in Don Ursulino's anxiety and in the correct but cautious attitude of the other bureaucrats.

He began to spend whole nights without sleeping a wink, planning how to distract the Leader's attention from the unfortunate incident which had caused so much talk in other countries. He remembered with satisfaction the Leader's birthday celebrations which had comprised a magnificent event, with a good number of foreign representatives present, and Augusto really convinced that he held the terrestrial globe in his hands...But the triumph had not lasted for long. With obvious vengeful intuition the journalists of the international press were featuring the Valverde incident and efforts to place the blame on Jacinto Brache were now fruitless.

Matters had reached this point when the news broke of the invasion which was about to take place. The critical moment had come, critical for Luis Jaramillo, who was playing his trump card. Now he would show Leader Augusto whom he could trust. Now he would really be close to the Leader! He realized that, for the moment, no one could overthrow the government; but if by some miracle the invasion should be successful, he could count on the support of a certain group of officers...At any rate, he arranged things so that he would not lose, no matter what the turn of events.

He immediately took advantage of the flight of the attorney Porfirio Uribe, to show the Leader why he had never trusted the Puerto Rican. The day before Uribe's disappearance, he had ordered his arrest, which was to be carried out the next morning. As luck would have it, Uribe had slipped through their fingers...

254

That same day the police arrested Don Joaquín Valverde in his own home.

"What's become of Juan Lorenzi?" Augusto asked Jaramillo.

"He didn't return on the date that he promised. Will the General allow me to tell him something?"

"Yes."

"Don't wait for Juan Lorenzi. I never did trust him."

"He offered his services..."

"He's very clever, General. Uribe's flight has something to do with the disappearance of Lorenzi."

Leader Augusto said nothing, but he felt betrayed. He never considered what he, as Leader, represented for those who loved freedom. He only thought in terms of personal friendship. He did not understand why Lorenzi had failed him as a friend, since he had always esteemed him and had even favored him with the exclusive rights to the export of mahogany. He found it hard to understand how any human being was capable of responding to such generosity with "treason". Naturally he was thinking as the mythical personage he now believed himself to be: the Field Marshal and Leader Augusto Cesar Luna del Valle. The chieftain Ursulino Cachola no longer existed for him.

Jaramillo believed that he had the crisis in hand. All that he needed was the Leader's backing, and at last he had it.

That afternoon several persons were decorated in a special ceremony in the barracks adjacent to the National Palace. Lieutenant Sebastián Brache was awarded another medal for his bravery and devotion in the fulfillment of his military duties. The Leader gave him, along with three other men, a special mission, which was to inspect certain detachments, using every possible means to detect and weed out traitors. He was given a safe conduct pass for the purpose.

"And I personally order you, quite specially, to bring

me that little lawyer and Juan Lorenzi back, alive."

"I'll capture them even if it costs me my own life," replied Lieutenant Brache.

"As soon as we have the information we need, we will deliver the rebels a crushing blow. But I want spies of that sort brought back alive."

Just as the Lieutenant was about to leave, the Leader dismissed him with the repeated order.

"Return with them! Your commander-in-chief orders you to, Colonel Brache!"

Without saying a word, the former Lieutenant, now Colonel Brache, came to attention and saluted. Augusto smiled and held out his hand. At the same time, he pinned on the new insignia.

The schooner had anchored far off the coast after nightfall. A motor boat loaded with arms was despatched towards a place on the beach which the revolutionaries had previously agreed upon. Aboard the launch were Lorenzi, Alfredo Laza and three other men, all armed with revolvers and hand grenades. They turned on no lights, but depended upon the skill of one of the men, who was familiar with this solitary stretch of sea, to bring them safely to shore.

From time to time Laza and Lorenzi talked in low voices, while keeping a sharp lookout.

"Considering the circumstances, it's the best we can do," Alfredo was saying. "The movement couldn't be postponed any longer. Not only were we putting a friendly government in a difficult position, but also the press was reporting our activities. Therefore it's only natural that our present objective should be to divide Augusto's armed forces and confuse them with rapid attacks here and there while we land arms. The truth is that the strikes haven't been as successful as we had hoped."

Four men were to carry out "Operation Hunt Down": Alfredo Laza, Porfirio Uribe and two others, one of whom was the mysterious officer in the National Army. Juan Lorenzi would have to return to his ship, not only to continue unloading arms, but also to make other voyages, if the initial operation proved successful.

It was a desperate mission which Laza himself had proposed to the revolutionary high command. Since it was impossible to confront the National Army, which was very well equipped, they would "hunt down the monster himself", at what they knew to be an enormous risk. Lorenzi had been a good candidate for the group which would carry out the operation, but it was decided that he was more valuable as the captain of his schooner.

Among others aboard was Rosana Cortines de Laza, who had offered her services as nurse. Laza could not prevent her from coming, and, after all, he liked soldier girls.

As Laza told Lorenzi, not even Doña Isabel knew anything about it. "But I feel flattered," he added, "and no one could reject a volunteer nurse."

"If we can't live together, we'll die together," she had said to him. He had tried to make her believe that the purpose of this mission was not to die, but to live. However, she was still pessimistic, and when he jumped from the schooner into the launch, he had seen a look of farewell on her face. For his part, there was no alteration in his usual calm manner. Nor did he feel that he was about to accomplish an epic feat. On the contrary, he believed that he was merely remaining true to his whole life.

He had not anticipated being able to count on Juan Lorenzi, much less on Porfirio Uribe, and he felt a quiet satisfaction in having won them over to a good cause.

"Look at Augusto's friend!" he said to Lorenzi, jestingly. "Look at the man who says that he's only concerned with his own individual freedom!"

"You're a fast talker, that's all."

"And you're the champion imposter, the kind that appears to be bad while being a good egg. Tell me, Juan, how did you win over Porfirio?"

"You don't have to win over people like Uribe. They're just waiting to join a cause like this one. I never did see that shadow he said he couldn't jump over."

"But we've put his life in danger. God knows what's happened to him!"

"One more soldier, what does it matter? Don't even more soldiers die for bad causes? In wartime life is worth nothing."

"To tell the truth, my conscience bothers me. Although from the beginning I was obsessed by the horror of a man's shutting himself away from the world for eight years of torturing study merely to become a little lawyer and politician in Coamo. Such a thing was inconceivable to me. Perhaps I'm too optimistic, perhaps I have too much faith in the human species. And perhaps I wanted to make a test case of Porfirio, at Porfirio's expense. Well, now, you see what's happened. I never dreamed he would join 'Operation Hunt Down.' "

"Nor did I. Besides, I even suspected Porfirio of being one of the Leader's spies."

"The man has a lot to give, he's naturally generous. All he needs is to be shown how to use those assets for his own and others' benefit. Prejudices and the urge to power are not innate, they are not an inherent part of man's incorruptible conscience, but are the result of social competition, the effort to keep up appearances. Even Augusto might have been the leader in a good cause if he hadn't let himself get all balled up in his superstitious hatred of the once powerful Valverde and Jaramillo families."

"Sorry, but what you say confirms me in the certainty of what I've always suspected: that you're completely insane."

Alfredo burst into a laugh.

"Probably. But the Jaramillos and Valverdes created a monster and then they couldn't control him. However, they can't wash their hands of him now that they're being persecuted, because they stand accused by their entire long history of oppressing others. We live in a crucial time, the time of the destructive vengeance of the Frankensteins. Who am I among the millions of oppressed human beings? What does my death matter? I'm just a drop of water in the barrel..."

"And why are you so dedicated? You don't have an investment in the future, you have no children."

"My very nature won't tolerate even the possibility that mankind may lose the rights it has acquired over a period of hundreds of thousands of years. I can't accept it, that's all. When those rights are threatened, I immediately want to add my puff of breath to the storm..."

Lorenzi, somewhat cynical and skeptical, did not know what to say, but he now understood a little more clearly why he had decided to join the expedition.

There were several revolutionaries waiting for them on the shore. They had liquidated two small detachments in the area by means of a careful ambush. It had not been necessary to fire a single shot. This left the door open to Palo Hincado, where they would meet Uribe and his guide.

"Let's go," said Laza. "Perhaps we won't be able to win the battle, but we'll arouse the people's courage."

He and four companions, disguised as farm hands, traveled along lonely paths over rough terrain covered with thick undergrowth. In Palo Hincado, a place not far from the capital, they gave the signal which had been agreed upon: a whistle imitating the hooting of an owl. Someone repeated the signal. A few moments afterwards, Alfredo Laza and Porfirio Uribe were hugging each other.

"We stayed in a cave all day," explained Porfirio. "We had one scare after another. Fortunately López is well acquainted with this part of the country."

But Laza had no illusions.

"The worst is yet to come," he murmured. "But now, I'm dying to ask you something: can the Lieutenant be trusted?"

259

"We think so. We had to take the chance, as Lorenzi has already told you, no doubt. We broached the matter to him the same day his brother was killed."

About an hour later they heard the sound of horses' hooves. Some riders were approaching. As one of the mounts reared, his rider exclaimed: "Damn this horse!"

It was another signal that had been agreed upon. In a few seconds the soldiers found themselves covered by the pistols of Laza and his companions.

"Don't move, anyone!" said Purificación López, the man who had guided Porfirio. "If you do, we'll blow you up with hand grenades."

The soldiers threw down their arms before dismounting. Sebastián Brache, their commander, walked over to Porfirio, who introduced him to Alfredo Laza.

"Alfredo, this is Lieutenant Brache."

"Colonel," said Sebastián, correcting him with an ironical smile. "They promoted me this very afternoon."

The three soldiers were still stunned with surprise.

"I thought that this midnight trip to San Nicolás was strange," muttered one of them.

"Do we kill them?" asked Purificación López.

"No," replied Laza. "We'll take them to the schooner and lock them up on board."

Colonel Brache approved Laza's decision. Laza regretted having intervened with his orders, since Brache was to be in charge of "Operation Hunt Down."

In a few minutes, everything was ready. Alfredo and Purificación had donned the uniforms of two of the soldiers and mounted their horses. The attorney Porfirio Uribe would ride surrounded by them and Colonel Brache, as "prisoner", the "spy" Brache was taking to the barracks to hand him over alive to his commander-in-chief.

"Operation Hunt Down" then set out towards the capital.

CHAPTER

XV

The newspapers were filled with the Niño Valverde case, as though it had happened but yesterday. Finally Augusto made up his mind.

"Luis Jaramillo has confessed his crime. Arrest him."

Thereupon Jaramillo was accused of the "despicable murder" of Joaquín Valverde, son and heir of Don Joaquín Valverde, and for the murder of others, unnamed.

"No one with more hatred served with more devotion," murmured Jaramillo as he entered the prison. "I who was so vigilant will die in darkness."

That very afternoon Don Joaquín Valverde walked out of the same prison, where he had been committed "through Jaramillo's false accusation."

From the beginning, Jaramillo knew what fate awaited him. Alone in prison, he untiringly reviewed the events of his life. Above all he was pursued by the recollection of how he had entered the Leader's service, how he had served him, and how he had been paid. Had he been given the opportunity to speak privately with Don Ursulino, perhaps the Leader's old father might have helped him to escape his terrible fate. But Don Ursulino was very ill, and could see no one. Jaramillo's only remaining hope was that the old man would have to call for his medical services, as he had done formerly. But no sooner had Luis suggested the possibility of seeing the patriarch than the commanding officer—a little Captain who three days before had fallen over himself doing favors for the Doctor—maliciously remarked that, clearly, "the illustrious patient had been the victim of an unscrupulous and scheming physician."

Repeatedly, in his reveries, Jaramillo tried to justify his past conduct. He told himself that he had only obeyed the orders of his superior. However, he regretted things he had done, particularly his treatment of Paulina. He was ready to beg her forgiveness, but would she now comprehend his words? Perhaps not. He remembered her lost look, that look of one who refuses to face reality.

But there was no doubt in his mind that his only sin had been in performing his duty too zealously. With difficulty he had broken the habit of commanding others and instead had learned to yield to the will of his enemy. Had the Jaramillos been justly deprived of their prerogatives? Luis now fancied himself as a martyr to a just cause...

The guards' footsteps, the jingling of keys, the barred windows all reminded him constantly of the four narrow walls. There was no one, no one at all to talk to. But after all, it was better this way. To be compelled to share a cell with people animated with hate would be frightful. They had no doubt deliberately isolated him as though he had the plague. Had he any intimate friends, any close relatives? Perhaps he had none. Friends and relatives have a way of ceasing to be friends and relatives after one has been accused, arrested, persecuted, exiled, perhaps executed. The bonds of friendship and kinship were weak threads which the least tension could easily break, Luis realized.

What more could he have done to slay the Chimera, to vanquish the Amazons? Perhaps Augusto would have respected their tradition as powerful landowners. A person who has once been a laborer always carries with him an almost superstitious respect for his former masters. But what could be done now? The Valverdes and the Jaramillos had decided to fight each other, competing for the ruler's favor. That had been their great mistake. Jaramillo now remembered with keen regret how he had treated Don Joaquín Valverde and how he had unhesitatingly killed Don Joaquín's son and driven his daughter close to insanity.

Without realizing it, this constant self-examination was Jaramillo's worst self-accusation. He thought nothing of the suffering of the populace, of the workers. He had always disregarded those who were outside his circle of acquaintances, comprised of members of the ruling class. It was his conviction that only landowners and employers had a right to rule. The way he saw it, there was scarcely any difference between the rabble and a herd of swine. Although he would never have gone so far as to express the thought aloud, it was often in his mind.

Jaramillo's rationalizations were a good example of the causes of the whole situation in the Republic and justified a pronouncement made by Alfredo Laza: "The Leader is not our only enemy. The forces which created him and now support him are still more formidable."

Luis Jaramillo had been in the antechamber of Olympus. From that eminence he had fallen into the antechamber of hell. He was the martyr of a cause! He was being crucified for defending the tradition of his predecessors! And that tradition was spoken of a great deal in books and depicted in paintings and statues and monuments. He felt that the only reason artists existed was to exalt the deeds—real or imaginary—of the powerful. What artist would exalt him, the man who could have been the new Leader upon Augusto's fall? If he should be executed, who would reclaim his body in order to protect it in a marble mausoleum?

Augusto went to live in the barracks, directing the military operations from that point of vantage. His air force

263

had already discovered some of the landings and destroyed them. When Augusto mounted his horse, he looked like the equestrian statue which he had promised himself.

When Jaramillo's extradition was formally requested, Augusto told the United States ambassador that the prisoner had committed suicide while awaiting trial for the assassinations. And Jaramillo had to commit suicide. That "head full of schemes" must vanish.

In the deserted streets of the capital the hoof-beats of cavalry horses on the cobble-stones rang out loudly. No one except the Leader knew what was happening on the coasts of the Republic. None of the officers had more than a partial knowledge of the situation. The silence stimulated the people's imagination, and fear spread into every home.

The Leader was waiting to strike one terrible blow which his enemies would never forget. The incipient strikes had all been crushed and proclamations reminded the workers that Augusto was the one who had freed them from their former ruthless masters.

In the first grey light of dawn, Colonel Sebastián Brache and his soldiers were taking the prisoner towards the capital. Brache was aware that none of his companions, neither Laza nor Purificación nor even Porfirio Uribe completely trusted him. During most of the first part of the journey, he remained silent, but finally he approached Alfredo to speak to him on the subject.

"You are right to doubt me. But consider this: you are all armed. If I make a suspicious move, shoot. I'm in front and you're behind. I'm sorry that I've had to put handcuffs on Uribe. But they can be opened easily.

That was true, because Porfirio had already proved it. But Brache's explanations didn't lessen their distrust of him, for they were acquainted with not a few cases of men who, just to stay in power, had become accomplices in the assassination of their brothers.

Uribe had never in fact been well-acquainted with Sebastián Brache. Unlike his brother Jacinto, he was intense and serious, and above all, he had always scrupulously performed his military duties. It was known, of course, that he just barely tolerated Jaramillo and that he resented Paulina's situation; but he had never spoken of it. Nevertheless, the day when Jacinto was killed, in spite of his bravery in defending the Leader, Uribe had observed a grimace of pain on Sebastián's face, as though he had suffered a deeper wound than the flesh-wound in his shoulder.

Without hesitation, Porfirio had told Lorenzi of this, and they had decided to approach Brache. Immediately Brache had joined their "Operation Hunt Down." The risk of betrayal was lessened when Lorenzi was allowed to leave the country, still unrestricted in his freedom of movement.

Porfirio spoke to Sebastián Brache several times about his brother Jacinto.

"If we come out of this alive, Jaramillo will have to crawl underground to escape me," Sebastián roundly declared, unconsciously digging his spurs into the flanks of his beautiful sorrel mare. "My brother and sister must be revenged!" And, as the mare trembled and reared, he flattered her mane, speaking to her soothingly. "Forgive me, old girl," he murmured, "I'm not angry with you."

Porfirio was struggling to overcome a feeling of plain fear, mingled with a dreamlike feeling of disbelief. His decision to join the conspirators had been so unexpected, so extraordinary, that it still seemed incredible. "Am I a legendary figure?" he asked himself. "Is this real? Am I the same man who aspired to become a majority leader, the same man who disregarded the enormous amount of suffering in the world and thought only of himself? Have I actually jumped over my shadow, am I about to escape the labyrinth by soaring above it?" No, this was not fiction, this was actuality. And he knew that were he given a choice now between personal freedom and risking his life for the ideal

265

of freedom, he would still take the risk and, if need be, die.

Now, journeying towards what might be certain death, he told himself, "We're in the middle of the river, it's too late to change horses, so be brave!"

But again he needed to be reassured. He turned towards Laza. "Will all this be in vain?" he asked.

"What?"

"Dying."

"So you think you're going to die? Well, I don't think I'm going to die! Does anyone ever die who influences others?"

Porfirio looked at Brache, hoping he would say something, but Brache merely nodded in agreement. However, Purificación, who had scarcely said a word for a long time, spoke at last.

"I put my enthusiasm into the revolution when General Cachola looked to us for support. He was one of us and I didn't think he'd betray us. In this one short life we're so often deceived! Now all I want is to come face to face with him..."

Alfredo Laza said nothing more. He was looking at the fading stars and enjoying the fresh early morning air, deep in his own thoughts. Why, he asked himself, did a man as absurd as Leader Augusto have to exist? How was it possible that mankind could set up conventional institutions in defiance of nature? Inconceivable that man, the new Frankenstein, should set himself in opposition to the very source of life! For surely, he thought, when life is no longer a beautiful experience everything is lost. And what else does inventing new means for enslaving and torturing humanity achieve except the most frightful anguish!

They were four men hunting the monster, determined to abolish death itself by living on in the memories of their fellowmen. The deed that was beginning to be clamored for in the hearts of a few men could perhaps change the fate of millions of human beings.

A sentinel's voice called out.

"Who goes there?"

They were approaching a military post.

"Colonel Sebastián Brache with the President's safe-conduct pass!" replied Sebastián.

"Halt and present your credentials."

They drew near the representatives of Law and Order.

"Here. I was sent on a special mission to capture this prisoner."

Laza, Porfirio and Purificación missed no detail in Sebastián Brache's attitude. Their attention was concentrated in their trigger fingers, for they were ready to sell their lives dearly if need be. Evidently Sebastián Brache, a professional army man, was a very well known person in the outposts.

"Forward!" the sentinel ordered, when he had examined the paper.

Just then an officer intervened.

"Colonel Brache, excuse me," he said. "I thought your grade was Lieutenant?"

"The Marshal promoted me yesterday afternoon."

Smiling, the officer approached Brache and whispered something in his ear. Purificación López, Alfredo Laza and Porfirio Uribe grew tense, ready to open fire.

Later, when they were again on the road, Sebastián explained.

"Jaramillo is in jail."

Naturally they knew nothing about the suicide. They continued their way in silence. Presently Sebastián Brache spoke again, in a tense undertone.

"We weren't born in the capital," he said. "As a child I'd always imagined the Leader on horseback, his chest plastered with medals and decorations, more like a statue than a man. I became a soldier. Shortly after I entered the army I saw him almost as I'd imagined him. It was after a parade. Then, suddenly, as we were entering the barracks, there he was,

267

still covered with medals and riding horseback, but he was pale and had lost his usual military bearing. He was anxious and hurried. You know why? He was on his way in a hurry to empty his bowels, he couldn't wait to get to the toilet! As he went through the doorway, to cross the big patio, his plumed hat fell off...Well, you know, during these days when I've been boiling with anger, I've remembered the sorry figure he cut as he went through the toilet door! In my mind he's no longer a glorious statue, but a man in a hurry to empty his bowels! And I think what a pleasure it will be to help him empty himself! What a pleasure!"

Imprudently, Purificación let out a loud laugh.

"Quiet!" ordered the Colonel.

"Excuse me, Colonel."

"There are no Colonels here. It just happens that I'm at the head of this little hunting expedition."

On they went. The first light of dawn promised a blue, almost violet sky. In the fields the many shades of green showed up vividly, the vegetation lush from recent showers. It was sad to think of the havoc wrought in such a world by man's base passions.

"How beautiful life would be," said Laza pensively, "if everyone were allowed really to live!"

The dawn light showed the usually hard face of Sebastián Brache in an expression of nostalgia.

"Porfirio knew my brother Jacinto," he said meditatively, "and you too knew him, Purificación." He turned towards Alfredo "You didn't know him. Well, he was an artist. While still only a boy he showed great talent for the violin. He might have been a famous concert violinist. But they sent him to provoke an 'accident', and he lost a finger in the scrimmage. You can imagine what such a loss must have meant to a violinist. Why wasn't I entrusted with that mission? It was one for a professional soldier to carry out! Why did they have to drain the life out of a talented musician?" He paused, then continued in a voice choked with emotion.

268

"He was a good boy. But after that disaster he found himself involved in other cases, like that of Niño Valverde. It was all so senseless! But the loss of that finger turned him into another person. And at last his mind went. Until..." He stopped, unable to say more.

"Rarely have I had as good a friend," said Porfirio.

"They've destroyed my family," Sebastián added, in a steadier voice. "We were poor, middle-class people in a country town. Our chief pride was our only sister, Paulina. And now see what she has become. The last time I saw her, she almost did not know who I was, I, her brother..."

Now they all became silent, for they were approaching the last outpost before reaching the capital. The face of Colonel Brache was again set in hard lines, and he was again an impeccable army officer, as the chief officer of the outpost questioned him.

"Why did you take this man prisoner? Isn't he the Puerto Rican bastard who turned desperado?"

"Yes, he is."

"Why didn't you eliminate him?"

"I know how to follow orders given me by the President himself, Captain!"

The Captain came to attention.

"Excuse me, Colonel! You may pass."

Relieved, they set out again, but their hearts sank when the Captain's voice brought them once more to a halt.

"Colonel!"

"Yes, Captain?"

"I just wanted to tell you, Colonel, that our aviation has wiped out the rebel landings. The news has been confirmed. Why, one of the rebel groups even brought a hospital staff for their wounded! Well, their wounded aren't even fit to be buried, now! The Leader is very pleased about it and has ordered the news to be proclaimed."

"The Leader is invincible," was all Brache said.

From that moment on, Alfredo Laza thought only of

269

Rosana, Rosana, now only a bloody rag of flesh. He remembered her last words to him: "Don't worry about your soldier girl. I'll wait on the little island. Carry out your mission. I'll be waiting for you where the wounded will be taken. May luck be with you."

The plan had been to set up tents for the wounded among some mangrove trees on a small off-shore island inhabitated by friendly fishermen. Lorenzi had planned to sail before dawn to try to get more arms and food. He was probably far out at sea by now.

Alfredo had to unburden himself to someone. He drew near Porfirio, who had also known her.

"That piece of news means that Rosana is dead."

"Rosana?"

"Yes, she came with us. She wanted to serve as a nurse. She was working in the hospital tents they destroyed. It wasn't the Rosana that you knew. Lorenzi has probably told you about her. You must know that from the minute she recovered she took up the study of nursing. And she couldn't let me come alone on this expedition. How pitiful to think that I was never able to make a home for her!"

They could see the capital now. Within a few minutes they would be in the streets on the way to the barracks. Thenceforth they spoke not a word to each other. They were going towards their death, perhaps. But there was still a chance that they might succeed in "hunting down the monster". The presence in their group of Sebastián Brache, a Colonel in the Presidential Guard, might enable them to achieve that wished-for end. But everything must happen quickly, before any of the officers could notice that the soldiers returning with Sebastián Brache were not the same as those who had left with him.

If anyone sounded the alarm before they reached Augusto, they were lost, and even if they managed to kill Augusto, it was more than likely that none of them would escape with his life. When they had set out on this mission they had already been aware that "Operation Hunt Down" was a suicidal endeavor. "It's all or nothing," Purificación López had calmly put it. All or nothing. But supposing they were able to bring about Augusto's death and with it the revolt of the people?

As they entered the streets of the capital, they were invaded by a feeling of great solemnity, and in low voices encouraged each other with a "Good luck, comrade!"

There were no civilians in the streets, which were empty except for police and military patrols. Forward the four men rode, the horses now going at a slow trot, and all four men were silent. Sebastián, Alfredo and Purificación pretended to hem in Porfirio, the "prisoner", while he assumed a dejected pose in the saddle. The horses seemed tired, as if weighed down by their heavy-hearted riders.

They slowed down to a walk as they approached the main entrance to the patio of the barracks. Step by step, they advanced..."Am I now about to escape from the labyrinth?" Porfirio wondered. He remembered his childhood, remembered Coamo. Had he thought of the law office he had once dreamed of having there, he would have lost courage. But no, he resolutely thought of the dangerous mission he was carrying out. Was he about to die? Perhaps. His parents— Lázaro, the tightrope walker and Juanita, the acrobat—had died in a fall under the canvas roof of a cheap circus. His godparents, Catalina and Estefano, had died inglorious deaths. And Estefano's baritone horn had sunk in the sea, gurgling as if with a death-rattle. He had no knowledge of his uncle, Florito Moya. He knew nothing of his relatives. He was alone, alone, "like a soul in purgatory", he reflected. It was natural, very natural, that he should join with his friends Laza and Lorenzi, in this just cause. And so, forward! For Paulina and Jacinto, for Rosana Cortines de Laza, the soldier girl! He had not studied law to receive a diploma in cowardice but to employ his talents generously for humanity.

271

Again the four men muttered encouragement to one another: "Good luck, comrade!" But their hearts were heavy, and the horses snorted and dragged their hooves as if weighed down by that heaviness.

It was clear, now, that Sebastián Brache would not betray them. Besides, he had more cause than any of them to fight the monster. It could be seen in his eyes that he was thinking with sadness of his wife and children, but his courage was bolstered by his resolve to avenge Jacinto and Paulina, his brother and sister. As for Alfredo Laza, his face was as if transfigured. Rosana Cortines, had she been alive and there to see him, would have found him beautiful. His physical ugliness had vanished, his head was held high, his face had the serenity only seen on the face of a man who is ready to die in a just cause and confronting eternity with eagerness. Purificación López, son of the Antilles, in whose veins ran the blood of three races, was the one who seemed most placid; indeed, an almost beatific smile hovered on his lips. His former friend, the overseer Ursulino Cachola, had frustrated his hope of redemption because as General Augusto C. Luna del Valle he had appropriated the oppressive powers of the Valverdes and the Jaramillos, had bent all his energies to avenge himself on his former masters and dazzle them with his wealth and power.

It was now a long time since Purificación López had stood face to face with his old friend, the overseer Cachola. One night years ago he had had to flee to a neighboring country. Now he had returned. With what pleasure would he ask Ursulino Cachola for an accounting! Purificación López smiled to himself as he reflected upon what he would say to him when at last he stood face to face with him. "Look, Ursulino," he would say, "we fought together to give the poor and oppressed a better life. We swore together to do that. But you turned away, became Marshal Augusto C. Luna del Valle, Leader Augusto, and now you oppress the people still more than the Valverdes and the Jaramillos

272

did. So your friend Purificación López invites you to take a little trip to the other world!"

At the main entrance to the barracks an officer asked, almost mechanically: "Were you only able to capture one of the spies?"

"I couldn't avoid making the traitor Lorenzi pay with his life," replied Colonel Brache.

"The Chief isn't going to like that. And you lost one of your own men, didn't you?"

"Yes."

Alfredo and Porfirio knew that Brache was trying to gain time by giving false information. Alfredo was now thinking about his friend Juan Lorenzi. "He undoubtedly escaped. He wanted to come with us. He always escapes from death, which he scoffs at. Hail and farewell, Juan Lorenzi..."

"Where is the President?" inquired Brache.

"They've already gone for him. He wants to see the spy."

In the barracks everyone was talking in low voices, but joyfully, about the triumphant air force, its prowess, and how it had decimated the invaders. The muted hum of voices sounded like a responsory for the dead.

Colonel Sebastián Brache, as he sat his horse, waiting for the Leader to arrive, looked impassive enough, but deep within himself a metamorphosis was taking place: he was becoming a man with but one single idea—vengeance. "Oh, my brother, oh, my sister," he thought with intensity, "you shall soon be avenged! I've waited in agony for this moment of vengeance which soon will be mine." Then, looking at his comrades and seeing how tense they were, he almost shouted aloud a thought that crossed his mind: "The rainy season has come!" He had recently read about an African fish which, in the dry season, buries itself in the mud of a dried-out pool to await the return of the rains. Then it awakes and swims again...He thought of himself, whim-

273

sically, as one of those African fish which had been waiting a long time to awaken and swim out of his hole. He would swim like a fish in the waters of his joy, once he had fired his pistol into Leader Augusto's heart. Yes, he wanted to shout, *"The rains are here!"*

Colonel Brache had still not ordered his men to dismount to receive the General. The soldiers stationed in the barracks were all lined up, standing at attention. Suddenly, almost as if by magic, Augusto appeared. He was surrounded by officers, two of them friends of Brache.

"There's the man!" said Alfredo Laza to himself, as if he already knew Augusto. The man was wearing a dress uniform to celebrate the victory of his air force. In spite of the medals there was space this time for bullets to penetrate his body somewhere between the two ends of his digestive tract. "There's the man!" He had known him before he was born! That man was the nightmare of more than one life.

Suddenly they were torn out of their reveries by a shout from one of the officers.

"Treason! Treason! That man is Purificacion López!"

An exchange of shots followed at close range.

Augusto grabbed his thigh with his left hand while he drew his pistol with the right. Sebastián Brache, Alfredo Laza, Porfirio Uribe and Purifiicación López fell, riddled with bullets.

The officer who had shouted turned to the Leader.

"Are you badly wounded, General?"

"I think not. Just a slight flesh-wound."

Another officer bent over to look through the dead men's pockets. In Laza's he found a paper with a note scribbled on it. He handed it to the Leader while the pistols and knives were being collected.

Augusto read the paper. Then, trembling in fury he shouted a preposterous order.

"Shoot those corpses!" he screamed.

There was one volley, and then another, into the bloody

274

and inert bodies. But Alfredo Laza, Porfirio Uribe, Sebastián Brache and Purificación López were alive, in another world, they had attained immortality. Their names would raise up armies in the future. For, as Alfredo Laza had written on that paper: "No one can kill us. Tyrant, be sure of it, we will return, our numbers multiplied, and in a thousand voices we will demand justice and freedom. For the world was not conceived by a monster."